ALSO BY MIKE HEPPNER

The Egg Code

Pike's Folly

Pike's Folly

MIKE HEPPNER

ALFRED A. KNOPF   NEW YORK   2006

THIS IS A BORZOI BOOK
PUBLISHED BY ALFRED A. KNOPF

Library of Congress Cataloging-in-Publication Data
Heppner, Mike, 1972–
Pike's folly / Mike Heppner.— 1st ed.
p. cm.
ISBN: 0-375-41289-1
1. Eccentrics and eccentricities—Fiction.   2. Wilderness
areas—Fiction.   3. New Hampshire—Fiction.
4. Millionaires—Fiction.   5. Rhode Island—Fiction.
6. Land tenure—Fiction.   I. Title.

PS3608.E67P55 2006
813'.6—dc22   2005044589

Manufactured in the United States of America
First Edition

For My Wife

I | Little Rhody

1

"They ate me alive," said the excitable man sitting across from Henry Savage's desk one June morning in Washington, D.C. "Absolutely tore me to bits. All I said was, 'Those people are no more Native American than I am,' which is *true*. Of course, you can't say things like that in Rhode Island, so everybody went nuts. The *Journal* took their usual self-righteous stance, the cannibals. I lost all of my old business contacts. Even Buddy wouldn't talk to me. People are so uptight these days, so goddamn conservative—and I say that to you as a fellow Republican."

"I'm not a Republican," Henry said.

"Oh. Then I say that to you as a fellow Democrat." Nathaniel Pike took off his sunglasses, cleaned them with a neatly folded handkerchief and put them back on. In the interim, Henry saw that Pike's eyes were a sparkling blue, like a beautiful woman's. "Anyway, here I am, still dreaming, still going strong, even twelve years later. You can hate me, Mr. Savage, but you can't keep me down, and you know why? Because I don't hate anyone. I refuse to. I hate fakery, I hate falseness, but I don't hate people."

Henry shifted in his seat. His erect posture behind his desk conveyed something about how he liked to conduct his business, with stiff formality and an unwillingness to be swayed by emotion. A similar bearing might've been useful in practicing meditation, if Henry had been inclined to such a thing.

"My problem is, I get restless," Pike confessed. "My mind's always going a million miles a minute, and I can't slow it down. It's terrible how I can't stay focused on any one thing, and even when I *do*, no one else gets it, you know? Whatever I think is beautiful, everyone else thinks is crazy."

Surrounded by his government-issue office furniture, Henry felt stifled by Mr. Pike's overlarge presence. Pike was one of the wealthiest men in the United States and, with his good looks and wild reputation, more charismatic than most. Trace wrinkles in the corners of his mouth were the only indications that he'd aged at all since dropping out of high school. He'd kept in good shape simply by living life at a frantic pace. His arms and legs were both longer than seemed in proportion to the rest of his body, and he carried himself with the assurance provided by a healthy, well-stoked ego.

The parcel of land Pike wanted to buy from Henry's department was one of several properties that the Bureau of Land Management made available each year to the private sector, largely acreage that the Interior Department deemed no longer suitable for public use. Most of it was out west, in such land-rich states as Arizona and Colorado. Pike's was the only parcel that the BLM still owned in the entire Northeast, and it consisted of seven and a half acres of untapped wilderness in the White Mountains of New Hampshire. Henry had no idea why Pike wanted the land, just that he was willing to pay top dollar for it.

Dressed smartly in his seven-thousand-dollar suit, Nathaniel patted down the top of his full head of brown hair and took a swig from a bottle of Poland Spring. "I'm not the kind of person

that you normally do business with, isn't that right, Mr. Savage?"
he asked.

"I don't know what kind of a person you are," Henry said.

"Visionary. Ambitious. Passionate. Not afraid to stick my
foot in my mouth. If I were a fruit, I'd be a banana. If I were a
car, I'd be a sleek limousine. If I were a . . ." Pike snapped his fingers. "Gimmie something else to compare myself to."

"A TV show."

"If I were a TV show, I'd be a ten-hour miniseries, like *Roots*
or *The Thorn Birds*. No Richard Chamberlain, though—that
guy's a joke."

Henry saw that Pike liked thinking of himself as a comedian,
so he did the polite thing and smiled. "I don't know, Mr. Pike. I
worry about what's in that head of yours."

"Well, *don't*. And don't listen to what other people say about
me. It's very easy to get a bad rap in a small state like Rhode
Island."

Pike chuckled at this. He'd lived in Rhode Island his entire
life, and over those forty-two years he'd built a reputation for
wasteful, eccentric behavior. Most notoriously, he'd bought an
old farmhouse in the East Bay, then surprised his neighbors by
demolishing the house and rebuilding it piece by piece, down to
the last detail—furniture included. No one knew why he did
what he did or said the things that he said. To call him a provocateur didn't quite capture it. A provocateur, yes, but a charming
one, a persuasive one, maybe even a dangerous one. Everyone in
the state had an opinion about him, usually either very good or
very bad.

Such audacity never failed to impress Henry. The playboy's
life was completely foreign to his own. He wondered, what
makes a person like Nathaniel Pike tick? No responsibilities, no
obstacles in his path. Is it just the money? Or is it some other
characteristic that he has and I don't?

"We'll have to do this properly, of course," Henry said. "You'll submit a bid, just like everyone else. I'm supposed to give preference to the neighboring landowners, so we'll need to act now."

"Fine, fine . . . anything else?" Pike asked.

"Yes. Just promise me that you won't do anything crazy up there," Henry said.

His old-fashioned sense of integrity amused Pike. "I'll promise you one thing. I will do nothing to that land that will not make it more beautiful."

"It's beautiful as it is," Henry protested.

"Damn right. Everyone should get a chance to hike the White Mountains. I've got a lady friend who runs a ski lodge in North Conway. I keep trying to get someone to go up with me, but no dice. People are intimidated by me, I think."

"Oh?"

"Sadly so. I've got to learn to tone it down. A little less tempest, a little more tact."

They spent the rest of the meeting discussing Rhode Island politics, about which Pike knew a great deal. He spoke of his friends in the state senate as if they all owed him money, and in fact many of them did. His life sounded so renegade, so unlike anything that Henry had experienced in D.C. It thrilled him to hear about it, and he suspected that Pike probably had a similar effect on others.

Leading him out of his office, Henry said, "I sure hope it cools off tonight. I'm taking my wife to a Beach Boys reunion concert in Annapolis. Do you like the Beach Boys?"

Pike responded with exaggerated enthusiasm. "Gee, I haven't thought about those guys in years. I once produced an independent film, you know, with Brian Wilson, back in the eighties."

"Really?"

"*Hell* yeah. That was a wild time."

Henry, feeling outclassed, retreated. "Their music's pretty corny, I suppose, but my wife won the tickets." He cleared his throat. "What time's your plane out of Reagan?"

"Three o'clock. Don't worry about me. I'm going to take a walk around the Mall. Strange name for it, don't you think?"

Henry escorted him as far as his outer office, then returned alone to brood behind his desk until lunch. His secretary, Rochelle, was still glowing from some compliment that Pike had paid her on his way out and was fairly useless to Henry for the rest of the morning.

Pike flew out on an afternoon direct to T. F. Green Airport, which got him home before the commuter rush. That night, he took his personal assistant, Stuart, out for a bite to eat at Café Nuovo and bragged about his trip to Washington. Over the bar, Gregg Reese was prattling on TV to the news anchor from Channel 6. Always selling something, that one, Pike thought. Well, at least he's trying.

2

Naked, Stuart Breen stood in the foyer of Siemens and McMasters, watching the foot traffic shuffle down College Hill into downtown Providence. It was late one morning in mid-November, and his head of curly black hair was still damp from the shower. A thin pane of glass separated him from the rain-dodging clusters of students and university professors trudging up the hill to their classes. No one noticed him, and he waited for what seemed like a minute before putting on his robe and stepping back into darkness, where the temperature differential between the inside and the outside of the building was so great that the windows had begun to fog. Stuart's employer, Nathaniel Pike, lived on the top floor of the five-story brownstone and kept the thermostat pumped to seventy-six to heat the whole house. Because Pike liked working in binges, Stuart would sometimes stay the night rather than walk back to his own apartment. The last time he'd seen his wife was two days ago. Besides Stuart and Nathaniel, no one else worked at Siemens and McMasters; the name referred to a corporate account set up to protect Mr. Pike's personal assets.

Stuart lifted the intercom in the kitchen, buzzed the fifth

floor, then listened to the thunderous sound of Pike bounding down the stairs. In the condensation of the kitchen windows, Stuart had scribbled an obscene sexual phrase, which he now wiped off with his sleeve.

"Get any sleep last night?" he asked as they settled down to a breakfast of bacon rashers and black coffee.

"A few hours." Pike sighed. "Henry Savage called around ten. That did it for me. Watched the Lifetime Channel until four a.m. I love that channel, Stuart—love it, love it. *Movies for women.*" He savored the words. "I'll bet that Cathy Diego watches the Lifetime Channel."

Cathy Diego was a representative from the Public Interest Research Group in Concord, New Hampshire. The NHPIRG was a consumer-based activist group that monitored the state's handling of its natural resources. State PIRGs kept in close contact with one another, collating information on land abusers from regions as diverse as New England and the Midwest.

"What did Savage want?" Stuart asked.

"Oh, he's just getting nervous. Most people, Stuart, don't have any vision. That's the difference between me and Henry Savage. Everything that guy stands for is sensible, sane, dull, and ordinary. I stand for magic. I stand for mystery. Why don't people like mysteries anymore?"

"I don't know. I've never written one."

Pike cracked up. "You should. Maybe *I* could be your mystery."

Stuart's face reddened. Working as Pike's personal assistant had been a humbling experience and quite a comedown from seeing his first book in print. Three years ago, he'd published an arty little novel, *My Private Apocalypse,* which had sold some four thousand copies and earned him a nice mention in the *Providence Journal.* He and his wife, Marlene, had met around the same time and were married two years later. Marlene worked at a Citizens Bank a few blocks from their house on the East Side. She was quiet, unassuming and always did her best not to upstage her husband; if she had any ambitions for herself, she was kind enough not to share them. Being married to a published author was good enough for her.

To the extent that it mattered, Stuart wondered what Marlene really thought of his book. The life that he'd described in *My Private Apocalypse* was as true to his own as he could make it. The main character, like Stuart himself, was an eastern-educated, narcissistic, sexually confused young man who—unlike Stuart—dealt with his confusion by consuming bits and pieces of his own body. This impossible premise now struck him as pretentious, but at the time he'd felt a keen empathy for his protagonist. He wanted his fiction to be dark and uncompromising because that was how he regarded himself. Writing the book was an act of literary exhibitionism, and like many such acts, he felt that once he'd completed it, he'd revealed too much.

Nathaniel pushed away his plate. "You look preoccupied, Stuart. You're not supposed to have any secrets from me, you know."

"And why's that?" Stuart asked.

"Why? Because it's not healthy. That's how you get cancer."

"Oh, really?"

"Yeah . . . brain cancer, anyway. Sexual repression causes dick cancer and brain cancer."

"There's no dick cancer."

"Sure there is. If you get it in your dick, it's dick cancer. Repression causes dick cancer, and too much fat in your diet gives you a heart attack—so eat your fucking bacon."

After breakfast, they climbed a flight of narrow and listing stairs and entered a small library that reeked of a cigar Pike had smoked the night before. It was here that he and Stuart had spent many hours making arrangements with contractors for the parking-lot project, taking bids from building suppliers as far north as Nova Scotia.

"How long are we going to be in New Hampshire?" Stuart asked as Pike bent to open a safe behind a panel in the bookshelves.

"A few weeks, who knows?" Pike spoke with his head deep in the vault. "I'm hoping we can break ground by New Year's."

"It's hard to do anything in the winter," Stuart observed, "particularly that far north."

Pike emerged from the safe clutching a fat, business-sized envelope. "We'll make it happen. Besides, it's just a parking lot. No foundation, so there's no need to dig more than a few inches."

"But if the elevation—"

"Oh, don't worry." Reaching into the envelope, he pulled out an arbitrary number of bills—fifties and hundreds—and transferred them to his pants pocket. "We'll have you back to your life of bohemian squalor in no time. Meanwhile, think of all the money you'll be making—really, Stuart—for doing next to nothing."

Stuart crept behind a Louis XV writing desk and sat down. The sight of so many books—voraciously collected, and most of them, he was certain, unread—exhausted him. The book that Stuart was reading right now was *Something Happened*. He'd never read Heller before but felt he ought to, particularly as it pertained to his own work. What had the author of *Catch-22* done, he wondered, during that decade-plus period between his first two novels? How did he make a living? How did he keep his spirits up? What had happened to Joseph Heller before *Something Happened*? Had he, like Stuart, spent the first few years of his career writing unpublishable garbage? How many novels had he started and never finished? How many had he finished but never published? Maybe *Something Happened* was just another book to him, one that he'd begun on New Year's Day 1962 and completed ten or eleven years later. It was possible; after all, some writers just worked slower than others, and *Something Happened* was an unusually long book. Five hundred sixty-nine pages. Assuming ten years to write it, 365 days times ten, that's 3,650 divided into 569, leaves you with roughly one-tenth of a page a day—not even a full sentence by Heller's standards. One sentence a day, for ten years. What kind of a life was that? But Stuart knew—it was the life he'd always wanted for himself. Still, when he thought of what writers actually did with their time, the ratio of the number of beautiful, meaningful, valuable words that they'd left on the page to the minutes and hours that they'd spent simply existing, it depressed him.

"Stuart! Look alive!" Stuart looked up to see Pike standing over him. "Quick: what are you thinking about right now?"

Because he had to say something, Stuart said, "Oh, I was just thinking about this interview with Gregg Reese in the *ProJo* today. 'Name three Americans who most influenced you as a young man,' that sort of thing. It's the usual puff piece. I'll show it to you when we go downstairs."

Pike grunted. "I'll tell you three Americans I'm *not* interested in. Susan Sarandon, Steven Spielberg, and everyone else on the planet. Everyone who has a *conscience,* because it's wrong to have a conscience. It's un-American. Emerson didn't have a conscience. Emerson was a self-centered, self-aggrandizing, loathsome little bastard, and I love him for it. My only heroes are freaks and eccentrics. New England, and Rhode Island in particular, is a hotbed for eccentrics. Charles Ives was an eccentric. So was Emily Dickinson, and Whitman and Thoreau. That's what makes being an American so unique: the right to live entirely for yourself."

"So you're a libertine?"

"*Hell* yes. It's everyone's duty as an American and a free-thinking New Englander to have as much lewd sex as possible, in every position, in every room of the house—and even fuck your family members if that's what you want, because it's all beautiful."

Hearing such licentious sermonizing reminded Stuart why he'd been drawn to Pike in the first place: his utter lack of self-consciousness. Stuart envied him his wit, his wicked tongue. What masqueraded as strong-willed convictions was really just the perverse ravings of a sadist. Pike didn't stand for anything, except maybe the need to stand for *something*.

"Everybody wants me to be like Gregg Reese," Pike said, "who has as much money as I do, and he's just as selfish as I am, but he feels *guilty* about it, and that's why there's the Reese Foundation, the Allison Fund, all that bullshit. What's wrong with people, Stuart?"

"Not enough lewd sex, I suppose."

"How's that?"

Stuart grumbled; he no longer felt like playing. "Never mind, I'm just acting like an idiot."

Pike grinned affectionately. "Well, anyway, you should get back to your wife."

"She's at work," Stuart said. He wasn't sure why he disliked talking about Marlene. Was he embarrassed by her? No. Well, a little. She made him angry sometimes, and impatient, and annoyed. She reminded him of that line in the old Flannery O'Connor story, "A Good Man Is Hard to Find": "*She would have been a good woman . . . if it had been somebody there to shoot her every minute of her life.*" It bothered him how much he liked that line.

He sighed. "Marlene can live without me."

"Of course she can, it's *you* I'm worried about." Pike knelt to close the safe, then came up again. "Next month won't be so bad. Once I get this straightened out with the DOI, we'll all be moving up to the White Mountains."

Stuart shrugged. Moving to the White Mountains made about as much sense as anything else—that is to say, none at all. "I wouldn't mind living in New Hampshire," he said. "But Marlene's tied to her job, so that's that."

"They have banks in New Hampshire. I'll build one." Pike chortled. "Now *there's* an idea—instead of a parking lot."

The parking-lot idea wasn't a new one; in fact, he'd been joking about it for years, developing it the way a comedian might shape a particular routine, taking a little out, then putting it back: "You know what I'd like to do? Buy up a thousand acres of who knows what, maybe Yellowstone National Park, and just pave the whole thing over," elaborating on it a few weeks later, "No, I'll build a parking lot in the middle of the woods, maybe up in Vermont or New Hampshire, miles and miles from the nearest access road," the idea growing on him until it began to wake him up at nights, this silly image of a pristine parking lot consigned to the rocky barrens of the White Mountains, never driven upon, each pointless parking space meticulously detailed in bold yellow lines, waiting for no one, an affront and an insult and a fantastic jest. Smiling in bed, he imagined blue-and-white handicap spaces, maybe three of them at the end of each row, the rows stopping where the smooth black macadam butted up against a wild, encroaching border of ragged beech and twisted pines.

Visions like these had delighted him ever since he was a boy. He'd grown up in South County, Rhode Island, a hodge-podge of small and diverse villages that included a range of economic classes, from the millwrights and construction workers who lived in old duplexes on Route 1 to the nouveau riche who'd bought up property on Wickford Harbor. He was hyperactive as a teenager, so his parents moved him out of the sticks and enrolled him in a private school on Providence's East Side. Surrounded by new classmates, he began to spend less time at home and more time chasing girls. He loved being popular but didn't lord it over anyone. One of his closest friends was a tomboy from the East Bay, Sarah Cranberry, who was far less pretty than most of the girls who would've gladly gone out with him. Years later, after he'd dropped out of school and spent a decade producing a handful of mildly scandalous art films for the European market—*Vanessa's Caress* and *The Succubus* among them—before bottoming out as a filmmaker and investing all his remaining funds in the commodity exchange, after he'd gleefully rounded second base with some eighty-plus women in Providence County alone, Pike still kept in touch with Sarah and visited her several times a year at her ski lodge in North Conway, New Hampshire. She was his favorite excuse to get away from the office.

Nowadays, he didn't like to work much, though every so often he forced himself onto a plane to make a circuit of the various corporate HQs where he held stock. All of the buildings were clean and boxy. One company manufactured computer chips for the defense industry. Another built payloads for NASA. The whole trip took about ten days, from Providence to New York, Washington to Dallas to Sacramento (*great* Vietnamese place in downtown Sacramento!) and then back to Providence. Work dispensed with, he returned to what he did best: enjoying himself, putting food and drink into his mouth, and plotting more ways to provoke Gregg Reese.

Gregg Reese was Rhode Island's other megamillionaire. The Reeses were an old Rhode Island family that had made a reputation for themselves as philanthropists, good-deed doers and, some might say, indiscriminate supporters of social causes. Every year, the Reese Foundation gave millions of dollars to parks and universities, museums and day-care centers, using any excuse to fork over another half-mil to anyone willing to change the name of their organization to the Gregg Reese Center for the Poor and Pathetic. Pike couldn't deny it: Gregg was a good man, a kind, civic-minded individual. In private, the two rather liked each other. On some level, Gregg appreciated Pike's little publicity stunts. Both he and Pike were making a commentary of sorts—on wealth, on being privileged in America. Gregg believed in an America founded on philanthropy, good works, and Christian charity. Pike took a darker view.

"The problem with this country," he told Stuart, "is that we no longer understand the impulses that brought us to America in the first place. This is a thieves' den, man! We're worse than Australia. Go down the list of names on the Declaration of Independence. *I'm* more like those guys than Gregg is. But if Ben Franklin were alive today, we'd put him behind bars just like the Unabomber or any other eccentric. We don't want eccentrics in this country anymore, we want *team players.* Government-controlled sycophants."

Stuart listened politely; today was payday, and he wanted to feel that he'd earned his money.

"Anyway, I'll let you go," Pike said. "Unless you're interested in sticking around for lunch. There's some crap in the fridge. We're allowed to have one beer before noon."

"No, thanks," Stuart said and followed his employer out of the library.

Heading downstairs, Pike suggested that Stuart and Marlene get out of town for the weekend.

"We are," Stuart said. "Not this weekend. Thanksgiving. We're taking a drive out to the Berkshires."

"What's in the Berkshires?"

"Nothing. Some expensive B&B that Marlene wanted to go to. We've had reservations since June."

Pike reached into his pocket, pulled out a wad of cash and gave it to Stuart. "Here, go buy yourself a good time."

Stuart took the money without thanking him. "I could get used to this," he said. Truth was, he'd *already* gotten used to it, months ago. Through no effort of his own, he'd come upon an easy way to coast through life and now felt disoriented to the point of paralysis.

Excusing himself, he got dressed in the first-floor guest room. Down the hall, he could hear Pike in the kitchen—eating again, judging from the smell of bacon frying and butter melting on toast. He dressed slowly, making frequent passes in front of the window. The shutters were open, and from a certain angle—perhaps from *that* lamppost, black and chilly on the opposite corner—one could see directly into the room, across a street of salmon-colored bricks, some askew and others oddly shaped to fit around manholes in the road. Half-naked, he placed his hand against the window; the chill of the outside world shocked him.

3

Later that afternoon, Stuart's wife, Marlene, was approached by her supervisor, Carla Marshall, as she was putting on her raincoat in preparation for the short walk home. Carla was younger than Marlene (twenty-seven to her thirty-two) and more attractive, more likely to entertain the hungry stares of young male customers as they waited in line to cash their paychecks. She'd gone to URI, gotten an MBA and now lived with her husband in an old townhouse near Brown. Marlene often saw her on weekends, dressed down, doing the groceries or returning a video.

"I can't wait to get out of these clothes," Carla said, leaning against the Plexiglas divider that separated Marlene's cubicle from the others. "I wish we could wear our pajamas to work." She waited for Marlene to say something, then asked, "What do you wear around the house?"

Marlene blushed. "Just this," she said.

Carla smiled, almost flirtatiously. "You're so conservative, Marlene. I think you'd look pretty in a tank top." She snapped her fingers. "Hey! How would you like to spend a week on Martha's Vineyard?"

Marlene glanced out the window at the cold drizzle slapping against the parking lot. "Now?"

"No, of course not *now*. In May. Bill and I are renting out a time-share in Chilmark." Bill, her husband, was a commercial photographer with a practice in Downcity. Stuart and Marlene had smoked pot with them after a fondue party a few months back, and ever since Carla had shown a strange, almost intrusive interest in Stuart's work, projecting a life for him that involved royalty checks in the tens of thousands. "The water'll still be cold, but at least getting around will be easy."

"I don't know." Marlene checked her watch; it was 3:05. Under her arms, she felt the jiggly sensation that always came at the end of a workday. "Money's a little tight right now."

Carla sighed disapprovingly. "You always use that excuse, and I never believe it." Moving away, she left a stack of loan applications on Marlene's desk. "Besides, the Big Money goes to Nantucket. We've been to both, and there's more to do on the Vineyard. Nantucket's too secluded."

"We'll think about it," Marlene said and fixed the last button on her raincoat. The coat was heavy and buttoned all the way to her throat. Many of her fantasies involved this raincoat—*at the grocery store, wearing nothing but the coat and a pair of black stiletto heels; Stuart coming up from behind, the cool mist from the produce aisle breezing against her skin as he loosens the belt, letting it fall to the floor, and people all around, staring . . .*

Man's voice: "Last one out!"

She took her purse and followed Carla across the banking floor, where a half-dozen tellers were also getting ready to leave for the day. One at a time, they filed past a security guard and out the front door. Most of the girls were in their early twenties, and they all shared connections—whether through college or childhood—that Marlene knew little about. She'd kept in touch with no one from her hometown of North Providence, only her parents, who'd both retired and were considering buying a place in Snug Harbor. No reason to go back, no need for old friends or even new ones. Marlene so thirsted for her husband that everything else was a distraction.

Heading home, she passed groups of university students smoking and slouching, oblivious to the rain, as they hung out on the front steps of two-hundred-year-old apartment buildings. They ignored her as she walked by; she was of another generation, straight and simple and no longer bursting with the potential of an Ivy League undergraduate. Marlene recognized this lack of potential in herself. Her own conservativeness continually frustrated her; it had become a self-defeating habit, like masturbating instead of going through the effort of having sex with your partner. Her mother, in particular, had always urged her to take chances, chances that Marlene ignored until, through her inattention, they eventually turned into missed opportunities. She'd acted during high school but gave it up as impractical when she went off to college. She could've gone to a conservatory—her parents would've paid for it—but didn't because it felt like an indulgence. Time and again she'd denied herself what other young people always took for granted: the right to make an honest mistake. Her adolescent rationales now escaped her, and she wondered what ultimate goal—*working in a bank?*—had made all the other sacrifices seem worthwhile.

Reaching her street, she let herself into her house without picking up the stack of mail on the front steps. She'd become absentminded in the year that she'd been married. She didn't consider herself a particularly good wife, though it wasn't for lack of trying. Her shortcomings were basic, God given. She wasn't smart, wasn't pretty, didn't know much about writers or literature. Getting her husband's attention and keeping it was a challenge she faced every day.

Other than the theater, Marlene had never had any real interests of her own. All of her favorite pictures of herself as a kid showed her dressed up as someone else: Miss Hannigan in *Annie,* Mrs. Paroo in *The Music Man,* Aunt Eller in *Oklahoma!* Being a senior member of the drama club had given her access to a social group that otherwise would've been inaccessible to her. Whenever she wasn't on stage, she was quiet, a hardworking yet average student. Her classmates were always surprised to see her come alive for the spring musicals, where she usually played the mayor's wife, the mother or the loudmouthed older sister; in other words, the fat chick's part. This wasn't a role she wished to pursue in real life, so after high school she traded in her artistic aspirations for something more conventional.

Passing through a dark hallway, she set down her purse, stepped out of her sneakers, and joined Stuart in the kitchen. He was doing the dishes; he'd been out of the house for two days, and of course she hadn't thought to do them herself.

"Boy, you really did a number on this place," he said, pausing just long enough to give her a quick kiss. "I took the trash out. It was starting to smell in here."

Marlene flashed her stupid-little-me smile. "I'm sorry. I don't know where my head's been lately." Feeling like a slob in the face of so much activity, she found a discrete corner of the room and sat down. The window above the kitchen table had its blinds down, and she yanked them open to let some light in. "It's raining harder now," she said.

He turned off the faucet. "What was that?"

"I said it's raining harder now."

He nodded vaguely. "Good night to stay inside."

Before he could get back to work, she went over to him and put her hands on his chest. "That wasn't a *real* kiss, you know."

Their second kiss lasted longer but seemed just as rushed as the first. "Something wrong?" she asked.

"No, not really. Nate always gives me a headache, that's all."

"Leave the dishes, then. I'll do them later." Leading him away from the counter, she tugged on his belt and began undoing his trousers. "Why don't I start some laundry?" she asked playfully.

Glancing toward the window, he said, "Careful. My wallet's still in there."

She took his wallet out of his pocket and saw that it was full of bills. "Hey, you've been holding out on me."

"No, I haven't. I just got paid today."

Marlene tossed the wallet onto the kitchen table, then went back to stripping off his clothes. Stuart helped her by taking off his shoes and socks. His mind was still stuck on the dirty dishes in the sink. He didn't like leaving a chore once he'd started on it. "How was work today?" he asked.

"Fine. Carla Marshall asked me what I liked wearing around the house."

Stuart winced. "What did you tell her?"

"Oh, nothing. I was a good girl."

She bundled his clothes and brought them downstairs to the laundry room. Before starting the washing machine, she took off her own clothes and added them to the load. Marlene loved being naked with Stuart, both in and out of the bedroom. They slept naked, watched TV naked, sometimes even ate dinner naked. Being naked made her feel like something important in the world revolved around her. Dressed, she didn't feel anything, just a lingering discontent with herself and her body.

Back upstairs, she boosted the thermostat in the hallway to seventy-four and went back to the kitchen. Stuart had resumed his chores and was cleaning the refrigerator with Fantastik spray. Marlene noticed that he'd closed the blinds.

"I'm glad you're home," she said. "I don't like sleeping by myself. I always think somebody's going to break into the house."

"They can break in whether I'm here or not."

"True. Anyway, it's good to have you here." She gazed down at her bare feet and her toenails, painted red. Her own nakedness seemed disappointing, even though she'd spent the whole day looking forward to it. She wanted more—not just to be naked but to talk about it as well. Watching his backside, she said, "You know something?"

"What?"

"Sometimes when I'm between clients at work, I wonder what it would be like if I took off all my clothes and everyone in the bank could see me. Is that weird?"

"Not particularly. I'm sure it's a fairly common fantasy."

She frowned. "Common" wasn't the word she'd wanted to hear. "I guess that makes me pretty predictable, then."

"You know that's not what I mean. I mean that other people probably think the same thing. That doesn't make you any less special."

The doorbell rang, and they looked around carefully, as if whoever it was had discovered a method, simply by ringing the bell, of morphing directly into the kitchen.

He sighed. "Where's my robe?"

She pointed upstairs, then went off to make herself decent. Grateful for the interruption, he hurried off and came back downstairs wearing his robe. Marlene was in the bathroom washing her hands. Through a window, he saw Celia Shriver standing on the front porch holding their mail. Celia lived across the street in a three-story colonial that anyone more desperate for money would've divided into apartments years ago. Looking at it from the outside, one imagined dusty rooms cluttered with yellowed bundles of newspapers, the whole place smelling like an unchanged litter box. She'd lived by herself for nearly two decades, and now, at sixty-seven, recently retired from the Textiles Department at the Rhode Island School of

Design, she'd begun to get out more often, going to fund-raisers and political rallies, always donating the bare minimum but also making the biggest racket.

Stuart opened the door. "Celia, hi, I was just"—he reached up, felt the dry hair on the top of his head, said it anyway—"getting out of the shower."

Celia handed over the mail, which he held dumbly against his chest. "I won't take up much of your time," she said. She'd left the house without her jacket, just a mouse brown cardigan over a black AC/DC T-shirt. Celia's face was elfin, and her out-of-sorts gray hair expressed the *up yours, asshole* persona commonly found in academia. "If I could just borrow your ear for one second."

"Sure." Stuart crossed his arms around the mail. From behind, he could hear Marlene taking her time in the bathroom, hands dashing under the faucet.

"I know you're a good person, Stuart, believe me, I'm a big fan of your work—"

"Oh, well, thank you."

"—and that's why I'm asking you to stay away from Nathaniel Pike, stay away from him like the *devil.* That man is a vulture and a parasite, and he exploits the goodness in everyone."

Stuart retreated into the foyer. "How so?"

"I know these things, Stuart. I know because I *care,* because I'm involved with this community." Meaning I'm *not,* Stuart thought. "Besides, it's in the papers. Read the *Providence Journal* front to back sometime. You think you can keep a secret in Rhode Island?"

He froze; the implications were too much for him—not today, not a mere six hours after he'd stood naked in front of the window on the first floor of Siemens and McMasters. "I'm actually doing research, Celia. It's for a book I'm writing about transgress—"

"That's no excuse." She reached into her cardigan, pulled out a Xeroxed flyer and thrust it at him. "Don't lose this," she warned, almost grabbing it out of his hands. "I'm trying to keep our copying costs down. We're a grassroots organization with an extremely limited budget."

Stuart looked at the flyer and immediately found that it bored him. "Well, then, here—I don't want it."

She refused it. "Think about what you're doing, Stuart. You don't know that man as well as I do. Ask Keeny Reese, she'll tell you."

Keeny Esther Reese was Gregg Reese's mother and the real head of the Reese Foundation. Other than Keeny, Gregg's only surviving blood relative was his daughter, Allison, with whom he lived on the East Side. Gregg's ex-wife, Renee, lived in London.

"Nathaniel Pike is nothing but an ignorant lowlife from South County," Celia hissed. "What business does he have owning a mountain in New Hampshire, anyway? What's he want to do with it? Build a casino? A strip club? I wouldn't put it past him."

"It's a free country, Celia."

"You're damn right it is! That's why I'm organizing an anti-Pike rally in Concord next month. I expect you to be there."

"In Concord?" He smiled, deliberately missing the point. "That's a pretty little town."

"Yes, and how would you like to see Nathaniel Pike come with his bulldozers and knock the whole goddamn thing down?" She crouched deep and swept both arms out in a giant leveling motion.

Again, he was struck by how much her passion, her political

commitments, bored him. Seeking a quick end to the conversation, he said, "How does dinner next Tuesday sound? I'd like to hear more about . . ."

Nothing honest came to mind, so he just smiled agreeably until Celia finally said, "I am occupied every night next week," and marched down the steps, adding at the foot of the drive, "Don't forget, Stuart, you have an obligation to the rest of the community."

"Okay," he said, waving cheerfully from the top step.

"You, as an artist, *you* should understand this."

"I do, I do." Closing the door.

"We all share the same respons—"

"Yep." Back inside the foyer, he told himself, *I did not just shut the door in that woman's face,* then slipped off his robe and joined Marlene in the bathroom just off the kitchen. She'd covered herself with a blue beach towel but took it off when she saw that the coast was clear. "Is that hard-on for me or for Celia Shriver?" she asked.

"Don't be ridiculous," he said.

They kissed, then went to the kitchen, where she poured them both a full glass of Chardonnay. Marlene poured wine like it was Coca-Cola, and Stuart had to make sure to pace himself correctly—one glass for every two of hers—or else he'd never be able to have sex after dinner.

Two glasses later—he'd lost track of how many she'd had— he pulled himself up from the living room sofa, where he'd been trying to read the uncorrected proofs of a first novel his agent had sent him ("Write more like *this*," he'd said over the phone), and set about preparing a Lean Cuisine for dinner. Marlene was in the kitchen, paying bills at the table.

"Hey, do you want to go to Martha's Vineyard next May?" she asked after some time had passed.

She was getting that dopey look in her eyes; somehow she'd

refilled her glass without his noticing. He didn't answer, just grumbled noncommittally as he pulled the Asian-style chicken out of the microwave and set it steaming on the counter. Wanting to be helpful, she got up and watched him slice through the TV dinner's cellophane wrapper with a pair of safety scissors. "This one's for you," he said, spooning the chicken over a desiccated lump of rice.

Marlene took the plate but didn't go back to the table. It was rude, she felt, to start before her husband, particularly since he'd gone to the trouble of making dinner. "Carla and Bill are renting a beach house, and they asked us to come along. It's a whole week, though, and I know you'll have a lot of work to do."

"Hardly."

They watched as the second round of Lean Cuisine quaked under the auburn glow of the microwave. The spicy smell of the food cooking was making them both hungry.

Marlene set her plate down on the range-top and edged his legs apart with her knee. "It might be fun. We could get naked on the beach." Her fingers crept down his back, pricking at the waxy hair under his balls. "There's a nude beach somewhere, I think. Right where the Kennedy plane crashed."

He laughed gruffly. "I have no interest in going to a nude beach."

She looked surprised. "Why not?"

"Because it's not sexy. There's nothing remotely erotic about it. You go to the beach, take off your clothes and wander around with a bunch of other naked people. Big deal. It's like going to the grocery store to buy groceries." He stared into the microwave, where the cellophane wrapper seemed to respirate as it swelled, shriveled, swelled and shriveled again. "I don't like nudists. There's too much bullshit philosophy involved. Back to nature and all that."

"Oysters are erotic. They have oysters on Martha's Vineyard."

"They have oysters in Providence. Oysters per se signify nothing."

She smiled, listening to him speak; he was teasing her, and she knew it.

"Besides," he said, "my editor has a summer house on the Vineyard. Or maybe it's Nantucket. Anyway, I don't want to risk it." The microwave dinged; he hit the button to give it another thirty seconds.

"I think it'd be fun," she said tentatively. "Knowing me, I'd probably bail out at the last minute. I wish that I could just turn off my brain and let myself go." Tired of waiting, she picked some chicken from her plate, blew on it, then popped it into her mouth, thinking as she chewed. "I wonder if you can have sex and masturbate and stuff like that."

"At a nude beach? I doubt it." He stopped the microwave and took out his serving. Slicing the wrapper, he arranged the chicken over the rice and mushed it up, quelling an urge to touch the hot fork to her skin. "Come on, let's eat," he said.

They dined in silence. It was dark outside, and something was going on at the church down the street.

After a few bites, Marlene pushed her plate aside and stared down at her breasts. Her nipples appeared slightly yellow, and she wondered if this made her more attractive or less. Her stare became a reverie; it felt good to see her breasts, just as it felt good to see her husband across the table with a paper napkin in his lap. "I started reading your book again yesterday," she said.

He didn't look up. "What on earth for?"

"Because you were gone, and I missed you."

"Marlene, my book isn't a substitute for me."

"I know, but it's a nice reminder. I'd forgotten all about the scene at the funeral home. I love that scene."

"You do?"

"Yes."

"I thought you said you'd forgotten all about it."

She laughed to hide her embarrassment. "I mean, I forgot about the *details.* You know what I mean."

His shoulders, which had been tense, slumped. "I know . . . I'm just being an asshole. I wrote that book a long time ago, Marlene. Words came easier to me then. I wish it wasn't so hard now. I guess that our minds just go soft after awhile." He paused. Sometimes he felt that these conversations would be a whole lot easier if he and Marlene weren't naked.

After dinner, they went up to bed and watched TV until eleven. During the commercials, he told her about his day at work. "I suppose it's hard not to admire Nate's spontaneity," he said. "The guy never seems to worry about anything."

She could tell from his tone of voice that something was bothering him. "We can be like that, too. We can be spontaneous," she said.

"No, we can't. We're boring."

"We're not boring! Look at us. Does this look like a boring couple to you?"

He glanced at their naked bodies, which in truth he was getting tired of seeing. "In a way, yeah," he said.

She sat up in bed. "Then let's make it exciting again. Let's do something dangerous."

"Like what?"

"Like . . . let's have sex in the backyard."

He laughed. "Oh, shut up."

"I mean it. Come on, right now."

She took his hand and started to rise, but he pulled her back down. "No. Next brilliant suggestion," he said.

Still high on the idea, she said, "All right, maybe not that. But let's just stick our necks out. For one minute, Stuart. It'll be fun."

"No, it won't."

No longer kidding, she said, "I'll go by myself."

"Oh, no." His grip tightened on her arm. "You're gonna get yourself in a lot of trouble."

"Come with me, then. You can protect me."

He sighed. Marlene's single-mindedness could be impressive at times. "All right . . . for *one* second. Not even that. A half-second."

Still unsure of himself, he followed her out of bed and down the stairs to the first floor. From behind, Marlene's body looked pale and shapeless, and he remembered how much he enjoyed pressing himself against her fleshy bottom, his erection fitting snugly in the crevice of her buttocks. This sense-memory helped to block out some of the doubts that were pervasive inside his head.

At the back door, they spoke in whispers:

"Should we leave it open?"

"Yes, but bring a key just in case."

"Just in case what?"

"Just to be safe. The wind might blow the door shut."

"But if we leave it unlocked—"

"Let's not get into an argument about it. Here—"

"Is there something wrong? Are you mad about something, baby? 'Cause we can—"

"No, let's just do it. But one second, and then we—"

"Shhh . . ."

Easing the door open, she placed one foot on the wet brick patio, then continued a few steps away from the house. Stuart followed but stopped where the light from a street lamp fell at his feet. He didn't feel safe out here. The area behind the house was enclosed by a six-foot-high fence that ran along the perimeter of the yard. Above the fence, the second and third floors of the neighbor's house lurked behind a thicket of bare trees. The rain had lessened somewhat; he could feel it on his back and chest.

Marlene walked purposefully to the edge of the lawn, then returned, smiling, radiant. "Where'd you put the keys?" she asked.

He nodded toward a window ledge near the door. "They're right there," he said, adding for his own sake, "they're not going anywhere."

Out in the church parking lot, a car door opened and closed, and both Stuart and Marlene watched as a man in a long rain-coat trod up the steps to the rectory entrance. She called out to him, "I'm naked!" but then, just as impulsively, scurried across the patio and into the house. Stuart didn't move, just stood in the gray glow of the streetlamp, letting the rain patter on his head, the same as it fell on the yard, the deck furniture, the unraked leaves. The wind blew sidelong across his body as he watched the man in the parking lot go into the church. He could feel the whole world looking at his penis, and he braved this prickly sensation for a full five seconds before sauntering across the wet brick patio and going inside.

An hour later, they were both still awake. The halogen track lighting over the bed cast ultraviolet rings across the stippled white-plaster ceiling; it all seemed a bit harsh for 12:23 in the morning, but with the booze wearing off—along with the shock of what they'd done—they craved a certain midday orderliness, the comfort of seeing definite shapes instead of blurs: the night-stand, the TV on top of the dresser, the closet door half open.

"Maybe we should've waited till later," Marlene said. She was sitting up in bed with three navy-blue pillows wedged between her back and the headboard. Her eyes had narrowed to anxious slits. "The Taylors still had their lights on. What do you think the chances are that someone saw us?"

Stuart didn't answer. He was trying to remember the past hour, but already it seemed like something that hadn't really happened, none of the sensory information—the wet leaves on the ground, the prick of the cold night air under his arms and between his legs—available to him except as mere description: the word "cold" but not the sense of it, the word "naked" but not the fact.

Marlene flung off the comforter and swung her legs over the side of the bed. "Damn it! This always happens. I always spoil things for myself. Maybe I should've had another glass of wine first."

"No more drinking, Marlene. Not if you're going to act like this."

His cautious interjections went unheard as she crossed to the dresser and began laying out clothes for work. "I'm tired of being such a scaredy-cat. I want to do everything, honey— streaking, public masturbation, you name it."

"All very much against the law," he warned.

She turned and beamed at him. "Nothing bad will happen to us as long as we're together. Trust me, Stuart."

As much as he wanted to believe her, he couldn't. "I admire your confidence," he said.

"I'm *not* confident," she insisted. "Not like you. My God, you *wrote* and *published* a *book*. That's amazing! I haven't done anything amazing." She looked down, and he followed her gaze to the floor. "I think . . . I want to start flashing people. I dunno."

She finished setting out her clothes, climbed into bed and, with the reluctance of a performer not wanting to leave the stage, turned off the lights. They kissed and held each other, but the spell was broken; neither felt like having sex. Ten minutes later, the sound of loud, masculine snoring from her side of the bed startled him.

Lying next to her—it was three in the morning, and he'd still not fallen asleep—he considered the smallness of the world, the connective fibers that existed for no other reason than to render a person self-conscious. This state in particular—the smallest, most insular one in the country—was a pressure cooker for self-consciousness. Everybody knew everybody else. Even Nathaniel Pike and Gregg Reese went to the same parties. In a growing panic—at 3:00 a.m., then at four and still unable to sleep—he remembered what Celia Shriver had said to him that afternoon:

You think you can keep a secret in Rhode Island?

Four-thirty, now . . . resisting the urge to go outside and do it again . . .

4

Allison Reese and her boyfriend, Heath, were arguing. It was one
in the afternoon, and neither had gotten dressed or even out of
bed. Heath's bedroom, one of two rooms in his East Providence
basement apartment, was cozy and cluttered, with film canisters
and videotapes piled on the floor, giant posters from gore and
exploitation flicks covering every inch of wall space, their corners curled where the tape had dried and come loose. Heath's
prized possession was a high-definition, wide-screen Panasonic
television, which he'd bought for three thousand dollars. Three
thousand dollars wasn't remotely in his price range, but he'd
done it anyway, and in the weeks since, he'd joined the Panasonic online mailing list, sent in the lifetime warranty and read
the sixty-eight-page owner's manual from cover to cover. He
wanted to be a good parent to his TV.

With the DVD player on pause, Allison sat up in bed and
blocked his view of the screen. "I don't see what's misogynous
about it, just because it shows one woman sexually dominating
another in front of a man. I mean, that's like saying sexuality is
misogynous. What's misogynous about Marguerite Duras, or
Anaïs Nin?"

"I'm not saying it's *bad*, I'm just saying it's misogynous," Heath replied. The film they'd been watching was *Ilsa: The Wicked Warden*, which showed a female warden sticking pins into a woman's breasts, another being suffocated to death in front of her sister, still another lying on a torture table while a prison guard injected acid into her vagina—all fairly typical of the 1970s women-in-prison genre but not, perhaps, the best choice for Thanksgiving Day entertainment. "I'm not making a value judgment about it," he continued. "I think misogyny is a perfectly valid form of artistic expression. Look at Philip Roth."

Allison, who'd never read anything by Roth, said, "There's a big difference between something like that and *Ilsa: The Wicked Warden*."

"Not necessarily. A Roth novel can be as fucked up as any sexploitation film. What you're reacting to is the difference between two art forms. Film is more visceral than print. There are things people will tolerate in a book that they'd never stand for in a movie."

"Whatever." She turned off the TV with the remote. "I think the whole idea of misogyny is misogynous, anyway. It's patronizing."

"Being misogynous?"

"No, always saying, 'Oh, that's misogynous,' just because you think I don't know how to stand up for myself."

He reached across the bed and took the remote out of her hands. "You know that's not what I think. I just don't want you to be offended by the film."

"I'm *not*." She rolled out of bed, threw on one of Heath's shirts and went into the tiny bathroom off the kitchen. Her muscles had tensed up during the movie, and she now found herself unable to pee. Flushing the toilet anyway, she washed her hands under a trickle of water and returned to the kitchen to make coffee. Heath had put on a Beach Boys CD, one of his several bootlegs from the legendary *Smile* sessions of late '66, early '67. Heath was a *Smile* fanatic, and his collection of memorabilia from that particular era in the band's history was extensive. Each bootleg was slightly different, and the same songs often had different titles—"Friday Night" was also "I'm in Great Shape," or "The Woodshop Song," even "I'll Be Around," depending on which reference work you consulted. As for the songs themselves, most were just brief, elliptical patterns— "feels," as Brian Wilson called them—more like backing tracks than finished compositions, as if all the rhythmic and harmonic sequences had been laid down without the melody. Part of *Smile*'s appeal was that, as a record, it only partially existed; various parts of it were lost, destroyed, never recorded, still sitting in a vault somewhere. Unlike the other relics of the sixties—*Sgt. Pepper,* even the Beach Boys' own *Pet Sounds*—*Smile*'s power came from its very inscrutability, the fact that it didn't exist in any definitive form. Much of what remained of the sessions sounded trite and sophomoric, hardly the stuff of myth. *Smile* was certainly not up to the refined level of Brian Wilson's other, better-known efforts like "California Girls" and "I Get Around." But at the same time, it *was* a masterpiece, because what he'd managed to capture on tape, however fleetingly, was the sound of his own mind coming apart. Even the titles suggested a young and once-brilliant Wilson struggling with his exhausted imagination: "I Love to Say Dada," "Do You Like Worms," "Tune X," "I Don't Know." *Smile*'s drama was real, not a fabrication. Heard over and over, those chants and ostinatos came to mimic the obsessive ruminations of a confused, broken man. It was music worth obsessing about: "Heroes and Villains," "Surf's Up," "Child Is Father of the Man." The most beautiful music ever.

To Allison, it sounded like noise. "Something else, please," she called across the room.

Heath turned off the music. "What do you want to hear?"

Focused on her task, she spooned three dark heaps of ground coffee into the basket filter of Heath's never-before-washed coffeemaker. "Actually, nothing right now. I'm still thinking about that movie." Starting the coffee, she pulled up a stool and sat down. Her feet were dirty from picking up dust and bits of uncooked rice from the floor. "I wonder why they don't make movies like that anymore. I mean, it's just *porn*. What's the big deal?"

"It's not porn, Allison." He moved in on her; this was a subject that he took *very* seriously, and his unshaven face—which Allison had once likened to a banana, an image she hadn't been able to shake since—regarded her with pity and concern. "Porn is its own thing. I'm not interested in porn. I'm interested in transgressive cinema."

She smiled at him. "No, I know you are, honey." Her eyes went dreamy as she appraised his body; his long, dyed-blond hair, black at the roots; the impressive musculature he'd built up from years of lugging camera equipment around and that now seemed wrong for his personality. She'd never dated a boy like Heath before. Two, maybe three nights a week, she stayed with him in East Providence, their dates consisting mostly of takeout pizza, one or two rounds of lovemaking (at twenty-one, Allison's sexual proclivities were still rooted in adolescence: candlewax and flavored condoms) interspersed with late-night screenings of *Zabriskie Point, I Am Curious (Yellow), I Am Curious (Blue), Salon Kitty, The Naked Ape, Last House on Dead End Street, Guyana: Cult of the Damned,* any number of Umberto Lenzi films, *Jungle Holocaust, Farewell Uncle Tom,* the uncut *Lolita,* the uncut *Caligula,* the European-only version of *Salo or the 120 Days of Sodom,* all preselected from his ever-growing library of rare and imported videos, DVDs, and even 16mm, which he showed against a baby-blue bedspread hung over the wall. For her part, Allison did her best not to draw any conclu-

sions about her boyfriend's sanity based on his cinematic prefer-
ences: banned films, films involving rape and torture and child
molestation, films at the very least rated NC-17 but generally not
rated all. She was beyond drawing conclusions about anything.
Besides, she didn't want to look like a wimp.

Ever since college—as expected, she'd graduated with hon-
ors in Comparative Literature, with a minor in Postfeminist
Theory—she'd been crafting a new persona for herself. Though
she still kept in touch with her former housemates, she now
considered almost everything about the Ivy League experience
distasteful. During those four years at Harvard, she'd gotten laid
exactly once and not since her first semester. The drugs were
good on campus, and easy to find, but the only place she liked to
get high was the aquarium—*check out the fishes, whoa*—and the
only clubs in town usually played too much eighties retro for her
taste. Freed from the bonds of academia, she wanted to explore
life a little, maybe get arrested, try heroin once, have a "lesbian
experience," read James Joyce and D. H. Lawrence, wear slinky
black dresses instead of sweaters and jeans, high-heeled sandals
instead of shapeless brown loafers, Poison instead of patchouli.

When she'd first met Heath back in June—the Wild Colonial
wasn't his usual hangout, but it was Bloomsday, and every year
the bar undertook a daylong reading of *Ulysses* in the back
room—some of those transformations were already in place.
She'd taken to wearing her sandy blond hair long, her bangs
trimmed in the front. If she was beautiful, she preferred not to
think of herself as such. *Striking,* perhaps, or *disarming,* both of
which qualified her looks in terms that she could understand. At
bars, she displayed proof of her education the way some women
flashed the pepper spray on their key chain: both as a warning
and, to the right man, a challenge. If you didn't "get it," you
didn't *get* it. Wherever she went, she carried a tattered copy of
The Golden Notebook in the pocket of her blood-red sweater-

coat. This, like everything else, was a test. The man she was looking for had to be smart, older (Heath was twenty-six), left wing and politically active, an artist, kind of cute, pot-friendly, acid-friendly, vegan-friendly but not militant about it. Heath was all of these things.

Best of all, he wasn't a Rhode Islander. Allison was tired of guys from Cranston, Warwick, East Providence. Heath had a vibe that set him apart from those losers. He'd left home, moved on with his life. He hardly even talked about his parents, who were both still down in North Carolina, where he'd grown up. Allison couldn't imagine making such a clean break from her past. Her family had always been a tight-knit crew, and not even her parents' divorce three years ago had done much to change that. Allison's mother, Renee, had since moved to an expensive flat in London, where Allison had spent recent summers. Her parents continued to get along, though seeing each other only occasionally. Renee, who'd turned into a bit of a fag hag in Europe, still called long-distance every few weeks, trying to fix Gregg up with one of the many pretty boys in her coterie. It was no big deal; these were modern times, and there was nothing anyone could do about it anyway.

Not surprisingly, the person most affected by the divorce was Allison. She'd begun to suspect something about herself recently that she could hardly believe, given that it contradicted everything she'd always regarded as fair and decent and open-minded. The truth was, she *didn't like* gay men. Being charitable, they made her uncomfortable; that's how she sold it to herself, by easing into the semantics of her own prejudice as a swimmer might enter cold water an inch at a time. Phrasing it thus, she acknowledged the problem was her own—the fact that all of the gay men she'd encountered in college had seemed like such stereotypes was a reflection of her own personal shortcomings, and not any fault of the men themselves.

"What should I wear tonight?" Heath asked, his arms around her waist while he nuzzled her in the kitchen.

The coffee was ready; Allison lifted the carafe and poured herself a cup. "Wear whatever you want. My father doesn't care. He'll probably wear a suit, but that's just his personality."

"Then I'll wear a suit."

"*Don't.*" She glared at him. "If you wear a suit, you have to get a haircut. That's the rule."

Climbing down from the stool, she took her coffee into the other room and said, peering out the high basement windows, "Maybe we should stay at my house tonight. We'll probably be too drunk to drive back after dinner."

"Is your dad a big drinker?" Heath asked, helping himself to the half-cup of coffee she'd left for him in the carafe.

"No, but *we* are." Taking off her shirt, she went to the closet and browsed through the three or four outfits she kept at his place. "Let's bring some pot, too. I want to get stoned."

An hour later, they'd both showered, dressed and walked up the broken cement steps to the parking lot behind the apartment. Allison drove them across the Washington Bridge to Fox Point, then down along the boulevard and past the mental hospital to where she and her father lived in a three-story brick and shingle Tudor, set off from the road by a tall hedge and a circular driveway. The BMW was parked in front of the house, along with a car she didn't recognize. Pulling up behind it, she turned to Heath and made a face. "I hope we're not having turkey."

Once inside the house, she led him through the smell of turkey cooking into a lamp-lit sun parlor, where her father and another man were sitting over drinks and appetizers. The other man was Nathaniel Pike; Allison hadn't expected to see him here.

"Honey." Gregg Reese got up from his wicker chaise lounge

and kissed his daughter on the cheek. The drink in his hand looked like a Scotch on the rocks. "Was the drive down easy?"

"Dad, it's five minutes." She smiled tightly at their guest. "Mr. Pike, this is my boyfriend, Heath. Heath . . ."

The man leaned out of his seat to shake the boy's hand. "Nathaniel Pike," he said.

Heath's face burned as he heard himself saying hello. It seemed an unlikely combination—Nathaniel Pike and Gregg Reese. Reese was the kind of middle-aged man that others referred to as "youthful-looking." His short, grayish-blond hair stood on end, wet-gelled to a punkish bristle, and his frosty blue eyes were set in deep dark sockets like lights inside a cave. As the public face of the Reese Foundation, he rarely appeared as anything other than rigidly uncomfortable in front of a camera, and he carried the same stiff, reading-the-cue-cards demeanor to his private life. The other man was a goof, a wasteful libertine. Every town, Heath supposed, had its Nathaniel Pike: the archetypal kook who resurfaced every few months, jabbering his opinions to local reporters about the issues of the day. Both Pike and Reese were so wealthy that the money seemed abstract—inexhaustible and therefore beyond reckoning. But to a basement dweller like Heath, who tended to regard the enlightened upper class with some suspicion, Nathaniel Pike was infinitely hipper than Gregg Reese.

"Mr. Pike," he managed, letting go of his hand. "It's an honor."

"I'm not staying," Pike explained, primarily for Allison's sake. "I just stopped by to drop off a bottle of something."

Politely, not wanting to make a big deal about it, Gregg protested, "No, Nate, I've already told you. We've got plenty of food."

"Oh, no, no. I don't want to ruin your Thanksgiving."

"You're not ruining anything." Gregg smiled, showing his teeth. Allison sometimes wondered how her father appeared to other men. Was he attractive? The idea freaked her out a little.

Turning to her, Gregg asked, "Allison, what would you and Heath like to drink?"

She answered coldly, "We'll help ourselves," and hurried off to the kitchen, where she waited for Heath to catch up. "God," she hissed, "I cannot *believe* he actually wants Nathaniel Pike to stay for dinner. Maybe we can sneak out early."

Heath still felt dazed from shaking Pike's hand. "I didn't know your father and Mr. Pike were friends."

"My father doesn't have any friends." Struggling with the corkscrew, she tried to open a bottle of Chardonnay. "Pike's been scamming off of my family for years. He used to hang out with my mom when I was little. He had her going on some lie about needing money to make a movie. I'm sure they probably fucked." The cork came out with a pop, and she poured them two brimming glasses, emptying most of the bottle. "The dude's completely bonkers," she said, "and he's a total perv."

When they returned from the kitchen, Pike asked, "Heath, what do you do?"

Embarrassed, Heath sat down, and Allison dropped into his lap. "I'm an independent filmmaker," he said.

"Heath has every film that's ever been made on videotape," she added.

He gave her a secret, disapproving look. Meeting Pike for the first time, he wanted to present himself on his own terms, without her girlfriendy interjections.

Smiling broadly, Pike said, "I used to produce movies—a long time ago. I tell you, that's a hell of a business."

"Didn't you do *Emmanuelle on Taboo Island*?" Heath asked. Some other titles then came back to him: *The Succubus. Fatal Warning II.* A whole video library's worth of glorious junk.

Pike looked pleased. "Not guilty. I made a cannibal flick with Laura Gemser, though, if that's what you're thinking about."

Heath told himself to quit fawning. "I'm writing a screenplay right now," he said. "It's sort of an homage to counterculture exploitation films like *Trash* and *Easy Rider*."

"It's a spoof?"

"No, not a spoof, although . . . I could *make* it a spoof."

"Something like a *funny* version of *Easy Rider*. But deliberately bad." Pike had a swallow of his drink. "That'd be interesting."

Gregg perked up. "Maybe you could get Mr. Pike to produce it for you, Heath."

Hearing his voice—bright and well intentioned—Allison felt a surge of love for her father.

"Oh, I don't think I'm quite ready for that," Heath demurred. Of the three, it seemed to him that only Pike was taking him seriously.

"I'll tell you an idea I once had," Pike said and helped himself to a brimming handful of mixed nuts. "Now, maybe you can do something with this. It's called *Boring Movie*. And the gag is, the whole film's tedious and dull for an hour and a half, then it's over."

"I see," Heath said, not following.

"A deliberately boring movie."

"But how would you—"

"You wouldn't! Don't play it for laughs. That would spoil the gag."

"That's stupid," Allison snapped. "What's the point in making a movie if it's just a waste of people's time?"

"But that's what's great about it!" Pike's voice rose to an indecorous level. "Your generation always takes things too literally, Allison. When Gregg and I were your age—well, maybe not Gregg, but . . ."

Allison glared, defending her father by ignoring the joke. "We knew how to have *fun*. Look at history. The only things worth doing are pointless things. Because if there's a *point*? Then that's all there is to it. 'And now *this* movie is going to show you how to comb your hair and be a good little American.' No!" Waving both hands, he nearly sloshed his drink onto the carpet. "I want a movie where the screen is blue for three hours."

Doing his best, Heath offered, "Kind of like a post-Warhol—"

"I want to read a book and be able to say, 'Now what the fuck was that?' when I get to the end of it. I want to have my expectations underwhelmed. I want to leave the theater dissatisfied."

Pike's bluster, his hyperbole and whiz-bang hand gestures left little room for discussion, but Gregg tried anyway. "There must be a way to tie it in with something else," he said, "because if you think about it, maybe the *film's* not really boring, maybe it's just that our attention spans are so—"

"No!" Pike slammed down his glass. "See, you're ruining it by talking about it too much. Everything beautiful has been ruined by critics and academics. It's not enough that something just *is*. It's got to mean something, too."

Heath nodded in appreciation; these were all points he'd made before, to college friends, to girls he was trying to impress.

Changing the subject, Pike asked Allison, "So, what have you been doing with yourself lately?"

She glanced at her father, then said, "Looking for a job, I guess."

"Why don't you work for your old man?" he suggested. "Hell, *I'd* hire you."

She briskly discarded the idea. "I think I'd rather work for my father, Mr. Pike, but thanks. Actually, I'm considering taking the year off."

Turning to Gregg, Pike asked, "What do you think of that?"

"Whatever she wants is fine with me," Gregg said. "I won't pressure her. Just as long as she gives something back to her community. That's what this family has done for generations, and when I go, Allison will be there to take my place."

Warmed by the alcohol, she reached for her boyfriend's hand. "We both will."

The whole room turned toward Heath, who, ever since sitting down, had become gradually more self-conscious about Allison's being in his lap. "I guess I'll try," he said, staring at her fingers interlocked with his own.

Pike came to the rescue. "You're scaring the kid, Gregg. Surely he doesn't want to go to fund-raisers for the rest of his life."

"Heath doesn't mind fund-raisers," Allison maintained.

Heath considered what to say for himself, then decided. "It depends what it's for."

That settled, Pike reached into his jacket pocket and pulled out a business card. "I should take you with me when I go up to New Hampshire next month, Heath. I'd like to shoot a little documentary before I get to work on that mountain. Have you got a decent camera?" Before Heath could answer, Pike handed him the card. "I'll buy you one. Nothing fancy—maybe a Betacam SP. All of my old shit's out of date."

Allison snatched the card away. "I don't like this," she said.

Pike smiled. "But Allison, this is a great opportunity for him. Besides, don't you want to see what I'm doing up there?"

The smug look on his face infuriated her. "Not really. Whatever it is, I'm sure it's disgusting. You're not proving anything to anyone, you know. So you've got a lot of money, so what? So do we. At least we give our money to people who deserve it."

"Don't be so certain about that. There's more than one way to spend a dollar. Me, I prefer to spend it on myself."

"Whatever." Shaken up, she got to her feet. "This wine isn't any good. I'm gonna open another bottle. Heath?"

Reluctantly, Heath followed Allison out of the room. With his daughter gone, Gregg saw fit to help himself to another splash of Scotch. He offered the bottle to Pike, who grunted and said, "Just a swig. I'm due at Mediterraneo in under an hour."

Pouring, Gregg felt compelled to fill Pike's glass all the way to the top. He didn't know why, but he wanted to get him drunk. "I don't see where you get the money to do these things," he said, thinking of the land Pike had recently acquired in New Hampshire.

Pike laughed. "Now, Gregg, don't go lecturing me about money. You're not exactly frugal yourself."

Gregg nodded judiciously. There was truth to this: whatever stunt Nathaniel pulled, however wasteful or eccentric, Gregg countered it with a very public act of generosity. He thrived on the idea that, in the twenty-plus years that they'd known each other, he was undeniably, unambiguously, on the side of the right. Inside, however, another Gregg Reese, the one who sometimes found his own family history too much to bear, watched with envy as Pike spent millions on unworthy causes, getting away with things that would've sunk the Reeses.

"You're lucky, Nate," he said. "You're all alone in the world. No expectations, no dynasty to uphold. No mother looking constantly over your shoulder."

This last was a topic of great amusement to Pike, who'd endured Keeny Reese's wrath from the time they first met. With Gregg's mother now well advanced in years and suffering from a variety of ailments, he preferred to think of her in a more forgiving light. He'd be around a lot longer than she would. "Don't take it out on your family," he said. "You've got a great kid, which is a blessing."

"Allison isn't the problem. It's people like Celia Shriver and those other old biddies who keep soaking me for charitable donations. On top of which, I'm getting taxed up the ass."

Anticipating Pike's response, he added, "I'm not like you, Nate. I'm sure you know all the loopholes, all the ways to get out of doing your part—I mean, no offense."

Pike shrugged. *Oh, none taken.* "You need a quick shot of cash? I can give you a hand, buddy."

"Forget it," Gregg snapped. "I'll be fine as long as this referendum goes through. I've got a solid budget until the end of next year, but that's when things get sketchy. Everything that's going to trickle down has trickled down already."

"Thus the Allison Fund."

"Yep." This was a referendum Gregg had proposed along with a few of his friends in the Rhode Island General Assembly. If approved, many of the charitable organizations supported by the Reese Foundation would receive their hefty subsidies from the state. Gregg didn't like talking about it. The fact that he'd done such a bad job of managing his finances—oh, no one would come right out and say it, of course, but he knew what they were thinking—filled him with a shame that was second only to the other shame in his life, the one that couldn't be named.

"I'm getting screwed on all sides," he said. "My mom's idea of what a dollar's worth is about twenty years out of date. I feel like I don't have anyone who I can talk to about this. Allison's too young—she doesn't get it. It's not her fault, it's mine. I never *taught* her anything."

Pike rose and, with a sigh of departure, chugged back the rest of his drink. He could take only so much of listening to Gregg before his thoughts began to wander.

Before leaving, he told Gregg, "You need to stop worrying so much about the Reese Foundation. It's all a lot of self-righteous bull, anyway. Every fortune—*especially* yours—has an evil source. Decades and generations won't change that. You might not be aware of this, Gregg, because you're too far from the source." He gritted his teeth. "But I made my own fortune. I *am* the evil source."

Gregg wondered what comfort he was supposed to take from this. Even after so many years, it still wasn't clear to him whether Pike really had his best interests at heart.

At the front door, Gregg thanked Pike for coming by. The weather had turned gray and blustery, with a patch of blue sky where the good weather had pushed off to the north.

"If you're interested in joining me," Pike said, "I'll be in Concord over the holidays. I know a woman who runs a ski lodge in North Conway. You'll like this gal—Sarah Cranberry. The Cranberrys are another old New England family, although," he laughed, unlocking his car door, "that's where the similarity ends."

Gregg stepped off the porch, trying to ignore the autumn wind circling around his ankles. "Okay, I'll think about it. Maybe I'll come up for a few days. But only to look around. I'll go shopping at the outlets while you're doing your business."

They shook hands. Glancing away, Pike spotted Allison in the kitchen window, her face partially blocked by a low swooping drape. Fleetingly, he wished he'd been more polite when he'd had the chance. Ah, well, dinner, some drinks, some talk, the comforting delight of good service in a five-star restaurant. "I'll give you a call," he said, then, forcing himself: "Tell Allison I'm sorry if I upset her."

Gregg didn't know what to say, so he just watched Pike climb into the car and speed away. The wind returned, this time with an infusion of cold rain. Looking back at his house, he saw a black stream of smoke lose its shape and disperse over the chimney. Chilled and wet, he hurried inside and shut the door.

Heath and Allison were still in the kitchen, rooting through the refrigerator and setting out half-eaten wedges of cheese. Allison skipped across the room and threw her arms around her father. For the first time, he could smell her perfume, a subtle hint of something tasteful and expensive.

"We found these mulling spices in the cupboard," she said. "We're going to make glogg after dinner."

He kissed her again. "You'll have to drink it by yourself. I can't handle that stuff anymore."

Going to the oven, he looked inside and saw the turkey basking in darkness, its juices catching in the drip pan with a sizzle. Dinner wouldn't be ready for another hour, but this only added to his lazy feelings of contentment, of being loved by his daughter. Thanksgiving was his favorite holiday; as much as he liked the food, what he most enjoyed was spending time with Allison, lingering over wine—even when she was a little girl, he'd always let her have a glass, maybe two—and leaving the dirty dishes until morning, instead trooping upstairs to watch videos on the large-screen TV. Thanksgiving was a slow-paced, low-key holiday. There was no point, beyond savoring the daily occurrences of family life, having dinner together, then quietly sending one another off to bed.

As Heath and Allison busied themselves in the kitchen, Gregg made a tour of the dining room, the table set for three, two candles flickering beside a glass decanter for the wine. Allison had put on some music—a Natalie Merchant CD, the volume set just a touch too loud. He went to the stereo and edged the music down, not so much that she'd notice and push it back up again.

Returning to the kitchen, he said to Heath, "I'm glad you could spend Thanksgiving with us."

"Thank you, Mr. Reese." Heath had tied his hair back in a ponytail, and Gregg could now see more of his face. Regrettably, the boy hadn't shaved, and the black speckle on his cheeks called attention to the fact that he'd dyed his hair blond. Next to him, Allison looked overdressed; her red evening gown, with its low back and frilly sleeves, was something her mother would have worn to a New Year's party.

Remembering his ex-wife, he asked, "How's Renee? I feel like I haven't spoken to her in ages."

"She's good," Allison said, busy arranging a half-dozen varieties of cheese on a cutting board. Although more than enough food had already been set out in the parlor, she'd taken it upon herself to assemble a tray of appetizers, complete with cheese and crackers, red caviar and smoked salmon. "I guess she's going to Ibiza next month."

"What's in Ibiza?" he asked, not even certain *where* it was.

Caught up in her work, she sucked a cheesy film of Brie from her fingers. "You should check it out sometime. Lots of gay bars."

Gregg winced but said nothing. Tonight he wanted only to eat and drink, to watch his lovely daughter at the dinner table. He wanted the conversation to be general and spirited, followed by the traditional movie upstairs. Lastly, he wanted to go to bed, content and just a little drunk, at eleven o'clock.

By the time dinner was ready, the candles had burned down to gnarled stubs, and the Natalie Merchant CD had restarted itself on autorepeat. Gregg, Allison and Heath passed the food around—Allison, who occasionally fancied herself a vegetarian, took a sliver of white meat just to be polite—and when the last silver serving platter finally came to a rest, Gregg lifted his glass of wine and offered a toast. "To you, Allison. I'm glad you picked me this year."

Feeling obliged to add something, Heath said, "Thanks for having me, Mr. Reese."

"Of course, Heath." Gregg kept his glass raised. This spirit of toast making, which in most families rarely lasted more than a few seconds, was something he liked to hold on to for as long as possible. "You know, when Allison was a little girl, Renee and I would bring her down to the soup kitchens on Thanksgiving."

"Thank God we don't do that anymore," she said affectionately.

To show that he didn't take himself too seriously, he laughed and set down his glass. "Well, we don't need to anymore, because you're a full-grown woman, and your mother always did a good job teaching you strong values."

Allison cracked up. "Mom didn't do shit. You were one who taught me everything, not her."

He shook his head but didn't argue the point; he was starting to lose his focus, and he could tell that Heath wanted to eat. "Anyway," he said, "I'm very proud of you, and I'm grateful for having both of you here on Thanksgiving."

She reached out and took his hand. "I'm grateful for you, too, Daddy."

Pleased, he gave her hand a squeeze. Across the table, Heath thought, *I can't believe I just met Nathaniel Pike.*

5

Sixty miles away, in the rolling hills of western Massachusetts, Marlene and Stuart were getting ready for their own Thanksgiving dinner. The inn where they were staying was packed with guests—young couples, mostly, weekenders from Boston, New York, Connecticut. According to the register, the Breens were the only guests from Rhode Island.

The view through their bedroom window was of a brown fallow field and, in the distance, a margin of trees—most of them bare but some still clinging to a hint of autumn orange and red. Staring out the window, Marlene pictured her naked body striding across the bright, empty field. From the time they'd arrived, she'd kept an eye out for streaking opportunities, whether a suggestive overpass or a bend in the road. Here in the Berkshires, she could stay outside for hours at a time, maybe even bring herself to orgasm by the banks of a gushing, foamy-cold millstream. She and Stuart could have sex if they wanted. In the country, the roads and streams and skirting trailways were a constant invitation to take off their clothes and show themselves to the world.

"We're going to have the best vacation, honey," she said,

inspecting herself in the bedroom mirror. Her skirt was a full size too tight around her waist, and her feet looked swollen where she'd stuffed them into a new pair of spiky heels. "Let's eat quickly, okay? The less we order, the better. I'm fat enough as it is."

A voice inside advised him to say something nice about her weight, but instead he began unpacking his suitcase. He wished that they could enjoy the evening one step at a time and not let whatever might happen after dinner preoccupy and distract them.

"What do you want to do tomorrow?" he asked. The thought of spending eight hours going to galleries and antique stands didn't appeal to him. The bookstores in the area didn't look like the sort to carry his book, either.

Marlene went to the dresser, picked up her brush and used it to chop the snarls out of her hair. "It's your call. We can go bumming, or we can have a nice leisurely lunch. I'll go anywhere you're not embarrassed to be seen with me."

"Why would I be embarrassed?"

She laughed. "No reason, Stuart. It's just a saying."

"No, it's not. I wish you'd stop putting yourself down."

"I'm not putting myself down," she said. With the same willfully calm expression, she tossed her brush onto the dresser and went to work on her makeup. "By the way, if you're looking for the cell phone, I left it at home. We're here to have fun. Let's not worry about work or money or anything."

"Sounds good," he said, "but someone may need to call us."

He knew that belaboring this would only hurt her feelings, so he didn't. This holiday was more for her sake than his, anyway. He was perfectly happy to stay in Providence, where at least there were limits to what they could or couldn't do.

Once they'd finished getting dressed, she said, "I'm sorry I'm so ugly and fat and bloated."

Stuart took her face in his hands and kissed her with as much tenderness as he could muster. "You're not ugly," he said. "You're the most beautiful woman in the world."

"You're crazy," she said, which was what she always said to him whenever he called her beautiful.

Taking their coats, they went outside and drove the quarter mile to the town's only restaurant. Two rooms—one screened-in and open only in the summertime—accommodated the guests of the inn, plus whoever else happened to stop by. With its chipped wooden floors and tarnished wall sconces, the dining room had the look of belonging in someone's old home.

All during dinner, Stuart kept wondering about their plans for later. The other couples in the restaurant would probably have dessert and an after-dinner drink, then drive back to their hotel, build a fire, make love and go to bed. Why wasn't that good enough for him and Marlene? Their expectations were too high for each other. Every night had to be as fresh and exciting as the first night they'd spent together.

Halfway through dinner, Marlene mentioned going to Martha's Vineyard in May with Bill and Carla Marshall. "I think we should do it," she said. For a main course, she'd selected an appetizer of poached quail eggs to go with her bottle's worth of white wine, which she'd ordered by the glass. "You'll need a break after dealing with Mr. Pike all winter."

"That's assuming we get the damn thing done on time," Stuart said. "We might still be working on it in May."

Looking down at her empty plate, she wished that she'd ordered something more substantial than just an appetizer. Still, she wanted to feel beautiful tonight, and that meant not having to worry about her weight. "Well, anyway," she said, "you can always take some time off. I know how hard you work. You work a lot harder than I do."

Stuart sulked as she asked the waiter for another glass of

wine. He hated hearing her say nice things about him. These things, he knew, were impersonal and based mostly on wishful thinking. They certainly didn't apply to him.

"I *don't* work harder," he said. "There was a time when I did, but that was long before you knew me. I don't even know *how* to work anymore. I think that's why Nate likes me. He doesn't like hard workers."

"Why not?"

"Why not? Because (a) Nathaniel Pike is a complete lunatic, but (b) he feels threatened by people who have conventional views about money. Nate never had to work hard for his money. He had to work *smart* but not hard. There's a difference."

When Marlene's drink arrived, she poured the little bit of wine left in her glass into her new one, then handed the empty to the waiter.

"I'm not a hard worker either," she said, "at least not compared to some people. Carla's a hard worker. I guess that's why she's my boss." She gazed at one of the nearby couples, a nice-looking man and woman who were sitting over their espressos while a busboy cleared their dirty dishes. "I feel like I haven't done anything with my life."

He didn't know what else to say, so he asked for the check and paid in cash, leaving a fat stack of bills under his water glass. Looking at the money, Marlene said, "That was wonderful," but then remembered she'd had almost nothing to eat. It depressed her, wasting Thanksgiving on a few lousy quail eggs.

When she was finished with her wine, she offered him her hand, which he held over the table. He could tell by the dullness in her eyes that she was drunk. He knew this Marlene as well as the other; they were like two different copies of the same picture—all the details matched up and yet, side by side, they suggested a difference.

"Do you think I'm a bad person?" she asked.

He let go of her hand. "Of course not."

"Because . . . I don't know. I was a good kid, and everything seemed okay when I got to be an adult, but then I just stopped wanting to do things." Something lit up inside, and she stared across the table. "I've got to do it, Stuart. Tonight. I want someone to see me."

He glanced nervously toward the maitre d', who was standing at the next table. "Take it easy, hon," he said.

"I'm not drunk, if that's what you're thinking."

His cheeks flushed hotly. "I never said that."

"I know exactly where I am and what I'm doing. I want to be naked."

"Shh, hon, you're raising your voice. Let's just go back to the inn. Trust me, you'll be glad in the morning."

Some heads were turning to look at them, so she said, "You're right, I'm sorry. I'll stop."

Oddly enough, that wasn't what he wanted to hear, either. He didn't know what he wanted. *I'm a mess,* he thought.

After a pause, she asked, "Stuart, are you sorry that you married me?"

He scowled. Questions like this always annoyed him. "No. Why?"

"Because I'm so boring."

"You don't need to entertain me. That's not why people get married." He squinted to see what she was doing with her right hand. Having already unbuttoned the top two buttons of her blouse, she'd gone to work on the third. "Cut it out," he snapped.

"I'm sorry," she said, dropping her hand.

"All right, Christ, fine . . . if you're so goddamned determined."

He pushed his chair away from the table, and she followed him out of the restaurant. Other couples were just arriving for the second seating; the men were older than Stuart, better

dressed, with an air of inherited wealth that reminded him of
the Reese family on local TV. As for their wives, Stuart counted a
number of lantern jaws, which he'd always associated with over-
bred, entitled women. He couldn't imagine any of them doing
what he and Marlene were about to.

Once outside, Marlene hurried across the parking lot, taking
tiny steps in her heels. The cold autumn air embraced her, and
she could feel an undefined, ethereal body racing a few steps
ahead of her own physical form. It was the same sensation as
when she'd streaked across the backyard with Stuart, only more
intense.

Sitting in the car, he reached over from the driver's side and
put his hand on her leg. Her pantyhose was rough, and her skin
felt hot through the material.

"Where should I get undressed?" she asked.

His ears pricked up; he felt as though he could experience
each second of time an instant before the rest of the world did.
He looked out the window, then behind him, across the backseat. The parking lot was lit up with yellow sodium lights. "I
don't know," he said. "Let's just drive for awhile."

"What are we looking for?" she asked. Her hand had moved
up her skirt as she touched herself through the fabric of her
pantyhose. She did this out of a compulsion, hardly aware of it
herself.

"I don't know," he repeated, then started the car and pulled
out of the lot. The roads were perfectly dark; the car's high
beams shone cones of hazy white light across the two-lane
street. Dense walls of trees flickered by, dissolving away to
expose a fenced-in field, a mill, an old pharmacy, a block of
antique shops—all of them closed down for the night—and
then just more trees and darkness, here and there a gravel trail
that led straight into the forest.

Marlene steeled herself and, in a thoughtless burst of energy,

tore off her clothes. Like Stuart's, her sense of time had acceler-
ated; all of this was happening much too fast for her to experience it in the present tense. As if from a distance, she observed
her naked body in the seat of the car, her bare feet raised
and pressed against the windshield, hands moving across her
breasts, her stomach, her thighs. "I can't believe I'm doing this,"
she said.

The road continued straight for another quarter mile or so.
When another car appeared, she spread her feet apart and thrust
out her chest, staring determinedly into the headlights that illuminated her body. She couldn't see the driver's face, but she was
fairly certain that he or she, whoever it was, could see her. She
had to believe it. *Look at me,* she thought, then said it out loud,
her right hand rubbing between her legs. Once the car had
passed, she tried to remember what it'd felt like. The only way
she could explain it to herself, and this revelation came much
later, was that she'd given the other person something so central
to herself—the sight of her naked body—that the stranger now
maintained a sexual control over her, control that was total and
could never be revoked.

By the time they'd reached the next little village, her need to
put herself in an even more dangerous situation had increased
to the point where she felt like a passenger inside her own body.
She had no choice over what her body decided to do, so she
had no accountability for any of its decisions. Swept along, she
unrolled the window and tossed her skirt and blouse outside.
Wind filled the car, wrapping around her torso like a pair of cold
hands.

The woods became more sparse as they drew closer to
Great Barrington, where a Mobil station stood at the junction
with Highway 7, a police car parked out front with its engine
running.

Marlene crouched under the level of the dashboard as Stuart

drove past. Her own thoughts confused her. As expected, she felt excited, aroused, a little dizzy—but also trapped, unable to control herself, filled with regret. Climbing back up to her seat, she rolled herself in a ball and thought, *Please stop doing this, please. I don't want to do this anymore.*

"Take a left here." She pointed at a sign marked To Mass Pike. Stuart veered the car onto an empty street and continued for another few miles before she told him to pull over. He hesitated; the breakdown lane was narrow and hard to see in the dark. As he eased to a stop, his tires kicked up a cloud of dust that hung suspended like fog in the headlights. He turned off the car, and they both sat quietly for a moment, almost too stunned to speak.

"How do you feel?" he asked.

With her arms wedged between her legs, she'd managed to cover both her breasts and her pubic hair, but this only made her look even more naked. "Scared," she admitted.

Stuart checked the rearview mirror. It reflected nothing, only black. "Do you want to go home?"

"Oh, no," she insisted but said nothing more.

He felt as though he were looking at and speaking to a very young girl. "What do you want to do?"

She pushed a lock of her dark hair behind one ear. Because the danger had passed—this was a quiet street, after all—being naked didn't feel special anymore. In fact, it struck her as depressingly banal. She hadn't risked enough, hadn't gone far enough. She lacked the courage to continue. From now on, her nakedness was a punishment—given by herself, to herself—for having a body and for being a bad person.

Stuart's voice prompted her. "Marlene?"

Feeling pressured, she asked him for his sports jacket, which he took off and handed to her. "Just turn around," she said. They'd both been through enough for one night—especially

Stuart, who wasn't as committed as she was. But it was a good start. She felt good about what she'd done.

It took them twenty minutes to get back to the inn. Stuart drove a few miles under the speed limit, keeping both hands on the wheel. Marlene's silence scared him; every now and then he said, "How're you doing, hon?" or "Would you like me to slow down?" or "We're almost there." She found that she couldn't speak to him just now. They'd debrief later, back in the room.

The grassy parking lot behind the inn was half-empty when they returned. Stuart noticed a young couple walking down a stone path to their car. "There's someone out there," he muttered. "Maybe I should run in and bring out some clothes." She handed him his jacket, which he refused. "You need it more than I do," he said.

She tossed it at him anyway. The parking lot was not well lit, and all he could see was the gray shape of her body in the passenger seat. "Just bring me my jeans and a T-shirt," she said.

Sighing, he climbed out of the car and walked across the lot. The couple wished him a happy Thanksgiving but cast a curious eye at his sports jacket, which was rumpled. He smiled and continued stiffly on. At the steps, he watched them pass behind his own car and squeeze into a silver Audi. The car started and pulled away; as it did, he unzipped his pants and took out his penis. Within seconds, an aching loneliness overwhelmed him—the night was made even more silent by the sound of crickets—so he stuffed it back and went inside.

Up in the bedroom, he opened Marlene's suitcase and brought out something for her to wear. Along with her clothes, she'd packed a hardcover novel, written by someone he'd once met while out promoting his own book on tour. The book surprised him, in that Marlene rarely read for pleasure. He felt as though he'd caught her cheating with another man—which, in a sense, he had. Still, he could hardly blame her; what this other man had accomplished was something beyond his own abilities and ambitions. He was creatively impotent, and J. Alan Sessions was not. She was better off without him, better off reading someone else's book.

When he looked up, he saw her standing naked in the doorway. "I left the car unlocked," she said. "I'm gonna take a quick shower, okay? My whole body's shaking."

For ten minutes, he listened to the sound of the shower running, then undressed and moved into the sitting area, where he halfheartedly fondled his cock by the window. Doing so gave him no pleasure, only the vague sense that he'd lost control of his life.

When she finally came out of the bathroom, she was wearing a towel around her midsection and another wrapped turban-style around her head. "We'll try it again tomorrow," she said, "but during the day. I think I'll stay in the car, if that's all right— at least just to get started. We'll see how it goes." Reaching up, she unwound the towel from around her head and dashed her fingers through her wet hair. "The best thing, honey, is that we're doing this together. You're the only one I can talk to, the only one I can share any of this with, because I know you feel the same way I do and would never judge me or think I'm weird."

He studied her carefully. "Of course you're not weird," he said.

They didn't have sex that night; instead, he watched her masturbate, then followed her into the bedroom, where they slept until morning. At seven, he rolled out of bed and got dressed. "I'll be right back," he whispered to her.

Her eyes opened partway. "Where are you going?"

"Coffee," he lied.

Outside, he started the car and drove back along last night's route, scanning the breakdown lane for Marlene's skirt and blouse. The highway appeared wider and less hemmed in by

trees than it had the night before, and its smooth blacktop—
white and yellow lines freshly painted—made his behavior seem
all the more appalling. It was, to Stuart, like looking at a page of
his own writing, then hearing it read aloud by someone else; he
couldn't relate to it, and every nuance, every wide-open curve in
the road, embarrassed and offended him.

6

The day after Thanksgiving, Allison and her dad paid a visit to his mother's house on Benefit Street, near Brown. Keeny hadn't felt well enough to join Gregg for Thanksgiving, though she'd rallied in time to have brunch with a few of her lady friends at the Rue, a popular spot on the East Side.

Allison and Gregg found Keeny in the living room, fiddling with the TV. "I'm taping this opera for a friend," she said and pushed a button on the VCR. "*You* know her, Gregg," she added. "Barbara Stevens, Kenneth's wife. We went on a bus tour to the Lincoln Center together. *Mozart.* She'd never been to an opera before. I said, 'You poor thing.' Some of these CEOs keep their wives under lock and key."

"I went to the Met last year," Allison said.

Keeny patted Allison's cheek. As much as she loved her granddaughter, she sometimes found it hard to take her seriously. "How's the young man?" she asked.

"Good."

"Job?"

"Still looking."

Keeny grinned; these were all coded questions, and Allison's responses were equally diplomatic.

"Let me give you some money," she said and hobbled into the kitchen, where she unlocked a cabinet and pulled out her purse.

Keeny looked especially frail this afternoon. Her bronchitis had worsened over the fall, and she'd recently begun a new regimen of medications to help control her blood pressure. With Keeny getting older, soon all of the Reese family's problems would fall squarely on Gregg's shoulders.

From inside her wallet, Keeny took a check she'd been waiting to give to Allison for some time, judging from its wrinkled and creased condition. "This is too much, Grandma," Allison said.

Keeny pshawed. She didn't expect gratitude from her own family. There was no need for it. Whatever she had belonged to all of the Reeses.

"Mom, you shouldn't throw your money around like that," Gregg said. "Whatever Allison needs, I'll give her."

Keeny frowned. "If Allison doesn't want the money, she can donate it to the Reese Foundation. I'm sure she knows that already."

Allison glared at her father. "God, *Dad*. It's not like I asked her for it."

"I know, I know." His face felt hot. "It's just that I've been so preoccupied with money these days, and . . . then this lousy *cleaning woman* comes in and takes you for a ride every week."

"What's wrong with my cleaning woman?" Keeny asked.

"She . . . just doesn't do a good job. Look." He pointed at the sink, which had a coffee cup in it. "Right there, and . . ." Actually, the room wasn't nearly as dirty as he'd thought it was. Little by little, he could feel his authority slipping away.

Keeny scoffed. "Oh, relax. It's only eighty dollars a week, which isn't much in Providence. Besides, she cleans both floors."

Allison chimed in. "If Grandma needs a new cleaning woman, I'm sure we can help her find someone else."

"*That's* right." Keeny reached for her granddaughter's hand. "Very sensible, as always."

"Thanks, Gram." Allison pointed down a dark hallway to the bathroom. "I'll be right back. I've just got to fix my contacts."

Suddenly more businesslike, Keeny led her son back into the den. Edging the volume down on the TV, she offered him a seat on the suede leather sofa she'd brought over from her old house on Wayland Square. Most of her furniture was familiar to Gregg from his childhood, and it looked odd to him in these new surroundings, where the rooms were smaller and the various tables and chairs didn't quite fit.

"I always forget how deep this sofa is when I sit down," he said.

With the air of depriving herself for the sake of a guest, Keeny took a seat on a hard ladder-back chair. On her head was a silver turban, which she wore to hide her baldness. As her hair had turned thin and straggly, she'd adopted the male custom of shaving her head every few days. The result had made her look younger, if unnaturally so. A recent face-lift added to the impression of alien perfection, a kind of "old woman of the future" as envisioned by a comic book.

"I didn't mean to go on about the cleaning lady like that," Gregg said. "I just think that you've got to be careful when you're spending a lot of money, particularly when you're a Reese."

Keeny squinted peculiarly. "What does being a Reese have to do with it?"

He laughed. He'd been saving this conversation for another time and didn't want to get into it now. "Nothing, I guess."

Under most circumstances, she would've taken this opportunity to lecture him about his predecessors at the Reese Foundation, who'd done so much for the needy people of Rhode Island, but a fit of coughing derailed her train of thought. "How's Allison?" she asked. "I suppose she must find living with you terribly boring."

"I don't think so," he said but allowed, "It's probably unrealistic to expect her to live at home forever."

Keeny reached deep into her cardigan pockets, pulled out a Kleenex and wiped her nose. "I remember, you were a real homebody when you were a kid. You hated going to summer camp because you didn't want to be away from me."

"No, I hated summer camp because nobody liked me there."

"That's not true."

"Not a single soul," he asserted. "And you made me get on that bus every day because you were convinced I was having the time of my life, and when your friends asked about me, you *lied* to them. You said, 'He's having a *wonderful* time,' when it was plainly obvious that I wasn't."

She stuffed the Kleenex back into her pocket. "You're remembering things wrong, but never mind."

At this impasse, Allison returned from the bathroom and plunked down next to her father on the sofa. "What are you guys watching?" she asked, squinting at the TV.

"Grandma just said she's taping a program for her—"

"Oh, right. I spaced." Turning to Keeny, she said, "Grandma, did Daddy tell you? Nathaniel Pike came over yesterday. He looked awful. Thinner."

This wasn't true, of course. She'd said it only to please her grandmother, who despised Pike. He'd been a hanger-on at the Reese Foundation some twenty years ago, when he was in his early twenties and still hustling all across the state. The foundation was at that time the biggest cash cow in Rhode Island and one that Pike had set his sights on. Keeny had always suspected him and Gregg's ex-wife of having a little fling—not that it mattered, given that her son was a homo.

Gregg sensed his mother's disapproval. "He invited us to New Hampshire next month," he said.

"You're not going, are you?" Keeny snapped.

"Yes, I *am* going, Mother. Just for a few days. A little rest. I think I deserve it. This is a hard job."

"Oh, I know how hard it is. Believe me, I managed the Reese Foundation for thirty-eight years, even when your father was still alive. All that time, we always stuck to what we believed in. Not once did we compromise or lower ourselves by associating with gangsters."

Gregg bristled. "Pike's not a gangster. He's just a guy who made a lot of cash when he was younger, and now he doesn't know what to do with it all."

"So he spends it on foolish indulgences—like a *mountain,* of all things—instead of following the *Reese* example, which we've upheld for more than three hundred years."

"Maybe he doesn't want to follow the Reese example."

The blinders were up; she refused to be persuaded. "You be careful of that man, Gregg. You don't know what he's up to. It might be dangerous. It might be illegal."

"Or it might be totally harmless. Give me a break." Gregg hadn't expected such a complete lack of sympathy from his own mother. He'd always believed that the Reeses were different from other families. Their loyalty to one another was old-fashioned, even romantic. *They* were the gangsters, not Nathaniel Pike.

Later that day, after Gregg and Allison had returned home, he sat alone in his study to recover some of the serenity that his mother had disrupted. Whenever he'd tried to assert himself, not just as a Reese but as his own person, Keeny would refute him with the usual guilt trip about his ancestors, who'd never once made a bad decision or failed to serve the public good.

Were *all* families like this? he wondered. Gregg actually knew very little about his family history. The past half-dozen generations were fairly well documented: surgeons and CEOs, even a state senator. But before the late eighteenth century, those accounts became more vague, until all that was left was a name scrawled in a yellowed store ledger, like those of so many other old New England dynasties—names that revealed nothing but suggested a great deal. Wealth's evil source.

The recorded history of the Reese family dates back to 1636, the year after Roger Williams left Massachusetts Bay to settle on the eastern banks of the Moshassuk River. Williams was exiled in late 1635, having been found guilty of espousing controversial views from his pulpit in Salem. He escaped before his sentence could be carried out and took shelter in present-day Bristol, Rhode Island, where he begged the help of the chief of the Wampanoag tribe, Ousamequin, whose winter headquarters were on Mount Hope.

Long a friend of the Wampanoags, Williams was the first white man to publish a linguistic study of Native American languages, Key into the Language of America. The Native Americans liked and respected him, and this mutual respect was the basis of their friendship. In the spring of 1636, Chief Ousamequin granted him a section of land ten miles north of Mount Hope, but the deed was challenged by the governor of Plymouth Colony, Edward Winslow, who claimed the land already belonged to him. Ousamequin provided Williams with a new deed, which stood up under scrutiny, and Providence was founded in May or June of 1636.

Two of the original settlers were Hugh Perry Reese and his wife, Ginny. They moved from Salem to Providence in 1636 and built a house next door to Williams. Ginny was a frequent presence at the church services Williams conducted from his private residence. Devout to the point of obsession, she spent her days and evenings attending his prayer sessions, until Hugh grew tired of her absences and asked her to stay at home. When she refused, he beat her. The couple's dispute was brought before a town council meeting, where the majority decided that Hugh Reese had violated his wife's rights. As a punishment, his voting privileges were rescinded until he offered a formal apology. He never did, and the Reeses left Providence the following month.

They were not heard from again until the next year, when their names appeared in a census document for Aquidneck Island, along with nineteen other families. The leader of the new settlement was Anne Hutchinson, an antinomian who'd run afoul of local authorities for preaching an unpopular form of Calvinism. Her quasi-mystical views were supported by a local magistrate in Boston named William Coddington, who followed her to Aquidneck in early 1638.

On balance, the settlers on Aquidneck were more worldly than their counterparts to the north. Though no less devout than Williams, Hutchinson and Coddington acknowledged the need for aggressive trade and commerce. As it was practiced, antinomianism (the name was pejorative, meaning "against law") stressed individuality over communal living and material success over piety. Unlike Williams's followers, who were each granted the same amount of land, the antinomians were awarded property on the basis of class and wealth. Such philosophies would have appealed to an ambitious merchant like Hugh Reese.

Relations between Reese and his wife seem to have improved after they moved to Aquidneck. The diary of one William Dyer records that on 3 March 1647, he "Saw Mr. & Mrs. Reece on Thames St., walking past the merchants house, holding hands in publick, and kissing on the mouth!"

II | The Independence Project

1

"Why are people always so quick to assume the worst of their government?" Henry Savage demanded. "We make mistakes, sure, but we're not fundamentally bad people. That's Hollywood."

It was early in December, and the view outside his office was a study in two shades of gray—the overcast sky, and the sleet-covered buildings across the street from the Federal Reserve. He was on the phone with Cathy Diego of the Public Interest Research Group in Concord, New Hampshire. A Clinton-era Democrat, Cathy had begun her career in Washington but was too raw and unabashedly partisan to make it inside the Beltway, where nothing ever happened without compromise. As much as Henry disliked dealing with her, he sometimes wished he had her job, which was closer to the roots-level activism he'd envisioned when signing on with the Feds.

"Have you seen it yet?" he asked, meaning the seven and a half acres of New Hampshire woodlands he'd sold to Nathaniel Pike in June. Circumstances had changed since their last face-to-face meeting, and Pike's subsequent behavior hadn't done much to inspire the confidence of Henry's department.

"No, he's got it all roped off, like he owns the place," Cathy said.

"He *does* own it."

"Thanks to you." Cathy's voice sounded scratchy on the phone, and he could hear her chewing gum, a sound he particularly detested. "You know, I can name a half dozen nonprofit agencies here in New Hampshire who would've loved to buy that land if you'd given them a chance. You could've donated the whole acreage to the local protection society instead of selling it to Pike. Alice Shepperton would've been glad to help you out."

Henry switched her over to speakerphone. He knew that his secretary, Rochelle, would be listening in from the outer office, and he wanted her to appreciate what he was up against. "You might not believe this," he said, "but I had no idea what Pike's intentions were when I sold that land to him. I hardly even knew him!"

"Everyone in Rhode Island knows all about Nathaniel Pike."

"I'm not from Rhode Island."

"That's no excuse. You can still pick up the phone and get all of the information you need from Irene Jacobs at the RIPIRG. That's how we keep tabs on these lunatics."

"I wouldn't exactly call Pike a lunatic." Henry'd had to defend himself to his colleagues so many times over the past few weeks that he almost felt as if he and Pike were in this together.

"Oh, no? Answer me this: why would someone buy a house, tear it down, then start rebuilding it two weeks later? I'll tell you why—because he's a *lunatic*."

"Maybe. At any rate, I'd really appreciate it if you'd just back off and let me handle this. You and Alice have a lot of sway with the college kids up there. I don't want every young person in this country thinking their government's a drag."

"You can't blame kids for siding against you. You're a bureaucrat."

"We're *all* bureaucrats! What's wrong with that? *This* bureaucracy—where I'm sitting right now—is responsible for more good in the world than Nathaniel Pike. It's thanks to us that we've managed to keep so many of our national forests in service. That's the Big Brother bureaucracy in action. Every man and woman in this building is deeply committed to his or her job. Yes, they're bureaucrats, and God bless them for it. These are people who love our parks, and our waterways, our national landmarks . . . including *you,* Cathy. I know I've been nasty to you in the past, but I've always respected you for doing your job."

"Don't even. I've got a migraine, my daughter has a dance recital in three weeks, and my husband forgot to pay the frickin' cable bill this month."

"Fine." Henry sighed. "You're probably right. Maybe I should do a little more research into what Pike's been up to lately."

"That's easy. One quick call to the IRS should tell you everything you need to know."

"Nah. If I'm gonna get through to him, I've got to do it honestly. This whole thing is about principles. Nathaniel Pike might not have any principles, but *I* do."

"Sounds like a pipe dream, but go ahead. Celia Shriver might be able to help you out. She works for the Reese Foundation. The only person who hates Pike more than Celia is Reese's mother, Keeny."

"Good. The Reese Foundation's in my Rolodex. I'll give 'em a call. And thanks for the tip."

"Don't even."

"Don't even what?"

"Just don't even."

2

They rode in two cars—Pike, Stuart and Gregg in Pike's hunter green SUV, Allison and Heath in her hatchback, which she'd picked up cheap right after college. Allison made a point of driving a modest vehicle, even though her father had offered to buy her something more expensive as a graduation gift. Instead she got a trip to Vail, which turned out to be a bummer; skiing season was long over and the Feds were out in swarms, busting crystal meth dealers or anyone who looked like a Deadhead. Allison spent the entire week by the pool, writing in her dream journal. There was a cute guy, she remembered; they made out one night but didn't have sex. Other than that, nothing doing.

"This would be a really cool state to live in," Allison said to Heath as they drove north into New Hampshire. They'd both packed light for the trip; Heath had taken along the digital video camera that Pike had given him for the purpose of following him around the mountains. "Maybe I'll move up here. I don't know what I'd do, though. Just hang out, I guess."

"I'll come with you," he said, then wished he hadn't. If they moved anywhere, it would be to Cranston, or North Providence, maybe Pawtucket. Equal rent, equal division of utilities. No help from Mr. Reese, either, unless Gregg wanted to pay her share.

Out of the blue, she said, "I think I'd like to join a writers' colony someday. What's a good one?"

Heath shrugged. "I dunno. Ask Stuart."

"Yeah, right," she laughed. Both of them were reading Stuart's novel, *My Private Apocalypse,* though she was about fifty pages further into it than he was. Heath's progress was slowed by his habit of flipping back to the author photo after nearly every paragraph, trying to find a connection between Stuart's face and his rather chilly prose style.

Allison checked both side-view mirrors before pulling into the passing lane. She'd been tailgating the same station wagon for miles, and when they went by, the driver glared accusingly at Heath. "I can't ask Stuart," she said. "Stuart Breen is a *real* writer. Real writers don't go to writers' colonies."

"Real writers go to colonies all the time."

"Yeah, but not like *Stuart.*" She veered in front of the station wagon and slowed to her original speed. "Maybe he teaches at one, but I'm sure he doesn't take classes."

Another mile up the road, they stopped at a rest area just outside of Nashua, where they saw Gregg and the others coming out of the refreshment kiosk. A dusting of snow swirled gently around them, settling on windshields before swooping across the turnpike, where an identical rest area catered to the stream of traffic heading south.

Joining the others, Alison said, "Hey, Stuart, did Heath tell you? He wants to make a movie out of your book."

Heath, who'd said no such thing, shrugged. "I still have to finish reading it."

"Don't bother," Stuart muttered. His thin dark hair wavered in the breeze that made the prominent tips of his ears turn red.

Watching him, Allison remembered nothing of his book, only the fact that he'd written one. His presence in the Pike camp continued to amaze her. How could a man with the sensitivity to write a novel waste his time with a sleazeball like Nathaniel Pike? It called into question the motivations of every creative person she'd ever met.

"Hurry and wash up, people," Pike said. "I don't want to keep Sarah waiting."

"I thought this was some old friend of yours," Allison said.

Pike looked annoyed. "That's right. I don't want to keep an old friend waiting."

They used the bathrooms, then returned to their cars and forged ahead. The main road was a smoothly paved highway that skirted east around Lake Winnipesaukee, then plowed through a straight, deep crevice, rising occasionally to break along a curve or a steep drop-off filled with snowy pines. Stuart sat in the back of Pike's SUV, directly behind Gregg, whose stiff, grayish-blondish hair he could see over the leather headrest. Riding in cars always made him nauseous, particularly at the speeds at which Pike liked to drive.

"I'm serious about your wife, Stuart," Pike called over his shoulder. "I'll fly her up for a few days. She deserves some time off. I can't imagine working in a bank, all that mindless paperwork, having to . . . fucking MOVE!" He honked his horn, and a squat Festiva pulled over so the SUV could pass. "Anyway, just let me know."

Stuart kept quiet—Pike wouldn't have listened to him anyway—and instead focused on the shops of North Conway blurring by, one parking lot after another, three or four outlets grouped together in strip malls identical to those in Seekonk or West Warwick. Pike's idea to pave over part of a foothill near Mount Independence, fifteen miles south of here, was, if anything, counterrevolutionary. The land was already spoiled, with parking lots as commonplace as anything else in the region, natural or man made. It occurred to Stuart how quaint his employer's conceits were—how ordinary and dull and ultimately old-fashioned. Yet he had to admit there was something fun about it. "Fun" was a word he had trouble relating to, even in his own writing. It scared him. To have fun was to acknowledge that nothing one might accomplish would ever amount to anything important. It was the spiritual equivalent of committing suicide.

Lighten the fuck up, he told himself and pulled a Certs out of his coat pocket.

Leaving town, they passed a brown, wedge-shaped sign announcing the entrance to the White Mountains National Forest. Restricted, the sign said. Pike smiled. "What the hell's that mean?" he asked.

"I think it's to make sure that people don't start forest fires," Gregg suggested.

True enough, another sign farther along informed them: Fire Risk Low. "Oh, that's a good idea," Pike said sarcastically. He watched the sign in his rearview mirror, then shifted his eyes to Stuart. "We really need a sign to tell us that."

Continuing on, they followed a gravel road that broke off from the highway. The sun was clouded over, and the shadows of bare branches crept across the hood of the SUV. Nathaniel drove past a clearing, where a steel lift cable rose out of view above them.

"Looks like we've got the place to ourselves," said Gregg. Up ahead, the Echo Lake Ski Lodge belched smoke from a stone chimney jutting from the center of its steeply pitched roof. For thirteen years, Pike's friend Sarah Cranberry had owned and operated the lodge, where she also lived during the off-season. A truck was parked on the lawn out front, and a small thicket of pines separated the main building from a row of cabins. A dark forest surrounded the premises.

Peering into the forest, Gregg felt the strain of his life at home—where everything seemed so cloistered, so oppressive—easing away from him. Providence was small enough that, standing outside the train station, one could pivot and take in a three-hundred-sixty-degree panorama of the entire downtown: the glass prow of the Providence Place shopping center, the old colonial homes perched on College Hill, the red lights atop the Biltmore Hotel, the Foundry, the Westin, then back to Providence Place. But when Gregg stood in the same spot, he felt—perhaps unique to anyone in Rhode Island—confronted by the various buildings and landmarks. The Gregg Reese Unitarian Chapel. The Gregg Reese Community Theater. Not to mention the Keeny Esther Reese Shelter for Abused Women and Children, or the Salmon Samuel Reese Center for World Hunger Relief. Everywhere he looked, he saw the name Reese on libraries and hospitals and public parks. In Providence, his forebears were preserved not in the typical New England–gothic fashion, as ghosts, but as institutions.

The men unloaded their bags and carried them into the lodge, where a fireplace glowed in the middle of the large room. Board games for kids to play with were stacked by the hearth; above them, a topographic map showed the many trails leading up and down the mountains. Another wall at the back of the room consisted entirely of sliding glass doors that looked out onto the meadow behind the lodge. The building was quiet, except for the remote sound of someone doing the dishes in another room.

The water shut off, and a woman called out, "Nate, is that you?"

Nathaniel proceeded a few steps ahead of Gregg and Stuart. "Hey, girl!" he shouted back.

The woman emerged from the kitchen, a look of happy,

sweaty exertion on her face. "Welcome home, chief," she said, and pressed her lips to Pike's cheek.

Nathaniel patted her on the butt. "We're hungry," he said, indicating the others.

Gregg blushed. "Oh, we're okay," he insisted.

The woman broke away from Pike to shake Stuart's hand. She looked in her mid-forties, with short, muscular legs that bulged in a pair of dark blue denims. She'd gathered her hair—black but white at the roots—into a wispy bun held in swirling disarray by a chopstick. "I'm Sarah," she said. "You've got two more coming, I know. We'll eat as soon as I get this ham out of the oven."

"No hurry," Gregg said. He'd been expecting someone younger than Sarah. In twenty years, he'd never known Pike to have a lady friend even remotely his own age.

"I'm taking jackets," she said, "and drink orders, if you're interested. I know what *you* want, chief." She nudged Pike, who'd put his arm around her waist. Gregg still didn't know what to make of her, except that she looked like a lesbian, according to his limited conception of what a lesbian looked like. She wasn't pretty; her face was apple shaped, with ruby dimples and a gently rolling double chin. Pike's former girl-friends had all been of a type: fawning waffle heads with size-two figures. He simply didn't associate with women who weren't exceptionally beautiful. Sarah's ordinary appearance was the most striking thing about her.

"Nathaniel was worried that we might be late," Gregg said, handing her his jacket.

She laughed. "He must still be on Rhode Island time. I keep telling him, the rules are different up here."

Allison and Heath joined them twenty minutes later in the dining room, where Sarah had laid the food out buffet-style on a sideboard. The ham smelled delicious, and it steamed in the center of the table. Sarah carved it with an electric knife, telling everyone to help themselves to wine and tossed salad. The knife tore into the meat with the razzing sound of a chainsaw, and she operated it manfully, peeling off thick deli-cut slices with one hand.

Allison stood in front of Heath at the end of the buffet line. The others had got a head start on the booze, and she watched their rowdy jostlings with the detached amusement of a social anthropologist. "I think my dad's drunk," she whispered to Heath. She was happy for him; as she saw it, her father rarely allowed himself to have the fun in life that he deserved. The feeling was contagious, and she said, "God, I want a toke *so* bad."

Heath smiled gamely but said nothing. Ever since leaving Providence, he'd regretted coming along on the trip. He could've used the time more productively by staying at home. Solitude was healthy for an artist. There was so much that he wanted to do—write "God Only Knows," produce *Pet Sounds,* learn to sing like Carl Wilson. What was he doing instead? Hanging out with his girlfriend.

Sarah cut herself a piece of ham and told her guests to sit down and eat. Gregg continued to mellow as the dinner progressed, and at times Allison even thought he might be flirting with their host.

"I can't believe you two went to school together," he said to Pike and Sarah, who were sitting next to each other at the head of the table. "You don't strike me as a Rhode Islander," he told Sarah.

She smiled, her mouth full of red wine. They'd gone through two bottles already, with another unopened bottle of Bordeaux on the sideboard. The bottle still had the price tag on it, a green sticker from the state-line liquor store. "I'm not—not anymore," she said. "There's a whole world out there, you know. There's Massachusetts, and Connecticut, and—"

"Don't forget Maine," Pike said to the general amusement of all. Only Allison wasn't laughing; she was too busy scrutinizing Pike for clues, wanting to find out exactly why she disliked him so much.

"What was Mr. Pike like in high school?" Heath asked. Allison gripped his right leg under the table and squeezed.

"Oh, kind of a rebel," Sarah said. "We were a pretty strange couple, he and I."

"So you guys actually dated?" Allison asked.

Pike took a moment to swallow a bite of ham. "Not really. But I did let her carry my books."

Sarah grinned, showing her wine-stained teeth. "Don't believe a word that he says, Allison. It's all lies."

Pike corrected her. "Not lies, dear—fabrications. Peasants *lie*. Gentlemen *fabricate*."

As their banter continued, Gregg began to understand why Pike had kept her as his secret friend for so long. Being with Sarah had freed up a part of him that was less informed by the public persona he'd taken such care to create in Rhode Island. Like she said, the rules were different up here.

At the end of the meal, Pike made a special announcement, one that he'd been saving all night. This was the first time he'd mentioned the parking-lot project to anyone who wasn't directly involved with it. That group now included Gregg, Allison, and Heath, whether they liked it or not.

"A parking lot?" Allison demanded, reaching for her wine. "What on earth for?"

"Wait and see, my pet, wait and see," Pike said, pleased with himself.

"How do you plan to get the equipment up there?" Gregg

asked. Being in the mountains had a transforming effect on him, and he found himself open to ideas that would've seemed ludicrous back home.

"We'll airlift it," Pike said, "to a staging area about fifty yards from the main site. It's expensive as hell, but we'll save in other ways."

Allison was less impressed. "But why a parking lot?"

Pike answered with relish. "The fact that it's a parking lot means nothing. A parking lot *defies* meaning. That's the beauty of it."

"Sounds pretty stupid to me." With a huff, she stood to help clear the dishes, while her father kept asking more questions. She could tell that Pike was reeling him in, and it disgusted her. "Are you finished?" she asked Heath.

"Oh, thanks," he said, glancing away from Stuart just long enough to pass her his plate. He'd hardly touched his food and had spent most of the dinner talking with Stuart, who'd also managed only a half-slice of ham.

"What about you, Stuart?" she asked.

Stuart handed her his plate but held on to his wineglass. The seating arrangements hadn't worked in his favor, with Heath on one side and Gregg on the other. Both expected more out of him—*the published author*—than he felt able to provide. Heath's questions hadn't let up since they'd sat down: about writing, getting an agent and editor, etc. These questions had continued even after dinner, until Stuart finally rose from the table and asked, "Hey, Nate, do you mind if I borrow the SUV? I want to pick up some wool socks. It's gonna be cold later on." The excuse sounded forced, but he didn't care.

"The Bean outlet's open all night," Heath said. "I'll come along."

With a paternal sigh, Pike reached into his pocket, brought out his car keys and said, "Don't get pulled over."

Stuart did what was expected and laughed. He'd driven the SUV before, usually bringing Pike to and from the airport. Every time, he'd heard the same lecture.

"If you get arrested, remember"—Pike winked, sliding the keys across the table—"I'm your one phone call."

Keys in hand, they stepped outside and headed off, Stuart ejecting the James Brown CD from the sound system and tuning the radio to a light classical station. As he drove, he wondered if he ought to call Marlene. She'd be drunk by now—she always drank too much whenever he wasn't home. Her neediness, her reluctance to assert herself except in the most futile ways, struck him as not endearing but pathetic. Her estimation of him was far too great, and her approval so easily won that it had almost no value. Stuart was tired of being the only bright spot in her life. Rather than put himself through this misery, he wondered, why hadn't he poured his energy into writing a new novel? That was his job, after all. He'd already written one book, and there was a realistic expectation he would write another. What the hell was he doing here in New Hampshire? He belonged back home, sitting at his desk. He never should've married Marlene to begin with. He should've *invented* her instead, plugged her into a story line and turned her loose.

"So what's it like to write a book?" Heath asked as they pulled into North Conway. The snow was falling harder now that they'd come out of the mountains. Stuart felt enthroned behind the wheel of the SUV, high above the ground, with an elevated view of the outlets and ski shops that were spread along the main drag.

He'd already answered the question once tonight but gave it another shot. The truth was, he didn't think much about his book anymore. All he remembered was that the actual writing entailed a lot of hard work, over the course of many years, and by the end of it, his experience of writing it was so diffuse that he felt unable to take credit for it. This was an honest answer.

My Private Apocalypse was, as they say, a flop. The premise of the book was too cerebral, the ending too abstruse. If he were to write another, he'd make it more genre-oriented than the first, maybe a spy novel, something that required less emotional investment on his part. Being emotionally invested hadn't paid off—not that he hadn't been compensated, because he had. No, what his emotions had failed to produce was a honest book. To write a piece of pulp would've been more truthful, in fact. Stuart's life had all the tawdry, dropped-in-the-bathtub flimsiness of a crappy paperback, clichés on every page.

"I found a typo," Heath said. "You probably know about it already."

"There's a lot of typos," Stuart admitted. The typos were all that still mattered to him. Unlike nearly everything else, he could relate to them objectively. "The hardest part about writing a book is proofreading it. The typos are all my fault. I just wanted to move on to something else by that point."

"Another novel?"

"I thought so. I wanted to be one of those book-a-year guys, like John Updike. But I got . . . sidetracked, I guess." He could tell that Heath wasn't particularly interested, so he said, "Thanks for reading it, though. You didn't have to do that."

He wheeled the SUV into the parking lot at L. L. Bean, which was three-quarters full even at this hour. When they got out, he sighed and said, "All right, so tell me about your screenplay."

Heath was shorter than Stuart, and he had to hurry to keep up. "Well, it's really an homage to—and I know this sounds pretentious, but—"

"Hold on." Just ahead, under a green awning, dozens of shoppers were streaming in and out of the store. Stuart ran the last few steps and held the door open for a woman who was staggering with her massive bags of purchases.

Heath continued, "It's sort of an homage to sixties counter-culture exploitation films like *The Libertine* and, um, *Venus in Furs*—"

"Dig it."

"*The Wild Angels,* that sort of thing."

"Dig it, dig it." Stuart stopped to get his bearings inside the store. Nearby, a man's orange flannel shirt hung on a skeletal rack, along with a dozen more just like it; the same style of shirt also came in red, blue and green, with each color displayed on its own separate carousel. "I tried writing screenplays for a while," he said, and they both nodded at having something in common. "I was never any good at it. Most of my ideas were pretty lame." The thought streamed away. Even as a rotten screenwriter, Stuart had liked himself better at age twenty-one, ten years ago, than he did now. "Let's check out the socks," he said.

Heath followed him into the men's department and tried not to watch as Stuart picked out some socks. This was intimate information—another man's socks—and it made him uncom-fortable. The implications were erotic, homosexual. Head down, he said, "I don't know what you're working on right now, but if you ever want to get back into screenwriting—"

"I don't."

The answer startled Heath. He couldn't imagine why some-one who'd been given a gift—and not just a gift but the oppor-tunity to use it—would be so reluctant to talk about his art. Heath's single desire was to make a film of such loving, emo-tional intensity that it would give people the same sense of spiritual well-being that Brian Wilson—whose autobiography he'd been reading sporadically on the toilet since September—talked about when describing some of his more advanced productions from the sixties. Heath's artistic analogues were all musical; he wanted to make a film that felt to his audience like "Good Vibrations," "Cabin-Essence," "Heroes and Villains," songs that functioned as near-static soundscapes to which one could return, as though to a physical, existing space: a room. He wanted to accomplish this in film.

The films that Heath most admired all contained an element of danger, not just in the subject matter but in the filmmaking process itself. The first *Ilsa* movie, for example, was secretly shot on the set of *Hogan's Heroes*—a TV show as wholesome as *Ilsa* was repellent. Sleaze-meister Jess Franco—director of, among hundreds of others, *Erotic Rites of Frankenstein* and *Bloodsucking Nazi Zombies*—covertly filmed his female cast members in the nude, then spliced the footage into the finished edit without their approval. The whole genre was tawdry and repulsive. But under the threat of danger, Heath felt, something worthwhile happened. These films were artifacts of a genuine experience rather than a simulated one. The tension resulted not from a script or a storyboard but from real off-screen menace.

"It's a genre of film that virtually doesn't exist anymore," he explained. "Some of it's proto-porn, but what I'm mainly interested in—and I know this sounds pretentious—is the social subtext. In Italy, for example, dozens of adult films were shot over a two-year period, from 1975 to 1976—some of the most grisly films ever made. Women being beaten, raped and experimented on by Nazi scientists. Graphic violence, genital mutilation, real sexual torture on camera. And these were mainstream movies, marketed as *erotic* cinema."

"They still make S&M movies."

"Yeah, but not with that kind of a budget. And *never* so overtly political. People used to eat this shit up in the seventies."

"Tastes change, I guess." Stuart started toward the checkout counter. "I know what you're talking about, though. I've definitely seen my share of it—*Salon Kitty, The Night Porter* and all that."

And more, he thought, remembering the hundreds of X-rated videos he'd watched as a younger man. In those pre-Marlene days, the amount of money he wasted on pornography was appalling. He preferred masturbation videos to sex videos because there wasn't as much interference between him and the performers; watching the women masturbate, he could interface with them directly, then dispose of them at will. The mail-order company he regularly patronized offered five new videos every month, each spotlighting a different model. The catalogue descriptions were often better than the videos themselves, 90 percent of which, when they arrived in a red, white and blue FedEx box, were disappointing. Working on his book, Stuart wished that he could write something as bluntly persua-sive as "Samantha, 19, 37DD, this stunning brunette strips from heels and garters to COMPLETELY NUDE in her own back-yard and brings herself to a HIP-THRUSTING, SCREAMING ORGASM!!!" Whereas the jacket description of *My Private Apocalypse* read: "A debut novel that shows, in finely crafted phrases both poetic and uncommonly expressive, the vanishing boundary between dreams and disillusionment, the teeming (and often confounded) hopes of a generation and the funda-mental power of language itself . . ."

They went over to a counter, where three cashiers were wait-ing to ring up the next purchase. Stuart handed his socks to one of the cashiers, who scanned each pair with an infrared sensor.

"Anyway," Heath said, "that's what I'm interested in. I want to re-create, with as much accuracy and sincerity as possible, the look and feel of an actual, late-sixties, early-seventies exploita-tion film."

"It sounds like a great idea." Stuart put a twenty-dollar bill on the counter. "Just don't expect to make a lot of money at it."

Pike's Folly

The cashier handed Stuart his change and the bag of socks. Walking ahead of Heath, he pushed the front door open with his shoulder, then caught the cold metal handle and held it open. "So what's this crap about turning my book into a movie?" he asked.

Heath was embarrassed. "Oh, Allison's just talking. She can be a little bossy at times."

"I hadn't noticed," Stuart remarked. Across the lot, Nathaniel's SUV looked enormous and out of place—taller and wider and more obnoxious than all the other cars parked around it. The breeze was bitter, and Stuart said, "Come on, let's get moving."

Back at the lodge, Heath found Allison packing her things in their cabin.

She was furious. "I don't know why I even bothered to come," she said. "Pike's obviously a scam artist. He scammed my mother, and now he's trying to scam my dad."

"What do you mean?" Heath asked.

"Don't you get it? He's fucking with us! He wants to turn my father into another rich asshole, just like him. That's why people don't like us, Heath. They see guys like Nathaniel Pike, and they think, 'See? All rich people are like that.' But we're not! At least *I'm* not." From the desk by the bed, she swiped up a twist-tie baggy of pot and stuffed it into her backpack. "I'm leaving."

Heath followed her out of the cabin. "It's too late to drive back to Rhode Island," he warned.

"I'm going to Concord. It's only an hour. I'll get a room."

"What's in Concord?"

"A whole bunch of Reese supporters. There's going to be a rally in front of the capitol building on Christmas Eve. Celia Shriver told me about it. I want to help out."

"I don't think that Mr. Reese is going to like that." Gently, he took her sleeve and pulled her toward him.

She jerked her arm away. "Too bad. I have to do *something*. Everyone back home is gonna flip out when they hear about this stupid parking lot." As a peace offering, she said, "You should come too. Take your camera and make a documentary."

"With Mr. Pike's camera," he pointed out.

"It's your camera. He gave it to you. Or *I'll* buy you one."

He looked toward the lodge, where Allison's car was parked. "I don't want to hurt your dad's feelings," he said.

She stared at him, incredulous. "What's with you guys? You're just like Daddy. He never wants to hurt anyone's feelings either. He didn't want to hurt my mom's feelings when they were married, which was why he ran around like a closet case for eighteen years without telling anyone about it."

Heath didn't argue with her. He had no business saying anything bad about Mr. Reese.

They walked to her car, where she gave his hand a squeeze. "I'll call you in the morning," she said and threw her bag into the backseat. "Hey, don't look so upset. You don't need me here anyway."

He felt like there was something more that he ought to say but didn't know what. Allison's moods were sometimes hard to predict. He almost didn't mind seeing her go.

3

Who's Christa McAuliffe? Allison wondered at the sign over the Christa McAuliffe Planetarium, a quarter mile from the Marriott Courtyard outside downtown Concord. The planetarium was the first thing that she'd noticed after getting off the highway, and she took it as a good omen. In Concord, they named buildings after women, not men. This Christa McAuliffe must be some kind of scientist, or an inventor. Whatever the case, Allison pictured herself in the heart of downtown Concord, fraternizing with dozens of independent-minded women, women who'd made the same mistakes that she had and who'd now emerged as better people, better women.

Pulling into the Marriott Courtyard parking lot, she upped the volume on her Tori Amos tape and sang along in a gritty, grainy voice. She felt like a badass.

The hotel lobby was crowded, and a sign listed the conferences taking place in the complex's seven meeting rooms. With an unlit cigarette dangling from her mouth, Allison plunked down her gold card for a room on the second floor. The desk attendant was a lanky young man with a fuzzy mustache and a stringy ponytail tucked under the neck of his red vest. Signing the charge slip, Allison asked, "How late's the bar open?"

"Till one a.m."

She thanked him and took the stairs to the second floor. Her room was near the landing, at the head of a long, red-carpeted hall. She opened the door with a digitally encoded key card, set down her bag and lay across the king-sized bed. The bed radiated coolness against her arms and back. When she sat up, she ran her hands across the comforter, the pillows, the shellacked nightstand. This was the first time she'd stayed in a hotel by herself. Everything inside the room was the result of her own decisions: money she'd spent, miles she'd driven.

A half hour later, she went down to the lounge, having changed into jeans and a sweater-coat she'd packed to go hiking in. A group of professional-looking men in their thirties and forties were at the bar, and one of them asked her for a smoke. "You go to Pierce?" he asked.

Trying not to do the obvious thing and blow him off, she invited him to sit down. "No way, man," she said. "I'm out of school. I don't dig that shit." She had no idea why she was saying this, but it sounded cool. "What's Pierce?"

"Franklin Pierce Law Center. We're having a departmental Christmas party. Would you like to join us?"

Allison shrugged but soon found herself sitting with her back to the bar, surrounded by guys in gray and blue suits, all law professors, all terribly interested in her opinion about every little thing.

Within twenty minutes, the one who'd asked for the cigarette was telling her about the Christmas Eve demonstration, which, as it concerned the law, interested him as well. "Whoever Pike's lawyer is," he said, "sure knows what he's doing. Just the other day, we had a call about Pike from the Society for the Protection of New Hampshire Forests. They own a lot of the land that the for-profits usually pass over. They're not too happy with Pike, as you can imagine. You should swing by their office on Portsmouth Street. Alice Shepperton's the big wheel down there. Also"—he paused to let her catch up in her note taking—"Cathy Diego at the New Hampshire Public Interest Research Group. They're on North Main. She'll put you to work."

"Thanks." Allison handed back his pen. Warmed by her second glass of white wine, she thought to ask him another question. She made him wait while she took a long drag on her cigarette, then said, "Hey, who's Christa McElroy?"

He tilted his head. "Christa McElroy?"

"The name, you know, on the planetarium." Casting down her eyes, she pretended to pick a strand of tobacco from her tongue.

The man looked disoriented. "Christa *McAuliffe*?"

Allison nodded impatiently, as if getting the name wrong didn't matter, and that he was being a square for pointing it out to her.

He chuckled. "Christa McAuliffe? The *Challenger*? The space shuttle?"

Allison sat perfectly still, afraid that anything she said would bring gales of derisive laughter from all corners of the room.

The man's smile broadened, and he asked, "How old are you?"

She didn't answer, although she couldn't think of a good reason not to just say, *I'm twenty-one*. Better stick to strategy rather than risk the dull, hard truth of it all. "How old are *you*?" she asked. The question sounded exactly wrong to her—coy and stupid, when all she'd wanted was to brush him back.

The man grinned at one of his associates, who'd come by with a drink for himself and one for Allison. "I pity our nation's undergraduates," the first man said to the other, then inclined his head toward Allison.

She turned away, wondering how to make herself seem more impressive, but everything that came to mind sounded either petulant or humorless in that awful, militant-feminist sort of way. The only thing would be to leave, or else sleep with one of them. She left.

The next morning, she drove downtown to the New Hampshire Public Interest Research Group. Cathy Diego's office was on the third floor, and the window behind her desk framed the dome of the Statehouse. Cathy was a squat, hefty woman in her early forties. Her light-brown hair was cut short, highlighted in blonds and reds. On her finger was an ostentatious wedding ring that seemed to lead her hand around like a marionette string whenever she reached for the phone, which rang incessantly during Allison's visit. Her ears were similarly bedecked with diamonds—although these, Allison could tell, were fakes. Even her glasses looked like jewelry—big and snazzy, with angular, rose-tinted lenses. Through the lenses, Allison could just barely see her eyes, which were blue and heavily made-up. A green ribbon was pinned to the lapel of her wool blazer: AIDS or breast cancer or gay rights—Allison could never tell which one was which.

"Uh!" Cathy groaned as the phone rang for the nth time. "Don't even . . ."

Allison let her eyes drift to the window as the woman took her call, speaking rudely to whomever was on the line:

"What now? Oh, give me a frickin' break . . . I DON'T CARE! . . . That's not coming out of *my* department . . . Now don't bother me, I *told* you." Once off the phone, she held her head in her hands and—just barely keeping it together—blindly reached for a thermos of coffee. "I am *so* over it," she muttered, making a perfunctory show of smiling at her guest.

"You guys are really busy around here," Allison said in what she'd meant to be a sympathetic voice.

Cathy snorted. "Don't even. This is nonprofit, hon. Get used to it."

In the interval between phone calls, Allison explained what she was doing in Concord. Little of what she said came as a surprise to Cathy, except for the part about the parking lot, which she didn't seem to believe. After so much anti-Pike sentiment had been unleashed, it was hard for people to accept that his intentions were relatively benign. There had to be a catch.

"If Reese wants to get in bed with that lunatic," Cathy snapped, "that's his choice. Henry Savage always tries to play the money card, and this time it's not going to work."

Allison wrinkled her forehead. "What do you mean, the money card?" She still hadn't made her mind up about Cathy Diego, but at the very least she hoped to learn something. Maybe she'd get a job in nonprofit someday. She could see herself snapping at underlings on the telephone, saying things like "Don't even."

"Savage runs his office like it's a business," Cathy explained. "He knows that most conservation groups like the SPNHF can't afford to bid against a tycoon like Pike. He doesn't care! All he cares about is money. Technically, he's not even supposed to sell to the private sector without holding a public hearing first."

"So how did he—?"

Cathy rubbed two fingers together, the universal sign for *Pay Up.* "And this state in particular is extremely volatile when it comes to bribes and backroom deals. Now, why is that, you might ask."

Allison scolded herself for *not* asking, for not even really understanding what the woman was talking about.

"Because," Cathy continued, "if you remember, every four years, this is where the first presidential primaries take place. So when you're dealing with politics in New Hampshire, you're dealing with the fact that everyone in the state's trying to kiss the federal government's ass, and vice versa. Right now, we're in the middle of a Republican cycle. And let me tell you—" She laughed. "There ain't a hell of a lot of Republicans in this building." Interrupting herself, she scowled at an office boy who'd stopped by with a box of flyers. At the sight of the box, she screeched, "Don't even. Don't *even!*" and the boy went away.

Such talk of money and bribes was making Allison nervous. It all seemed to implicate her father. She most often associated bribery with the mayor of Providence, Vincent "Buddy" Cianci, who'd recently been indicted for swapping bribes with, it seemed, every cop and garbage collector in the city. Many in Rhode Island, Allison's father included, considered him a gangster, probably because he was Italian and looked like a typical wiseguy. Was Gregg Reese, like the mayor, a person who gave and took bribes? Did being from a rich family also imply being a crook?

To get away from the phone, Cathy brought Allison out of the office and into a larger room where a half dozen volunteers, all elderly women, were seated around a table stuffing flyers into envelopes. Allison spotted Celia Shriver among them; she was immediately recognizable in her moth-eaten cardigan and Megadeth T-shirt. She had long been an ardent supporter of Gregg Reese's; in fact, her enthusiasm often exceeded his own, and she'd been known to call him at home, even past ten at night, indignant over some organizational snafu. Allison particularly admired eccentric old women like Celia: women in their sixties who signed up for continuing education classes and listened to seventies-era New York punk and generally acted cool.

"Well, *Allison Reese,*" Celia said, "this is a surprise. Keeny told me that you and your father were spending the week with Nathaniel Pike. How nice." Hearing Allison's name, the other ladies looked up from their work as Celia scooted her chair to make room at the table. "Have you been dispatched by your pa-*pah* or did you come on your own?"

Allison glanced from face to face and saw that the women were not smiling. She tried to think of something witty to say, but Celia didn't give her a chance. "It's one thing if your father wants to leave us in the lurch at the last minute," she said, "even though some of us have been stuffing these envelopes since last Thursday."

The other women muttered their own tales of overwork and underappreciation. "We'll make do," Cathy said, "but I'd counted on more support from Mr. Reese. We've been keeping an eye on this Pike character ever since he built that crazy house in Rhode Island."

Celia put her hand on Allison's shoulder. "It's good that you're here, though. We're going to need lots of help recruiting volunteers from New England College. That's in Henniker, where I'm staying. You should come back with us tonight. Alice Shepperton has a farm near Henniker. We're using it as a staging area for the rally on Thursday. How old are you—nineteen?"

"I'm twenty-one," Allison said.

"Oh, well—good enough."

All afternoon, Allison did her best to help stuff the envelopes, believing that the harder she worked, the more forgiving Celia and Cathy would feel toward her father. She'd never had a real job before, short of running errands for the Reese Foundation. Watching the other women—Celia in particular—she imagined doing the same work and leading the same lifestyle. Women like Cathy and Celia were rare in that they'd remained politically active at an age when most people generally lost their edge. Celia may have been in her sixties, but she still cared about the environment, questioned the news media, attended pickets and rallies, actually gave a damn about things. Life hadn't worn her down, just made her more focused, more committed, more impressive to Allison.

Just before five o'clock, Cathy finally announced, "That's enough, ladies. Let's go home. My daughter's got tap dancing in twenty minutes."

Cathy had taken Celia in to work that morning, so when the group split up, Allison gave her a ride—first to the hotel to collect her things, then to the small town of Henniker, fifteen miles west of Concord. En route, Celia said, "How's the new stud?"

It took Allison a moment to realize that she was asking about Heath. "Oh, he's good. He's still up in North Conway with my father."

"He's a filmmaker?"

"Yes." A few hundred yards of state highway went by before she added, "At least he'd like to be. I think he wants to make a documentary. It's hard to tell."

"Do you *need* him?" Celia asked.

Surprised, Allison looked over at her. Celia had taken off her baseball cap and was working her fingers through her gray, shoulder-length hair. What bothered Allison was how completely obvious the answer should've been. She didn't need Heath, any more than she needed any man. But why wasn't it obvious to Celia? So far as Allison knew, she had been married only briefly, and that was a long time ago. With Celia, there didn't seem to be any question of need; she was clearly self-sufficient. Only Allison had to justify herself, because she was young and well-off and reasonably attractive. "It's not a matter of need, I guess," she said. "It's just nice to have the physical thing every now and then. I like to be assertive, you know? And Heath's cool, because he's not macho. But he also doesn't always let me get what I want. So there's some give and take." She finished her explanation with the awareness of having meant nothing of what she'd said.

Pike's Folly

When they arrived at Alice Shepperton's farmhouse, she felt drained by the conversation. Every comment of hers—even those that she'd screened carefully beforehand—was challenged, Celia extrapolating from them all manner of political subtext until Allison began to feel categorized, stereotyped and completely written-off. Celia's judgments were nothing that Allison hadn't heard before. She was naive like her father, spoiled rotten like her mother. Like Mom, a ditzy throwback to the 1950s; like Dad, a limousine liberal with decades of guilt to burn. Coming from Celia, this hurt more than it would've from Nathaniel Pike. Allison didn't care what Pike thought, but Celia—Celia was cool! Funky and sassy, a badass bitch. Allison wanted to be a Celia when she got to be that age. Not a Renee, or a Gregg Reese. Not a Reese at all.

The farmhouse was at the end of a long gravel road that curved through the forest until it came out onto a few acres of lawn covered with a dirty-looking layer of snow. A smaller cabin was connected to the main house by a trail of many footprints, and from a stone chimney rose smoke that looked pale against the black sky. Five cars were lined up in front of the house, and Allison parked next to a green-and-white Microbus. "Are you sure this is okay?" she asked, but Celia had already pushed the door open and was moving around to the front of the car. Allison grabbed her bag and followed.

The door to the house was unlocked, and Celia made quick business of introducing Allison to Alice Shepperton, who was stirring something in a mixing bowl with a long wooden spoon.

"We're having an all-dessert dinner tonight," Alice said, setting the spoon down to shake Allison's hand. "I'm making banana brownies, Leah's got a batch of sugar-nut cookies in the oven, and *someone's* supposed to bring a cheesecake."

Looking ahead into a vast and dark hearth, Allison could see a gathering of young people slumped in front of the fireplace, some lying prone on the furniture and others sitting cross-legged on the bare wood floor playing Trivial Pursuit. The warm smell of the cookies—and the sweet cedar fire, and the varnish on the cherry-plank walls—made her smile, and she proceeded farther into the house, leaving her bag and her wet boots by the door. Alice hurried ahead to introduce her to the other kids, none of whom seemed particularly interested, beyond a nod and a casual " 'Sup?" A giant bong rose like a minaret in the middle of the group, surrounded by beer cans and plastic soda bottles. Up close, Allison could tell that the kids weren't her age but more like sixteen or seventeen, nineteen tops. To them she was a grown-up, an intruder from a generation that had already failed, unlike their own generation, which was unique and would never fail.

Alice and Celia went off to attend to their brownies, and Allison was left to watch the Trivial Pursuit players move their colored tokens around the circular board. After a long dry spell during which no one was able to answer a single question, a girl with blond dreadlocks finally won the game (Q: What early member of the Beatles died of a brain hemorrhage in 1962?). Allison soon grew tired of being ignored, so she ventured back to the kitchen, where the kids' boots were lined up along one wall. Alice and Celia were sitting at a butcher-block table with a bottle of Chianti between them.

Alice offered her a glass of wine, but even here she didn't feel completely welcome. For all the drinking and smoking, no one seemed to be having any fun. She wondered what her mother was up to. With her mom, Allison was free to do anything she pleased. If she wanted to put on a tight dress and vampy high heels, Renee would put on her own dress and pumps, and together they'd head down to the West End, take in a show, then go for dessert and drinks, then more drinks and dancing at another club across town. If, the next morning, Allison felt like chilling in her jeans and a T-shirt, her mom would be cool with that, too, and Allison wouldn't have to worry about maintaining the same persona from the night before. Renee was the least judgmental person in the world. She expected a certain inconsistency out of life and, like Allison, mistrusted those who went from day to day in the same earnest, predictable fashion.

Catching herself, Allison decided not to think about her mom. For all of her good qualities, Renee lacked the traits Allison always associated with independent women—like Celia, or even Cathy Diego. They had strong points of view; if you asked one of them about, say, NAFTA, they'd offer a strong opinion, good, bad or otherwise. It didn't matter what the opinion *was*. It was enough just to have one. Allison wanted to be like Celia, not like her mother, who had no opinions except of restaurants and orchestra conductors and the best places to score coke.

Sitting down at the table, Allison peeked at a stack of paperwork that the women had set aside. The sheet on the top had a picture of Pike with the caption, "This man is a war criminal."

"We're disagreeing about the flyers, Allison, so maybe you can help." Alice took a page from the stack and passed it to her. "I think it's too strident."

"Not strident enough," Celia grumbled. "I think it should say, 'This man, this *canker sore,* this *son of a bitch,* has made a career out of throwing his money around without any care or thought of the consequences.' "

Just like my father, Allison thought.

"Even if that's true," Alice said, "let's not lose the high road to Nathaniel Pike."

"Don't worry about it." Celia poured herself some more Chianti, giving Allison the last little splash from the bottle. "The only people who listen to Pike are freaks and malcontents. And highly impressionable multimillionaires."

Allison knew that this was her cue to come to her father's defense, but she didn't feel like it. It wasn't that she didn't care about the parking lot anymore; she just wanted it to go away for a while.

"We need to be careful," Alice warned Celia. "We've got our own radical factions at the SPNHF. That old-school agitprop ain't gonna cut it. It did when *we* were in school but not today. Let's just have a nice, orderly demonstration." She turned to Allison. "What do you think?"

A nice, orderly demonstration sounded about right to Allison. "I agree," she said. "I'd rather not go to jail over a parking lot."

Celia slapped the table. "No, no! This isn't about a *parking lot*. This strikes at the heart of who we are as Americans."

Too late, Allison caught her mistake. "I didn't mean—"

"If Nathaniel Pike wants to spend his money, let him give it to a worthy cause. This is not a worthy cause. This is a perversion."

"No, I know, it totally is."

"As Americans, we have an obligation to lead responsible lives. No one's going to *make* us do it. There's no Hitler, no Stalin. No one's sticking a gun down our throats. It's all up to us. This country is ours to preserve or to squander, and that is why we must *squash* men like Nathaniel Pike, who don't respect their own responsibilities and who live in decadence when they should be helping others."

"Without a doubt." Not for the first time today, Allison realized, she'd said the wrong thing. "I mean, it's like . . . he's such an asshole."

She excused herself and went back to the main room, where the kids had left the Trivial Pursuit pieces and quiz cards on the floor and had brought out an acoustic guitar, along with a few bongos and tambourines. An electric bass was plugged into an amp, and its booming sound overwhelmed all the other instruments.

Putting on her jacket, she took her cell phone outside and called her mother. It would be past midnight in London, but Renee usually stayed up until two or three. They hadn't spoken in over a week, so it took a few minutes to bring her up to speed. When Allison finished talking, Renee said, "Sounds perfectly awful. Why don't you spend Christmas with me?"

Allison moved farther down the porch to get away from the music. Even though she'd been hoping that her mother would invite her over, she felt bad anyway. She didn't want to think of herself as running away from a challenge. Being a strong, independent woman meant sticking with something, not just flitting from one distraction to another. "Mom, I can't just leave. Everyone's talking about Daddy like he's some kind of monster—like he's Nathaniel Pike. It's so unfair."

As expected, Renee had no sympathy for this. "Allie, let your father fight his own battles. Now, look, I can wire you a plane ticket. I think there's a direct from Logan to Heathrow."

"Not *now*, Mom."

"Then later in the week. I'll pay for the ticket, and you can pick whatever date you'd like. Come out for New Year's."

Allison could tell that a definite no was out of the question, so she said, "I'll think about it. It's expensive to fly to London."

"I said I'd pay for it."

"I know you did." Allison cupped her hand around the cell phone and turned her back to the wind. "I don't want you to spend that much money."

"Don't you want to see me?"

"Of course I do. I just want to have a quiet holiday."

"We will!"

"On Ibiza?"

"I can cancel that. We don't have to go to Ibiza. We can stay right here. We'll find something to do around the house."

"I already have something to do. I'm not in college anymore, Mom. I can't just hang out and go to clubs and . . . live off my parents."

"But for *Christmas,* honey." The English accent was showing in Renee's voice.

Allison snapped, "I *told* you, I can't—"

"New Year's! I'm sorry, I meant to say New Year's. Actually, I believe I'm spending Christmas in the country with Fabrice. You'll have to take the train to Gloucester if you come before Boxing Day."

Having put up enough resistance, Allison no longer felt so guilty about humoring her mother, and she even allowed herself to enjoy the idea of spending a few days—days, weeks, whatever—in Europe. "Well, maybe. But don't spend a lot of money on a ticket, because depending on what goes on down here, I may have to back out."

"That's fine," Renee chirped. "Tourist on BA is just as good as first class. Pity about what happened in New York. You'll have a long wait at security."

It was agreed that a ticket would be waiting for Allison at Logan; if she needed to cancel or change the date, she could do it either online or in person. When she got off the phone, Allison felt that she hadn't done wrong since she hadn't committed to anything.

Back inside, she told Alice and Celia that she was tired and wanted to go to bed. Alice gave her a sleeping bag, then showed her to the guest cabin, where the other kids were also staying. It was heated by a giant space heater, but she could still feel the cold wind seeping in through cracks in the walls.

Saying good night, Alice left a Coleman lantern by the door and went back to the house. Allison kept her clothes on at first but stripped down to her T-shirt and panties when it got too warm inside the bag. For nearly an hour she listened to the distant strum and bang of the jam session across the yard. A year ago she would've stayed at the party, passing the bong and sharing philosophies with the other kids, but tonight's experience had made her feel old and obsolete. Tonight, all she wanted was to fall asleep. She would've been better off at the Marriott—or, if not that, on a plane to London. Allison had options available to her that most people her age, she suspected, did not. But because she did, it was harder to decide what to do. Far better not to have a choice and just feel, like Celia Shriver, that she had a place and a purpose, and beyond that the rest of the world could go to hell. She wished that she didn't care so much about what other people thought of her; that someone—if not Celia, then one of the others—had been nice to her.

She woke early the next morning and left a note thanking Alice and Celia for letting her crash at the farmhouse. By seven, she was back on the road. Everything that she'd been through in recent days now seemed so pointless, so adolescent. Whatever it took to be a strong, independent woman, she didn't have it. She'd tried to prove her mettle to everyone she'd met in Concord and failed. These women didn't want to bother with her, and neither, she supposed, did she with them.

Driving toward Boston, she headed straight for the airport and left her car in the long-term parking lot. She'd packed only enough clothes for a few days, and most of them were dirty. No matter, she thought; she could always borrow something from her mom.

4

After so many demands, outraged statements and cries for blood from within the anti-Pike organization, something unexpected happened: nothing. In the end, the weather proved too much for even the likes of Celia Shriver and Cathy Diego. Christmas Eve was bitter cold, and temperatures remained below freezing through New Year's. Attendance at that year's First Night in Providence was lower than expected because of a near nor'easter that dumped fourteen inches of snow all along the Cape. Even the rally in Concord had to be canceled due to snow and high winds. For the next three weeks, no one much felt like going outside.

Then in mid-January, the weather took a mysterious turn for the better, and Rhode Islanders enjoyed a period of record highs, with readings in the balmy low-fifties. Every day, newspapers carried pictures of people walking around Bristol and Newport in shorts and shirtsleeves. While heavy snows continued to fall in Connecticut, northern New England, even parts of western Massachusetts, a halo of clear skies had settled over Rhode Island and stayed there.

Late in January, Stuart invited Heath over to the house for

dinner. For weeks he'd been trying to introduce Marlene to some new people. Other than Bill and Carla Marshall, the Breens didn't have any real friends. All she had was him, and all he had was her overwhelming need for him.

About twenty minutes before Heath was to arrive, Stuart went downstairs to check on the lasagna he'd put in the oven. He was wearing an argyle sweater and a pair of gray permanent-press slacks. When he entered the kitchen, he was surprised to find Marlene naked. "You'd better put on some clothes," he said. "Heath's a pretty conscientious guy. He's bound to be early."

"Oh . . . right." She hesitated. The backs of her bare legs stuck to her chair when she got up from the table. "I suppose you're right," she said, taking her wine with her into the hall.

He stopped her at the bottom of the stairs. "Wait a minute. Were you planning on staying like that?"

"Of course not. I'm not crazy, Stuart. I don't want to upset your friend."

She was still getting dressed ten minutes later when Heath arrived for dinner. Stuart led him into the living room, where he'd set out some cheese and crackers, an ice bucket and an assortment of soft drinks and hard liquor. "Marlene will be down in a second," Stuart said. "Fix yourself a drink. We also have wine and beer."

"No, this is fine." Heath poured himself a soda and stood by the coffee table, waiting for Stuart to offer him a seat.

Stuart eyed his virgin drink. "You're welcome to some rum with that, or whiskey," he said.

"Oh . . . okay." Heath took a sip of his drink to bring it down a level, then added a splash of Bacardi, careful not to spill anything on the carpet.

"How's Nate?" Stuart asked, plunking down on the sofa. Through the ceiling, he could hear Marlene pacing around in her high heels. *What the hell is she doing?* he wondered.

Heath blushed, as he always did when the subject of Pike came up. "He's good, I guess. He's been spending a lot of time on the phone with Allison's dad."

Stuart nodded. Other than the weather, the big news around town was Pike's decision to come out in support of Gregg Reese's pet project, the Allison Fund. The public perception of Pike and Reese was that they weren't exactly the best of friends, so the announcement had come as a surprise to everyone. With Pike's help, the Allison Fund had a marginally better chance of surviving the fall elections. "I don't get this Allison Fund business," Stuart said. "I don't see why the state should have to subsidize the Reese Foundation. I mean, I know they've done plenty of good in the past, but it still makes no sense."

"Neither does building a parking lot in the middle of the White Mountains," Heath said. "By the way, you really should take another drive up there. They've done a lot of work on it since last week."

"And it actually looks like a parking lot?" Stuart asked.

"Yep. Exactly like a parking lot. Hard to believe."

Marlene soon appeared at the foot of the stairs, and Stuart got up to introduce her. "Heath, this is my wife, Marlene." He chuckled to himself. "I always feel so old when I say that."

His comment rattled Marlene, whose silver-blue eye shadow had the jarring effect of stage makeup.

"Marlene, are you sticking with wine?" Stuart asked.

"Yes," she whispered and handed him her half-empty glass. Heath's rum and Coke was still fine, so Stuart went off to refill Marlene's drink in the kitchen. He'd planned on having a beer but on impulse poured himself a glass of wine instead.

When he returned to the living room, Marlene was talking to Heath about the weather. "I hope it stays like this," she said. "I hate winter. I like being outdoors."

Stuart tensed his jaw. "It's pretty unlikely that we've seen the last of winter, hon. Enjoy it while you can, because we're due for another snowstorm."

"That's not what they said on the Weather Channel. They said that it was going to be the warmest February on record."

"Well, we won't know until it happens, I guess," Heath said.

Marlene agreed. "That's right. You never know what's going to happen next."

"Good. A toast to that," Stuart said pleasantly, and they all clinked their glasses. Marlene took a big gulp of wine, then another. Stuart felt embarrassed watching her drink. "Have you heard anything from Gregg's daughter?" he asked Heath.

"Allison? Yeah, she calls me every day." Heath turned to Marlene. "My girlfriend's staying with her mom in London."

"When's she coming back?" Stuart asked.

"I dunno. Maybe next month. I think she's been partying a lot over there. You know, getting it out of her system."

Marlene touched Heath's knee. "You must miss her," she said.

Stuart noticed how quickly she'd warmed up to Heath and attributed some of it to the wine.

"I guess I do," Heath said. "I've got more time on my hands now—when I'm not working for Mr. Pike."

"Oh? What do you do for Mr. Pike?" she asked.

"Marlene, we've been over this," Stuart said. "Heath's making a documentary about Nate in the White Mountains."

She took another thirsty gulp of wine. "Is that what you do for a living?"

Heath shrugged. "Sort of. I don't really do anything for a living. I just like making movies."

The simplicity of this delighted her. "Good for you. That's great. Don't let anyone tell you otherwise."

"Oh, I won't," Heath said.

"Ask Stuart. He knows. Don't you, Stuart?"

Stuart came to; he'd been staring at the back of Marlene's neck. "Hmm?"

"Tell Heath what you went through to get your book published."

It would've been easy enough to humor them both, but he chose not to. "No, Marlene. You can tell him, if you'd like. I've got some work to do in the kitchen."

He left them in the living room and went to finish preparing dinner. He stayed in the kitchen for ten minutes, getting some plates down from the cupboard, rinsing out the water glasses, checking on the lasagna, checking on it again, turning down the oven, turning it off, washing his hands, cutting into the lasagna with the flat edge of a spatula. Once everything was ready, he went back to the living room and called Heath and Marlene to the table.

"Stuart, Heath and I have decided to make a movie together," Marlene said, stumbling a bit as Stuart helped her to her feet.

"Oh? What kind of a movie?" he asked warily.

"We don't know yet. We haven't gotten to that part. Something about us. We're interesting people. Well, *you* are," she said, nudging Stuart. "I'm not, but we can work around me."

"You're interesting, Marlene," Heath said as they sat down at the table. No one commented on the food, and Stuart sulkily took his chair at the end. "Tell me something interesting about yourself," Heath prompted her.

She kept her eyes downcast. "Oh, gosh, let me see. I work in a *bank* . . . not much exciting there."

"Here, who wants to get started?" Stuart asked, offering the lasagna to Heath and Marlene. They both passed on it, so he served himself the first piece.

"It doesn't have to be work related," Heath said. "How about a hobby? What do you like to do in your spare time?"

Stuart's throat began to ache. "Food's getting cold," he said weakly, handing the serving platter to Heath.

Marlene didn't lift her head. "Nope, no hobbies. Like I told you before, I'm boring."

Stuart said, "She's right, Heath. Marlene's the most boring person in the world." Marlene looked hurt. "Oh, come on. I'm kidding! You're always going on about how boring you are. No one's buying it, Marlene."

An awkward silence ensued, which Heath didn't dare to interrupt. Finally she said, "I'm not boring, Stuart. *You* should know that."

"I do. That's what I've been saying all along. Now come on, let's pass this salad around," he said.

She took the bowl from him but didn't put any salad on her plate. "Maybe Heath would like to know what we're talking about," she suggested.

Stuart shot her a warning look, then turned to their guest. "Maybe Heath would like to eat," he said, rolling his eyes, trying to enlist Heath's support. "Hey, you look like you need a new drink," he said, but Heath covered his glass with his hand.

"I don't want to make trouble for you guys," he said, more to Stuart than to Marlene. "I was just kidding about the movie thing. I don't want to pry into your personal lives."

"You're not prying," Marlene said. "We don't have any secrets around here. Isn't that right, Stuart?"

Stuart put down his fork. "Hon. Stop."

She continued in her easygoing voice, "There's one thing you should know about us, Heath. We're not normally this formal around the house."

"Hon . . ." The word died in Stuart's throat.

"I mean, we're not this dressed up," she said, smiling now. "The fact is we're not normally dressed at all."

"All right, that's enough," Stuart snapped. "You're being silly, Marlene. Heath doesn't need to hear this."

"We haven't actually been to a nude beach yet. I want to go, but Stuart says—"

"Just zip it, okay?" he hissed.

Her moment of courage left her. "I'm sorry. I'm spoiling the night."

Feeling sorry for her, Heath said, "Hey, no, you're not spoiling anything. Really. I think I understand."

"No, you don't," she sighed.

"I do. I've met people like you before."

Stuart turned his anger on Heath. "Like who?" he asked.

As Marlene fought back tears, Heath insisted, "It's okay, guys. You don't have to explain. Trust me, it's a lot more common than you'd think. I used to live near this special camp when I was a kid. I had a good friend who went there with his family every summer. It was cool."

Marlene wiped her eyes. "It was?"

"Totally! I even ran the naked mile when I was at UNC. All my friends did. There was a guy in my dorm who was a nudist. He used to hang out in the hallway, and no one ever said anything."

"All right, I'm not listening to this anymore. You two can finish eating by yourselves," Stuart said, pushing back his chair.

"Then let's talk about something else," Heath said. "I'm just saying you guys shouldn't be ashamed. You should be proud of it. I've got a lot of respect for the nudist community . . . or whatever it's called. The nudism community. Nudist, nudism. Nudist."

Marlene laughed gratefully through her tears. "That's nice of you to say," she said.

"Speak for yourself," Stuart barked. "No one's a nudist here."

"So," Heath asked Marlene, "what about streaking? Have you ever done any streaking?"

She blushed. "Not much. Well, not yet."

"Not much. What does 'not much' mean?"

"You know . . . we've been out to the backyard a few times."

Heath slapped the table. "Oh, dude! I've *got* to get this on tape!"

"Nope," Stuart said. "No movies, nothing. Marlene, knock it off, okay?"

Heath set aside his plate, no longer interested in eating. "Think about it, guys. We could make a streaking video. We could even use Mr. Pike's camera. We'd shoot it on the weekends."

Marlene turned the idea over in her head. "Where would we go?"

"Here, there, wherever you'd like. We'd go all over the state. It'd be like"—he fumbled for the right words—"a naked tour of Rhode Island. And you'd be the perfect host for it, Marlene."

Flustered, she asked, "Me? Why?"

"Because you're a nice person. People can relate to you," Heath said.

Stuart was eager to deflate their growing enthusiasm. "People? What people? You're not actually taking this crackpot idea seriously, are you?" he asked Marlene.

She reached across the table for his hand. In a quiet, pleading voice, she said, "We wouldn't have to show it to anyone, Stuart. It could be just our little thing."

"No."

"I'd even edit the master tape for you," Heath added. "You'd really be doing me a favor. I could use the extra practice time in the studio."

Stuart didn't know what to say. Much as the idea repulsed him, he also saw some sense in it. If they had a few of their naked

adventures preserved on videotape, maybe they could stop tor-
turing themselves like this. They could take the tape out once
a year, watch it for a laugh, then put it back on its shelf. "This
is crazy," he said, mostly to reassure himself. At least he still
knew what crazy was. If not his dignity, he still had his self-
consciousness, which distinguished him from Marlene.

"Please, Stuart," she said.

"All right, don't nag me. I'll think about it. But you have to
promise me one thing." He grasped Marlene's hand tighter until
it hurt her a little.

"What?" she asked.

"This is all you, Marlene. Understand? Not me. This is your
thing."

She nodded gladly, not wanting him to change his mind.

"Tell Heath," he said.

She turned to Heath. "He's right, Heath. This is all me. I'm
the crazy one."

Stuart took his hand away. "All right, fine. Now let's eat. This
dinner took me two hours to make."

"Wait! When do we get started?" she asked.

"The first warm weekend," Heath said cheerfully. "Keep an
eye on the temperature. As soon as it hits sixty, I'll be right over."

The first warm weekend came in late February, and not a day
too soon. The winter had been especially hard on Marlene, and
it was all she could do to not take off her clothes at work. Carla
Marshall had noticed something strange about her and considered it another good reason for Marlene and Stuart to come
along to Martha's Vineyard.

"Our time-share's right on a private beach," she said that
Friday, about an hour before the close of business. "We'll go
skinny-dipping!" Marlene looked unhappy behind her desk, so

Carla added, "Unless that sort of thing makes you nervous. We can just go to the regular beach instead of the nude beach. But like I always say, it's fun to try new things. And it's not like you'd be the only one doing it."

That's the problem, Marlene thought. I *want* to be the only one. If everyone else is doing it, then it's not special, and if it's not special, then *I'm* not special. But there was no telling Carla this, so she just said, "I'm not sure if Stuart will be able to join us. He's working on a new novel."

This was the only excuse Carla would ever accept, as she held Stuart's writing in such high esteem that one might assume (wrongly) that she'd read his book. "It'll be just us, then," she said and slipped a manila folder into the tinted plastic in-box screwed to the wall of Marlene's cubicle. "Bill will probably be working in the darkroom all week anyway. But I hope you can twist Stuart's arm. I don't want him to think that I'm just this boring person who works in a bank."

"He doesn't," Marlene said. "Stuart likes you."

Carla smiled; she was used to hearing this. "Stu's a great guy. Anyway, I've got to run. I'm meeting Bill in a half hour. We're driving up to Vermont for his birthday. What are you and Stuart doing this weekend?"

"Oh, nothing exciting," Marlene said. "Hey, don't worry about us. You two have fun up north. Wish Bill a happy birthday for me."

The next morning, Heath arrived at the Breens' with his video camera and a case of special lenses and filters. Stuart brought him into the living room and went upstairs to fetch Marlene. Furrowed lines on her forehead were the only signs of the argument she'd been having with herself all morning. "Why aren't you ready?" he asked, annoyed to find her exactly as he'd left her ten minutes earlier, sitting at the foot of the bed.

Marlene looked up from her lap. "Is he here?"

"Yes, didn't you hear us talking just now?"

"No."

"That's funny. I can usually hear people downstairs when I'm in the bedroom."

He ducked out of the room and left her to finish getting dressed. Rousing herself, she put on sweatpants and a T-shirt, came down the stairs with her sneakers in her hands and tiptoed into the kitchen, where she eased open the refrigerator, pulled out a bottle of Chardonnay and poured some into a juice tumbler. Gulping down the wine, she ran the glass under the sink, rinsed out her mouth with lukewarm water and stepped into her shoes, which squeaked against the linoleum tile.

"Marlene?" Stuart called from the front steps.

"Coming!" She wiped her lips on the back of her trembling right hand and joined the men outside.

From Providence, they drove twenty minutes to Brenton Point in Newport, just south of the Newport Bridge. A two-lane road curved around a lighthouse and continued along a stretch of coastal grass. Past a low seawall, big blocks of broken shale tumbled to the beach. The place was largely abandoned, and the usual reek of kelp and dead fish was as strong as ever.

Heath pulled onto the grass and stopped the car. He'd expected to have a better sense of what to do next—where to shoot, what to tell his talent—but now couldn't think clearly. He felt like he'd never picked up a camera before. Through the windshield and across the blue hood of the car, he saw a thicket of autumn olive trees, then an opening where a narrow trail led into the scrub. About as inspiring as staring at a brick wall.

"Well, it's a start," he said and stepped out of the car. The others followed. Heath knew that if he didn't start asserting himself, the whole project would fall apart. Think big, he told himself. Think different. Think like Brian Wilson.

As Heath unloaded his equipment, he decided that the world

was divided into two camps—those who were like Brian Wilson and those who were like Mike Love, the Beach Boy who, of all the others, had been most opposed to the *Smile* project. It wasn't a stretch to imagine that if Love had been more supportive, the album might've actually been finished, despite the drugs and Wilson's dementia and dwindling self-confidence. Countless times on countless tapes, Love undermined Wilson by repeatedly dismissing his latest efforts as avant-garde crap. "Do You Like Worms" was crap, and "Heroes and Villains" and "Mrs. O'Leary's Cow." In a sense, he was right. "I Love to Say Dada" was certainly not as polished as "In My Room," or "Help Me, Rhonda." Perhaps it was too much to ask Love to appreciate the abstract lyrics and inscrutable structures of *Smile*. His reasons for being a Beach Boy weren't the same as Brian Wilson's. Wilson believed that art, at its most spiritually honest, was assembled rather than produced, discovered rather than contrived. Thus the elliptical fragments, the hours of apparently incompatible riffs and patterns collected on tape. The purpose in spending so much time in the studio was to create not a heady, impenetrable masterwork but a simple, beautiful collection of popular music. "A teenage symphony to God," he'd called it. But in 1967, Mike Love was less fragile than Brian Wilson, so he won the battle. *Smile* was lost.

Like Brian Wilson, Heath had encountered more than his share of Mike Loves. Mike Love was anyone who said to him, "Huh?" or "*What* are you talking about?" or "Who'd ever want to see a movie about *that*?" The fact that Heath couldn't answer these doubters didn't matter. Brian Wilson couldn't answer Mike Love either. All he knew was that something beautiful was going on here. He'd worry about the whys later.

While Stuart stood lookout by the car, Heath took his camera and led Marlene into the woods. With every step, he felt more and more ridiculous, and his goal of creating something beautiful—his own "teenage symphony to God"—more absurd.

They stopped short of a clearing, where three men in rubber boots were fishing on the beach. The temperature was cool, and the blanketing sound of the wind had an eerie note to it. "This looks good," Heath said. "Maybe we'll have you start here, then I'll follow you back to the road."

Marlene hesitated before taking off her shoes. Her sweat-pants came next, followed by the rest of her clothes. As she undressed, Heath felt nothing—not arousal, not even mild interest. He was too nervous about doing his job to think of her as anything other than his subject.

Once naked, Marlene looked down at the men on the beach. One of them was crouched at a tackle box, fixing his rig. A dog had entered the picture, a golden retriever that was splashing around in the shallows among the rocks. The men were drink-ing beer.

A trance lifted, and she realized she'd covered her breasts with her hands. This was a natural reaction, of course, but still disappointing. She wanted to believe that she had no inhibi-tions, yet here she was, unable to be as brazen, as shameless, as superhuman as she'd have liked. So, she *did* have inhibitions. Whenever she thought of the people that she most admired—and Stuart was at the top of the list—what they all had in com-mon was a confidence she lacked herself. Stuart wouldn't agree, but she knew him better than he did. He was her idol, her role model. Whenever she introduced him to one of her friends, she would say, "He's a writer," and her friend would invariably look dubious until she produced a copy of his book. But whenever he introduced her, no one ever asked what she did, and if it came up, no one doubted it, or looked dubious, or demanded proof. The fact that he'd written a book still amazed her, and it wouldn't matter even if he never wrote another, because he'd *done* something with his life, something definite and tangible and beyond the immediate confines of where he was or who he was with at any given time. If you typed in his name on the Internet, something happened; it wasn't much—just a list of reviews and books for sale on eBay—but it was better than nothing. The invisible world registered and reaffirmed his existence every day, whereas Marlene's name brought up only a single reference to another Marlene Breen, who lived in Oregon and sold real estate.

Making a decision, she lowered her hands and showed her breasts to the men on the beach. When one of them looked up, she stepped back and hid in the shade of the autumn olives. "I think they saw me," she said.

"Do you want to stop?" Heath asked.

She shook her head but said, "Just go check, okay?"

He went to the clearing and pointed his camera down the beach. The fishermen looked the same as before, concerned only with their beer and their lures and the golden retriever dodging between their legs. Heath focused on the three men, then pulled up to show Marlene hiding in the woods. He wanted to highlight the proximity between the naked woman and her surroundings. "You want to take a walk?" he asked.

Still worried about the men, she crept back into the open. Gradually, she became less afraid. Her body looked more beautiful than ever before. Her breasts were lovely, her stomach tight, her legs firm and muscular. Again, she went to the edge of the clearing, but didn't hide when the men glanced her way. Instead, she stuck her hip out at them, and the cool ocean air tightened around her waist.

"I can see the bridge from here," she said. Farther up the beach, the Newport Bridge looked as familiar as a picture from a travel brochure. Seeing it made her feel both small and powerful; small, because the bridge was so enormous, and she was nothing compared to it, but powerful, because no one else near the bridge was naked, only she, and that made her equal to it. "All right, let's go," she said. Bundling up her clothes, she stashed them between two large rocks.

In the ten minutes he'd been waiting by the car, Stuart had seen about half a dozen vehicles drive past the park entrance. One was a state trooper's, another a Coast Guard van. Just as the van was driving away, he heard what sounded like his wife's voice in the distance. His cock stiffened, and he reached down and massaged himself through his pants.

Marlene came out of the woods, followed closely by Heath, who said, "We got some great shots."

For Marlene, the thrill of the experience was already wearing off. "Oh, it was okay," she said, "but I chickened out at the end. I should've gone down to the beach. There were these guys fishing there. I should've flashed them."

"Don't worry about it," Heath said. "You got as close as you could. Any closer, we would've blown it."

She shook her head. "No, you can always get closer."

Oh, like you're some fucking expert, Stuart thought. Marlene's professionalism was starting to annoy him. "Come on," he said, roughly hustling her into the car. "Let's try not to get arrested."

Driving back to Providence, Stuart wondered why he was in such a bad mood. Was it because of Heath? No, both Heath and Marlene had done a fine job. His problem was with himself. To be honest, he would've said the same thing if he were Marlene: *I should've flashed those guys on the beach. I should've done more.*

Over the following weekends, they'd have several more chances to do just that. Every Saturday and Sunday, Marlene, Heath and Stuart went out in search of new locations, whether to shoot a quick flash 'n' dash or a full-scale outdoor masturbation scene. By mid-March, they'd collected more than twenty scenes, nearly two hours' worth.

Somewhere in the midst of this, Allison returned from London. She and Heath had been apart for three months, during which she'd switched from smoking pot to snorting coke, resulting in her dropping ten pounds she really couldn't afford to lose. In her absence, Heath had started working on a screenplay loosely based on her experiences in Europe, which she'd told him about over the phone. Showing the script to Allison had turned out to be a mistake; she didn't like seeing herself through someone else's eyes and resented Heath for trying.

"It's easier for me to use people's real names when I write the first draft," he told Stuart as they sat in the living room of the Breens' apartment, waiting for Marlene to get out of the shower. They'd just returned from another long weekend expedition. After each session, Stuart always insisted on watching the raw footage at home, before Heath took it back to the editing lab in Warwick. "I was going to change it later, but she doesn't believe me."

Stuart plugged a cord into Heath's video camera, having run the other end into the back of the TV set. "Well, people get upset."

Heath looked at him curiously. "Who did you base your characters on for *My Private Apocalypse?*"

Stuart hit play on the camera. "No one, really." Leaving it at that, he brought his drink over to the sofa.

"I guess it's taking the easy way out," Heath said, "just to write about things that really happened."

"Not at all." Stuart paused the tape. "You should stop using me as an example, Heath."

Heath smiled. "I don't know any other writers. Everyone always says, 'Oh, I'm writing a book,' but you're the only one I've known who's actually done it."

"Yep. And here I am." Stuart made a grand gesture with his gin and tonic.

"That's awesome."

The shower turned off, and Stuart could hear Marlene open and close the stall door behind her. He didn't want to talk about this in front of her. "You should trust your own instincts, Heath. If you want to write a screenplay about your girlfriend tramping around England, do it. And don't worry if she gets angry, because that's what happens."

"Is that what happened to you?"

"No." Stuart stared into his drink. "Actually, nothing happened. I don't know what I expected." Puzzled, he took another sip. What *did* I expect? For the world to change. For people to look different to me.

After a few minutes, Marlene came into the room and started the video. The opening scene was a quickie. They'd gone down to the Exchange Street Bridge and filmed her in the backseat of Heath's car—a little light masturbation, no big deal.

Watching herself on TV, Marlene was critical as usual. "I should've kept going when that old man walked by." She moved closer to the set and pointed at an elderly pedestrian hobbling across the bridge. On the screen, Marlene had stopped masturbating and was waiting for the old man to pass. "It's like I get scared at the last minute and then pull back."

She looked at Heath, who told her, "No, you did a good job." He was used to giving her pep talks after a day's shoot. "You gotta keep in mind that when you get scared like that, it's a natural reaction, and it just makes the scene even more erotic."

"I shouldn't get scared at all," she said. "I don't know what my problem is. It all makes sense when I'm sitting here, but then when I actually go out and do it, I choke."

"Hon, relax," Stuart grumbled. "It's not like it's a professional sport."

He might as well have punched her in the stomach. "I didn't say it was a professional sport, Stuart. I'm just trying to analyze what happened."

He sipped his drink. Between them, the TV continued to play the scene of her masturbating in the car. Tentative moans came through the speakers. *I'm touching myself,* the voice said. *I can't believe I'm touching myself . . .*

Marlene stared at him. "What do you mean, it's not a professional sport?"

He glanced at Heath, who was trying to watch the tape. "Not now, Marlene. We've got company."

"If you're trying to hurt my feelings, it's working."

"Forget it."

. . . touching myself, touching myself . . .

"I just want to make this perfect for you, Stuart."

"Don't do it for me, do it for yourself."

"I'm doing it for the both of us!"

"Fine, end of conversation. Heath?" Stuart snapped his fingers. "Turn that off."

Heath stopped the video, and the screen reverted to cable mode. "How 'bout we just call it a day," he said, "and then we'll pick it up again next week."

Stuart and Marlene agreed. They were fighting over nothing. The day had gone well, and neither had any reason to be angry with the other.

Later that night, Stuart got a phone call from Mr. Pike, who was still in New Hampshire. Stuart had made several trips up north since Christmas, mostly to help with local contractors who found Pike too flaky to deal with.

After hanging up, he told Marlene, "Sorry, hon, it looks like I have to go back up next Thursday."

"Why?" she asked. Both she and Stuart were naked in the living room, drinking wine and staring at the TV.

"The parking lot's finished. A bunch of writers are flying in for a press conference, guys from the *New York Times* and the *Washington Post*. Nate wants me to be there."

She paled. "Can't you get out of it?"

"No, I can't. Anyway, it's only for a few days. I've left you alone before."

"I know, Stuart, but not when you're angry with me." Her eyes were watery, and she clutched at his hand.

He laughed. "I'm not angry with you. What are you talking about?"

"I don't want you to go away when you're angry with me."

"Marlene, I'm not leaving until Thursday. That's five days from now."

She continued to insist that he was angry with her until he couldn't stand hearing it anymore and stormed upstairs. Once he was alone, he put on his robe and tied the belt tightly around his waist. Being naked all the time was getting to be a drag.

5

Can't read, can't sleep, can't watch TV. Jesus, look at me, I'm shaking. Called Stuart a half hour ago—no answer. I'll try again at noon. No, don't, he's busy. Was it today or tomorrow? Today. I'm sure that's what he said. Yes, that's right—the press conference's today, then he's back on Saturday. No . . . Sunday! Today, then Saturday, then back on Sunday. The ceremony's at noon, so I can't call him at the lodge. They'll all be gone. I'll wait until one, then try him on the cell phone.

Come on, Marlene. Just hold on till Sunday. Three days and two nights. No big deal.

"I should've gone to work today."

It's easier for guys—they just jerk off and they're done, but I always feel it, and I always feel like coming, and I always feel like making myself come.

"Oh, I wish somebody could see me."

If I come right now, I think I can last until mid afternoon. And then I'll come again when it's rush hour. I wanna flash that guy in the red Jeep Grand Cherokee, when he's right *there*. Ooo, that's hot. He usually comes home at five o'clock. So I'll start at five to five.

I like it when I push up like that.

"Right like that."

Makes me look sexy.

"I wanna come right now. I wanna come in front of a bunch of people."

Wait until after lunch. Make a sandwich or something. There's some tuna in the fridge. I'll have a beer, too—one beer to calm down—or else, I don't know, maybe go outside and show off and everyone can see me and I can't get away.

Do it/don't make me.

One flash, that's it. One flash before lunch, then I'll stop. Three good flashes—but *good* ones, so I know they're watching and I'm watching them. No running away, even if they notice and there's eye contact. Total exposure. And stand close enough so that they can see I'm naked.

"Look at me. Look at me. Look at my body. Look at my—"

Fuck! Nope, get down, get down . . . even more. I think he saw me. Tits and bush and hands on my pussy. Shit. What do I do? I'm dead.

"Oh, fuck, I fucked up."

Good, he's going.

I shouldn't be so scared all the time. I should just go out and do it. Just for a second. For one little second, then I'll turn around and come back in. That's not so bad. Or try the back-yard, because it's safer. No, save that for tonight, so I can stay outside. I hate dashing in and out like that. Wait till dark—and maybe in the front yard too. I won't be able to masturbate unless it's real late. *Only* if it's late. Oh, please don't make me do this.

Quick to the curb. Come on. Leave the key on the step.

Wait, let me check—

Look at me, look at my body.

No one—good, so I'm safe. Open the door first, then take a peek.

Do it / don't make me.

"Okay. I'm going. Going."

That's it, there I am—now I'm nuts. Touch and go. Feet on the pavement.

Do it/don't make me.

If I keep going straight, I should be all right. A few more steps, then stop. Just past this next house. And another. More, more.

I'm naked, I'm naked, I'm naked, I'm naked.

How far to Main Street? Three blocks, I think. What if I went left, then down to Wickenden? No, that's crazy. If it's only been a few seconds, I could—

Say something.

"Hi."

That's good, with the laugh like that—makes it look like it's a joke, like a Candid Camera thing. Was that a man or a woman? I didn't notice. A woman. Blue jacket, brown boots. I hope she saw me—pussy and bush and cunt, all nude.

"I can't believe it."

I'd better try a side street, then wind my way back home. Where's Hope? Come on, think "north." There's the church, so let's see . . . fuck, it doesn't matter, just run.

"Sorry, sorry, hold on."

If I can get back to Hope, or Brook. Which one's Brook?

"Sorry. Sorry."

I don't know anymore. I thought this was Brook, but that's the liquor store, so it can't be. No, the liquor store's *on* Brook! Campus Liquors, that's right. So that's north and that's south, good. But where's—what happened?

"No, I'm just looking for something."

Get away from this guy. Bus-stop bully.

"That's okay, no thank you, I'm fine."

There, that's Sheldon Street. One up and one over and I'm

home. Maybe I should cut across someone's yard. No, stay here—down on the sidewalk, ass bucking, and my fingers on my clit and everyone can see me and I can't believe I'm doing this.

Do it/don't make me.

"Nothing."

Shit, right in front of a kid. I gotta get out of here. He'll probably run and tell his mother.

"I'm sorry."

Stop talking, stop thinking, just stop it, stop everything.

Do it/don't make me.

"I had an *accident,* okay?"

It's okay. Everything's okay. Just a little farther.

Do it/don't make me.

From here to Brook Street, that's how long? Back two blocks across the bridge and then under the overpass, it's . . . wait. This is Empire, right, and there's I-95, or 195, where it breaks off, so I must've kept going. Did I do that? Right on Empire, that's right, so here's Weybosset Street. Westminster, Weybosset, down to Kennedy Plaza. Oh my God. Oh my God, no, please help, please help me. I don't know where I am.

"Can you help me?"

Just keep your hands up and they won't see.

"Why are you *looking*?"

No one. There's no one. Is that the sidewalk?

"No, I'm okay."

This isn't happening. It isn't. I'm not here. I'm at home watching TV, and I'm going to the kitchen to make a sandwich. See? I'm opening the refrigerator, looking inside—hmm, so many choices. There's chicken, and roast beef, and tuna, and salami. I think I'll have a salami—

"Sorry."

—a salami sandwich, on pumpernickel. With Swiss cheese and Dijon mustard, that's good. And potato chips. Chips are in the cupboard. Chips and pretzels and microwave popcorn. Maybe I'll microwave some popcorn. How many minutes? Two. Two minutes in the microwave. One, two. Pop pop pop pop—

"*Please,* I'm sorry."

Ding! Now I'm reaching into the microwave and taking the bag out. Oops, I haven't made my sandwich yet. Go back to the refrigerator. Okay, I'm opening the refrigerator—salami, got it, and cheese, and I've got the bread and the mustard.

Fuck, I've gotta cross at Waterman. I guess it's the only . . . Shit!

"Leave me *alone!*"

If I can just stick to the boardwalk, I should be able to get back to the East Side, no problem.

I'm naked, I'm naked, I'm naked, I'm naked.

Do it/don't make me.

Let's see . . . close the refrigerator. I think I'll start with the mustard. Spread it directly onto the bread, nice and thick. That's good, and now add three slices of cheese. Cheese and salami. Cut it in half. And don't forget the popcorn.

Do it / don't make me.

On the ground, yes, that's better. Keep touching it, keep touching. Touch my legs and my body and my breasts and along the insides of my thighs, and my bare feet against the blue sky, and everything's tense and shaking.

Whoo—what just happened?

Shadow on the sun.

It's okay. You're beautiful. You're sexy and beautiful.

I'm sexy. I'm beautiful.

Watch me. Watch me.

It's like the first time I masturbated in front of Stuart, when he stepped outside and looked through the bathroom window, and I felt like a free and beautiful woman because I knew that he was out there, and I was naked, and he was outside watching me.

I can feel it.

And then I was alone at night, and I left the back door open and sat on the grass, and I wondered who might be watching from one of the other houses, spying on me, seeing everything, the look on my face and every inch of my naked body, my hand going like mad between my legs.

I feel . . . close.

No!

There—good, I'm gone, goodbye.

"I'm sorry. I think I screwed up."

Please don't tell my parents. Don't tell anyone.

"I don't know. I'm sorry."

Stop saying that. He doesn't care.

"Thank you."

Take it. Put it on.

"I must've blacked out, I guess."

Here comes another one. Why? What did I do?

"Marlene. Marlene Breen."

Answer him. If I keep talking, maybe it won't seem so bad. Make it sound reasonable.

"No, I haven't been drinking."

What happened to my clothes? It's hot under this thing. Did I go out like this? No, I remember, because I was sitting in the living room and was going to make a sandwich, and then . . . I don't remember. Nothing happened.

"I'm sorry, I'm just upset."

Take it one step at a time. I was sitting at home, and I got up to make a sandwich. *That* for sure. Tell him that.

"I was making a sandwich."

I got up to make a sandwich, and then I . . . nothing.

"I'm sorry. I'm listening."

Pay attention. Listen and answer, listen and answer.

"I don't know. I feel awful. I hope everyone's okay."

Oh, God. I know what I did. I know what I did. Jesus. Did I?

"Where are we going?"

I know what I did.

"Look, I know you don't believe me, but please, just let me go home. I'm so scared. I don't know what's wrong with me, but I'll work it out on my own."

I'm going to lose my job. My parents are never going to speak to me again.

"Why can't I go home? You can see for yourselves, I'm not going to hurt anyone."

Don't argue with them. That's the worst thing you can do. Wait until we get in the car. Let them cool down first. They're nice people, and I'm just a poor, pathetic, ugly . . . who cares, I might as well die or jump off a bridge or blow my brains out.

"I'm coming."

Good, let's get out of here. Too many people around. I hope that no one saw my face. Please go away, I'm not worth looking at.

"I'm sorry. I'm so sorry."

They're not listening. Let them do their jobs first, then say something. They've got their routine, and I need to be sensitive to that and not be too pushy, because *I'm* the one who's in trouble, not them.

"Who are you talking to?"

Oh, this is so unnecessary. Put that down. Don't talk, don't *brag* about it. What's the point in wasting everyone's time? Look, it's a joke. Ha ha, the ugly woman, isn't it funny?

"Who were you just talking to?"

Eyes in the mirror. Handsome. He doesn't like me.

"What did she say?"

They're taking me down to the station. Well, how long is *that* going to take? Hours, days, years, I'm never gonna get out.

"How long is it going to take?"

Don't just *smile*, I've got a right to know. Dumb cop thinks he's so great. I bet he'd like to see my body, big breasts and hairy pussy, stroking, and everyone all around—

"Okay, I'm sorry, I just got hot. This blanket's heavy."

Stop it. You've got to realize that this isn't normal. Can you understand that? These men have every right to do what they're doing. They're totally in the right, and you're totally in the wrong. You need to listen, and be courteous, and try to get through this. And then never, *never* do it again.

"In case you're wondering, I'm not too happy with myself right now. I mean, I'm really scared. Whatever you guys need to do, that's fine, because I just want to get better. I don't know what I was thinking, or if I even *was* thinking. I guess I wasn't, because I don't even remember most of it. I've got a problem where I go into these trances, and I can't control myself, and I think I'm ugly."

Crying's not going to make it better.

"I'm sorry. But this is the end of it. And if I have to go to jail or a hospital or wherever, then that's fine. I'll accept that."

They're listening now. I'm getting through to them.

"I just wanted to . . . *do* something, you know? Do you know what I mean?"

Yes, of course they do. Good.

"I feel like when I go to bed at night, I haven't done anything. And the days are so long. I mean, there's work and my husband."

Stuart's a writer.

"My husband is a writer. Stuart Breen. He wrote a book called *My Private Apocalypse.*"

Stop smirking, you big, dumb . . . Oh, the world is so awful.

"I'm sure that you haven't heard of it. It wasn't a best seller, didn't get made into a movie. But it's real. It really happened."

Come on, Marlene. You're saying crazy things.

"Pardon?"

Listen and answer, listen and answer.

"Oh, he's in New Hampshire, on a business trip. He'll be back on Sunday."

Why doesn't he believe me? If you're going to blame some-one, blame me, don't blame Stuart. Stuart has nothing to do with this.

"What do you mean? He's a writer. He's doing research."

LEAVE HIM ALONE! LEAVE HIM ALONE!

"Why? You're not going to call him, are you?"

6

Pike barged into the common room of Sarah Cranberry's ski lodge and waved a newspaper at Stuart, who'd just got off the phone with his wife. "How're we going to spin this?" he demanded. In his excitement, he didn't notice that Stuart's hands were shaking.

Head buried in the paper, Pike read, " 'What gives the Independence Project its special mystique lies in its refusal to impose a set of values on the surrounding landscape. It is, quite simply, a parking lot. One approaches it with apprehension, but comes away feeling strangely renewed.' " He interrupted himself. "What the *fuck* kind of nonsense is that, Stuart?"

No response.

Pike sat down with the paper and continued to read. " 'In this context, Mr. Pike has redefined what is organic—and, in turn, essential—to the American experience. Such Yankee bluster has never been politically correct and probably never will be. In a nation that owes a terrible debt to its indigenous populations, the idea of questioning what "indigenous" means can seem in poor taste. But in Nathaniel Pike's world, *nothing* is indigenous. Everything is imposed, and through such impositions, the ugly and the practical, the base and the utilitarian, are redeemed and made beautiful.' This is the *Globe*," he said malevolently, and read on. " 'To some, such rhetoric deliberately misses the point. These same critics generally focus on the project's more sensational aspects—its hubris, its (ultimately negligible) physical impact on the environment—and fail to accept the parking lot on its own terms.' "

Pike folded the paper and handed it to Stuart. "Whoever decided to call it the Independence Project, anyway?" he asked. "Not me. I never called it that. I never called it anything. It's just a goddamn parking lot." Snapping his fingers, he hurried into the next room and returned with a stack of newspaper articles that had appeared in advance of today's reception. Everyone, it seemed, had something to say about him. The *Village Voice* offered this rousing defense: "Get off the guy's ass. So he's nuts—so what? So was Frank Lloyd Wright." The *L.A. Times* commented: "America has always had an uneasy relationship with dadaism, and Nathaniel Pike's Independence Project is no exception. Perhaps what bothers his critics the most is his apparent disregard for his own work. This is part of the charm, the fact that not even Mr. Pike quite 'gets it.' " *Entertainment Weekly:* "And speaking of weird—Rhode Island's leading megabillionaire, Nathaniel Pike, this week unveiled his two-million-dollar-plus creation, Independence, to a chorus of acclaim. Consisting of little more than a slab of blacktop in the foothills of the White Mountains, Pike has called his parking-lot-in-the-sky 'A tribute to the men and women who lost their lives in the Spanish Civil War.' We don't know what it all means, but we think it's pretty cool. GRADE: B+."

Pike read each article out loud, until Stuart lost his patience and snapped, "What did you expect, Nate? This is what you wanted. Attention."

"Not *this* kind of attention!" Pike tossed the reviews onto the bear rug under his feet. Of all the possible scenarios, this was one that he hadn't considered—getting good reviews, being accepted instead of scorned. "I don't want praise, I don't want criticism. I want dumb, mute awe." Feeling melancholy, he settled into a leather easy chair and glanced through the reviews again. Even after so many years, he still found it strange to see his name in print. What would it be like to lead an entirely private life? he wondered. To his surprise, the idea didn't bother him—so long as he had his drink, plus all the material comforts money could buy.

When he looked up, Stuart's face was pale, which Pike took to mean that he was upset about the reviews as well. "Don't worry about it, Stuart. I don't care who thinks I'm crazy. I consider that a compliment, coming from these assholes. Is it crazy to dream?"

"No, Nate, it's not," Stuart muttered.

"That's right. Everyone dreams. You go to bed, you dream— it's that simple. Who cares what any of it means? These books they've got, *1001 Dreams Decoded* . . . I don't want my dreams decoded. I don't want to think that hard."

Stuart left Pike brooding with the stack of reviews in his lap. The question returned to him: *What did you expect, Nate?* He didn't know. Playing the part of Nathaniel Pike had made it difficult for him to think of himself as anything other than a provocateur. For the first time, he noticed how quiet it was inside the lodge. Except for a single lamp next to the easy chair, the room was entirely dark, and he could almost forget that Sarah was in the kitchen making his dinner for him. *This* is what I want, he thought. Not loud but soft. Not big but tiny. I want to stop acting like such a jerk. The thought was so foreign to him, however, that once he became aware of it, he rejected it.

One thing was certain: he hadn't taken the project far enough. Reflecting on all that he'd learned, he decided that whatever he replaced the parking lot with, it would have to be immune to interpretation, so that not even the most astute critic could say anything about it.

That same evening, Gregg Reese was sitting at home, watching the local news. The story about the naked woman had taken up the first three minutes of the broadcast. He'd never met her before, but he'd spent some time with her husband, Stuart, both in New Hampshire and Rhode Island. Stuart worked for Siemens and McMasters, which meant he worked for Nathaniel Pike. Everyone associated with Pike seemed to exist on the deviant fringes of society: literary novelists, experimental filmmakers, now streakers. Keeny Reese would not have approved. But what about Gregg himself? He was a friend of Pike's, no less involved than Stuart. There weren't enough degrees of separation between himself and these wackos. His mother was right: Pike was bad news. Gregg was used to his mother's being right. She was right when she'd told him not to divorce Renee, to keep his little secret a secret, if only for the sake of public relations. The very fact of his existence was a lingering embarrassment. The Reeses deserved better than him. They deserved a patriarch, like his father, or Martin Kelley Reese, or Daniel Foster Reese, or Parker Davis Reese, who died in 1841. It wasn't fair. What was so great about being a Reese? Did these people ever really exist? Or just their legends?

By 1639, Hugh and Ginny Reese had established a successful mercantile operation in the newly founded harbor town of Newport, Rhode Island. Prosperity came naturally to Reese, whose keen business sense led him to experiment with different forms of trade. From 1640 to 1643 he dealt mostly in such crops as corn and peas, and in 1644 he switched to cattle. By decade's end, he was one of the wealthiest merchants in New England.

Despite his good fortune, we can assume that he wasn't satisfied, for in 1649 he embarked on a capital venture that was new to the region: the slave trade. Rhode Islanders were split on the issue of slavery, with opposing sides falling along the dividing line between merchants and Puritans. Hugh presided over a vast trade monopoly that flourished for many years before social pressures forced him to move on. The first blow to his empire came in the 1650s, when the towns of Providence and Warwick passed an ordinance outlawing hereditary black slavery. Though the law had little practical effect, it indicated the political dangers inherent in trading such a risky commodity. Along with those who admired Reese for his business acumen, many more despised him for how he made his living.

Pike's Folly

The slave trade grew over the years until Newport ranked as the largest slaveholding port in New England. Unfortunately for Hugh, he'd created considerable ill will among the Puritans, many of whom were friends of his wife. When Ginny died in 1669, he decided to bring his investments west to the Great Swamp, which was at that time in disputed territory claimed both by Rhode Island and Connecticut. What the area lacked in navigable shoreline, it made up for in other resources, such as timber and orchards. Using the money from his Newport ventures, Hugh built a grand home for himself and his daughter, Maggie, on an estate of seventy acres.

After a few lean years, he came up with a diabolical scheme to increase his holdings. His plan was to raise a militia, support it with his own finances and use it to stir up unrest among the clashing tribes of Indians in the region, who hardly needed any further encouragement to kill one another. After each skirmish between the tribes, Reese's men would round up the male survivors and send them back to Newport, where they were auctioned off and shipped to the West Indies. As for the females, they remained on the property as Hugh's personal slaves.

To provide shelter for the girls, Hugh had a team of laborers construct a giant shed on the estate, which served as a makeshift holding cell. They used cheap materials and worked in great haste. The conditions inside the shed were unsanitary at best, the ground was muddy, and the shingle roof leaked constantly. There were no windows, and the only light bled in through spaces in the walls where the boards failed to overlap.

In addition to cleaning house and tending to the grounds, the girls were expected to entertain the men on the estate. Hugh allowed his frequent guests to rape and abuse them to their hearts' delight. Whenever a girl died from disease or exhaustion, he simply replaced her. He recorded all this in his diary, no doubt assuming that future readers would not judge him too harshly.

After Hugh's death in 1680, his daughter took over the family business. Maggie Reese did not keep a diary, so her thoughts on slavery are lost to us. As a woman, her feelings about forced prostitution may have differed from Hugh's, or perhaps not. Regardless, the shed remained standing until 1685, when Maggie replaced it with a more permanent stone structure. Apparently, she had more of her father than her mother in her.

III | The Ocean State

1

A woman met Henry near the security check at T. F. Green Airport in Warwick, Rhode Island, ten minutes outside of Providence. She was wearing a black Mötley Crüe T-shirt, and her eyes were wild and blue with menace. "Savage," she said.

"That's me."

Celia introduced herself as they both moved in the direction of the exit. "Let me guess. You're a Republican."

"Actually, no. I vote Independent."

She looked disappointed. "I'm not as good at pickin' them as I used to be. First time in New England?"

"First time in Rhode Island but not New England. I used to come up to the White Mountains with my son every summer."

"Ah, so it's a personal vendetta."

They left the terminal through an automatic revolving door. The same spring breeze that had tossed Henry's plane around on approach now blew him off-balance. "It's no vendetta," he said. "I don't let my personal life interfere with my work."

He followed her across a pedestrian walkway and down to the short-term parking lot. When they reached her car, she said,

"Well, since this is your first time, I'll have to give you a little introduction. Cabinets are milkshakes."

"Excuse me?"

"Cabinets are milkshakes. Grinders are deli sandwiches. When you're ordering a coffee, ask for extra extra. Extra cream, extra sugar."

"Extra extra," he said, throwing his bag into Celia's trunk. "Anything else?"

"Don't rush me. There are thirty-nine towns in the entire state, including Block Island. East Bay means east of Narragansett Bay. South County is actually Washington County, but no one calls it that." She unlocked the car door, and they both got in. "Joe Mollicone is the most hated man in the state, then Patrick Kennedy. Don't speak ill of Buddy Cianci on Federal Hill unless you want to wind up in a body bag." Without looking behind her, she backed out of the parking space. "South Providence is black, Fox Point is Portuguese. Total population's just over a million. The mob runs everything, including this airport. Everyone knows everyone else." Once past the toll booth, she began to free-associate. "The hurricane of thirty-eight. The blizzard of seventy-eight. The Patriots, the PawSox. Newport Jai Alai. We are, without a doubt, the greatest state in the Union."

"I didn't realize that Rhode Island was such a unique place."

"Oh, we are. It's the size, it's the history. Most of our town centers were laid out before the Revolutionary War."

As they drove along the expressway, Henry had to restrain himself from pointing out the Red Roof Inn next to the airport and the many gas stations and chain restaurants, none of which could've been more than ten years old. From here, Rhode Island looked about the same as any midsized metropolitan area on the eastern seaboard. "Where does Mr. Pike live?" he asked, staring out the window at the approaching skyline.

"Pike? When he's in *town,* he's on the East Side, just like Reese and all the other bigwigs."

"What do you mean, when he's in town?"

"I haven't seen him for weeks. Last I heard, he was staying up in New Hampshire with some woman named Cranberry. Sounds like a bimbo to me." Celia's hands tightened on the steering wheel. "It just makes me so mad. I want to *kill* that man, I'm telling you. I absolutely want to kill him."

Henry cracked the window. "First things first. I'd like to take a look at that old house in . . . what's the name of the town again?"

She frowned. "Little Compton. I don't know what you intend to find there. The house itself isn't spectacular. Pike obviously doesn't know anything about real estate."

"And why's that?"

"Well, the East Bay's great, provided you don't have to go anywhere. You've got one road leading in and out, and that's it. As an investment, it stinks."

"Maybe he bought it for some other reason."

"What reason?"

"I don't know yet. At any rate, it's worth checking out. It strains credulity that a man would spend that much money on a house, tear the whole thing down, then have it rebuilt, for no reason at all. Whatever the reason is, it might also be why he's up in New Hampshire doing God knows what."

She sighed. "You people in D.C. always have to make everything so damn complicated."

At the I-195 turnoff, a green highway sign read To Cape Cod, and even though Cape Cod was still an hour away, he wished he was going there instead of Providence. He imagined himself on the slow ferry to Nantucket, drinking a beer on the foredeck with the cold gray ocean spray in his face.

They stopped at Kennedy Plaza, and soon he was standing in front of the Biltmore Hotel, thanking Celia for the ride. "I'll call you in the morning," he said, waving at her through the open car window.

She didn't wave back, just saluted mock officiously and drove off, leaving him there with his bag and his briefcase. *Well, screw you, too,* he thought. Being away from Washington always made him feel like an outsider. A savage. Don't take it personally, he told himself. You're here to do your job.

2

For days, Marlene wouldn't step out of the house. She'd lost her job, so there was no need to get up at any particular time. No need to do anything, really. She would've killed herself if there'd been a point to it, which there wasn't. She ate only one meal— a can of Campbell's Chunky Soup—and that was it for the day. At first she'd stopped drinking, then went back to it with a vengeance. Her own body disgusted her. She was paranoid and frightened of the telephone. Her parents had called several times, but she was too embarrassed to talk to them. Stuart couldn't get through to her either, and she feared he'd stopped trying. They still slept together but hadn't once had sex since her arrest.

The police, as it turned out, had been exceptionally nice to her. She'd already made her court appearance, where she'd pleaded guilty to one count of public indecency. She'd offered no excuse, just looked at the courtroom floor and let the tears fall as Judge Caprio sentenced her to a small fine and sixty hours of community service. The judge was not a cruel man; he knew a broken woman when he saw one. Imposing his punishment, he ordered her to report back in the morning for her work assignment. The task was fairly easy and involved canvassing for voter registration, which both parties in the statehouse had made an election-year priority. Her spiel was written out on an index card, along with half a dozen follow-up questions, so there was no way to screw it up. The job appealed to her, and even after the sixty hours were up, she continued to solicit people from her phone at home. She herself had no opinions about political issues; she'd never voted in her life and didn't consider herself qualified to make such important decisions.

As to her previous habits, she'd stopped—simple as that. She stopped lounging naked around the house and even slept in her clothes, undressing only to take a bath or a shower. She hated her body. It hurt that people thought of her as a sexual deviant.

Almost as a penance, she went up to Stuart's office one day and logged onto the Internet. Surely she wasn't the only person who'd gone down this same confused path. Public nudity wasn't the worst crime in the world; there was rape, and bestiality, and premeditated murder. Googling "public lewdness" had brought up a fairly uninspiring list of legal briefs and court cases, nothing that she could really sink her teeth into. She wanted testimonials, firsthand accounts from people just like her.

By chance, she stumbled upon a page called secret-exhibitionist.org, a very popular site, judging by the number of hits on its counter. The main page originated in Britain, with postings from all over the world, some dating back more than three years. A full three-quarters of these were from men, but the ladies chimed in as well, just as shamelessly and aggressively. One wrote: "I discovered this website today, and I can't tell you how delighted I am. I used to think that I was the only person who liked to go au naturel in public, but I can tell that there's a lot of us out there. Thank you! Thank you!"

Other friendly, supportive contributors forwarded their responses to the woman's story:

"Welcome!!! Sounds like you had one hell of a night. Keep it up, and let us know the next time you do something crazy."

"I had a similar experience when I was in La Junta, Colorado. One word of advice: you should always keep an extra change of clothes hidden if you plan on going out for more than a few miles. It can take a little preparation, but it'll save you a lot of trouble in the end. Other than that, good work. BTW: Anyone want to trade pix of PN in urban settings? I have construction sites, abandoned factories, highway overpasses. Daytime only, please. No shoes."

"SandyS, you are a *madwoman.* I'd love to live in your building. Good for you. Don't let anyone tell you otherwise. Have you ever considered doing a 48-hour nude? It can get boring but it's a fun way to spend the weekend."

For several minutes, all Marlene could do was stare at the screen. The sheer quantity of the postings was impressive. Public nudity was everywhere, in stores, parking lots, every conceivable mode of mass transit. The idea bothered her. She felt as though something tiny and fragile had been taken from her and stretched out of shape, made grotesque. According to these people, public nudity was like a sporting event, with its own lingo and code of ethics. "Secret exhibitionism"—a term Marlene had never heard before—was defined as "the display of the unclothed human body in places and situations where nudity is not permitted by law or social custom." Fair enough. But why sound so clinical about it? This was a *compulsion,* not a sport. No equipment, no qualifying rounds, no tips from the experts. Just nightmares, and anxiety, and self-doubts. One or two brief glorious moments, but that was it.

While Marlene began spending all her time on the Net, Stuart had worries of his own. He still owed his publisher what his contract referred to as "The Work," for which he'd been paid more than half of the money promised him as an advance against royalties. Weeks ago, his agent had given him a new deadline for the book. Write an outline, he'd suggested, something to get the ol' wheels spinning. Problem was, Stuart didn't know where to begin. An outline? Whatever for? Why not outline the stages of his emotional breakdown instead? His mounting depression, the chapter-by-chapter dissolution of his marriage. That'd thrill everyone. Stu, his agent would say, whaddaya doin' to me here? You're giving me garbage. I've got cookbooks to sell, self-help guides, stop smoking, stop eating, stop jerking off ten times a day. You're too depressing, man. Too wrapped up in your own head. There's gotta be some sizzle, an element of fun. Don't judge people just because they don't want to read about your miserable life. *I* don't want to read about your miserable life either, about your wife's kinky sex hang-ups or the fact you can't keep your clothes on for more than five minutes. That's icky, man. Gross. Too much fuckin' information. Write a book about George Washington. Write about the history of prostitution. Gene splicing, Jacques Cousteau. Something specific. When people read a book, they want to feel like they're learning something. What are they learning from you? They're learning dick, they're learning cock, they're learning ass, they're learning fucking on the front lawn. This is advice from a friend, Stu. You did the self-indulgent thing once. You can't do it again. Write about big-band music. Sophocles. Sophocles' sister. Write about art!

These days, Stuart didn't want to write about anything. When it came right down to it, even he could see through his own act. He knew he wasn't the "sharp, smart voice of his generation," as his publicist had once described him. He wasn't smart or sharp or any of that. He was an airhead. A dodo, a moron. Whatever those other geniuses had, he didn't have it. It was an easy enough matter to get the publicity blurbs together and make everything look peachy from a distance, but up close, there wasn't much there. He was lucky, that was all. His book was a souvenir. His career, a joke.

Still, he did his best. He tried writing an outline, just as his agent had suggested. After a few days, he gave it a title, changed Characters A, B and C to real names and got started on a draft. Marlene was so out of it that he could easily imagine she wasn't even there, and his mind returned to when he was writing *My Private Apocalypse,* living as a single man in his single-room apartment. Then as now, writing helped to ground and protect him; if not for his work, he would've succumbed to worse habits.

One spring morning, he set his notebook aside and walked to the Citizens Bank on Brook Street. Marlene had been dismissed six weeks ago, but neither of them had worked up the courage to pick up her belongings. She certainly wasn't going to do it, so that left him with the job. The walk was peaceful and pleasant; now that the college kids had all gone home, the locals could reclaim the area around Brook and Thayer. He smiled as he walked past a sushi restaurant near campus. His stomach was growling, and he weighed the happy idea of treating himself to a nice lunch.

Carla Marshall was working at the bank that morning and waved when he entered the building. The other tellers and financial consultants looked up from their desks and stared. He could feel his face turn red, so he made a direct diagonal across the banking floor to Marlene's old office. Someone had put her things in an open cardboard box that sat in the middle of the otherwise bare desk. The cubicle walls afforded him some privacy, so he sat down and looked through the box: a calendar; a coffee mug with a brown halo-stain in the bottom; pictures of Stuart, her parents, someone's baby—probably a coworker's; pens, paperweights and an unopened pack of chewing gum.

A voice interrupted him. "We thought we'd never see you again."

Carla was standing inside the cubicle. He blushed, wondering how long she'd been watching him. She'd always struck him as an exceptionally sexy woman, in a trashy, ex-stripper sort of way. She and her husband, Bill, were both huge stoners, and generally good for some high-quality hash whenever Stuart and Marlene came over for drinks.

"How's Marlene?" she asked.

Stuart gazed down and saw she was pumping her right foot in and out of her shoe. No point in pretending; he stared at it, then back up at her face. "Not too good," he said. "We hardly talk anymore, and when we do, she's out to lunch."

She tsked sympathetically. "Poor kid. Marlene always takes it on the chin. And what about you?"

He shrugged. "I'm all right. We're just trying to get through this together."

Stepping back into her shoe, she sat in the empty chair across from Marlene's desk. "To be honest with you, Stuart, I tried convincing our regional managers not to let her go but no dice. You know how conservative bankers are."

It'd been so long since he'd spoken to a woman other than Marlene that he felt like flirting with her. "You're not conservative," he said.

She laughed. "No, I'm not. I think what Marlene did was really cool. I could never do that. I'm so self-conscious about my body."

Sure you are, he thought.

"By the way," she said, "my offer about Martha's Vineyard still stands. We're going up this weekend."

He hesitated. "I don't know, Carla. I don't know if she's ready for that yet."

"Ask her. She needs to get out of the house. You both do." Carla's bright, super alert blue eyes held his own for a moment, then blinked away. "I don't see what the big deal is. In Europe, people walk around naked all the time. One of Bill's friends is a photographer from Paris. He's got a whole Web site filled with pictures of girls wandering around Europe without any clothes on. City streets, parks, everything. It sounds like fun to me."

Stuart smiled. "Well, maybe we'll move to Europe someday."

Carla's laughter sounded forced, as if she hadn't actually heard him. "Look at it like this—at least it'll give you something to write about."

Ah, yes: good advice. Even a passing conversation with Carla wasn't possible without his writing coming up. Because she'd once seen a profile of John Grisham on *60 Minutes,* she believed that all writers were the near-equivalent of movie stars, if slightly less recognizable on the street. He'd tried explaining that, unlike John Grisham, he wasn't swimming in royalty checks, and that only a handful of people had actually read his book from beginning to end. She didn't buy it and felt he was being falsely modest. Why argue with her? he wondered. Let her think what she wants. At least someone's impressed.

Carla's habit of slipping her shoe on and off was making him horny, so he said goodbye and hurried home to his wife. Marlene was in the kitchen when he returned, frying an egg on the stove. He crept up behind her, then reached out and turned off the burner.

"Hon, don't do that," she said. "It's not finished cooking."

"I don't care." His kisses were everywhere: her mouth, her chin, the side of her neck. "I need you. Right now. Please, hon, I'm going crazy."

"Cut it out, Stuart. Now I'm going to have to start all over."

"Who cares? Let's go upstairs. I want to see you naked."

"It's too soon." Squirming away, she carried the frying pan over to the sink and dumped the egg down the drain. "I've been through a lot, Stuart. Don't blame me for being upset."

"I *don't,* Jesus, but come on—you weren't raped, Marlene.

You were arrested. It happens." He followed her to the kitchen counter. "I'm sorry, this is just driving me insane. I've got cabin fever. It's just you and me in this little apartment, and . . . you won't let me touch you. You won't talk to me, you won't even look at me. You're not looking at me right now." She glanced up at him, then down again. "Let's go away for awhile. We need a change of pace. *I* do."

"You can go without me," she muttered.

"I don't want to. Look." He took both of her hands in his. "Let's go to Martha's Vineyard. This weekend. I ran into Carla Marshall at the bank. She wants us to come, both her and Bill. You can bring a book and lie on the beach. Whatever you want to do. Please, Marlene."

"Go by yourself."

"Why do you keep saying that?"

"Because no one likes me."

"Carla does. She told me just today. She even said that she tried to get your job back, but her bosses wouldn't listen." This ought to have made her feel better, but it didn't seem to. "What can it hurt? We'll go for a few days—a week, if you want. Come on, you've been talking about this for months."

Her eyes avoided his. "It's just too much right now. I'm sorry, Stuart." She knew she was disappointing him but couldn't help it. "I don't deserve you. You should be with someone else. Someone who's beautiful and intelligent, who doesn't complain all the time and isn't a big drunk."

"Oh, stop being so goddamned hard on yourself. We both fucked up. You did and I did. We're both guilty."

"No, only me. I'm the bad guy."

She was looking for sympathy, though he didn't feel much like giving it to her. "You think *you're* bad? You're an angel, sweetheart. You don't know what bad is. *I'm* the one who's bad. I shouldn't even be in the same room as you. I shouldn't be in the same house. Don't tell me about who deserves who and who doesn't. I don't deserve anything."

He stormed off, leaving her alone in the kitchen. He'd never yelled at her like that before. Marlene was used to thinking of Stuart as a steady, stabilizing presence. She felt she owed him an apology, though she wasn't sure for what.

Later, in his office, she turned on the computer and logged onto secret-exhibitionist.org. Stuart had left for a walk an hour earlier, and she hadn't decided whether to start worrying or not. As a distraction, she went to the open forum page and browsed through the latest postings. About two dozen entries had been added since the last time she'd checked. Reading them quickly began to bore her. So many reports of flashing, streaking and masturbating in front of windows became monotonous after awhile, and she wondered if everyone else who visited the site eventually came to the same conclusion: there was only so much you could do, so many different variations before the stories began to repeat and break down into categories. She never thought she'd find the topic boring, but there she was—bored stiff.

Then, at the bottom of the page, she noticed a posting whose title, *Female Streaker Busted in RI*, intrigued her. The message went on, "Attention! Check out this article. Her name's Marlene Breen, and she lives in Rhode Island. This is, without a doubt, the ultimate streak!!!"

The posting contained a link to an article in the *Providence Journal* about Marlene's arrest. In response, other contributors added their own comments: "Cool! Who is this person? Is she a member?" "Does anyone have a picture? I tried doing a search on AOL, but nothing came up. I will pay cash for top-quality jpegs. Urgent!" "Any ideas on how to track her down? Maybe s-e.org could do a profile—or, better yet, let's set up a live twenty-four-hour webcam feed. I *have* to meet this woman."

Marlene reread the entry several times. To her, this was like receiving a glowing review in the *New York Times*—the ultimate expression of respect from her peers. I'm famous! she thought. People are talking about me. People I've never met, never seen before. Streakers, nudists, perverts, exhibitionists. People in different states, in different countries. They all want to meet me. *Me*. Marlene.

I'm on the Internet!

Alone in the empty house, she leaned back in her chair and, for the first time in many days, smiled: a great, glowing, sunshiny *smile*.

3

A few weeks after Marlene's arrest, Heath and Allison went up to New Hampshire for a sneak peek at phase two of the Independence Project. Unlike with phase one, Pike hadn't allowed cameras on the site until it was nearly finished. Allison didn't particularly want to go, but she didn't want Heath making the trip by himself either. They'd become much more clingy in the days since she'd returned from London, and less spontaneous. Their relationship had all of the hallmarks of two people who were either about to break up or get engaged.

Just outside of North Conway, she asked, "Do you know if Stuart's going to be there?"

"Beats me," Heath said. "I think he's got a lot on his hands right now."

"Oh . . . right. Have you ever met his wife?"

He didn't want to get into that, so he said, "Not really."

"I feel sorry for her. People in this country are so fucked up. So goddamn conservative. You should see some of the sex clubs in Soho. Even the English are more hip than we are."

"You went to a sex club?" he asked.

"Not a real sex club. It was more like a rave."

"A dance club."

"No, a rave. A fucking rave. You know?"

It wasn't worth fighting about, so he closed his eyes and listened to the music on the tape deck. As the driver, Allison had agreed to let him play his music for the second half of the trip, much as it annoyed her. Allison liked *songs,* finished songs, not half-baked works in progress.

"How can you stand this junk?" she asked.

Heath reluctantly turned down the volume. He'd brought along a box of *Smile* bootlegs for the three-hour trip, most of which consisted of multiple takes of melodic fragments: the same xylophone passage repeated sixteen times, or a vocal line sung a cappella, then overdubbed ad infinitum. This particular session, "Surf's Up," was one of his favorites. In late '66, Brian Wilson was working with a lyricist named Van Dyke Parks, and "Surf's Up" was their greatest collaboration, a multipart suite featuring sleigh bells, horns and Brian's own wide-ranging vocals. Unlike a lot of *Smile,* "Surf's Up" sounded fully realized, even on the session tapes. This alone made the song unique. Avid *Smile* fanatics had learned how to deal with disappointment; "Mrs. O'Leary's Cow" might've been an interesting title, but as a song it wasn't much. "Surf's Up" didn't disappoint. The demo version of Brian playing the middle movement on the piano was gorgeous, complete in itself.

"I'm sorry," Allison said. "I just need silence for a few minutes." Shutting off the tape, she concentrated on the traffic, which had picked up considerably since they'd arrived in North Conway. During the warmer months, the roads leading in and out of town were always bumper to bumper—quite a change from her last time in New Hampshire.

"Why are you so uptight?" Heath asked.

"I'm not."

"Okay."

"What does that mean?"

"Okay, you're not uptight."

"That's right, I'm not. I'm just tired, and I've been driving all day, and I want to get off the road. My bra's killing me."

"Would you like me to drive?" he offered.

"No, we're almost there. You should've asked me an hour ago. What's the point in only driving the last five miles? None, nothing, there's no point."

"Okay."

"What do you mean, *Okay*?"

"Okay, there's no point. I'm sorry."

Allison leaned on the horn and flipped off the driver in front of them. She grumbled, "Why are you sorry? You've got nothing to be sorry about."

Leaving town, they continued north to the ski lodge, where Pike was waiting to take them to the top of Mount Independence. When she pulled in, he was standing in front of Sarah Cranberry's place, which he'd commandeered for the duration of the project. Heath and Allison joined him on the porch.

"You're just in time," Pike said. He looked as upbeat as ever, and his bright blue camouflage jumpsuit made him stand out in the woods. "We're meeting a pilot to take us to the construction site. Anyone afraid of flying?"

"What kind of a plane is it?" Allison asked.

Pike smiled at her worried expression. "It's an MD-600. Have you ever been in a helicopter before?"

"A helicopter? No." She looked at Heath, who was busy prepping his camera bag and didn't notice her. "Is it safe?"

Pike clapped her on the shoulder. "Of course it is! Would I let you ride in it if it wasn't? Give me a little credit, Allison. I'm not going to let anything happen to you."

They piled into Pike's SUV and drove to a nearby airstrip, where the helicopter was sitting on the tarmac, its blades circling slowly above the cabin. Pike gave a thumbs-up to the pilot, who signaled back. Allison was the last to board. Neither she nor Heath was looking forward to the ride, but at least Heath had his video camera to distract him; Allison had nothing.

The Plexiglas-domed helicopter took off and flew west over the Kancamagus Pass. Allison did her best not to let the mild turbulence get to her. Her nerves were frayed and her pulse was pounding in her wrists and throat, thanks to the three lines of coke she'd ingested earlier that morning.

Doing drugs, like a lot of things, wasn't much fun anymore. Back in London, she'd first tried coke because her mother had enjoyed it, and initially she did, too. Cocaine was expensive, exciting and upscale compared to pot, which was common and teenager-cheap. Allison associated smoking pot with being in college, whereas snorting coke seemed like a more adult thing to do. She was feeling impatient with her life—confused, bored, nervous—and cocaine suited her perfectly. It was the right drug for the right time.

Unfortunately, her body couldn't handle it, and within weeks she'd developed migraines, insomnia and inflammations of the nose and throat. She'd even lost some of her hair. For Heath, being around Allison was like dating a junkie or a crackhead. There wasn't a morally sound rationale for doing coke like there was for pot. Brian Wilson had shown him that pot and LSD could serve as conduits for creative expression. Not cocaine. So far as Heath was concerned, she might as well have stayed in London.

"There it is," Pike said, pointing out the canopy at the green mountainside two hundred feet below. "Heath, get a shot of that."

Heath leaned forward and aimed his camera down the steadily ascending slope. Allison also rose, but the chopper hit a rough spot, and she fell into Heath's lap.

"Ow!" He glared at her. "You spoiled my composition."

Pike called out, "Hey, everybody shut up back there. We're almost right over it."

As their altitude dropped, a trail became visible through the dense cover of trees. About a thousand yards east of the trail, they saw what appeared to be the top of a building, which was rectangular and fairly low to the ground. The roof was flat and wide enough for the helicopter to land on it. Circling closer now, they looked down on Pike's parking lot, which flanked the building on one side. A sign jutted above the building's entrance, but they could see only the back of it.

"Now, check this out," Pike said.

The helicopter descended and banked steeply to the right. Coming about hard, Allison and Heath got their first head-on view of the building. It was quite large and appeared to be constructed for commercial or industrial purposes. Tall, broad windows extended from either side of the multiple doors that provided access.

Allison squinted but couldn't see through the windows. "What is it?"

The roar of the propeller decreased as the pilot hovered fifty feet over the ground. She wondered if he planned on landing, or if this was as close as they were going to get.

"Look at the sign," Heath said.

She did. She'd seen it somewhere before—so many times, in fact, that it'd stopped making an impression on her. This was an icon, an image anyone over a certain age associated with suburban sprawl, strip malls and commercial overdevelopment.

Kmart, it said.

She couldn't believe it. "Fucking Christ . . ."

"Take us down," Pike told the pilot. "You really have to see it close up."

They landed in a field about a hundred yards south of the

building and disembarked. Once Allison, Heath and Pike were safely clear of the rotor blades, the pilot gave a jaunty salute and lifted off.

"Where's he going?" she asked.

Pike smiled. "Don't worry, he's on call. Come on."

He plunged into the woods, where a poorly cut trail wound up a hill to the construction site. Heath and Allison hustled to keep up.

"Can you deal with this?" she whispered to Heath, who'd taken a break from filming to have a look around. "This is beyond crazy. This is fucking certifiable."

"I think it's pretty amazing," he said.

"Oh, there's no doubt about that. I mean, a parking lot is one thing. But why a Kmart? I thought Kmart filed for bankruptcy."

Pike overheard her. "They did. That's how clever I am, Allison. No other company was willing to sell their licensing rights to me. You should file that away for future reference, both of you. It's easier to negotiate when the other party's strapped for cash."

At the end of the trail, the ground rose sharply to the level of the parking lot, which was still in pristine condition. A wall of trees surrounded the lot, some of them so tall that they loomed several feet above the rooftop, where workers on ladders and scaffoldings were applying finishing touches to the weather-proofing.

"The stadium lights just arrived a week ago," Pike said, indicating a rack of lights near the construction site, behind which pink and black electrical cords were plugged into a massive generator. "Used to be, we couldn't work after nine p.m."

Heath panned with his camera across the lot. He stopped on Allison, who looked wistful inside his viewfinder. "Are you just going to leave it empty like that?" she asked Pike.

"Hell no! As soon as these workers get out of here, we're

gonna receive our first shipment from the DC in Columbus. DC—that's Distribution Center. It'll probably take two weeks to fill the shelves, but it'll be worth it. I'm even going to hire a full-time staff. Stockboys, cashiers, you name it."

"But *why*?" Allison demanded.

He grinned savagely. "Stop asking that. I hate 'why.' A kid your age shouldn't ask why all the time." Across the lot, many of the workers had set down their tools to listen. "I declare war on why. If I do nothing else, that's my goal. My one cause in life. No more why."

With his camera raised, Heath had a hard time keeping Pike in focus, so impulsive were his gestures. It occurred to him that this scene would fit in nicely with some of the bits he'd shot with Stuart and Marlene earlier in the spring. The two projects were basically incompatible, of course, but in an ideal world he could intercut them. He thought back to some of the earliest footage that he'd taken of Marlene, when they'd brought the camera down to Brenton Point in Newport and she'd walked naked to the edge of the seawall and gazed out at the Newport Bridge. If there was a link at all, it was that both Pike and Marlene were well-known eccentrics—marginal figures, ultimately, but no less interesting for that. Like Brian Wilson, Heath primarily saw himself as a collage artist; the individual components weren't as important as what they created together. On a certain track from *Smile,* for example, it was the juxtaposition between Hawaiian chants, a thundering motif for kettle drums and steel guitars, and the Beach Boys singing cyclical riffs about early American history. In Heath's film, the juxtaposition wasn't musical but visual, ideological rather than psychedelic. He had no idea what any of it meant but tried not to think about it. He, too, was on an anti-why crusade.

"Let's go," Pike said and led them into the building. A pair of automatic sliding glass doors opened and closed behind them, just like in a real Kmart. Once inside, the drilling, sawing and buzzing sounds of construction became louder as carpenters installed huge shelving units that extended to the back of the building. The cash registers had already been set up, along with a numbered banner above each checkout station.

They proceeded as far as the customer-service desk, where Pike opened a box of ad-prep and pulled out a banner that read Save While You Shop. "Look at that," he said. "An authentic, Kmart-approved aisle banner, and I own it." Allison didn't want to touch it, so he offered it to Heath, who handled it with care. Seeing the inside of a Kmart in its semiconstructed state seemed to him a rare opportunity, like watching heart surgery.

"Who do you think will actually shop here?" Allison asked.

Pike took the sign from Heath and put it back in its box. "I don't know. That's the mystery of it. Short of a chopper, the only way in's on foot, and that's a three-hour climb up rough trail." He paused for the punch line. "I don't think we'll be selling much office furniture."

Both he and Heath laughed, but Allison didn't join them. "I don't get it. Don't you care what people are going to think of you when they see this?" she asked.

"Not particularly. Don't worry about me, Allison. My sterling reputation isn't worth losing any beauty sleep over."

"Whatever," she said. Arguing with him was pointless, since he had an answer for everything. Still, she had to give him some credit; he did what he wanted, and damn the consequences. Pike didn't believe in denying himself anything, even if it made him look bad. She supposed that this was what so many women had found attractive about him—not just his good looks but his fearlessness. How unlike her father, she thought; how unlike herself, for that matter.

She turned to leave, but a sudden pain inside her head

stopped her. Everywhere she looked, she saw a haze of blue, then purple, then green.

Pike cut out his clowning. "Allison, what's wrong? You look like hell," he said.

She swallowed with effort. Her face was pale, and her skin felt clammy. "Oh, I'm okay. I just think the altitude's getting to me," she said.

"Well, don't get sick on my nice new floor." Pike didn't know what to do with her, so he said, "Why don't you take a walk? There's some fresh air near the back door."

She nodded weakly and stumbled along to find a quiet spot to sit. Her joints hurt, and something in the back of her throat tasted corrosive. A chill came over her as the pounding in her head gradually died down a bit. With a shock, she realized her nose was bleeding.

4

One hundred fifty miles to the south, Celia Shriver picked up Henry Savage and drove him to Nathaniel Pike's old house in Little Compton, Rhode Island, through vineyards, fallow fields and ranchettes along the rural route leading into blackberry country. The house itself stood far back from the road and was shielded by a row of tall evergreens, some of which were dead. A low stone wall surrounded the property, giving it an uniquely New England character.

In the days since he'd arrived, Henry had had few opportunities to experience the real New England, apart from what Celia had shown him. Overall, the trip wasn't going well. The people he'd interviewed about Pike were wary of Henry's government credentials, and not even Celia could accept that there was anything more to him beyond what she thought of the agency he represented.

All of which frustrated him greatly. Henry wanted people to feel about their government as he had when he'd started working for it nearly three decades ago: that the United States, for all its faults, was still the most open and compassionate country in the world; that the men and women who comprised its agencies were not evil automatons with computer chips planted in their brains, merely fallible human beings whose faults were the result of their own personal limitations and not some overriding conspiracy within the system. If they fucked up seven times out of ten, it was only because that's what people did: fuck things up. In hospitals and muffler shops, loan offices and fast-food restaurants, the people of America were busy fucking things up, every hour, every second—putting the decimal point in the wrong place, giving you extra onions when you asked for extra pickles. Why should those same people expect a higher degree of competence from their government? Why, Henry wondered, blame *me* for everything?

Outside the house, he waited at a discreet distance as Celia rang the doorbell. She had a vague connection to the homeowner—they'd taught together at the Rhode Island School of Design—and had set up the appointment herself.

The man who answered the door was gray-haired and elderly, with a feeble squint that became more prominent the longer he stayed in the sunlight. Introducing himself as Parker—whether first name or last, Henry wasn't sure—he led them into the living room, where a tray with some cheese was set out, along with a stack of cocktail napkins. He'd made some effort to welcome his guests, and Henry assumed he didn't get out much.

"How long have you lived here?" Henry asked.

"Seven years, sir." Parker's voice was as watery as his blue eyes, which looked disproportionately large behind his thick glasses. "We moved out of Providence shortly after my wife retired. Most of our friends thought we were pretty cuckoo when they heard whom we'd bought it from." The thought of Nathaniel Pike brought a smile to his thin, creased lips. "I always say, if it weren't for Mr. Pike, we never could've afforded this place. The realtor's original asking price was way too high."

Henry frowned. "Did you know the history of the house before you bought it?"

"Of course. It was in all the papers. Nathaniel Pike *this,* Nathaniel Pike *that.* He's quite an eccentric. I remember one time—"

Celia coughed impatiently. "Can we please stay on topic, gentlemen?"

A door at the back of the room opened, and a woman about Parker's age came in. "What kind of lies are you telling these people?" she asked him.

"Oh, the usual." Parker's body language became more formal when he offered her his seat. "Mr. Savage, this is my wife, Barbara."

She remained standing. Like Parker, she was gray-haired, but with a stronger, more compact build. She nodded at Henry, then acknowledged Celia by name.

"Barbara," Celia said, "whose idea was it to buy this place, yours or your husband's?"

"Both of us. I had more questions about it than Parker did."

Henry perked up. "Did you get any answers?"

"Not from Mr. Pike. But I found a few things out on my own."

Her husband looked embarrassed. "Honey, it's not important."

"I know it's not important, but the man might be interested."

"What's this, Mrs. . . . ?" Henry's voice trailed off. He'd wanted to say Parker, but knew that wasn't right. Mrs. Parker? Parker Parker?

Barbara motioned for him to follow. "It's out back," she said, then led him, Parker and Celia out the back door to a field behind the house. A gravel trail continued into the outlying woodlands, where many of the trees were still bare.

Henry turned around to look at the house. Its most distinguishing feature was the balcony on the second floor, which had no railing around it, just a low brick ledge about knee-high. The roof was dark brown, and the upstairs windows were all cut out of it, like eyeholes in a ski mask. For all its history, the house looked plain, even homely. Whatever mystery it contained didn't show on the surface.

Up ahead, Barbara left the trail and plunged straight into the woods, and within a few steps they reached a clearing where the ground was still covered with yellow and black leaves from the previous autumn. Barbara kicked them aside, and they swirled and blew against her legs.

"I did a little research," she said. "Parker and I know a guy who collects old maps of southern New England. We were both out here six months ago." Crouching, she pointed to a stone foundation, which the mossy undergrowth partially concealed. The stones described a perfect rectangle, with a single opening for a doorway.

"What is it?" Henry asked.

"A pen of some kind. A free-standing cellar. I'd guess it's about three hundred years old. These property lines haven't changed since the seventeen hundreds, so it's safe to say it's always been part of the estate."

Celia stood in the center of the foundation. "It's big," she said. "What do you suppose they kept in it?"

"Possibly dry goods. We're on an elevation, so the ground stays dry most of the year. They could've stored grain or cured meats, maybe even ammunition. Many of the wealthier families down in South County moved over to the East Bay to get away from the Narragansett Indians, and most of them kept an arsenal."

Henry chipped away at the ground with his shoe. "There's probably some pretty heavy artillery under all this dirt."

"I found something better. Look." She pointed at a second

pile of leaves, about twenty feet from the first. When they went over to it, they saw more rocks from the foundation lying in rubble. The dank smell of dirt and decaying wood was particularly strong here.

"Ruins," Henry said. "I don't see the point, unless—"

"They're not ruins." She hefted one of the smaller rocks. "Nathaniel Pike did this. I checked my friend's map against a more recent one. This building was still standing ten years ago. When Pike had the main house bulldozed, he tore down this pen, too."

"So?"

"Why would someone go through the trouble of making an exact copy of a house, down to the last stick of furniture, except for this one structure?"

That question "why" again. It came up a lot where Pike was concerned.

"Maybe he just lost interest," Celia suggested. "Pike's got the attention span of a two-year-old."

Both women looked at Henry, who admitted, "I'm clueless. My only guess is that something bothered him about this place. Maybe that's why he sold it to you so cheaply. He wanted to get rid of it."

Barbara said, "Oh, there's no doubt about that."

They walked back to the house, where Henry thanked the old couple and left with Celia. Instead of heading directly back to Providence, they made a quick swing through the village square. Like many communities in the East Bay, Little Compton consisted of a small commons area lined with tiny markets and steepled churches, quaint and old-fashioned for these few short blocks. A brick-and-glass police station stood next to the firehouse around the corner from the high school and across the street from a green patch of cemetery. It was hard to believe that Providence was only thirty minutes away.

Celia parallel-parked in front of the town hall and squinted at her watch. "It's almost four. If we hurry, we can have a look at Federal Hill before the traffic picks up."

Checking out Federal Hill—Providence's Italian district—probably made sense, but it wasn't what Henry was interested in now. "This'll just take a few minutes," he said. "I want to find out who owned that house before Pike."

Celia relented, and they climbed a short flight of steps to a door with a 9/11 memorial flag taped to the window. Once inside, they had trouble finding anyone to help them. The front desk was unattended, and when a receptionist came out of the ladies' room, she seemed at a loss as to where the town kept its records. Eventually, an older woman led them down a dark, mahogany-trimmed corridor to a surprisingly vast room marked Archives. A long worktable stood in the center of the room, under a wicker ceiling fan that remained motionless until the woman turned on the lights.

"Looks like we're the only ones here," Henry observed.

"Only ones all week," the woman said. "We're one of the smaller towns in the East Bay—probably the whole state. The population's held pretty steady so there's not much need to update the records more than once every few years." She became rueful. "Mr. Pike, though, I know all about *that* guy."

"So you spoke to him?"

"Many times. But I was as surprised as anyone else when I'd heard what he did to that house."

"Didn't the town council object?"

"Nothing to object to. The house wasn't a landmark, so as far as we were concerned he was free to do whatever he wanted."

Henry reached for a chair and slowly sank into it. "That seems odd to me. We just spoke to the house's current owners."

"Yes, the Parkers," she said.

His brain did a little flip. "That's right, the Parkers. They told us that the house—I mean, the original house—was three hundred years old. That should've qualified it for landmark status."

"Not necessarily. As you know, Mr. . . . . Savage, is it?" She tittered. "I like that. I hope you're *not* a savage."

Henry smiled tolerantly, having heard worse. "Call me Henry."

"Henry, fine. As you know, the National Register of Historic Places keeps a fairly strict watch over its membership. Most homes on the list are at least fifty years old. That's been the guideline for ages, and it's pretty rare that the Feds break their own rules. But it seems Mr. Pike didn't want to go through with the application process."

"Why?" Celia asked. "Is it complicated?"

"It can be, depending on who your State Historic Preservation Officer is. Some of them like to inspect the properties themselves. They'd at least order a thorough investigation. Whatever documents pertained to the house would be catalogued, evaluated and eventually made public."

"So Nathaniel Pike buys a three-hundred-year-old house," Henry mused, "tears it down, then reconstructs it from new materials. Therefore it's no longer eligible for the register. It's a brand-new house."

"Pretty crazy, huh? Here, let me see what else I've got on file."

The woman left to pull a stack of records from the back room. While she was gone, Celia said, "It's just like Pike to pick a fight with the National Register. I'm sure this whole thing was done to spite the Reeses."

"Why do you say that?" he asked.

She regarded him as one might a naive child. "Gregg's mother, Keeny, has been president of the State Historic Preservation Society for years. It's a passion of hers. If Keeny had wanted that house on the list, I can't imagine her just giving up on it—not without a good reason."

The woman returned ten minutes later with a bundle of papers and set it on the table. The sheets were dog-eared—some yellowed, some not. The first few pages were out of order; Henry saw the names "Parker," then "Pike," then "Parker" again.

Celia peered over his shoulder. "What are we looking at?" she asked.

"That's all I could find," the woman said. "The state passed a paper-reduction act, so it's liable to be incomplete."

Leafing through the pages, Henry's eyes began to glaze over. Most of the sheets were records of local tax assessments and conveyed little of interest. "This is going to take awhile," he sighed. "All I want to know is who owned that property before Pike."

"That's simple," she said brightly. "The Johnsons. Danny Johnson and Willie Johnson. They were brothers. Moved to California, I believe."

Deeper into the stack, he came upon a reference to the Johnsons, whose tenure had been brief. "How long were the Johnsons in town?"

"Oh, since eighty-eight, eighty-nine, thereabouts. That's when I moved down from Boston. If I remember right, they were both interior designers. *Lots* of money, but of course you'd need it. This is an affluent community. I suppose that's what designers do—they buy houses, keep them for a couple of years, then turn 'em around for a profit."

Thinking out loud, Henry said, "So, the Johnsons bought the place, sold it to Nathaniel Pike for a quick dollar, then Pike all but gave it to the Parkers, who've owned it for seven years. Who came before the Johnsons?"

"That's before my time. Ask me anything since eighty-eight, and I've got it down cold. Photographic memory, almost." She didn't want to disappoint him, so she added, "I do remember talking to Willie Johnson once. He mentioned a name, but . . . nope, I lost it."

Henry's patience with the town's primitive filing system was wearing thin. Back home, this information would've been stored in a database, and he could've found it without rummaging through so much moldy paperwork.

"It's probably nothing," he said, "but I want to make sure that before we leave—" He froze. The name on the next page so startled him, it was as if Pike himself had snuck up from behind and tapped him on the shoulder.

The two women glanced down to see what he was staring at.

"I *know* that name," Celia muttered.

"Cranberry!" The woman snapped her fingers. "Oh, *that's* right. Sure, the Cranberrys have been here *forever.*"

5

That same morning, Marlene and Stuart took the ferry from Woods Hole to Vineyard Haven, where later they'd meet up with Bill and Carla Marshall, who'd already been on the island for two days. The day had started off overcast but cleared up once the ferry pulled out of port. Neither the landing nor the ferry itself was as crowded as both would be in another week, after Memorial Day.

The ferry maneuvered between a row of red and green channel markers and into open water. Stuart felt like having a beer, so he bought a Heineken for himself and a Coke for Marlene. They huddled close together on the top deck, where the breeze was strong and gusty. Marlene's black hair, which she'd had cut for the occasion, blew into his eyes. Midway across, he ventured, "What do you think Bill and Carla will be wearing?"

"Why?" she asked. "Are you hoping to see Carla in a bikini?"

In fact, he was. Bearing her in mind, he'd brought along a Speedo swimsuit, one that showed off every contour through its skintight fabric. Wearing it around Carla would be like being naked in front of her, and being naked in front of her was his big goal this week. Much as he hated to admit it, there were still cravings he hadn't quite mastered. "Actually," he said, "I'm look-ing forward to seeing *you* in a bikini."

She smiled and snuggled against him. On the horizon, a line of beach began to rise out of the water—their first sight of the Vineyard.

"It's strange," she said, "but a year ago, all I would've been thinking about was taking off my clothes and running around in front of people."

"And now what are you thinking?" he asked.

She knew that telling the truth would only make him upset, so she lied. "About how much fun we're going to have."

The boat docked at Vineyard Haven, and they could see Bill and Carla waiting at the edge of the landing. Carla was wearing a bikini top and a sarong, with her light-colored hair piled up and tucked under a straw hat. Bill looked as though he'd come directly from work, in khaki slacks and a blue oxford shirt. At forty-five, he was the oldest of the four. His brown hair was thin-ning on top, and his suntan looked glazed on.

Carla spotted them coming down the gangplank and ran ahead of Bill. "Welcome to the island," she said—*just like a native,* Stuart thought as she drew him close to give him a kiss. He could feel her breasts flatten against his chest.

They were standing in the flow of arriving passengers, and Bill called out to Carla from the pier, "Kid, you're in the way."

Carla took Marlene's hand, leaving Stuart to schlep their bags. At the bottom of the plank, Bill muttered, "Hey, Stu," then relieved him of the larger bag and gave Marlene a much warmer welcome. "Our car's parked a couple of blocks down the road. We hadn't counted on so much beach traffic, otherwise we would've left earlier."

They proceeded up a ramp to the edge of a rocky seawall, where they walked to Bill's champagne-colored Mitsubishi. The ferry was getting ready to take off; a long, low toot from its horn blew across the water, and a fleet of cars began to creep single-file into a hold on the lower deck.

"You girls are going to have to squeeze in back," Bill said as he tossed their bags into the trunk. "Carla and I were taking some pictures down at Aquinnah, and we didn't get a chance to unload our stuff."

Marlene peered into the car and saw a tripod lying flat across the backseat, along with a camera bag and what looked like a shiny silver umbrella, the kind used by professional photographers to bounce light around a studio. "Where's Aquinnah?" she asked.

"Don't worry, we'll get there," Bill said. He pushed a button on his key chain to unlock the car. "Not today, though. We've got a full schedule."

Carla slid into the backseat and righted the tripod, standing it evenly between her and Marlene, who'd climbed in behind Bill. With everyone settled, Carla grabbed Stuart's shoulder through the headrest. "Good, I get to play with your husband," she said to Marlene.

Bill hit the gas, and once they were clear of the Vineyard Haven traffic, he told Stuart, "We brought along the *best* hash, man. Fresh from Vermont. I'm telling you, it really makes a difference if you're willing to spend a little more."

"A beer sounds about my speed," Stuart said. They'd turned onto a back road, amid trees and tall grass growing up from the dusty median. Bill drove with authority, not bothering to keep both hands on the wheel. His nonchalance vexed Stuart, who thought, *Dude, you don't live* here. *You're on vacation. Get over yourself.*

Carla spoke up from the backseat. "Honey, did you tell Stuart and Marlene about Lucien?"

Stuart frowned. "Lucien?"

"Lucky's an old studio friend of mine," Bill said. "We met in

Paris back in ninety-one, when I was teaching a summer course on scientific photography. He's staying in the guesthouse."

"The guesthouse," Carla repeated. "Doesn't that sound cool?"

Marlene smiled politely but said nothing. The news that someone else would be staying with them was jarring to her. She'd come expecting a safe place where she could drink wine on the beach, smoke some grass and surround herself with familiar, friendly faces. She needed to be nursed back to life, slowly, one little baby step at a time.

Bill grinned. "Lucky's a great cook, and a really good guy. He's especially looking forward to meeting *you*, Marlene."

"Me?" She felt pinned to the seat cushion. "Why?"

No one knew how to answer her. *Because you're a freak. A sex addict.*

Finally, Stuart said, "Who *wouldn't* want to meet you, hon?"

The others laughed, and Marlene halfheartedly joined in. Just in time, they slowed in front of a mailbox at the end of a long, wooded driveway. "We're here," Bill said and turned into the woods.

The time-share was smaller than either Marlene or Stuart had expected—an old country cottage with gray clapboard walls, a flat roof and an open porch where the paint was peeling. When they stepped out of the car, they could hear the ocean but couldn't see it. Past the house and driveway, a footpath plunged straight into a dense wall of beach grass, which hid the house from its neighbors. The air was lukewarm and smelled of salt-water and vegetables rotting in the garden.

Bill and Stuart left the bags on the porch and waited for the ladies, who were dallying in the yard. "Where's your friend?" Stuart asked.

Bill stepped out of his leather flip-flops and sat down. "We'll join up with him later. He's probably still taking pictures on the beach. The water's just down that trail," he said, waving in the direction of the beach grass.

Near to where he was pointing, Stuart noticed another cottage, similar in construction to the main house but smaller. The front door was wide-open, and a royal-blue beach towel was drying from the rafters. "It sounds nice," he said.

Bill stretched to crack his back, a habit Stuart particularly abhorred. "You get what you pay for, Stu. If you think this is nice, you should check out Lucy Vincent's."

"What's that?"

"That's the nude beach. It's a ten-minute walk." Bill crossed his legs, and Stuart could see the dirty bottom of his right foot. "Think you guys are up for it?"

Stuart tensed; over his shoulder, he could hear Carla and his wife approaching. "Oh, I don't—"

"Maybe just Marlene, then." Abruptly, Bill jumped out of his chair and danced over to his wife, who was standing with Marlene at the edge of the porch. "Hey, kid. We were just talking about going over to Lucy Vincent's this afternoon."

Echoing her husband, Marlene asked, "Who's Lucy Vincent?"

Carla blushed. "Oh, nothing. It's just a . . . tourist attraction. We'll see."

The subject was forgotten, and Bill went inside to fix them all drinks. Stuart couldn't tell whether Marlene was enjoying herself but preferred to think she was. She looked tired and in no shape for going to the beach.

When she caught him staring at her, she asked, "What are you looking at?"

He almost said, "How pretty you are," but didn't feel like it. Instead, he said, "Just you."

"That's nice." She smiled sadly, as if she didn't consider herself worthy of him.

After banging around inside the kitchen, Bill kicked open the screen door and came out carrying a tray of glasses filled with white wine. "Give me a hand," he said to Carla, who took two glasses from the tray and passed them to Marlene and Stuart. The two remaining glasses upset the tray's balance, and it crashed to the ground, the glasses shattering around Bill's bare feet. "Damn it, kid. Those don't belong to us."

Carla bowed her head. "I'm sorry. I'll pay for them."

"That's not the point. What are we going to use for wineglasses now?"

Stuart could tell Carla was used to being yelled at, and he felt awful for her. "Bill, it's okay," he said. "I'm sure there's a store in town."

"Yeah, that's right," said Carla. "Listen to Stuart. And besides, we can always use paper cups. There's a whole bunch in the kitchen."

Excusing himself, Stuart set down his wineglass and went off to fetch the cups. He hadn't expected Carla to side with him so aggressively against her husband. Great, he thought—we're here five minutes, and already everyone's pissed off at each other.

The kitchen was small and cluttered, with wooden cupboards and a shallow Formica counter on which sat a spiral of green foil from the bottle of wine that Bill had opened. Stuart pitched the foil into the trash under the sink, then found a stack of paper cups. Pouring Bill and Carla each a fresh cup of wine killed off the bottle, so he threw it away, too.

When he returned to the porch, the others were in a better mood. "We should all drink up and change into our swimsuits," Bill said. "Lucien's going to wonder what happened to us."

Everyone seemed agreeable, so they hurried the rest of their drinks and went inside. Carla showed Marlene and Stuart to their room, which was across the hall from the one she and Bill were using. The house was dark, lacking light fixtures in the ceilings. The only illumination came from floor lamps, which they switched on one at a time as they passed through the hall.

"It's an old house," Carla said, "so the doors don't shut all the way." She demonstrated with the door to Marlene and Stuart's room. "I hope that's okay."

"Sure," Stuart said, "that's fine. We're all friends."

Leaving the door open, Carla left to get changed in the bathroom. Marlene had slung her bag onto the bed but just stood there staring at it. When he asked her what was wrong, she said, "I don't think I want to go swimming today. I'll just sit with a book."

"Whatever you want, hon. But you're going to be hot in those clothes."

"I'll roll up my pants. They're baggy, see?" She lifted her right pant leg. "Besides, it was chilly on the ferry. I think it's too cold for swimming."

"Marlene, it's perfectly nice out. It was cold on the ferry because of the breeze off the open water."

"I'm sure you're right. I'll see you outside." Her force field went up, and she took her purse and left.

Stuart had to laugh—this wasn't going as well as he'd hoped—and then began to undress. The door was still wide open, and he could hear Carla finishing up in the bathroom. He quickly tugged off his pants, socks, underwear and T-shirt as a rapid pulse filled his throat at the thought of Carla's seeing his naked body. He wanted her to catch him unawares, in the act of bending over or reaching for his swimsuit, but it had to appear entirely unintentional, otherwise the effect would be ruined.

With his back to the door, he waited for her to come out of the bathroom. His Speedo swimsuit lay in a black lump on the floor, just inches away from his right little toe. At the sound of footsteps, he bent over, stuck his ass high in the air and picked up the suit. The footsteps slowed in front of the doorway and stopped.

She's looking at it, he thought. Carla Marshall is looking at my ass!

"What are you doing?" Marlene inquired.

Whirling around, he covered his penis with his hands. "Just putting on my swimsuit," he said.

Her brow wrinkled suspiciously. Her new, shorter haircut showed off more of her face, revealing expressions he'd never seen before. This was one of them, this spinsterish look of disapproval.

"At least shut the door." Brushing past him, she took a pair of sunglasses out of her bag and transferred them to her purse. Apparently, his being naked merited no more comment than that. Like any old wife, she crossed the room and pulled the door closed behind her, saying, "Come on, they're waiting."

For a long time, he stared at the tarnished brass coat hook on the back of the door. With a sigh, he retrieved the Speedo from the floor and stepped heavily into it, first the left leg, then the right.

When he got outside, Bill was wearing a pair of navy-blue trunks that came down to his knees. "What the hell's that?" he asked, smirking at Stuart's swimsuit. "You look like Greg fucking Louganis, man."

"I thought I'd get a tan," Stuart explained. Feeling every inch the loser, he followed the other three through the tall grass to a marsh, where they took off their flip-flops and crossed an ankle-deep inlet of mud to the other side. Stuart kept his eye on Carla and Marlene ahead of him. The one on the right is my wife, he thought, and the one on the left is not.

Past the inlet, a row of warped birch boards served as stairs down a sandy hill to the beach. The day wasn't quite right for sunbathing, so they had the place more or less to themselves.

"Does anyone see Lucien?" Carla asked. Shielding her eyes from the sun, she stared down the beach. "Oh! There he is. Hey, Lucky!"

A man in cotton pants and a white unbuttoned shirt ran over to introduce himself. He looked about forty, with a salmon-colored complexion and golden hair parted wet to one side. Taking Stuart's hand, he said, "Mr. Breen, the novelist. Carla told me all about you. Your book is widely read in Europe."

Stuart frowned; this wasn't true, and they both knew it. "Are you sure?" he asked. "It was never published there."

The Frenchman made a trifling gesture and moved on to Marlene. "And Mrs. Breen. I hope I'm not intruding on your holiday."

"Of course not," she said. It was the first thing that Stuart had heard her say since they'd set out for the beach, and probably the most animated she'd sounded the whole trip. "We hear that you're an excellent chef," she added.

"No, no." Thinking himself rather charming, he said, "I am an excellent photographer but a *wonderful* chef."

Stuart rolled his eyes. "A man of many talents," he said. "Hey, where are we in relation to Chappaquiddick?"

"It's not far," Lucien said. "We'll drive to Edgartown in the morning. Don't worry, we'll see *everything.*"

Stuart resisted the man's allure but listened with the others as Lucien led them down the beach, regaling them with his knowledge of the island. "The best place to watch the sunrise is ten miles from here, in Oak Bluffs. Of course, I am primarily interested as a photographer."

Marlene asked, "What kind of photography do you do, Mr. . . . ?"

He said a word that sounded like *Zhean-Zhahn.* "But call me Lucien. I like to take pictures of people—women, mostly."

"Lucky took a beautiful picture of Carla," Bill said, winking at Stuart. "*You* can't see that one, though."

"Of course he can," Carla said. "What's the big deal? It's just *art*, you know. Everyone gets all freaked out in this country."

Bill challenged her. "What other countries have you been to?"

"I've been to Bermuda, and Jamaica, Barbados—"

"Those aren't countries, kid, those are *islands.* Like this one. *This* is an island."

As the resident exotic, it was Lucien's job to make peace. "Carla is right, though. In Europe, particularly in my country, there is a different attitude toward the human body. Less of a taboo. If you want to show your cock, you show your cock." Carla tittered, and he asked, "Is that not the right word? 'Cock,' you say?"

"Nope, that's the right word," Stuart grumbled. He didn't like where the conversation was going, so he said, "Actually, Jamaica *is* a country, I believe. Bermuda's part of Great Britain."

"Regardless," Lucien said, "it's true the world over. My first wife, Victoria, was Swedish, from Uppsala. Naked all the time—outside, in the backyard. They say, 'Look at my body,' you know? And no one cares."

"Isn't it against the law?" Marlene asked.

He shrugged. "Sure, but so is murder, no? It happens."

By this point, Marlene, Lucien and Carla were walking together, with Bill and Stuart a few steps behind. Stuart watched his wife carefully. Marlene was in a dangerous mood—he could tell just by looking at her.

At the front of the group, Carla was saying, "You should go to Paris, Marlene. Stuart, too. Stuart could write a book about it. Wouldn't that be a great idea?"

Marlene glanced behind her. They'd moved far enough ahead where Stuart couldn't hear what they were saying. "Oh, I don't know. We've already been through a lot this year. I wouldn't want to cause any more trouble for him."

"You should listen to your friend," said Lucien. "Paris will welcome you with open arms. I will put you up myself—and your husband, of course."

She blushed. "That's very nice of you."

He continued in a lower voice. "You must forgive me, but I have a business proposition that I hope you will consider. You see, Marlene, in my country, in *France*, you are what the Parisians call—" He said a word that sounded like *Zhee-Zhean-Fvay*. "You know, 'Big hot stuff.' "

"I am?" she asked.

Carla interrupted. "Marlene, I'm so sorry. This happened at the last minute."

"Yes, Carla is not to blame." From inside his shirt pocket, he pulled out a long, brown cigarette and offered it to Marlene. When she declined, he stuck it between his lips and lit it with a match.

"What kind of a proposition?" Marlene asked.

"It's for a personal venture—online. I call it *Nude-About-Town*." As an afterthought, he added, "dot-com."

"It's a huge commercial Web site," Carla said. "Subscription only. Lucien could make you a *star*."

"It will be difficult, of course," Lucien warned. "The world is filled with naked women. One public-nudity Web site is as good as another. That's why I need you, Marlene."

She didn't know what to say. "Why me? Why not Carla? She's beautiful, and I'm not."

He reassured her. "But Marlene, you are a *notorious nude*. A famous nude, the Bettie Page of nude. You have gone where no nude has gone before."

Marlene stopped walking, and the others waited on her. Fortunately, Bill and Stuart were nowhere in earshot, having wandered farther down to walk in the surf. "Me?" she asked.

Lucien nodded yes. "Please understand, Marlene. You are a role model. Maybe not to everyone but to some people. Think about your husband. How many people have actually read his little novel?"

Marlene looked toward the water, where Stuart was standing in the shallows, watching the sea foam bubble around his ankles. "I don't know . . ."

"A few dozen, who cares? But you . . . you, my dear." Lost in the vision, he simply shook his head—no words to express it. "Today, a handful of lonely souls on the Internet. But tomorrow? The possibilities are limitless." He put his hands on her shoulders. "Listen. Are you comfortable in front of a camera?"

She answered haltingly. "I guess so. I made a silly little video a few months ago, in Providence."

This news pleased him greatly. "Ah! I *must* see it. We will make our own video, of course. Video, still photos. I will film you naked in Times Square, Central Park, the Champs-Elysées."

His enthusiasm was hard to resist, but she said, "I don't have it anymore, Mr. . . . Lucien. I mean, I've got a cheap copy at home, but that's it. Heath has the rest of it."

"Who's Heath?"

"Oh, just a friend. He's a very talented film director."

Lucien instinctively reached for his wallet. "He will sell it to me, this Heath. Whatever the cost. Your adoring public must have a sense of where it all began. For historical purposes."

Her eyelids fluttered. "My *public*?"

Carla nudged her in the ribs. "Hey, you've got a public, Marlene. Isn't that cool? I don't have a public. Just you and Stuart."

Both women gazed across the beach at Stuart, who'd moved

away from Bill to find a dry spot to sit down. His back was to them, and he had his knees drawn to his chest. He looked cold, even though the temperature was in the upper seventies.

My public, Marlene thought, and continued along the beach. Carla and Lucien followed.

They went as far out as a breakwater, then retraced their steps and returned home. Bill and Stuart had gone back early— Stuart to lie down, Bill to lift weights in the yard. They decided to do some shopping before it got too late, so Bill toweled off and fetched his keys. Carla and Lucien went along, and Marlene stayed behind with Stuart.

Once the others left, Stuart emerged from the bedroom and joined her on the porch. She'd opened a can of beer and was sitting with her legs propped up, facing the vegetable garden.

"Lucien's such a nice man," she said.

"Sounds like a pretentious prick to me." He mimicked Lucien's voice. " 'Oh, your book's doing so well in *Frahnce.*' I hate being patronized like that." Stepping down from the porch, he leaned against a corner post and glared at the guesthouse. Lucien's royal-blue beach towel was still hanging out to dry.

"Maybe he wasn't patronizing you," she suggested. "Maybe he was just trying to be nice."

"Unlikely."

She sighed. The afternoon had been pleasant up until now, and she was angry at him for spoiling it. "You might've not liked him, but I did. He made me feel good about myself."

"Don't I make you feel good about yourself?"

"Sometimes. Usually. Not right now." She set down her beer and followed him into the yard. "Stuart, listen. Lucien wants to buy our video."

"No."

"Wait—"

"No. How the hell does he know about it, anyway?"

"I told him."

"You *what*?"

Her voice warbled out of control. "Yes, I told him. I *told* him, Stuart. I told him because he asked and was interested . . . in me. And now he wants to make another video, only not just in Providence—all over."

"That's crazy."

"He wants to start a Web site—"

"No."

"Don't just say *no*. You can't tell me no."

He smiled to placate her. "I know I can't, but Marlene, listen to yourself. This is insane."

She'd never known this kind of feeling before, this outraged, seething anger. "Why is it any more insane than *you*, with your stupid *book* that nobody reads." Her anger ran out, and she suddenly felt ashamed. "Stuart, I'm sorry."

"Well, Marlene, I'm sorry if you think my book's stupid. I think it's pretty stupid, too, but so what? You've gotten plenty of mileage out of it."

"What do you mean?"

"You didn't think it was stupid when you married me. Remember? Stuart Breen, the big-time, hot-shot novelist."

"That's not why I married you."

"But it *was* a reason, wasn't it? What if I weren't a big-time, hot-shot novelist? What if I were just another poor schmuck trying to write a book and failing at it, like most people? How cool would that be?"

She put her hands up to block his face from hers. "Look, just forget it. It was a stupid thing to say, and I'm sorry."

He took both her arms and held them at her sides. "Marlene, I am not going to let you get involved with another harebrained scheme like the last one. No video, no Web site. As soon as we get back to Providence, I'm going to call Heath and tell him to get rid of those tapes."

She twisted away from him. "We still have our own copy, Stuart."

"I'll junk that one, too."

"Not if I get to it first." Both she and Stuart were standing with their fists balled, their foreheads almost touching.

He laughed. "Come on, Marlene, get real. You don't know what's best for you."

"I have a right to do whatever I want to with my own life. No one told you not to write your book."

"Oh, a whole lot of people did, Marlene."

"I don't care. This is what *I* want. I want to do something that matters. I don't just want to be your wife, or some fat old bag who works at the bank. I want to be *famous.* I want to be naked all the time." Their argument then turned into a scuffle, with Marlene running away from him as she pulled her shirt up over her head.

He reached for her, but his arms fell short. "Put your fucking shirt back on."

Her bra came off next, and she threw it at him. "That's me!" she said, bunching her breasts in her hands. "I want everyone to see me. I want to be *naked!*"

He waited for her to calm down, and when she finally did, they both looked and felt equally helpless. "Just put your shirt back on," he said.

She went inside with her clothes, and by the time the others returned with the groceries, she and Stuart had managed to pull themselves together. Lucien took charge of the kitchen, dispatching Carla and Marlene to chop vegetables, while Bill and Stuart hovered nearby, drinking more aggressively now that it was after six. The Frenchman cooked with a high flame, pouring sherry and blended egg yolks into a saucepan and stirring it with a whisk. The choice of music was also Lucien's—fucking Billie Holiday, Stuart moped, of all things. So predictable, so bourgeois. Yes, let's listen to Billie Holiday, and then Bessie Smith and Dinah Washington, and then some fucking *Sting*, and goddamn *Joni Mitchell*, and then we'll all congratulate ourselves on how sophisticated we are. To get away from the music, he took his drink out onto the porch, then continued across the yard, past the vegetable garden, to the guesthouse. Lucien's blue beach towel had fallen from the rafter, and he kicked it into the weeds.

At the dinner table, Marlene said to Lucien, "This is absolutely delicious. Thank you *so* much."

Lucien set down his fork and gave her hand a squeeze. "It's a recipe from the region of Burgundy, where my family lived during the German Occupation. The secret is, you add a . . . lemon? To seal the flavor. But just a drop."

"Add a lemon." She tapped her forehead. "I'll remember that."

Stuart stared at her over his hardly touched *blanquette de veau*, thinking, *Oh, like you're ever going to make this.*

After they'd cleared the dishes, they went outside to smoke a joint. Various stupid philosophies circulated during the course of conversation, most of them Carla's and Lucien's. When they started talking about acupuncture, Stuart said, "I hate to bag out on you guys, but I'm beat."

Four pairs of red-rimmed eyes looked at him, but Carla was the only one to wish him a good night. "Be sure to find the right room," she said. "You don't want to wind up in bed with the wrong person."

Oh, but I do, he thought. For Marlene's sake, as much as my own. Let her sleep with Lucien, and I'll sleep with you, Carla, and we'll let Bill be the odd man out. Or better yet, let's all five of us go our separate ways tonight. We'll keep it real simple. No

sex, no pressure, no human interaction whatsoever. Just darkness, and silence.

Alone in bed, he listened to the party drone on without him.
One last thought came to him before he drifted off to sleep. Like
hell, he told himself. Marlene's never getting her hands on that
fucking videotape.

6

Pike and Sarah were alone for the first time in many weeks, and to celebrate she cooked him his favorite meal of roasted venison with chestnuts. Pike fidgeted all during the evening. He wasn't used to accepting her hospitality, no matter how long they'd known each other. Though he liked doing people favors, he wasn't so good at receiving them.

After dinner, they went into the den for coffee. "What do you want to do next?" he asked. He was lying on the couch in his stockinged feet, while she sat across from him in a tall wing chair.

She looked out the front door, which stood open, with only the screen closed to keep the flies out. Beyond, a moonless country night had settled in the foothills. "We could sit on the porch," she offered.

He stretched and undid one of the buttons of his oxford shirt, the first wave of postprandial fatigue weighing down on him. "I guess that's not what I meant. I mean, what do you want to do next *month*, next year, that sort of thing?"

"Hmm, I see. The eternal Nathaniel Pike question." She rose from the chair and pushed aside his legs to make room on the couch. "We don't have to do anything, I suppose. I'm happy doing nothing."

"I know you are," he mused. "That's a good quality. Whatever the opposite of restless is."

"True enough. You're still restless. Forty-three years old, and you haven't slowed down a bit."

"I'm not forty-three," he said.

She smiled familiarly at him and took his hand. "I know how old you are, chief. I've always been a year older than you. Older, uglier, lazier——"

"Now cut that out." He sat up straight and held both her hands. He couldn't tell whether she was kidding or not. "How about smarter, huh? You're an ace compared to me. Ask me anything, any fact—I *guarantee* I don't know it."

"You sound like you're proud of yourself."

"No, I'm not. It's true, though. 'Who was the third president of the United States?' *I* don't know. Some asshole with a wig. See what I mean? I must be dyslexic or something—the thing where everything looks backward."

"Does everything look backward?"

"No."

"Then I guess you're not dyslexic."

He snapped his fingers. "Autistic, then, or ADD. There's gotta be something wrong with me."

"Why? You're just a little eccentric, that's all."

"Yeah, me and John Wayne Gacy, right?" He sighed. Lately, he'd resolved not to spend so much time talking about himself, particularly when he was around Sarah. "I wish you'd move back to Rhode Island," he said.

"Why? I'm happy here."

"Why can't you be happy in Rhode Island?"

"I probably *could* be happy in Rhode Island, Nate, but I'm here, and I'm happy staying here."

"I'll buy you a house."

"You will *not*. You don't need to take care of me all the time, you know. We're friends. If I really needed your help, I'd ask."

"You make it hard for a guy to do something nice for you."

She kissed his forehead. "I just don't like to see you throwing your money away."

"That's what it's there for. Besides, it all goes back into my pocket. I'm like a money magnet, Sarah. I can't get rid of it. When I was a kid, hookers used to blow me for free. True story." She was smiling at him, so he went on. "I'm the luckiest man in the universe. Why me? Of all the kind, deserving souls."

"You're a kind, deserving soul."

"No, I'm not. I'm a prick, a scumbag . . . Hey, don't rush to contradict me or anything."

She laughed. "Well, you're no Gregg Reese, that's for sure."

"No, and thank God for that. The poor guy. Always butting into other people's business. I keep telling Allison, that's no way to live."

"Well . . ."

"Am I wrong? You know better than I do. What do you think old Keeny Reese would've done if she'd had her way with you back in Little Compton? I'll tell you. Your folks' house would be in the National Register by now, and you *know* what that means. Instant crucifixion in the *Providence Journal*."

"Oh, I don't know about that."

"It happens. Look at what happened to me. I made one stupid crack to the *ProJo* and went from saint to sinner in twenty-four hours. There are still folks who ask, *Aren't you the guy who said, 'Those people are no more Native American than I am?'* Yeah, I am—and so what?" He stopped and realized that he was yelling. In a softer voice, he said, "I just didn't want you to go through the same thing. People are strange in New England.

Everybody's out to get everybody else. I'm the only person in the entire state of Rhode Island who's moving forward instead of backward."

"I know you are, chief. You don't have to prove anything to me." After a long, moody silence, she said, "You just don't think these things through. My mother had a hard enough time selling that house to a couple of total strangers. We certainly didn't expect you to buy it from them. And then to tear it down, Nate. Think of the waste."

"It's like I told you, money means nothing to me."

"Maybe it should. What would your daughter say if she—" Sarah knew that this was forbidden territory, so she backed off. "You just should've left it alone."

"I *did* leave it alone eventually, once I saw how upset you were. It took a lot of hard work to put that house back together."

"All of which could've been avoided if you'd just consulted me. Even now. Think about all the time and money you've wasted up here."

"Time well spent, I might add." With his nose in the air, he looked like an obstinate little boy.

"You should've asked me first," she insisted. "I'm quite happy managing my little ski lodge. I don't need to own a mountain, too."

He roared back. "I thought you'd like it. You've always talked about putting up another ski lift."

"You can't ski down that mountain, Nate. You can barely walk down it."

He blushed. "Well, I didn't know that."

"And now you're stuck with seven and a half acres of junk property that no one wants—not even *you*."

He forced himself to laugh. "No, now, Sarah . . . not quite. I've been planning on building that parking lot for a long time. At least three years. The reason I *offered* it to you was because . . . I figured I'd give you first crack at it. You know, as a friend."

"As a friend, you could've just bought me dinner," she said. Rather than argue with him, she sipped her coffee and reclined against him on the sofa.

Pike's combative instincts had always prompted him to keep talking until his opponent, whether due to sheer fatigue or the strength of his persuasion, had to admit he was right; but this time, he accepted her gift of silence and said nothing.

Minutes later, an animal's paws scratched against the screen door. "What the hell's that?" he asked.

"Oh, we've got coyotes this year. They keep trying to get into the house."

"What do you do with 'em?"

With a heavy sigh, she got up from the couch and hobbled toward the door. "Shoot 'em, if I can," she said, then snarled at the coyote, "Get the hell away from there!"

Pike jumped, nearly dropping his coffee. "Holy Christ, Sarah. My nerves are shot as it is."

She laughed and pushed open the door. The coyote was long gone; only a cluster of fireflies was left swirling under the lights above the porch. "Come on, chief. It's nice out," she said.

He joined her on the porch, where the air had turned chilly since nightfall. Sarah felt warm in his arms, and he liked the fruity, girlish smell of her hair. Walking his fingers down her stomach, he gently held her around the waist. "There's a nice, meaty woman," he said.

She smiled and settled deeper into his arms. "Why me, chief? Why do you keep pestering me?"

Instead of offering a clever one-liner, he just let the question stand. She knew the answer as well as he did. She was the only normal person who'd ever cared for him. Placing his lips to her ear, he whispered, "What do you want to do next?"

Eyes closed, she began to move against his body. "Next year?" she asked.

"No," he said. "Right now."

Meanwhile, in Providence, Gregg Reese was a nervous wreck. Reaching out to Siemens and McMasters had increased voter interest in the Allison Fund, although broad-based approval remained a longshot. Reese's own people no longer supported him. Celia Shriver had even criticized him in public for spending too much time with Nathaniel Pike. Without Celia, the Reese Foundation would lose most of its grassroots appeal, and without the Reese Foundation, the Reese family itself wouldn't survive. He couldn't allow that to happen—not on his watch, not while his mother was still alive. Oh, to unburden himself of this millstone, this terrible "Reese"! No hope for it. Once again, he'd proven himself unworthy of his own last name.

Maggie Reese's eldest son, Joseph, assumed control of the family in 1686, six years after his grandfather's death. Joseph bucked convention by taking his mother's maiden name. The word "Reese" didn't merely denote a family; it was a product, an industry. It was status itself. One of the most prolific Reeses ever, Joseph was known to have fathered more than a dozen children, all born to his own slaves. The males he named Joseph II, III, IV; the girls were all named Josephine. Accounts written by Joseph Reese III, the only one of the sons to learn to read and write, described his father as "crazed with liquor, spells, and whores."

By the early eighteenth century, prevailing attitudes toward slavery had not changed significantly. The number of slaves belonging to the Reeses was thirty-six in 1692, twenty-nine in 1698, thirty-five in 1701. Of those slaves, more than half were young girls, few of them older than fourteen. Despite the bitter South County winters, the girls were given only rags to wear and forced to sleep on the bare earth inside the Reeses' pen made of stone. When not working in the fields, they were little more than playthings for the Reese men. As violence periodically broke out in the region, hundreds of soldiers visited the estate, eating and drinking and enjoying their fill of women, whom they raped, sodomized and even tortured for amusement.

An Anglican church was built in 1707 in nearby Wickford, but no attempt was made by parishioners to intervene on the slaves' behalf. Even the very devout owned slaves in Rhode Island, particularly in the southwestern corner of the state, home to several dairy plantations. The Reeses were hardly the largest slaveholders in South County. Some kept as many as fifty slaves, but those were typically black, not Indian. By mid-century, the number of slaves in South County was 17 percent of the total population. The only thing unusual about the Reeses was that so many of their slaves were girls, and so many were Native Americans.

Change came gradually as the century wore on, and various efforts on the part of reformers to limit the slave trade met with some success. Also, churches began opening their doors to blacks and Native Americans. Though Rhode Island was still a long way from emancipating its slaves, these were steps in the right direction. They had little impact on the Reeses, however, except to make their practices more covert. With so much religious zeal in the air, the Reeses were careful to keep a low profile so as not to arouse the suspicions of their neighbors. Aside from those in the know— chiefly young soldiers whose grandfathers had been guests of Hugh Reese—the entertainments on tap at the Reese estate remained New England's most carefully guarded secret.

IV | The Evil Source

1

"How's it going down there?" Henry asked a man in an orange jumpsuit, who said, "We've moved about three feet of dirt. Nothing so far."

Both men were standing in the fields behind the Parker house in Little Compton, where a hastily organized investigation was still in its early stages. Most of the activity was centered on the remains of the stone storage pen, which had monopolized Henry's attention.

"Keep digging," Henry said. "Tell the others to start near the perimeter, then work back. I'll be right there."

The man left just as the owner of the house, Barbara Parker, came up. "Thanks again for letting us do this," Henry told her. "We'll restore everything as soon as we're finished."

She laughed. "What would you have done if I'd said no?"

"I guess I would've been stuck."

"No, I'm sure you would have figured something out. You don't strike me as the kind of guy who takes no for an answer." She yelled at her husband: "Parker! Stop gettin' in the way!"

The old man came over from the excavation site. "I'm just making sure they don't puncture the septic tank," he explained.

"We're not going anywhere near it, Mr. Parker," Henry assured him. "What we're looking for isn't going to be that close to the house."

"What *are* we looking for, anyway?" he asked.

Barbara sighed. "Parker, we've been over this."

"I want to know what's under that rubble," Henry said. "I think it's a marker of some kind."

Three days had passed since Henry's first visit with the Parkers, and in that time he'd developed two theories. First, the reason that Nathaniel Pike had torn down the original house in Little Compton was to keep Keeny Reese, as the head of the State Historic Preservation Society, from nominating it to the National Register of Historic Places. It wasn't the nomination itself that troubled Pike so much as the scrutiny that went along with it. If he had something to hide, the last thing he wanted was a bunch of local historians and insurance appraisers snooping around the property.

The question remained, however, as to why he was so concerned about the house in the first place. The most likely explanation was that he was protecting someone else, a friend. Sarah Cranberry. This brought Henry to his second theory, which was that Pike wasn't nearly as eccentric as his reputation suggested. In fact, he was quite sane, and his extravagances had a reasonable and coherent design—a pattern, if you like. Building a new storage pen would've involved digging several feet into the earth to set a new foundation. Whatever Pike was afraid of, Henry believed that it lay underground.

A voice called out from the woods, "Mr. Savage, take a look at this."

Henry walked back to the excavation site, where an investigator handed him a round object still partially encrusted in dirt. As the Parkers looked on, Henry realized he was holding a skull. "Jesus," he said, quickly returning it. "How old is it?"

The investigator studied the damaged cranium. "I don't know yet. All of the cartilage is gone, so we're not talking recent."

"Ten years?"

"Easy. The teeth are still intact, which is strange. Judging from the shape and size, I'd say this was an adolescent girl, maybe thirteen years old."

Henry glanced over the mountain of rubble at their feet. "Where's the rest of her?"

"Gone, but we're still looking. Our tools aren't worth shit in this hard earth. Whoever left her here must've had some help."

"Good, good." Hastily, he added, "I mean, *not* good, but let's keep at it."

As the digging continued, Barbara demanded, "You're not going to tear apart our whole yard, are you?"

"It's a skull, ma'am," Henry said. "That could mean any number of things. For all we know, it could be three hundred years old."

"Let's just stop this right now," Parker said. "I don't want anyone getting in trouble."

"I'm afraid we can't do that, Mr. Parker," Henry said.

"I thought you told us—"

"That was then. I've got to treat this as a potential crime scene. We've discovered human remains on the property."

A commotion under the rubble caught their attention, and Henry called down to the workers, "Kenny, what'd you find?"

The man held up a chunk of debris. "Here's another one!"

Henry and the Parkers moved closer for a better look. The investigator got there first and gently handled the second skull. "It's similar to the other," he said. "Same bone structure. This one's got an impact crater, I'd say from a rifle butt or a shovel."

Deeper into the unearthed ruins, another worker exclaimed, "Holy shit!"

"What is it?" Henry shouted.

A second man said, "You'd better come here, sir."

"Let me check that out," Henry told an assistant. "You take care of the Parkers."

"We're not going anywhere," Barbara insisted. She headed after Henry, but a man blocked her way.

"I'm sorry," he said, "this area is off-limits."

At the base of the ruins, Henry pushed past the workers who'd gathered around what they could now see was a mass grave, filled with skeletons that looked like they'd been trapped in a mudslide. "Good God," one of them said, "there's dozens of 'em."

2

Gregg Reese woke up one morning in late May to discover he wasn't alone in bed. A shape stirred next to him, but he couldn't determine who or what it was. The light coming through his bedroom window stung his eyes, making it hard for him to see. He must've slept late, something he never did. He was always the first person up in the morning and usually beat Allison downstairs by a good three hours. But Allison wasn't here. She was in New Hampshire. Who *was* this person?

"Good morning, sleepyhead," said the stirring shape, who sat up to block the window light. Gregg blinked madly until his eyes focused on the figure of a young boy, maybe nineteen, lying naked above the satin covers. Feeling under the sheets, Gregg realized that he was naked, too. His gentle headache told him he'd had too much to drink the night before.

"Oh, hi." Gregg's voice sounded husky, and he cleared his throat. "I thought I'd set the alarm."

The boy smiled and kissed his cheek. "It's okay, I understand. Let me introduce myself. My name is Ferdinand. I'm an exchange student from Ecuador. We met at Viva last night, you bought me drinks, you took me home, I sucked your gorgeous penis, and we both fell asleep." He laughed. "I think you are a very nice man."

Gregg wasn't sure whether to kiss him or run screaming out of the room. Instead, he scratched his thinning gray hair and mumbled, "Oh . . . Ferdinand, is it? I'm sorry, I must've dozed off. Did we . . . ?"

"Not yet. But there's still time." Gregg must've looked petrified, because the boy let him off the hook. "Seriously, though, I understand if you're busy. Just the cab fare home would be nice."

Giving the boy a second look, Gregg admired his firm chest and stomach, his slender waist and the tangled patch of hair above his genitals, which Gregg felt compelled to touch. "You're lovely," he said, then caught sight of the alarm clock on Ferdinand's side of the bed. "Oh, shit, is that the time? I've got a meeting with my mother in forty-five minutes. Do you mind? I need to take a shower."

Taking some of the covers with him, he wrapped them around his waist, trotted off to the bathroom and took a ninety-second shower. He was afraid that if he left the boy unattended for too long, he might start snooping around the house. When he finished toweling off, he called through the wall, "I'll be right there! You're welcome to use the shower downstairs."

Emerging from the bathroom, he found the boy naked in the hallway and looking at framed photographs on the wall.

Pointing at one of them, Ferdinand asked, "Is that your daughter?"

Gregg stood behind him. "Yes, that's Allison. And that's Allison's mother."

"You were married, then?" Ferdinand asked.

Gregg nodded. "Twenty-three years."

Ferdinand sighed as he leaned against Gregg, who reluctantly embraced him. "I would like to have a child one day," he said. "I could sleep with a woman just once."

Gregg could tell Ferdinand still wanted to make love but did nothing to encourage him; instead, he maintained the formal posture and good manners that had protected him all his adult life. He wished he could be as carefree as the boy—no responsibilities, no shame, no secrets, nothing to do all day but lie naked in his lover's arms. Even when Gregg was nineteen, he wasn't like that. He'd never lived entirely without shame.

Ferdinand turned and put his arms around Gregg's neck. "How could you stay married to one woman for so long? Didn't you cheat on her?"

Gregg lowered his head. "No, I didn't. My daughter means too much to me. I didn't want to upset her. She doesn't like people like us."

Ferdinand pressed his lips to Gregg's and when their kiss was over said, "This has been a good one-night stand, yes?"

Gregg nodded. "I think so," he said and walked away to finish getting dressed.

After a rushed farewell, Gregg sent the boy away in a cab and drove to his mother's place, where she intercepted him at the side door and led him into the oppressive comfort of the living room. The whole house was stifling, and she'd set out a serving tray with cookies and crackers and petits fours, along with a carafe of hot coffee.

"Did you see the *Journal* this morning?" she asked, brandishing a newspaper clipping headlined "Reese Calls Independence Project 'A Shocking Waste.'" "I would've preferred better coverage, but this damn murder-suicide in Coventry has been stealing the spotlight."

Gregg averted his eyes from his mother, who looked hideous under her gleaming silver turban. Keeny's health had further declined over the winter, and her weakened condition made it difficult for him to argue with her. "Please, Ma," he said, "let's just drop it. I did what you wanted, and it's over. I haven't spoken to Nate in over a week. Except for Allison's still being up there, it's been a clean break."

"Good. Let's keep it that way."

He reached for a bottle of sambuca and poured a splash into his coffee. "Look, don't rub my face in it, all right? I don't see why you're so dead set against him, anyway. Nate was a good ally. I'll be damned if we're going to get much support for the Allison Fund without some help from Siemens and McMasters."

"We don't need anyone's charity, Gregg, especially not *his*. People love you in this state. More important, they respect you. No one respects Nathaniel Pike."

"*I* do," he objected. "Nate's made something of himself. What have I done? Nothing."

"Oh, bosh."

"Name something, then—and don't say the Friends of Walter Greevy Society, because that was Dad's idea, and don't say the Ocean State Arts Collaborative, because that was yours."

Keeny drew herself up until the top of her turban pressed against the wall behind her. Her patrician arrogance could be colossal. "There's no sense in comparing yourself to Pike. He isn't half the man you are," she sniffed.

No, Mom, he thought, you're wrong. He's twice, ten times, a hundred. Even Allison knows that.

"When's Allie coming back?" asked Keeny, who'd always had a knack for intruding on Gregg's thoughts.

He shrugged. "Why?"

"Tell her to hurry home. She's not going to want to be up there in a few days."

The spiked coffee turned to gall inside his mouth. "What do you mean?" he asked.

"I received a call this morning from your favorite person, Celia Shriver. She's been showing a man from the federal government around town. According to Celia, things are about to get pretty sticky for Nathaniel Pike, and for this Sarah Cranberry person too."

Gregg's face became flushed at the mention of Sarah's name. "What about Sarah?" he asked.

Keeny told him what Henry Savage's men had found in Little Compton: nearly three dozen skeletons, along with various munitions, chains and restraints, all of it dating back before the Revolutionary War. A mass grave, she said, on good old Cranberry soil.

Gregg refused to listen. "This is an old country, Mom. I'm sure the Reeses have their fair share of secrets, too."

She considered this in passing, then dismissed it. "I found it quite interesting, actually. It explains a lot of pretty strange behavior."

"No, it doesn't. It explains nothing. I don't care what the Cranberrys did in the past, any more than I care about what my own family did. It's totally irrelevant to the fact that Sarah Cranberry is a decent person and was incredibly nice to me in New Hampshire and treated me like a human being and didn't fawn over me or hit me up for money or ask me to do anything other than sit back and enjoy the holidays."

"Don't be so sure of that. How well do you know her?"

"She and Nate are friends, that's all. They might even be dating. What does it matter?"

"It matters because this man from the federal government wants Nathaniel Pike out of the White Mountains just as much as the Reese Foundation does."

Gregg looked dubious. "And how does he propose to do that?"

Henry's plan was simple: convince Pike to relinquish his holdings in New Hampshire by threatening to make public the information about the remains he'd found in Little Compton—remains buried on land the Cranberrys had owned for generations.

Gregg interrupted. "I'm sorry, Mom. You and Celia can do what you want, but leave me out of it."

She glared at him. "You have got *some* nerve, Gregg, to turn against your family at a time like this."

"I'm not turning against my family."

"Like hell you're not! Regardless of your personal limitations, you still have a responsibility to the Reese Foundation, above everything else."

For once, Keeny's usual taunt didn't work. "Mom, as far as that goes, I've already blown it, haven't I? I mean, I've been a pretty lousy benchwarmer—certainly compared to you and Dad."

"I didn't say that. On the contrary, you've been a wonderful leader, maybe the best ever. You *are* the Reese Foundation, Gregg."

"No, I'm not."

"Yes, you are. You're the soul and spirit and conscience of the city of Providence and the state of Rhode Island, and no one can ever take that away from you."

Please, Ma, he thought, let's stop kidding ourselves. We both know what I really am. I'm a dirty little fag. Don't sit there and pretend like you've dealt with it and everything's fine now. Get real, okay? I embarrass you. I'm not the soul and conscience of *anything*. All I am is a huge disappointment, to you, to Allison, to the whole family. The worst Reese ever.

"Do you remember when your father died," Keeny asked, "and I almost bought that house on the Cape? I *would've* bought it if you hadn't talked me out of it."

"I didn't talk you out of it. You talked yourself out of it."

"Ultimately, yes. But you were the one who made me realize

what I was doing. I was running away. That's what living in Rhode Island means to this family, Gregg. It's a promise, a commitment. We're special here. We're not special anywhere else."

It was time for her lunch, so they went into the kitchen, where she heated up a can of condensed tomato soup. Gregg's temper had cooled somewhat, and he apologized. "I'm sorry I got so upset, Mom. I just hope that nothing bad happens to Sarah."

She answered distractedly, "Mmm? Oh, the Cranberry woman. I'd appreciate it if you didn't call her by her first name."

His anger returned. "Why not? She's got one, just like everyone else." He stepped between her and the stove. "I'll have you know something. That woman is one of the nicest, least stuck-up people I've ever met."

"I need to stir my soup."

"I don't care. I want to talk about Sarah."

"Move, please."

He reluctantly stepped aside, marveling at her utter lack of concern for what might happen to Sarah. "I think that it's terrible to use an innocent person to settle a score with Nathaniel Pike."

"There are worse things in the world, Gregg."

"Such as?"

"Use your imagination. Or better yet, ask Renee."

His jaw dropped. "You're being ridiculous," he said.

She turned her soup down to simmer, then sat with him at the kitchen table. "I can be as ridiculous as the next person. You just haven't seen that side of me. Allison has, which reminds me—I've been meaning to ask about her money situation. If you were smart, you'd find a place for her at the Reese Foundation. I think that she'd be a real natural at public relations."

Gregg slapped the table. "I'd rather have Allison work for McDonald's than the Reese Foundation. I'd rather have her do nothing, just stay in the mountains with her boyfriend for the rest of her life. At least then I could talk to her about something other than this stage play we've built up around ourselves."

Keeny sat very low in her seat. "Don't yell at me, Gregg."

He made an effort to control his voice but couldn't. "I'm not yelling, I'm just saying maybe it's time we put the Reese Foundation to bed. I'll call Celia this afternoon." He laughed. "She'll probably have a stroke, but that's her problem."

"Celia is a friend of mine," Keeny said icily.

"No, she's not. We don't have any friends, Mom. Celia Shriver, Walter Greevy . . . none of 'em. They're all business associates. They may look like friends, but they're not. Martha Friedkin—"

"You're not being fair to any of those people, Gregg. You're certainly not being fair to *me*. Running the Reese Foundation is hard work. I've carried this family for thirty-eight years, when your father wouldn't do it, when *you* wouldn't do it."

"What would be the harm in letting go, huh? Instead of living in the past and constantly invoking the names of our forefathers—like anyone gives a damn about those people."

Keeny bustled out of her seat and went to turn off the stove. He could tell that he'd hurt her feelings, and in the quiet that followed she ladled the soup into a bowl and brought it to the table. The soup was so thin that he could see the bowl's rose pattern clearly through the steaming red liquid. She had one spoonful, then said, "When I'm dead, this is the conversation you'll remember—"

"Ma—"

"*This* is the conversation you'll remember, and I hope that you'll think very hard about what you said to me, because quite frankly, I'm extremely disgusted with you right now."

She picked her spoon back up and continued eating. What Gregg now perceived, in a flash that momentarily blinded him, was the thought of his mother's absence in the years ahead. The time would come when he would want her forgiveness, and she wouldn't be there to give it to him. Why not ask for it now? Mom, I'm sorry. You did your best with me. Let's just leave it in the past, okay? That's where it belongs. Buried.

3

Marlene and Stuart returned from Martha's Vineyard feeling even more distant from each other than they had the week before. As soon as they got home, he marched upstairs, found their VHS copy of Heath's video and smashed it to pieces. Marlene didn't try to stop him; he was stronger than she was, physically, mentally, emotionally, in every way.

They didn't sleep together that night. After Stuart had gone to bed, Marlene took a bottle of Clos du Bois to the back porch and spent the next few hours drinking and feeling sorry for herself. With fatigue came a dismal sort of clarity. What she wanted wasn't so particularly extravagant, after all—just to add one or two little sentences to the paragraph that ultimately described her life. She wondered what would've happened if she'd stayed in the theater, if she'd gone to the conservatory as her mother had suggested. Probably nothing. She wasn't pretty enough to make it as an actress. Even those women who specialized in "ugly" roles were, when you saw them interviewed on TV, beautiful. Marlene's kind of ordinary wasn't permitted anywhere but here in the ordinary world.

The next morning, she waited until Stuart left on his daily hour long walk, then took his car keys and drove out of Providence. With no particular destination in mind, she felt a strange pull leading her north into the mountains. Heath would be there and Nathaniel Pike, too. Maybe *they* would accept her, if no one else would.

She wasn't good at reading maps, so she pulled off the freeway and went into a Dunkin' Donuts to ask for directions. The middle-aged woman behind the counter answered her pleasantly at first, then lost patience when Marlene kept repeating the same questions, causing the line of customers to back up.

"It's another twenty miles to New Hampshire," the woman said for the third time. "Just keep on Ninety-three past Methuen. It's impossible to miss."

"Ninety-three past Methuen." Marlene tried committing the words to memory, but there was so much clutter inside her brain that nothing seemed to stick. "Ninety-three, Ninety-three, Ninety-three. I keep getting Ninety-three mixed up with Ninety-five." She smiled apologetically. "You must think I'm an idiot."

The woman remained silent behind her cash register, so Marlene looked up at the menu board and frowned at the selections. "I guess I'd better order something, now that I've wasted your time."

On the counter were various donuts and muffins, none of which looked especially appealing. In the end, she chose a blueberry muffin and gratefully put an extra buck in the woman's tip cup. Back in the car, she set the bag with the muffin in it on the floor of the passenger seat and promptly forgot about it.

True to the cashier's word, Ninety-three led into New Hampshire, where it turned into a toll road just north of the state line. Three lanes fed into the toll booths, and she picked the one with the longest line. When it was her turn, she drove up, put her car in park and reached into the backseat for her purse. "How much is it?" she asked.

The toll taker barely glanced at her. "Seventy-five cents, ma'am."

His tone was the same as the cashier's back at the Dunkin' Donuts—bored and contemptuous. She could sense his impatience as she rifled through her wallet for a small bill. "Is it the same amount driving the other way?" she asked, handing him a dollar.

He said that it was. She'd hoped to pry a few more words of conversation out of him, but he just gave her her change and waved her through.

By the time she'd arrived in the mountains, she was a basket case. Three hours of freeway driving had given her heart palpitations and a tension headache. The other motorists didn't approve of her, apparently; they crowded her in the slow lane, then made a big, arrogant show of speeding ahead to cut her off. Whatever standards existed for the road, she didn't measure up.

At least the number of cars had dropped off, which allowed her to slow to a crawl in the breakdown lane as she looked for a trail marker. Finally she stopped at a roadside diner to ask for help.

Inside, an elderly male patron said, "If you're looking for that guy Pike, he's about a mile south of the Kancamagus Pass. You can't get to it by a trail. You've gotta wish for it."

A waitress, who was pouring his coffee, laughed. "He's pulling your leg, dear. Nathaniel Pike's the big joke around here." She set her coffee carafe down on a hot plate, then took Marlene's map and spread it across the breakfast counter. "You're going to park here, at White Ledge, then follow the blue blazes for about two and a quarter miles until you come to a riverbed with a footbridge running across it. Go over the bridge, walk another ten, twenty paces, then head due east off the trail for another eighth of a mile. Don't worry if you get lost. Just give a shout, and someone'll come looking for you."

Marlene took the map back and folded it up. "Have you seen it? I mean—"

"No, but my son's been up there six times already. He just started working for Pike last week." She smiled aggressively. "Pays pretty good, too. Pays better than this dump."

Marlene thanked both the waitress and her customer and hurried back to her car. The afternoon was waning, and it soon would be too late to start up the trail. But she knew she had to do this today, while she still had it in her.

After another ten minutes of driving, she spotted the trailhead and turned into a dirt lot just off the road, parking under the trees near a pickup with a camper on back. At the rear of the lot was a picnic table, a cast-iron cooking grill and a rusted-out garbage drum filled to the brim with beer cans and paper plates. Other than these few signs of life, the place looked abandoned.

When she got out, she reflected on what had brought her here, not merely to New Hampshire but to this point in her life: the thrill of being seen naked by another person, that terrible, awesome, impossible-to-hold-on-to moment in time. Locked inside that moment was a reality she wished to commit herself to. She wanted to leave all the other realities behind and accept the fate that was predestined by her body.

Do it/don't make me.

Like a woman undressing at home, she took off her shoes and socks, rolled the socks into a ball and stuffed them into the heel of one of her shoes, which she left in the car.

Do it/don't make me.

Everything else followed—her bra, her jeans, her faded yellow panties. As a final casting-off, she threw the bundle of clothes into the backseat, left the keys in the ignition, locked the door and slammed it shut. She felt as though a quantity in the world she hadn't noticed before—a sound, perhaps—had suddenly increased, and she could hear it all around her. Leaving her car, she tiptoed across the lot and started up the trail.

Within a quarter-hour, her feet were cut and dirty, so she stopped to rest on a flat, shelflike outcropping of rock. The forest was still except for the shiver of the wind filling the Kancamagus. With her knees tucked, she picked the black mud from her feet. To her amazement, she found that the keen, hyper-real sense of being naked hadn't worn off yet.

Farther up the trail, she heard voices and turned her head to listen. Through the trees she could see three men and three women proceeding single file. Defying her own instincts, she remained in plain view, waiting for the group to pass.

When the first hiker saw her, she stopped about ten yards from Marlene and stared, slack jawed, as the others caught up to her. The hikers were all in their twenties and thirties; one might think they were college friends who'd kept in touch after school. The men all wore beards, and the women were muscular, prim and simple looking. One of them said, "Hey, what's the matter? Are you all right?"

Marlene didn't answer. All of her attention was focused on certain pinpoints scattered on the surface of her body: her left nipple, a fingernail, a spot above her right knee. With her skin a creamy white, she seemed to have taken off more than just her clothes but also an invisible layer she'd always worn up until now.

The woman asked again, "Are you okay? Has someone hurt you?"

The man next to her added, "Do you need a doctor? Do you want us to get help?"

These questions were echoed by the other hikers. Marlene

felt her confidence dwindle. She didn't want their concern or pity. She wanted their admiration.

In a breaking voice, she whispered, "Just look at me."

One of the women said to her friends, "Come on, let's go. This lady's giving me the creeps."

The hikers filed past and continued down the trail. The women regarded her more severely than the men, but even the men avoided looking directly at her, preferring to stare down at her feet. Long after they'd passed out of sight, Marlene could hear their scornful laughter rising through the forest. This aroused her, since part of her liked being treated with contempt.

On and on she hiked, until she came to the riverbed the waitress had told her about. The footbridge was narrow and splintery, and she nearly fell into the muddy river as she crossed to the far bank. This high up the mountain, the trees gave way to scrub brush and boulders, and the open terrain made her feel even more naked than before.

Following the waitress's instructions, she went ahead another twenty paces, then turned off the trail and skipped across a field of broken rocks. The ground was murder on her feet, but there was nothing she could do about it. Mercifully, the mountainside sloped downward again, and soon she was back in the forest, only this time without the benefit of a trail. The sun was low in the sky, and she began to worry that she might not find Pike's lair before nightfall.

She eventually came to a small clearing, where she noticed a faint humming noise. The sound was so out of place that she thought at first she was hallucinating, but no—she distinctly picked out the dull roar of a motor, and voices conversing in low, lackluster tones. When she peered deeper into the woods, she saw nothing to indicate where the noise might be coming from. No point in standing here forever, she thought, and called out, "Hello? Anyone? Where are you?"

Like two armed sentries, a pair of young boys appeared, both carrying flashlights and dressed in identical uniforms with name tags pinned to their chests. "Shit!" one of them said. "It's a naked lady!"

Marlene covered her breasts with her hands. "It's okay," she said. "I'm not going to hurt you. I'm just trying to find Heath Baxter."

The boys recognized the name. The one who'd already spoken said, "He's working in sporting goods. We'll take you to him."

"Sporting goods?" Marlene wondered but came out of hiding to follow the boys through the woods.

They walked for another few hundred yards until a faint light, like a will-o'-the-wisp, glowed up ahead. Marlene stopped to catch her breath. "What is it?" she asked.

Neither boy answered. Instead, they swung their flashlight beams around, picking her out in the darkness.

"I'm sorry," she said and lowered her head. "I know I look disgusting to you."

The boys didn't understand her, so they turned and trudged on.

At a certain point, the trees thinned out, revealing a vast expanse unlike anything she'd ever seen before. Moving past the boys, she stepped onto a surface of newly spread blacktop. Its smoothness came as a relief after walking on the trail all afternoon. The area around the parking lot was lit up with giant stadium lights that ran on power generators—the motor sound that she'd heard earlier. Beyond this nimbus of light, a deep blue forest extended on all sides, sloping upward to the mountains, which looked remote and two dimensional, like scenery in a stage play.

In the foreground stood Mr. Pike's fully functional Kmart.

The sign hung over the main entrance, which consisted of slid-ing glass doors that opened onto the foyer. Through the display windows, she could see dozens of cashiers standing idle at their workstations. They appeared lifeless behind the glass.

A handsome man welcomed her, and she read the solid gold name tag on his jersey: Nathaniel Pike, Store Manager. "You must be Stuart's wife," he said. He took little notice of Marlene's nudity, except to glance down at her breasts. His eyes gleamed cheerfully. "You've got balls, lady. I've never met a nudist before."

Marlene instinctively brought her arms around her chest. The blazing glare of the stadium lights made her feel visible from a great distance. "I'm sorry," she said.

"Don't be. Hey, you've got nothing to apologize for. I've seen far worse, believe me."

Pike's creation had a hypnotic effect on Marlene, and she found herself forgetting herself entirely, even as she began to attract the attention of the people inside the store. "It's beautiful here," she said.

"Come on, I'll give you a tour." He presented her with his arm, which she hesitated to take. "It's okay, Marlene. No one's going to hurt you."

Reluctantly, she slid her hand into the crook of his arm, and they crossed the parking lot together. It was all Marlene could do not to cover herself, particularly when they entered the store and the cashiers who'd noticed her through the display window came forward for a better look.

Pike led her farther into the building, past aisles and aisles of shelf stock that looked picked-over, like the day after a clearance sale. Marlene began to suspect that the employees weren't really working for Pike but were living off of the merchandise inside the store. In one section, cashiers who'd gone off shift for the night slept on displays of Sealy Posturepedic mattresses, while nearby a group of stockboys made good use of an electric grill to cook their dinners. The entire store was its own, self-sufficient universe.

"I've got fifty-one employees right now," Pike explained, "including myself. Of course, anyone's always welcome, but I'm not actively looking for new hires at the moment. Maybe I'll open a superstore next year."

They'd come as far as the women's clothing department, where a salesgirl with long, sandy blond hair was sale-tagging a display of floral-print blouses, each identical to the one that she was wearing.

Marlene halted before the display. "If you don't mind, Mr. Pike, I think I'll get dressed now. I just . . . feel weird all of a sudden."

Nathaniel withdrew politely. "Of course. Help yourself to whatever you need. It's all for the taking."

She thanked him and went to find her size at the end of the sale rack. Her choices were all arbitrary; the important thing was to cover herself with as many layers as possible. With trembling hands, she tore open a package of plain cotton panties and put them on. Likewise, she picked out a bra, a pair of jeans, a T-shirt and a cable-stitch sweater. Most of the items had security tags on them, so she brought them up to the salesgirl in the floral-print blouse. "Can you pull these tags off for me?" she asked.

The girl took the bundle of clothes and set it by her register. "You're Stuart's wife, right?" she asked. "Marlene, the nudist?"

The question startled Marlene, who took a closer look at the salesgirl's name tag. Hers wasn't gold, like Pike's, but a blue and white plastic card that read Allison Reese, Sales Associate. Marlene felt embarrassed at meeting Allison under such awkward circumstances. Having spent so many weeks hearing about her from Heath, Marlene wanted the real Allison to like her. "That's me," she admitted softly.

Like Nathaniel, Allison appeared unfazed by Marlene's nudity. "Hey, don't look so freaked out. This isn't Providence. No one's gonna call the cops."

The thought hadn't occurred to Marlene until now. "My husband might," she said.

Allison laughed. "Stuart? Nah. He might be a little uptight, but he's not an asshole."

Marlene found it strange that anyone would think of Stuart as "uptight." He'd never been uptight with her, only patient and understanding. *She* was the problem, not him. If he'd ever acted uptight, it must've been because she'd done something to upset him.

Allison took off the security tags and passed each item across the sales counter to Marlene, who gratefully put them on. "Is Heath around?" Marlene asked.

"I don't know. He was supposed to meet me twenty minutes ago for dinner." Allison frowned. "How do you know Heath?"

Marlene explained as best she could the many weekends they'd spent working on the video that Lucien had offered to buy from Heath. Allison listened attentively, feeling intensely betrayed that Heath hadn't told her any of this.

"I knew that I shouldn't have gone to England," Allison said. "Bad things happen when I'm not around. That's why my parents got divorced, because I went off to college. I've gotta learn to just stay put. My father's lived in Providence his whole life, and he's happy enough."

Marlene couldn't understand why Allison had to take the blame for anything. This was *her* fault, no one else's—her fault that she'd been arrested and lost her job; her fault that Stuart wasn't talking to her anymore, and even that Allison's parents were divorced; her fault about 9/11, and the recession, and every bad thing that had ever happened since the day she was born, April 7, 1969, and probably even before that, too.

"We'll get your videotape back," Allison assured her. "Heath's not going to do anything with it, anyway. He's a total type A personality. Or type B. I always forget which one's which. But the one that never gets anything done."

After Marlene finished getting dressed, she and Allison found Heath in the sporting goods department and led him out of the store to a copse of tall grass growing on the leeward side of the building. The evening air hung heavy with a kind of blue, suspended mist.

Understandably, Heath wasn't pleased to hear about Lucien. "Who is this guy, anyway?" he asked Marlene. "I mean, if he's a *producer,* that's one thing."

"What do you mean, 'That's one thing?' " Allison snapped. "It's her body. Don't be so fucking . . . what's the word?"

"Paternalistic?" he guessed, and she rolled her eyes at him.

"Lucien would pay you for the video, Heath," Marlene said. "He's a decent, trustworthy man."

"See?" Allison said. "He's a decent, trustworthy man. This sort of thing happens all the time. Like in that musical, *Rent,* where the kid shot the video and CNN wanted to buy it, but he was stupid and said no. Don't be stupid, Heath. You'll make other videos."

He didn't want to argue with her. After many days of careful consideration, he'd finally decided that the raw footage that he'd shot with Marlene and Stuart was too good to waste. He had larger designs for it, though he wasn't sure exactly what. But he certainly couldn't do anything without Marlene's video. The core element of his film had to be genuine for the rest of it to carry any weight.

Allison nudged him. "Come on, Heath. That video camera doesn't even belong to you. It's Pike's."

He hated being reminded of this. "I know, it's just . . . I wanted to finish that project on my own," he said lamely.

"Why? What for?" Allison folded her arms, clearly prepared to reject whatever reasons he might propose.

"I can't tell you," he muttered.

"Why not?"

"Not when you ask me like that. You're just going to make me feel stupid."

Marlene took pity on him. "Look, just forget it. I'm sorry I even came up here," she said.

Allison turned on her. "Don't say that. Don't ever apologize for doing what you want to do."

Heath stared at the ground as Allison continued to badger him. *What would Brian Wilson do?* he wondered but found no answer. This was the same kind of adversity that had finally killed off the *Smile* album in May of 1967. With the exception of Brian's younger brother, Dennis, who shared some of Brian's eclecticism, the other Beach Boys were by degree either perplexed by the tracks that Brian had assembled or else completely opposed to them. At any rate, the consensus was that he'd lost his touch, and in the months following *Smile*, a new, more democratic Beach Boys emerged. They recorded a very fine album in late '67 called *Wild Honey*, then another, equally fine, record the following year, *Friends*. The albums appeared regularly throughout the next decade before drying up in the early eighties. Dennis drowned in '83; Carl died of a brain tumor in '98; Mike, Al and Bruce continued to work the festival circuit; and Brian, the boy genius who at twenty-four had seemed invincible, came to regard his long-lost "teenage symphony to God" as "dated sounding." If there was a moral to any of this, Heath didn't know what it was.

"Just think about it, Heath," Marlene said. "I don't know what kind of money Lucien has, but I'll bet it's a lot."

"It's not the money," Heath said. "I don't need the money."

Allison shouted, "What are you talking about? Pike's not

going to support you for the rest of your life, Heath. I'm sure he's got other things on his agenda."

"I know that. Look, let's not talk about this right now. I don't feel so good."

"Whatever. I've got work to do." Allison glanced at Marlene, then stormed back into the building.

Marlene gave Heath's arm an encouraging squeeze. She wanted to say something wise to cheer him up, but she feared that any advice of hers must be cursed.

Once both women had gone inside, Heath wandered away from the building and lay down in the grass. The ground felt cool and lumpy through his thin work shirt. As he gazed up at the darkening sky, another Beach Boys song came to him, this one from 1964. The song was one of Brian's miniature masterpieces, with harmonies so beautiful that Heath hadn't really thought about the lyrics until now. The title said it all, though: *Don't Back Down.*

4

The next morning, Pike tracked down Heath in sporting goods and announced that he'd arranged a birthday surprise for him. Heath's birthday wasn't for another two weeks, but Pike insisted it couldn't wait.

At eleven o'clock, a helicopter landed at the staging area just north of the Kmart, and Pike went to meet it by himself. When he returned thirty minutes later, he asked Heath to follow him. "Quickly, now, we're on a tight schedule," he said.

They crossed the parking lot and plunged into the outlying forest, where they followed a trail that the staff used to bring supplies in from the helicopters.

Pike stopped a few steps short of the staging area and pointed left off the trail. "Walk straight until you come to a clearing," he said. "You'll see a couple of folding chairs. Stop and take a seat."

"Then what?" Heath asked. As much as he trusted Pike, he felt uneasy about this.

Pike smiled mysteriously. "Just you wait."

Heath followed his instructions and soon was standing between two folding chairs that were facing each other. As they were identical, he picked one at random and sat down. Ten minutes went by before he heard a rustling sound and saw motion in the trees. Someone was coming toward him. He watched apprehensively as the figure drew closer, stepping uncertainly over the rocks and tangled roots on the ground.

With a last push forward, a man emerged in the clearing and smiled at Heath. "Are you Heath Baxter?" he asked.

The blood drained from Heath's face. He nodded.

The man offered his hand to Heath, who felt so detached from his own body that he could hardly move to shake it.

"I'm Brian," the man said. "Nate tells me it's your birthday."

They shook hands, and the man took a seat in the other chair. He wore slate-blue, ultralight hiking boots, a pair of khakis and an oxford shirt with wide maroon stripes. Over the shirt was a tan windbreaker with a wrinkled hood that hung loosely from the neck. Heath knew from reading his biography that Brian Wilson was a few days shy of his sixtieth birthday, but he easily could've passed for fifty. His face was hard and thin, and his brown hair looked like someone had combed it for him. There was something monstrous about him, Heath decided. He looked a bit like Frankenstein, although human, more handsome. His eyes had the same tortured, lovesick quality, and they penetrated inquisitively from two craggy sockets. Despite his weathered features, his body was trim and muscular—a triumph of personal determination, dieting and exercise, pop psychology and, one would assume, a fair number of green and yellow pills. He spoke out of the corner of his mouth, and one side of his face even looked slightly spastic, as if he might've had a stroke. Yet his voice was the same one that on Heath's *Smile* bootlegs told the musicians to make the percussion sound more "like jewelry."

"My birthday's comin' up, too," Brian said. "I guess that means we're both Gemini."

"June 20, 1942," Heath said quickly, then added, "I mean you, not me."

His nervousness amused Brian, who sang a few lines of "Birthday" by the Beatles. He laughed to himself, letting his eyes drift. "I remember wanting to do that song with the Beach Boys back in the seventies but . . . I just couldn't get my act together."

Heath still couldn't believe that this was happening. "What are you doing in New Hampshire?"

Words came slowly to Brian, but he eventually said, "We're playin' a show down in Concord on the third. Nate bought a couple tickets for you and your girlfriend. Then we're playin' a double-bill with Elvis Costello on the fourth. I think you're really gonna like it. We've got a smokin' band this time, some of the best touring musicians in L.A."

Heath couldn't resist asking, "Are you going to do any songs from *Smile*?"

Brian cocked his head slightly, as if trying to recollect the name of an old friend. "The problem with a lot of those songs, Heath, is that I don't remember how most of 'em go. I mean, I can remember the words, and the melodies . . . but that's about it."

And then a miraculous thing happened. Closing his eyes, he leaned back in his chair, took a quick, shallow breath and sang, *"She laughs and stays in her one, one, one, wonderful."*

And Heath felt the mountain drop out from under him, and the wind was silent, and a sparkling firmament settled softly on the trees.

When he finished singing, Brian said, "It was good to see Nate again. We haven't worked together since the eighties. I've lost a lot of weight since then."

"You look great, Mr. Wilson," Heath said.

Brian pointed at himself, and those deep, Frankenstein eyes sparkled hideously. "Who's Mr. Wilson? I'm not Mr. Wilson."

From this, Heath understood he was to call him Brian. "Mr. Wilson was my father," he said, "not me."

Murry Wilson, Heath thought: the Beach Boys' first manager and the man who, once Brian's talents began to outstrip his own, so berated his eldest son in the studio that on a 1965 session tape he could be heard screaming, "You see, Brian? I can be a genius, too." It was Murry who'd done the most to undermine Brian's self-confidence. Two years after *Smile,* Brian produced one of his best songs from the late sixties, "Break Away," and on the label, his songwriting partner was credited as "Reggie Dunbar," a pseudonym for Murry. It was almost as if Brian were saying, "You're right, Dad. I'd be nothing without you."

Feeling uncomfortable, Heath asked, "How did you meet Mr. Pike?"

Brian had to think about it for a while. "Well, that was when my brother Dennis was still alive. Denny'd done some acting during the Beach Boys days, and Nate wanted him to be in one of his movies. We were all gonna produce it together. I don't remember if the movie ever got made, but Nate was fun to hang around with. He's a good drummer."

Heath stared. "Mr. Pike?"

"Yeah! Nate always reminded me of Denny on the drums. Denny never thought he was a good drummer, either, but man, he could *swing* it!"

Brian went back to talking about his current band, his fans and some of the new songs he was trying out on tour. "I never thought I'd get so much enjoyment from playin' every night. I find it very therapeutic. For a long time, I didn't want to go out on the road because I was in so much psychological pain, and I didn't want to inflict any of that bad karma on the audience. You know, that's not good for the music, and it's not good for the soul either—and the *soul* is what's important. I always try to write soulful music. It's not 'soul music,' but it's soulful."

Listening to him, Heath wanted Brian to know that, as an artist himself, he could sympathize with what he was telling him. "I feel the same way," he said, "when I'm working on a screenplay or writing a script . . ." *Same thing, you idiot,* he thought, then realized he'd inadvertently picked up Brian's rambling, redundant speech patterns, and even a hint of his southern California accent. He didn't want Brian to think he was mimicking him, so he spoke clearly and precisely in his regular voice. "I think that a lot of younger artists are afraid of expressing themselves," he said, "because they think they'll be criticized for it. But I *want* to express myself. I want to make myself open to people, like you did with your music."

Brian regarded him thoughtfully. He'd obviously done this as a favor to Pike, but he also seemed to be genuinely enjoying Heath's company. "I always tell people," he said, " 'Man, I *still* believe in the power of music.' That's what the Beach Boys were all about. Every song that we ever recorded was about the same thing: love. Sharin' it, spreadin' it, *believin'* in it. And that's why those songs are still popular today."

Heath saw an opportunity to ask a *Smile* question. "But what about 'Cabin-Essence,' or 'Child Is Father of the Man'? I mean, both of those songs seem a little abstract for pop music."

Brian couldn't suppress a pained expression. Every successful artist, Heath supposed, had his own albatross to contend with, and this was Brian's.

"I reached a point when I was a lot younger," he said confidentially, "when I began to question my own spirituality. It was . . . a bad scene. And I stopped seein' things clearly. I wasn't exercising, I wasn't eatin' right. And after awhile it began to affect how I heard things inside my head. Instead of writing spiritually joyful music, I was writing acid music and marijuana music. I wasn't thinking about God anymore." He paused. "And then I realized that God isn't about what's in your head. That's not where God lives. God lives in your feet, and your arms, and your hands, and your muscles. God is what happens to you when you hear a Sam Cooke song on the radio and you have to stop what you're doin' and just groove to the music. That's a *spiritual* celebration. That's why I love disco music, because disco music is spiritual. Anything that makes you move your feet."

Heath had to disagree. "But that's not what's so great about it, I mean, what you were doing on that album. I feel like when I listen to those songs—'Heroes and Villains,' and 'I Love to Say Dada'—that it *is* spiritual music, because it's so pure and strange and beautiful, and it makes me think about . . ." He stammered, aware that he wasn't making much sense. "About myself, and what I want to do with my life, and it . . . *inspires* me. I mean, I'm not saying you're wrong, because obviously you're not, but when I think about your albums—and I love all of them, even *Orange Crate Art*—it's always *Smile* that I come back to, because it's more than just an album, it's this *thing*, this concept I can't put into words. It's pure experience. It's like this vacant space that swallows everything up."

Heath felt dismayed that Brian didn't share his enthusiasm for *Smile*. On a purely intellectual level, he understood that artists were often the worst judges of their own work, but to apologize for something that had given him so much pleasure seemed almost obscene.

Brian looked wistful. "I sometimes think if I *had* finished that record, people wouldn't be so interested in it. As hard as I try, I can't write the perfect song. I can't say all there is to say in a three-minute piece of music. I tried once, and I almost went crazy doin' it."

Heath wondered what song he might be referring to, but Brian didn't elaborate.

"A song is really just a means of communicating with people," he said. "That's why I wrote those surf songs back in the sixties—'cause that's what kids were doin', and I wanted to write happy music about things that other people cared about, like surfin' and hangin' out with your friends. It wasn't art music per se, it was religious music." He sighed. "But the fact is, once a song's over, it's over. You can listen to it as many times as you want, but you're never gonna get any closer to the *essence* of the song itself. The only way to get truly close to a song is to stop listening to it. There are some songs I won't listen to anymore, because I don't want to ruin them. I haven't heard 'River Deep, Mountain High' in over ten years, but I remember every note of it."

Heath asked, "So if you had to do it over again, you wouldn't have written *any* music at all?"

Brian gave the question serious consideration. "No. I couldn't live without music. Music's my big brother. I've always been everyone else's big brother, but music is *my* big brother." This statement was made more poignant by the fact that both of Brian's brothers were dead, and that he probably could've used a real big brother when he was younger, instead of an intangible one.

"Believe me," he said, "a day doesn't go by that somebody doesn't ask me about that record. And as much as that might upset me, it's also kind of cool. There's something mysterious about an unfinished work of art—'mysterious' in the old sense of the word, meaning that which relates to the mystical or inexpressible. Because I couldn't finish the record, the music still belongs to God. And that's what I wanted to do in the first place. When I went in the studio to make *Smile,* all I knew was I wanted it to sound joyful, and childlike, and honest. I didn't have any idea what the single was gonna be, or even what any of the individual songs were gonna sound like. I just wanted to *play*, you know, like little kids play. Have you ever watched kids playin' in a sandbox, and they make a mound over here and another little mound over there, and pretty soon it's a castle or a dragon or, you know, a sports car? They don't sit down and say, 'Now I'm gonna make a sports car.' They let the *sand* talk to them. And I wanted to do that with my music. Same thing with 'Good Vibrations.' That was all about the *sand*, man. That was about listening to the sand and lettin' the music do its own thing."

Heath appreciated what Brian was saying but couldn't relate to it himself. "It's hard to make a film like that, though. You need to have a plan of some kind—if not a screenplay, at least a rough outline."

"That's not important. Don't worry so much about the process. Songwriting is all about discovering beauty, not creating it. And that's also true of filmmaking. If you can't finish something honestly, leave it unfinished. That's what I did with *Smile*."

Heath, who'd been staring down at his shoes, looked up. "You did?"

Brian's face became very serious, as if he'd never spoken of this before. "*Smile* wouldn't have worked as a real record—not the kind that you hold in your hands and put on a turntable. It wouldn't have made it."

"That's not true. What about 'Surf's Up'? That song kills 'A Day in the Life.' And 'Cabin-Essence,' and 'Do You Like Worms,' and—"

"No," Brian insisted. "It wasn't good enough. Hey, I was stoned out of my mind. I was fat and depressed and I couldn't write anymore. I *blew* it, man, you know? There I was: twenty-four years old, I'd just had a number-one hit single, the Beach

Boys were the most popular band in England—more popular than the Beatles—and everyone in the world was waiting to hear what I'd do next. I couldn't just come out with another *album,* could I? I had to do something amazing. A super album! So that's what I did. I went into the studio and kept the tapes rolling . . . and went fucking nuts, man. It's as simple as that. That's what *Smile* is—it's me going nuts. Playin' with fire trucks and makin' barnyard sounds and gettin' on my brothers' nerves and"—he laughed—"and just gettin' it all on tape, you know? And all the while, people were asking me, 'When's the next Beach Boys record comin' out?' And I kept saying, 'It's gonna be great, man, it's gonna be great!' But I had no idea."

Heath had stopped listening. He'd heard enough already. Up until now, his own project—the hours of footage that he'd shot with Pike and Marlene—had failed to cohere. It lacked structure, lacked a thesis. But after talking to Brian, he knew what his thesis was. The lost movie. The unfinished work of art.

When their meeting was over, Heath and Brian walked out of the clearing and back to the staging area, where a helicopter was waiting to take Brian to a sound check in Concord. Before leaving, he said, "Denny had a lost album, too, called *Bamboo.* He never finished it. I don't like it when a person finishes everything he starts. It means he's not tryin' hard enough."

Heath smiled. "Sounds like Mike Love."

Brian was surprisingly generous toward his cousin. "Let me tell you something—Mike Love *is* the Beach Boys. Without Mike there wouldn't have been a group. I love that guy. Every one of those fellas—Mike, Carl, Dennis, even Al and Bruce—was more responsible for the Beach Boys' success than I ever was. They played the *concerts,* man. They went on the road, they took the music to the *people.* I'm grateful to each one of 'em, and I miss Carl and Dennis somethin' terrible." He held out his hand.

"Look, if you need anything else, just let me know. Nate's got my number. I'll be on tour through August, but any time after that's cool."

"There might be *one* thing," Heath began, but then the helicopter pilot shouted, "Brian, we've got to go."

Brian waved for the pilot to hold on. Putting his arm around Heath's shoulder, he said, "I wrote a little tune once. I think it made it on to one of our records. It's more like a Boy Scout chant than a real song. It goes"—he sang in his nearly worn-out falsetto—"*Eat a lot, sleep a lot, brush 'em like crazy. Run a lot, do a lot, never be lazy.*"

Heath knew the song, of course. " 'Mama Says,' from *Wild Honey.* The original version was supposed to be on *Smile.*"

"It's good advice," Brian said, maintaining a strong grip on Heath's shoulder. "Don't forget it." Then, releasing him, he jogged across the field and climbed into the helicopter, which took off almost immediately. Heath watched the chopper rise, hover at a low altitude and make a 180-degree turn toward its destination. He couldn't see Brian through the glass canopy but kept waving anyway, until the helicopter dipped over the mountains and the sound of the chopper blades faded into silence.

Thanks, Mr. Pike, Heath thought, and walked back to the store.

5

Foreword

—by Brian Wilson

Man, I wish you could've seen it.

Most of what you're about to read doesn't exist anymore; some of it does, though who knows what happened to it—ask Heath. I was one of a few invited guests who happened to get a peek at Heath Baxter's unfinished masterpiece, and I can tell you that I haven't been so blown away by a movie since the first time I saw *2001*. Heath's movie is hard to describe—part guerrilla documentary, part sex film and part time capsule, it manages to incorporate a staggering array of visual techniques as it offers a glimpse into the lives of its famous, real-life characters. For now, all we can do is savor these collected fragments—adapted from the director's own transcripts—and to hope that, one day, Heath will come to his senses and release the rest of it.

Man, I wish you could've seen it.

Love and Mercy,
BW, Summer '02.

Pike's Folly

Fragment #3b—"Ich bin der Zorn Gottes!" (1:13)

(NATHANIEL PIKE, 43, *stands beside a construction site in a heavily wooded area, where workers are deforesting the land to make room for a parking lot. He looks uncomfortable in front of the camera, which slowly tightens in from a wide shot.*)

PIKE: (*Speaking directly into the camera.*) Welcome to my kingdom. My little, uh . . . this is where I like to take my clothes off and run around naked. (*He laughs.*) No, I don't . . . but I *would*, if I wanted to. Nothing wrong with that. (*Getting impatient.*) Hey, Heath, is this gonna take all day?

HEATH: (*Behind the camera.*) I'm just practicing my zoom. (*The camera pulls back as twice more,* HEATH BAXTER, 26, *rehearses his technique. Pike checks his watch, then fiddles with his shirtsleeves.*)

PIKE: All right, let me tell you a joke. You wanna hear a joke? I'm gonna make up a joke. Two guys walk into a bar, and one of 'em says, "Hey, you know what? I just got laid." And the other one says, "So did I." (*He pauses, thinking of a punch line.*) And then the first one says, "Was it good?" And the other one says, "I don't know . . . was it good for you?" (*He smiles, proud of himself.*) Hey, Heath, did you hear that? (*No reply, so he asks again.*) My joke. Did you hear my joke?

HEATH: (*Preoccupied.*) I'm sorry, I was just practicing my zoom.

PIKE: Well, screw you, then . . . he don't listen to my jokes. (*Pike lapses into a ponderous silence, as again, Heath zooms in with his camera, then pulls quickly back out.*)

Fragment #7a—"Have You Seen Me?" (2:57)

(MARLENE BREEN, *32, poses at the entrance to the Sakonnet Bridge, a small link of state highway that crosses the Sakonnet River near Tiverton. The day is gray and breezy, and she's bundled up in a long winter coat. About twenty yards down the empty road,* STUART BREEN, *31, keeps an anxious lookout for approaching cars. After a truck passes, he signals to Marlene, who slips off her coat and stands naked. She looks very cold as she smiles for Heath's camera.*)

HEATH: Hold it. Hold it. Good.
(*A gust sweeps up from the river, blowing Marlene's hair in her face. Both she and Heath laugh.*)
MARLENE: Ooo, it's cold!
HEATH: You wanna stop?
MARLENE: (*With the wind dying down.*) No, it's okay. (*Looking over her shoulder, she gets an idea and starts across the bridge, walking away from the camera.*) Let's go over here.
HEATH: (*Laughing.*) Oh, shit . . .
(*He follows her, stops to frame his shot, then runs to catch up. Stuart yells at them from far off, but his words are unintelligible.*)
HEATH: (*Teasing her.*) Damn, girl, you've got a nice ass!
(*She smiles back at him and keeps walking. For several seconds, all we hear is the wind, Heath's breathing and Stuart's distant shouts.*)
HEATH: All right, we should probably head back.
(*She ignores him and picks up the pace.*)
HEATH: I can't believe this. (*A few steps later.*) This is *so* fucked up.
(*Midway across the bridge, she stops and leans back against the guardrail.*)

MARLENE: This looks like a good place.

HEATH: A good place for what?

MARLENE: *(Shrugging.)* What do you want to talk about?
(The picture goes in and out of focus as Heath makes an adjustment to his camera.)

HEATH: Uh . . . whatever you want to talk about, Marlene. You're doing fine.

MARLENE: *(Holding her breasts.)* How about how fucking *hot* I am?

HEATH: *(Good-natured but without much enthusiasm.)* You are pretty fucking hot, ma'am.
(Footsteps approach as Stuart runs in from the corner of the screen and covers her with her jacket.)

STUART: What the hell are you doing?

MARLENE: Jesus, Stuart, you're gonna push me right off the bridge!
(Stunned, she holds the jacket in front of her but doesn't put it on. Off camera, a car whooshes by.)

STUART: *(Pointing at the jacket.)* Get that on, and let's go.

MARLENE: All *right*! Ask nicely.

HEATH: Yeah, Stu's probably right. Let's not push it.
(Heath puts his camera down; the rest of the scene is a close-up of his pant leg.)

HEATH: *(To himself.)* I think I fucked up the audio when I—
(Marlene and Stuart argue in the background.)

STUART:—when I'm telling you something!

MARLENE: Well, I'm sorry! Heath was here, and I was having a good time—

STUART: I don't care. Let's go. It's too goddamn cold anyway.

MARLENE: Why do you always have to make me feel so awful?

STUART: I'm *trying* to help you, Marlene.

MARLENE: Fine, just ask nicely when you—
(Heath swoops up the camera and turns it off.)

Fragment #7b—"Old Friends" (1:43)

(The scene opens on a bare table in a firelit breakfast room. Pike sits across the table from his old friend, SARAH CRANBERRY, *44. Behind him, a four-paned window looks out on a meadow, where snow is falling. As the scene starts, Stuart is setting a mug of coffee in front of Pike. He points at Sarah.)*

STUART: You want me to make another pot?
(She half-rises from her chair.)
SARAH: I can do it.
STUART: No, no . . . you sit.
(He leaves the room, and Pike smiles pleasantly at Sarah.)
PIKE: That's right, Sarah, let someone else do the work for a change. *(He presents his best public relations smile to the camera.)* Sarah's the real reason why I'm here, you know. There's not a woman alive who can keep me away from Providence for more than forty-eight hours.
(She looks pleased but speaks softly into her lap.)
SARAH: Don't joke about it, Nate.
PIKE: I'm *not*, I'm just saying *(turning back to the camera)* that Sarah's the best short-order cook in New England. She can do more with one hand than most women with—
(She slugs him.)
SARAH: Don't say it.
PIKE: *(Laughing.)* What? What'd I say?
SARAH: *(Also laughing, gesturing at the camera.)* He's trying to ask a question.
PIKE: Oh, right. Of course. *(He composes himself.)* Heath, what was your question?
HEATH: *(Off-camera.)* Are you—
PIKE: Too slow! Gotta do better than that.

SARAH: You didn't let him finish. Go ahead, Heath. What's
   your question?
HEATH: *(Mildly piqued.)* That's okay.
SARAH: *(To Pike.)* See? You hurt his feelings.
PIKE: No, I didn't. Heath knows I'm just screwing around.
   Don't you, Heath? *(The camera nods.)* See? Now shake
   your head. *(The camera does.)* Good. Now roll over.
HEATH: Fuck you.
(All laugh as Stuart returns from the kitchen.)

Fragment #11a—"Boys' Turn" (:48)

*(Marlene points the camera at Heath, who stands in front of
a nondescript brick wall. She laughs continuously
throughout the scene.)*

MARLENE: All right . . . go!
   *(Trying to be a good sport, Heath unzips his pants and
   flashes his dick at the camera. Marlene gleefully zooms in for
   a better shot.)*
MARLENE: Oh, good, good—that's good!
*(He holds the pose for a two-count, then stuffs himself back into
   his pants and walks out of frame.)*
MARLENE: *(Disappointed.)* Aw, you moved too soon!
   *(As she sets up another shot, we hear the garbled sound of
   Heath coaxing Stuart in front of the camera. Except for the
   brick wall, the screen is empty. Finally, Stuart comes on, led
   by Heath.)*
MARLENE: And now, the man of the hour . . .
HEATH: Yeah, Stuart!
   *(After some hesitation, Stuart pulls down his sweatpants and
   lets them bunch around his ankles.)*
MARLENE: Whoo! Look at that sexy cock!

(He tolerates this for a few seconds, then yanks his pants back up and walks off-screen. Marlene calls to him.)
MARLENE: Wait, hon, if you—
(Black.)

Fragment #12a—"Masturbation Fantasy #1" (2:35)

(Early evening on Mount Independence. Shovel in hand, Pike digs a shallow hole in one corner of the construction site, which is covered with trees and underbrush. Someone has made him angry, and he's taken up the shovel to let off steam.)

PIKE: *(To himself but in a loud enough voice for others to hear.)* As long as I'm out here, no one goes home. I don't give a damn. I'll build the fucking thing myself. *(He stops digging and calls out to a small group of workers who are also working with shovels.)* Who wants to quit, right now? Any takers? Come on, you hotshots. Who wants to go back to Concord? *(One of the workers shouts something antagonistic to Pike.)*
PIKE: That's fine! Talk all you want, buddy. I gotcha right here *(makes a fist)* in the ball sack.
(The worker continues to shout at Pike, who waves sarcastically.)
PIKE: Bye-bye! Bye-bye! *(He briefly goes back to work, then throws down his shovel and marches toward the workers.)* Who wants to go home? Tell me now—who wants to go home?
(His voice becomes garbled as he storms away from the camera. When Heath finally catches up to him, Pike is arguing with three hostile workers.)
PIKE: You're nothing but shit, man. Your mother was embarrassed to give birth to you.

WORKER: Is that right?

(Pike's rage is centered on one of them, who in turn seems hesitant to confront him directly. The other two maintain a cautious distance, not daring to speak.)

PIKE: Do you know what you are? Let me tell you, this is funny. You are a retarded piece of cow crap. You can eat my fucking turds—right out of my asshole, fuckwad.

WORKER: *(Laughing.)* All right . . .

PIKE: You shut up! I'm not finished with you.

WORKER: It sounds like you are.

(The workers chuckle to themselves but stop when Pike flies into a new tirade.)

PIKE: Oh, HA HA, right! HA HA! There, I can say it, too.

(The most recalcitrant worker spits at Pike, who doesn't hesitate to slap his cheek. All three workers freeze.)

PIKE: *(Jabbing his finger in the man's face.)* Don't you *ever* fucking do that to me again. I'll stab your fucking eyes out, man. I'll pull your prison records. You want that? You wanna get raped?

(There's an abrupt cut, and when the scene resumes, Pike has gone back to his original spot. He speaks in a soft, conversational tone to Heath, who is behind the camera.)

PIKE: The fact is, Heath, I don't always know what I'm talking about. Hey, I'll admit it. That's all right—that's part of being a good leader. The important thing is to just keep dreaming. And if some people don't share my dream, then there's compromise. And I don't like compromise.

Fragment #12b—"Masturbation Fantasy #2" (1:35)

(Marlene lies naked in bed and speaks to Heath and Stuart, who are behind the camera.)

MARLENE: I guess I don't understand this scene.

HEATH: Okay. What don't you understand?

(She's reluctant to say anything critical but finally does.)

MARLENE: It's just that we've been shooting outside all this time, and now *(looking around the bedroom)* we're *here.* I don't get it.

HEATH: Don't you feel comfortable here?

MARLENE: No, I do. It's just different. I like it better when there's people watching.

HEATH: I'm watching. Stuart's watching.

MARLENE: Strangers, I mean.

(Stuart has less patience than Heath, and he snaps.)

STUART: Why don't you try it in front of the window, hon?

MARLENE: No, here's fine. *(She looks expectantly into the camera, as if waiting for further instructions.)* What do you want me to do?

HEATH: Whatever feels good.

(As directed, she opens her legs and starts to masturbate. Her mind quickly wanders, though, and she comes to a stop.)

HEATH: *(Prompting her.)* Marlene?

MARLENE: Hm? Oh—

(She resumes, but with the same empty look in her eyes. Again she slows, and again she stops. Black.)

Fragment #17b—"Vive la Trance" (:34)

(Pike, Heath and Stuart are riding around North Conway in Pike's SUV. It is early in the project, judging by the winter colors outside. Pike sings "I'm a Yankee Doodle Dandy" as he drives. Heath has the camera, and he points it at Stuart, who sits alone in the backseat.)

HEATH: Hey, Stuart? What're you thinking about?
  (Stuart looks out the window. His eyes don't move, even as the SUV slows, stops and speeds up again.)
HEATH: Stuart?
STUART: *(Shifting his gaze toward Heath.)* Mm?
HEATH: What're you thinking about?
STUART: Oh . . .
  (He stammers, shakes his head and goes back to staring out the window.)

Etc.

6

They came from all directions: Stuart from the south, Cathy Diego and Alice Shepperton from the north, Henry Savage and Celia Shriver from the west, and a whole team of PIRG activists from Augusta, Maine, seventy miles east of Mount Independence. All parties converging on Nathaniel Pike.

Stuart had spent most of the previous afternoon sitting by the phone, waiting for news from Marlene. The call finally came at 7:00 p.m., some ten hours after he'd last seen her. A voice informed him that she'd turned up in New Hampshire and was resting safely in Pike's camp. When he asked to speak with her, he was told this wasn't a good idea.

She'd left him without a car, so he rented one in the morning and drove north to White Ledge. When he arrived at the trailhead, he was surprised to find Cathy Diego and Alice Shepperton, who'd come down from Pinkham Notch, where the Appalachian Mountain Club operated a shelter for hikers. With them were a handful of AMC recruits, along with two armed rangers.

"We're moving in on Pike today," Cathy told Stuart as a crowd gathered at the foot of the trail. "I ain't playin' with this creep anymore. He doesn't own the whole frickin' mountain. We've got a right to know what's going on up there."

Stuart looked toward the parking area and saw his car, which Marlene had abandoned. He approached the car and peered inside. The doors were locked, but he could see his keys, a bag from Dunkin' Donuts and a pile of laundry in the backseat. This last item caught his attention, and he squinted for a better look. *That's not laundry,* he realized, and backed away from the car, nearly tripping on his own feet.

"Hey," Cathy called. "You coming with us?"

"S-sure," he said, and hurried to rejoin the group.

If Cathy seemed particularly on edge, her past twenty-four hours had been hectic. Rumor had it that Pike was entrenched, David Koresh–style, with fifty of his supporters, whose own mental conditions were unknown. In addition, one of Cathy's assistants had seen Henry Savage at a Bickford's in Concord the night before. Something was up, and Cathy didn't like the smell of it.

The motley assemblage started up the mountain just before one o'clock, wanting to surprise Pike in the middle of the afternoon. Both Alice and Cathy were adept at handling the trail, which varied between long, muddy stretches of nearly flat terrain and steep hills of broken granite, where the hikers had to use their hands.

Coming out of a deep, brooding silence, Cathy said, "I can't *believe* that Reese girl is actually working for Fuckface." *Fuckface* was her nickname for Pike, which she also used to describe many of the men in her life, including her husband.

"Really? Who told you that?" Alice asked.

Cathy glanced at her over the rims of her purple-tinted sunglasses. "Who do you think? Pike only calls me on the phone every five frickin' seconds to brag about it. I should've seen it coming. She bailed on us back in Concord, and now she's completely flaked out."

"I'm sure she's just confused," Alice said. "Men like Nathaniel Pike have very seductive personalities."

The trail became steep and rocky, and they took turns hoisting one another to a higher level before going on.

Back on flat ground, Cathy said, "I am *so* over these snotty Ivy League kids. They get the nonprofit bug, and once I've gone through all the trouble of training 'em, they're on to the next thing."

"Surely not all of them."

Cathy scoffed. "Don't even—I deal with it every frickin' year. As soon as the novelty wears off, they're on the next plane to Cancún."

They'd reached a difficult stretch of trail, where they stopped talking and concentrated on getting up the mountain. Cathy was never much of an outdoors person, unlike her husband, who loved hiking and camping and fly-fishing with his friends in Manitoba. As she climbed, she paid little attention to the surrounding scenery, which, as the forest thinned out, had begun to show itself through the trees. It wasn't that she disliked the outdoors, just that working for the NHPIRG had spoiled her enjoyment of it. Where other people saw rivers and snow-covered summits, Cathy saw hills of paperwork and flowing streams of red tape. She was one of those permanently aggrieved women who was always running twenty minutes behind schedule. She thought of the men she worked with as morons; the women— if they were younger—as Barbie dolls, and if older as merely invisible. She wasn't unlikable per se, just impossible to warm up to. Having a conversation with her was like watching a sarcastic comedienne do her routine, only with all of the funny bits taken out.

At the tree line, she stopped the group and told the two rangers, "You guys go first. Let's give him a good scare."

"We don't want to provoke him," Alice warned. "We still aren't sure what he's got up there. He might have weapons, too."

A worried voice from the back of the group spoke up. "No one said anything about weapons."

To a general din of dissent, Cathy said, "Come on, we're wasting time. For all we know, Henry Savage has already beaten us to the punch."

Before she could give the rangers any more instructions, Stuart intervened. "Let me go first," he said. "I know this place better than anyone else."

Cathy still preferred her own idea but reluctantly agreed. With Stuart now in the lead, they left the trail and continued across a rocky, alpine meadow. Seeing the meadow brought back memories, and Stuart reflected on the first time he'd taken this path, in those pre-Kmart, pre–parking lot days. What would've happened if he hadn't started working for Pike? He didn't even want to think about it. He'd given a year of his life to this folly when he could've devoted it to something more constructive, like writing another book or spending more time with his wife.

On the other side of the mountain, Henry Savage and Celia Shriver were also closing in on Pike. They'd taken the western route, which wasn't as steep and wouldn't be as demanding on Celia's old legs. They walked in tense silence, stopping every few hundred yards to comment on what they saw: crowded thickets of zebra-white birch trees; giant slabs of rock embedded in the muck and gravel; blue and yellow blazes painted on tree trunks by volunteers of the AMC; sections of trail where emerald moss formed a slippery carpet under their feet; pellets of dung lying in neat pyramids that resembled piles of musket balls; a length of rubber tubing that ran between the maples where some crafty entrepreneur, legitimate or otherwise, had set up a makeshift syrup factory. Other than the dung pellets, the only evidence of an animal presence was an occasional rustling in the shadows, a furtive movement that could've been the wind or a black bear or another person.

"I like your style, Mr. Savage," Celia said. "You're decisive, and that's a good thing. Most D.C. bureaucrats wouldn't have the guts to confront Pike all alone."

"I'm not confronting him, Celia. I'm initiating a dialogue. If he feels under pressure, he'll balk," Henry explained for the third time that afternoon.

"Let him balk. Pike's a dog, a mangy mutt. What he needs is a good kick in the ass."

Henry put his canteen to his lips and drank. They still had another hour to get to the summit, but the air was thin and his lack of physical fitness was starting to slow him down. It would be so easy to give up and go back to Washington. His actual presence wasn't required here; he could've sent Pike a letter or called him on the phone, as he'd done many times before. He was curious, that was all. Out of sheer interest, he wanted to see the Independence Project for himself.

They finally reached the summit at three o'clock, and from a quarter mile away they could barely distinguish Pike's hideout through the forest. Even with his binoculars, Henry discerned no clear path to their destination. "Do you hear that?" he asked.

They listened again for the sound to carry across the valley. There it was: people talking, laughing, shouting happily, a radio playing loud, jangly, sixties pop/rock. It sounded like a party.

Celia obstinately stuck out her chin. "What's wrong with *silence*, Mr. Savage? They're ruining a perfectly good summer afternoon. Are we so neurotic that we can't enjoy a moment's peace?"

Pike's Folly

How 'bout one right now, he thought as he squinted through his binoculars. "I'm not seeing a parking lot—more like a warehouse, or an airplane hangar. I'm not sure."

He handed the binoculars to Celia, who had a look for herself. She scowled. "That prick. That little *prick.* Come on! Let's go get 'em."

Nathaniel Pike was sitting alone in his manager's office, staring out a window at the Kmart's giant, single-room sales floor. The smile lines that normally creased his face were gone, and his eyes lacked their usual sparkle. Now that the store was up and running, he felt like the Independence Project had finally exhausted itself. It just wasn't interesting anymore. He missed his brownstone, and his favorite restaurants and having dinner with his high-rolling friends on Federal Hill. He wanted to go back to being good ol' Nathaniel Pike, local eccentric.

Not that he wasn't proud of what he'd accomplished here, because he was. His goal had been to create an utterly vacuous monument, an ode to nothing, and he'd done it. Even the *Village Voice* had little positive to say when they'd reviewed his "installation" piece (as they'd laughably called it) back in May. Most of the popular press had written him off as an incorrigible loony, right up there with Jim Jones and Charlie Manson. *Entertainment Weekly* had downgraded his report card to a C−, while the *New York Times* could only marvel at what had happened to the same artist whose Independence Project, Phase One, "had demonstrated all of the elements of simplicity and restraint that this new, super-sized version lacks." Given his stated objective, the Independence Project was a success. It was time to move on.

But to what? The building would fall apart without him.

Weeds would push through the floor, and mold would gather on the merchandise. Left in ruins, the store would inevitably take on a metaphoric dimension, as his parking lot once had. The only way to preserve its basic meaninglessness was to keep it running. It had to remain as it was—just a Kmart, just a Kmart, just a Kmart.

This is crazy, he thought. Look at yourself! You've been living in a dream for the past ten years. You're sitting in a fucking *Kmart* in the middle of the fucking *White Mountains* and you've spent a fucking *fortune* on fucking *nothing,* and all those people out there—he got up from his desk and looked down at the sales floor—all think you're a total *wacko*. And they're right! They're absolutely right. Someone should put you in straitjacket, man. You're a fucking *freak.*

When Heath knocked on the door and let himself into the office, Pike brightened. His birthday surprise had been a hit, and it was good to know he could still make someone happy.

"Do you have a minute?" Heath asked.

"Of course."

Pike waved at him to close the door. Heath did, and both men took a seat.

"I've been thinking about our video," Heath began. He'd practiced this speech before, about fifteen minutes ago, but found it harder to say with Pike looking right at him. "I know that you were kind of hoping that I'd have it finished by now, and I'm sorry about that. Every time I get into the editing lab, the computer keeps crashing."

"Don't worry about it," Pike said. "What's important is that you're learning something and having a good time."

"Is it?" Heath asked, now skeptical, since Pike wasn't always this accommodating.

"Come on, Heath, you know me better than that. It's *your*

show. Personally, I don't care what you do with it. I won't inter-fere." As if one subject necessarily implied the other, Pike asked, "What do you *really* think about this place?"

Heath didn't know what to say. "Gee, Mr. Pike, I love it up here. I feel like we're doing something different, something worthwhile."

Pike took this in. "Go on," he urged him.

"That's it, I guess. I've always been interested in things that most people think are just weird."

"Do you think *I'm* weird?"

"No, I mean . . . maybe weird's not the right word. Whatever. I get the same vibe from Brian. He says that you're a really good drummer, by the way. Just like his brother."

This answer still didn't satisfy Pike. "You don't think I'm, you know, crazy, like a mental case?"

"Oh, no! Not at all."

"You're not afraid of me, are you?"

Heath shook his head, and Pike let it go. Turning to the win-dow that looked over the store, he asked, "Do you think *those* people think I'm crazy?"

Heath glanced behind him, out the window, then back at Pike. He lied. "No, they all think you're really cool."

The phone rang, and Heath retreated to give him some pri-vacy. As he waited, he studied the backs of his hands, his palms, the bluish tangle of veins in his wrists. Brian's hands were larger than Heath's, stronger, more distinctive. His fingernails were sharp and almond shaped—more like Count Dracula's than Frankenstein's. By contrast, Heath's fingernails were chewed to nubs, and he'd written someone's e-mail address on his left palm.

Pike slammed down the phone and snarled, "That was your girlfriend. Thank God she had her cell phone on her. She just saw that Diego bitch coming up from White Ledge. Looks like Henry Savage is with her, and about twenty others."

"I thought those guys didn't like each other," Heath said.

Pike shouted, "Damn it, Heath, don't ask me questions when I don't know the answers!" Shaking, he pulled his manager's jacket off the back of his chair and thrust his arms through the sleeves. "Let's see what's going on."

Heath followed him out of the office and across the sales floor to the front door. Several workers had also heard the news and were convening near the cash registers. One of them was naked, another down to her bra and panties. Thanks to Marlene, the Independence Project was turning into a nudist camp.

Once outside, they spotted Allison hurrying toward them.

"Where's Marlene?" Heath asked.

"She's hiding," Allison said coldly. "Stuart's here, too. She doesn't want him to see her."

"Wonderful," Pike grumbled. "After all that I've done for that guy, now he's working for that douche-bag Diego." The more he thought about it, the more it pissed him off. "Terrible book, too," he added. "Never got past page twenty."

They could see no signs of either Henry's party or Celia's, which were either still some distance off or else waiting for a better moment to reveal themselves. Meanwhile, more and more employees had come out of the store, filling an entire section of the lot.

"I need to get back to Marlene," Allison said, and before Heath could stop her, she ran back into the woods and scampered down a muddy incline. Her footing was poor, but she let her forward momentum carry her to the bottom of the hill, where she caught her breath.

Nothing of the surrounding vegetation looked familiar. She and Marlene had spent the morning exploring this area together, seeing how far they could go without getting lost. Marlene had been naked the entire time; it had bothered Allison at first, but she soon found herself admiring her for it.

Deeper into the woods, she spotted a fallen tree she recognized. "Marlene?" she called out softly.

Leaves rustled up ahead, and a pale arm waved to her from twenty feet away. Allison came a few steps closer, then stopped.

Marlene was standing ankle deep in mud and wet leaves. She looked frightened. "Where's Stuart?" she asked. She'd been crying, and her eye shadow was running down her cheeks.

"You're shivering," Allison said. "Here, you can wear my jeans. I don't mind going in my underwear."

She started to take off her pants, but Marlene shook her head and put her hand on Allison's waist.

"Come on, Marlene. Why are you doing this to yourself?"

Marlene burrowed her wet nose into Allison's shoulder. "I'm scared. I don't want to go alone."

"You won't have to. We'll go together."

Neither spoke for some time; all they did was hold each other. Marlene went limp, giving all of her dead weight for Allison to support.

"Stuart hates me," she blubbered. "He thinks I'm crazy. I'm no good for him. He's good, and I'm not. He's smart, and I'm not. I'm nothing."

"No one thinks you're crazy, especially not Stuart."

Marlene wiped her nose. "What about you?"

"I don't think you're crazy, either."

"Yeah, you do. I'm a crazy old witch. Don't lie to me."

Allison blushed. Honesty didn't come naturally to her, a fault she'd picked up from her father. Spontaneity and candor weren't Reese traits, but self-criticism was. "We're all crazy up here," she said. "You're no more crazy than Pike or me or anyone else."

Marlene was amazed. "You think *you're* crazy?"

"Yeah, I can be," Allison said, another lie. What *wasn't* a lie? she wondered. Allison felt like her head had been spun around so many times that she no longer knew. Life was too ambiguous. Instead of "crazy," she could've just as easily described herself as "serious," "obnoxious," "daring" or "conservative." You could take your pick. Even her basic moral sense varied from day to day. There was nothing that she stood for that she couldn't be talked out of by a five-hundred-word article in a magazine or a blurb on the Internet. She was exactly the kind of shallow, pseudo-enlightened kid of wealthy parents she'd always abhorred. Maybe "crazy" was the right word after all.

"How are you crazy?" Marlene asked.

"Oh, you know, being in my family can drive you kind of nuts." Allison nearly made a joke at her parents' expense but didn't. "Actually, I'm not crazy at all, and neither are you. I think you're wonderful."

"No, I'm not."

"Yes you are. I think you're a strong, independent woman."

Marlene stared down at her feet, which were submerged in muck. "You're nice," she said. With sheer effort, she kept her hands at her sides, leaving her body uncovered. "Please, Allison, I want you to look at me. I know that I'm ugly. I just want you to look . . . and not say anything."

Allison glanced down at Marlene and made a quick survey of her body. Marlene could feel her skin tingle, a wave of sensation that started in the middle of her chest and spread outward to her armpits and the backs of her knees. She thought: *Someone is looking at me. Someone is looking at my naked body.* She hadn't felt like this since the first time she'd undressed in front of Stuart—when he, too, was just a stranger to her.

Back at the store, all parties had spilled onto the parking lot: Pike, Heath, the cashiers and stockboys (clothed and otherwise), Henry and Celia, Cathy and Alice, Stuart, the two armed rangers, the AMC recruits, and the PIRG activists from Maine.

Pike's Folly

Everyone was yelling, though Pike's voice boomed above the rest.

"This is private property," he screamed in Henry's face. "All of you are trespassing. Go back to Washington."

Cathy Diego fought her way to the head of the group and pushed Henry aside. "I'm warning you, Pike. I've been up since three-frickin'-thirty in the morning, I'm PMSing, and I'm maxed out on overtime this week. So don't even."

"Let's all take turns," Alice said.

Her suggestion went largely ignored as a new shouting match flared up between the stockboys and the AMC recruits. Stuart stood apart from the others, refusing to participate.

"Oh, boy, I've been waiting for this day," Celia told Pike. "You could've saved yourself a lot of trouble if you'd just been honest with people."

"Can it, bitch," he said, and looked condescendingly at Henry. "What the hell is she talking about?"

Henry piped up over Cathy's shoulder. "Sarah Cranberry. Your friend from North Conway."

"Sarah's not a *friend*," Pike countered.

"Oh, I don't know about that. She seemed a friend to me. Regardless, I'm offering you a deal. Pick up your stuff and go back to Providence. We'll nullify your purchase of this land and forget that it ever happened."

"Take the man's advice, Nathaniel," Alice said. "You're a good person, just a little eccentric."

Henry nodded in agreement, but Pike showed only more contempt. "I'm not eccentric, Henry—*you're* boring. I'm not crazy—*you're* afraid. You're afraid of yourself. Not me, I know who I am. You can be as meek and cowardly, as humorless and puritanical and self-righteous as you fucking well want. Have a goddamn ball."

Henry refused to let Pike mock him. "The choice is yours, Nate. Just say the word and I'll have that pile of bones in Little Compton crawling with journalists."

Pike sneered. "I don't care what you do. Sarah and I are above it all. We're above *you*, and the Reese Foundation and the whole goddamned state of Rhode Island."

Henry looked from Celia to Alice, then back to Pike. "I don't get it. Then why did you—"

"No, you *don't* get it. And you want to know why? Because you don't have a soul. You're a bit part. You do what you're told, and that's it. You think you're some kind of fucking detective— searching for clues, huh? There *are* no clues, Henry, because I'm not a criminal. I don't have a motive. I've got no more reason to fear my past than you do."

"Well, I'm sorry, I guess I'll just have to—"

A commotion broke out on the other end of the parking lot, and those who'd been watching the argument ran over to investigate. Henry came last, just as the mob of cashiers and angry environmentalists parted down the center to make room for two women who'd emerged together from the forest. Both women were naked. Henry had already noticed a small handful of naked men and women on the premises, but they seemed like peripheral figures by comparison with these two. One of them had short dark hair, a pear-shaped figure and large, heavy breasts. As she stepped onto the blacktop, she kept her head down, her eyes on her feet. The other woman was tall and fair, with slender hips and a bony frame. She walked lightly on the balls of her feet and looked continuously around, as if searching for someone.

"Allison!" a male voice called out. The taller woman didn't react, except to take the other woman's hand and keep moving resolutely forward.

When they came to Henry, they stopped. He didn't know

what to do or where to rest his eyes. The sight of the naked women intimidated him, and he wondered why they'd singled him out, out of so many people.

The taller woman spoke. "This is my friend, Marlene," she said. "She's not hurting anyone. Please, just leave us alone."

Henry tried to resist but found his eyes continually drawn to the taller woman's body.

Marlene hid her face in Allison's shoulder. "Where's Stuart?" she asked.

The question traveled to the back of the crowd, where Stuart was standing by himself. Once he saw Marlene come out of the forest, he'd felt so detached that he found himself looking at her not from the perspective of a husband but as someone who'd never seen her before. Pushing his way through the crowd, he stopped in front of her and said, "Hi, Marlene."

Marlene's grip tightened around Allison's hand. "I'm sorry," she whispered, still not looking at him.

"It's okay," he said. "Don't be sorry."

When she finally raised her head, she said, "I'm so scared of myself, Stuart. Please don't go away."

"I won't," he said.

The activists and the cashiers were no longer fighting with one another, and even the rangers had put away their guns. All eyes were on Marlene and Stuart.

Marlene let go of Allison's hand and threw herself at Stuart, who had no choice but to catch her. "I'm sorry," she said over and over again. *I'm sorry I'm sorry I'm sorry I'm sorry . . .*

He cut her off. "Let's go home, hon. We've both done enough for one day." Catching Henry's eye, he laughed apologetically, as if to say, *So now you know what I've been dealing with all this time.*

Henry didn't laugh back. His throat had seized up, and he couldn't speak, could hardly breathe. All he knew was that more than anything else, he, too, wanted to take off his clothes and run naked in the woods with these two. He was tired of always being on the side of lawfulness and decency. He wanted to be the *pursued* for a change, not the pursuer.

Turning away from Stuart, he announced to the shocked faces of Celia Shriver, Cathy Diego and Alice Shepperton, plus some two dozen others, "He's right, people. We've all done enough for one day. Let's just go home."

Back in Providence, Gregg Reese had just received the news that his mother, Keeny, had died that morning in her sleep. He'd seen her the night before, when they'd spoken about an upcoming fund-raiser for a mayoral candidate the Reese Foundation was supporting in the fall. Their meeting had been businesslike but cordial. Keeny had looked better than she had in weeks, and Gregg left planning to visit her again in a few days. Now, along with his surprise, he felt oddly relieved. A cord had been severed that had once joined him to his ancestors. The last of the great Reeses was dead. Without Keeny, he was free to do as he pleased.

Of the many Indian girls that the Reeses kept on their property, one remarkable example distinguished herself by marrying into the family: Nummauchenem, who changed her name to Nancy when she wed Joseph Reese III in 1720. Under her guidance, the family increased its earnings by a hundredfold from 1720 to 1730. Rhode Island's wealth in the first half of the eighteenth century derived from three principal sources: sugar, slaves and fishing. The Reeses had a hand in all three, but Nancy concentrated on the first two, which were closely related. Slaves were usually exported to the West Indies in exchange for sugar that was distilled into rum. Of the thirty-three distilleries in Rhode Island, twelve belonged to the Reeses.

Nancy's own tenure in the Reeses' storage pen had hardened her heart to the plight of her slaves, who were still tortured and killed on a whim. Some of her cruelty was justified by the demands of her occupation, one of the most dangerous in New England. Rebellions were frequent, whether on the plantations or on board the trading ships. It took a strong hand to control so many unruly subjects. Hesitate or show weakness, and the margin for error evaporated.

Sickness also plagued the slave trade and ate into the traders' *profits. One ship, run out of Providence by Nicholas Brown, lost 109 of its 167 slaves to disease. With so many risks involved, Nancy made sure that she asked a high price for every slave she exported. The going rate for a healthy male ranged anywhere from $250 to $400. In a pinch, the Reeses could also buy their own breeding slaves with rum from their distilleries. Males went for two hundred gallons apiece, while females sold for one hundred eighty—quite a bargain, in that the rum cost only twenty-five cents a gallon to make.*

When Nancy wasn't seeing to her business, she indulged herself on the estate. Her husband apparently had difficulty controlling her and wrote in his journal, "Nancy is too bold in her wayes . . . in the morning she coupl's with the gardener, then with the gardener's wive at night . . ." Nancy became even more promiscuous after Joseph's death in 1733 and eventually took one of her own offspring to bed. Her favorite son, Irving, was sixteen when Nancy initiated sexual relations with him. They would have a child together, a boy, Sander, who was only three years old when his mother died of venereal disease. So ended the brief life of this extraordinary woman, thanks to whose ingenuity the Reese family fortune endured well into the twentieth century.

V | Hope

1

Four months after his encounter with Nathaniel Pike, Henry Savage opened the sliding glass door to his brick patio in North Potomac, Maryland, and walked across the cool grass of his backyard, skirting the six-foot-tall fence that separated his property from his neighbor's. He was on the phone with his former associate Danny Pittman, who'd called to see how Henry was holding up now that he no longer worked for the Interior Department.

"I'm doing fine," Henry told him. "Kate's teaching an extra class this semester, which should get us through the rest of the year."

"Then what?" From Danny's tone of voice, he clearly believed that Henry had been crazy to quit his job, particularly after he'd invested so many years in it.

Henry smiled up at the sunshine, which felt warm and summery on his face. "Who knows? Maybe I'll go back to school. I've always wanted to study Eastern philosophy." To further annoy his old colleague, he said, "I've been reading up on a lot of occult religions lately. Did you know that there are as many Zen Buddhists in San Francisco as there are registered voters in the state of Rhode Island?"

"I'm waiting for the punch line."

Henry laughed. "Don't worry, I haven't completely flipped out yet. I'm just trying to broaden myself a little. Examine different ways of thinking." His bare toes clenched at the grass, which stuck up in sharp, bristly sprigs around the outlines of his feet. A large black ant crawled across the top of his right foot, but he made no move to disturb it.

"What happened to you, anyway?" Danny asked. "The last I'd heard, you were flying up to the White Mountains to tear Nathaniel Pike a new asshole."

The ant scurried off, and Henry walked across the lawn with his head down. The direct sunlight cast shadows on his bare chest, making him look well toned and muscular. "Nothing happened," he said. "The whole trip was a bust. Nate's a harmless ol' kook—a little eccentric, but that's about it."

Danny didn't buy it. "Sounds to me like you chickened out. And what's all this crap I keep hearing about Pike's old house in Rhode Island? Someone told me that the FBI was looking into it."

"Oh." Henry paused. "That was a false lead. Nothing turned up. I'm telling you, the guy's clean. Just like his taxes."

As Danny droned on, Henry crossed to the center of the lawn and looked back at his house. His reflection in the sliding glass door was blurry, and all he could see was his face and his bare legs up to the thighs. Taking a step closer, he admired his lean torso, proud of the many hours he'd spent working out at the gym. On the other side of the house, he could hear neighborhood children playing in the street.

"You still haven't answered my question," Danny said.

"What question's that?"

"What *happened* to you? You used to live for that department. Is this some kind of fucked-up midlife crisis? Because if it is, let me know, and I'll tell Barry Baker to keep your spot open for another six months."

Henry sat cross-legged on the lawn, still staring at his reflection in the glass door. Beyond the fence, the neighborhood sounds continued: high-school girls chattering like birds on their way home from school; a car radio blaring pittery-pattery dance music, then fading mercifully down the street; Julie Watson sliding her minivan door open, calling to her kids to help out with the groceries.

Henry answered Danny with another question. "Have you ever felt like a bit player in someone else's movie?"

"All the time, my friend. It's called having kids. You get used to it—or if you don't, you should."

"I guess it's hard to explain. I just wanted to try some new things. I feel like I know myself too well, if that makes any sense."

"Not really, but that's okay. Just make sure to monitor your investments strictly from now on. You don't realize how much you're spending until the money stops coming in."

"Sage advice."

"Don't be sarcastic. I'm only trying to help out."

Henry stretched out on his back and kept his eyes closed to the sun. Just within his range of hearing, Julie Watson was poking around her own backyard as her two kids chased each other in and out of the house. Every five seconds, the screen door swung open, then slammed shut.

"Sounds like Kate's home," Henry lied. "I've gotta go. Keep in touch, all right?"

"Sure. We'll do Applebee's sometime."

Henry said goodbye, set down the phone and rested his arms

at his sides. A breeze blew across his body, and his skin prickled with the nearness of Julie Watson on the other side of the fence.

Now I get it, he thought. *Now I understand.*

Raising up on his elbows, he took firm hold of his hard-on and—quick, before she goes indoors!—cranked off under the hot October sun.

2

After such a busy summer, the start of autumn signaled a welcome return to normal. For Marlene, this meant getting a job at
the Providence Place Mall, where she worked three days a week
as a salesclerk at Zales Jewelers. The store was run by a family of
Lebanese merchants who'd hired her on a probationary basis,
given her criminal record. These days, Marlene felt like she was
on probation everywhere, which was fine with her. Nothing
wrong with hanging out in purgatory for a while.

As a new hire, Marlene was expected to work the worst shifts,
with the least chance of earning a decent commission. This, too,
she accepted. The women from the store were kind to her, albeit
in a reserved, territorial way. On Wednesdays, she and three
other clerks went to lunch at the food court in the mall, where
they ordered salads and Diet Cokes and talked about their lives
outside of work. Marlene rarely said anything except in response
to the most direct questions. When asked about her husband,
she would say, "He's a writer," and leave it at that.

While she was at work, Stuart used the time alone to catch up
on some reading. He'd been neglecting this lately, a symptom of
his general funk. If he couldn't write, then at least he could read,

which might lead to something down the road. He read Jerzy Kosinski, John Updike, Henry Green, John Kennedy Toole. He'd forgotten how to recognize a really fine piece of fiction, but once he'd become reacquainted with the authors on his shelves— Richard Yates, Graham Greene, Malcolm Lowry—he began to see the point in writing again.

As for the Independence Project, the Kmart finally closed its doors in late July, and Pike went back to leading a quieter life, spending most of his time in North Conway and visiting Providence only to keep the occasional dinner date. Though his friends didn't see much of him anymore, he remained a frequent subject of speculation. The city seemed grayer and smaller, less dynamic without him.

Heath and Allison broke up right before he went to L.A. to work on his first feature-length film for Miramax. Ever since fragments of his *Independence Project* movie began to circulate online—first as transcripts, then as downloadable video clips— his following had grown exponentially until it encompassed a sizable swath of the eighteen-to-thirty age bracket, a demographic known for its willingness to embrace any passing fancy, no matter how shallow or derivative. No one complained that the content of the material was severely lacking or that the video quality was minimal at best. Heath was young, cool and reasonably well connected, thanks to his friend and sometimes angel, Nathaniel Pike. The very fact that he had nothing to offer made him even more attractive from a marketing point of view.

Celia Shriver, Alice Shepperton and Cathy Diego found new causes to champion as the year wore on. Cathy scaled back to part time at the NHPIRG, while Alice battled a misdemeanor charge stemming from a traffic violation in August. Closer to home, Celia enrolled in a Bikram yoga class that kept her in Tiverton three afternoons a week. Even more than spring, autumn was a time of new beginnings.

One day in early fall, Stuart got a call from Gregg Reese asking him to come over for a visit. Gregg was reluctant to state his business over the phone, but Stuart agreed to meet with him. Gregg wasn't the sort of person Stuart heard from on any regular basis, so the call was especially intriguing.

Stuart arrived at the Reese house dressed in casual work clothes: brown loafers, a pair of khakis, an off-the-rack sports jacket and a blue oxford shirt, open at the neck. In his jacket pocket was a wadded-up tie, which he'd decided against at the last minute. Driving across town, he felt like he was going to a job interview.

Gregg was alone when he led him into his large, Tudor-style house and to a sunroom that overlooked the backyard. Like Stuart, he was wearing a sports jacket and an oxford shirt unbuttoned at the neck.

"You look like you've been on vacation," Stuart said, observing Gregg's sunburn, which had started to peel on his nose.

"Yes, I was just down in Florida with . . . friends of the family. Would you like something to drink?"

Stuart had learned never to say no to free booze, so he nodded and asked for whatever was easy.

"I'll get us both a beer," Gregg said, and hurried off to the kitchen. While he was gone, Stuart noticed a copy of *My Private Apocalypse* sitting on a table next to a wicker settee. Gregg's reading glasses were on top of the book, and a scrap from a newspaper marked his place about halfway through. The temptation to pick up the book tugged at Stuart's heart, but he resisted it.

Gregg returned with two bottles of Sam Adams. Before handing one to Stuart, he lowered his head and assumed a more casual tone. "Yes, as I was saying, I was in Florida with a man I've been seeing."

"Great," Stuart replied, not in the least bit surprised. Funny of Gregg to think it wasn't obvious he was gay.

Gregg looked relieved. "Cheers," he said and gave Stuart a beer. They both took long swigs from the bottles. Stuart could tell that Gregg wasn't a regular beer drinker by the inexpert way he held the bottle by the neck.

"I've been reading your novel," Gregg said and went over to get the book. Stuart felt a surge of dread as he tilted the book to let the reading glasses slide off. "My daughter left it here when she moved out of the house."

"Oh? Where's she now?" Stuart asked, grateful for the chance to talk about something else.

Gregg kept his eyes on the book, which to Stuart looked thin and ordinary. "Allison has her own apartment in Downcity. It's a very nice loft—perfect for her, really. She moved there right after Heath went out to California." His attention shifted to a framed photograph of her. He sighed. "Anyway, she's gone."

"Does she like living on her own?" Stuart asked, picturing a messy bathroom, pizza boxes stacked up in the hallway, dirty dishes in the sink, shoes and underwear piled on the living room floor. Much like his own apartment when he was her age.

Gregg chuckled. "Who knows? I never see her anymore. Her grandmother left her a lot of money when she passed away. I assume she's saving some of it." He went back to the book. "This is quite a remarkable accomplishment, Stuart. Based on your own experiences, yes?"

Stuart took another sip of beer. "Yeah, some," he said.

Gregg hadn't expected such a curt response, and he wondered if he'd said something to offend Stuart. "I suppose that's okay sometimes. To embellish, to stretch the truth a little."

"What do you mean?" Stuart asked.

"Well, just that . . . it happens all the time, doesn't it? The stories we tell about our families. It's all pretty much myth to begin with. For example, the character of the father in your book. I'm sure your own father wasn't really like that. There might've been some shade of truth to it, but the rest is just made up, isn't it?"

Stuart wasn't sure how much he wanted to go into this with Gregg. "Actually, whenever I try writing about my father, I usually wind up writing about my mother, and whenever I try writing about my mother, I wind up writing about my father." Now why did I say that, he wondered. Is it true, and maybe I'm just now realizing it for the first time?

Outside, a commercial jet began its descent into T. F. Green. Engine noise trailed after it, sounding faint through the windows. In Rhode Island, *everyone* lived near the airport.

"I'd like to write a book someday," Gregg said. "There's a small publisher in Boston that keeps asking me to write my memoirs, though I can't imagine anyone outside of Rhode Island would be interested." He was approaching his subject cautiously, and Stuart began to suspect a hidden motive. "I suppose if I *were* to write a book, I'd need some help."

"Is this a business proposition?" Stuart asked.

Gregg gestured for him to sit down and did so himself. "If you like. You wouldn't have to do much research. In fact, you wouldn't have to do any research at all."

Looking down at his beer, Stuart saw he'd already drunk half of it. *Pace yourself,* he thought. *You want to be sober tonight for Marlene.*

"Our family's always been a little sketchy on its history," Gregg explained. "Go back two, three hundred years, and you're pretty much relying on hearsay. No one really knows what the Reeses were up to before the nineteenth century. My mother always insisted it was a family of lawyers, but we could've been anything—sailors, craftsmen, spies. We could've been slave traders, for all I know. In fact"—he snapped his fingers—"I like that. We could use that for our book."

"You're kidding, right?" Stuart asked.

"Not at all. A little creative license never hurt anyone. Besides, it makes sense. All this money had to come from *somewhere*, you know." Gregg frowned at the elaborate furnishings in the room: the set of mahogany shelves his father had bought at auction back in the sixties; the hand-painted ceramic lamp his mother had brought back from a trip to Portugal; several large paintings in ornate, gilded frames. His face looked aged, sad, bitter, eager, excited and vengeful—all at once. "I want people to know the *real* Reese family, Stuart, even if it's not precisely real. That's what this book should be about—*my* reality. I can't keep living like the pope or . . ."

"Mother Teresa?"

"That's right. I can't keep living like that. The reality is that we've all got blood on our hands, including me and you. You can have all the best intentions in the world, but you have to know—you *have* to know, Stuart—that you're still guilty of something. And the better your intentions, the more guilty you are."

"Why's that?"

"Because you're lying. Some people never stop lying until the day they die, and I don't want to be one of them. I'm tired of the parties and the fund-raisers and the public service announcements. I'm tired of everyone admiring me and telling me how wonderful my parents were. I just want to be normal."

"And what's normal?"

Gregg began to rock in his chair. "I'll tell you what normal is. Having *flaws*. My mother didn't understand that. She refused to accept flaws in herself or me or anyone else for that matter. Isn't that crazy?" He laughed, and Stuart, feeling uncomfortable, laughed, too. "I just want some peace. I want some peace for myself."

As he listened, Stuart wondered why Gregg had chosen to open up to *him*, of all people. "I'm still not certain what you're trying to accomplish by writing this . . . book of yours. It's not going to do much for your reputation."

Gregg brought his beer to his lips but didn't drink. "That's the point. Picture the worst thing imaginable, something utterly depraved and appalling. Now *that's* what I want people to think of when they hear the name Reese. Not the Gregg Reese School for the Developmentally Challenged or the Gregg Reese Center for the Visual Arts. You get it?"

"I think so," Stuart said, though he really didn't.

"That's the thing about me, Stuart, which you probably don't understand, but you should. *Everyone* should understand it. All I am is me. I don't want to slink around anymore."

"Slink around?"

"That's right. And that's for Allison's sake, too. We all need to get back to being real people."

Stuart looked away. For all of Gregg's complaints about his public image, Stuart had a hard time sympathizing with him. What reputation did Marlene have except as a freak show on page eight of the *Providence Journal*? There were worse things in the world than having people think well of you. "I've never actually ghostwritten anything before," he said. "I have a hard enough time writing as Stuart Breen, let alone as someone else."

"Oh, you'll do fine. This my last act of philanthropy, Stuart, so let's make it a good one. All my life, I've always had to make other people happy. My mother, Renee, even Allison. I want to make myself happy now."

"And *this* will make you happy?"

"Being alive makes me happy, and this makes me feel alive."

Stuart didn't want to spoil his good mood but said, "Well, I'll be honest with you. There's not going to be much support for the Reese Foundation once a book like this comes out."

Gregg smiled. "It's not called the Reese Foundation anymore. Starting next year, we're calling it the People's Foundation. Celia

Shriver's taking it over." He winked. "Don't tell anyone you heard it from me."

After some more talk about Celia, Allison, the book—whatever was on Gregg's mind—it was time for another beer, so they went into the kitchen and pulled a couple of Sam Adamses from the refrigerator.

"Let's drink them out of frosty mugs," Gregg said. He opened the freezer door and brought out two glass mugs that frosted up once he set them on the counter. Inside the freezer, he'd left room for the turkey he'd already ordered at the butcher's. Thanksgiving was Gregg's favorite holiday, and he liked preparing for it early. Last November, he'd had Allison and Heath over for dinner, and he hoped she'd want to do it again this year. He wanted to introduce her to Donald Kress, the man he'd been dating since August.

Gregg poured their beers and handed Stuart a mug. "It's been one hell of a year, hasn't it?"

"Yep," Stuart said, tasting his beer.

"I'm excited about this book. Are you?"

Stuart nodded, and a trace of his old irritation returned. What do you expect me to say? No?

"Don thinks I'm crazy. Don—that's my friend. He's a worrier. I told him, I've done enough worrying. I'm trying to be less cautious these days."

They took their drinks into the sunroom and nursed them for the next half hour. The beer made them both sleepy, until finally Gregg looked at his watch and said, "I need to change clothes. I'm meeting Don for dinner."

"Yep. I should see what the old woman's up to," Stuart said and set his empty mug down on the tile table next to his chair.

3

While some relationships floundered that summer, others flourished. Marlene continued to see Allison around town, most frequently at a bar and grill called Jake's near the hurricane barrier. Along with Carla Marshall, they went out once a week, usually for dinner at one of the restaurants on Thayer Street. Marlene enjoyed having such beautiful and vibrant friends, especially since having friends of any kind was something of a breakthrough for her. They were like Charlie's Angels together: the sexy one, the sweet one and the other one.

One night in mid-October, Allison suggested going to Paragon, a dimly lit eatery with a Eurotrash theme in the music and décor. Carla picked up Marlene and drove to Allison's loft in Downcity. She'd moved in a month ago but hadn't felt ready to receive visitors until now.

Outside the guarded entrance to the apartment building, Carla said to Marlene, "Lucky girl. I wish I had that kind of bread."

Marlene detected something not so nice in her tone of voice, but chose to keep quiet.

Allison had left word with the guard, so they proceeded to the elevator and took it to the eighth floor. Looking down at herself, Marlene saw a brown smudge of foundation on her blouse and hoped no one else would notice. All three ladies liked dressing up for dinner; they enjoyed the reactions of their waiters, who invariably became flustered at the sight of three pretty women in short skirts and heels. Marlene knew that most of this attention was for Carla and Allison, but she appreciated being included.

The elevator opened on a pale yellow corridor, and they followed Allison's directions to the second of only two doors on the floor. Allison answered the door before they could knock, as if she'd been watching for them through the peephole. "Sorry it's a mess," she said. "I just got back from Pottery Barn."

She led them into the loft, which wasn't a mess in the slightest. The walls were exposed brick, and huge windows gave panoramic views of the city: the illuminated statehouse, the Providence Place Mall and the rivers that divided the East Side from the financial district. Allison had put a lot of work into the place, and it showed. The main piece of furniture was a camel-colored suede sofa with a sisal rug underneath it. An iron spiral staircase rose like a corkscrew through the floor of the loft bedroom, which had a skylight and beamed ceilings. The kitchen was directly under the bedroom, with a long, continuous countertop of pink marble.

"Oh, it's beautiful!" Marlene exclaimed. She and Carla took turns giving Allison a hug and a kiss.

"Here, let's sit and have a glass of wine before we go," Allison said. "I'm sorry it's so cold. The landlord's supposed to fix the furnace tomorrow."

"Stop apologizing," Carla said. "The apartment's lovely. God, I can remember my first place after college. I lived in this dump with three other girls down in Bonnet Shores. What about you, Marlene?"

Marlene was still looking up at the high cathedral ceilings and didn't hear her. "Huh?"

"What was your first apartment after college like?"

"Oh." Marlene barely remembered it at all, except that she had to share the driveway with the woman on the second floor, and the broken screen door always used to snag her skirt on the way to work. She laughed. "Not like this."

Allison poured some wine, and once they'd all had a chance to get settled on the sofa, Carla brought out a baggy of pot. "Should we be bad tonight?" she asked.

Allison hesitated. She'd been clean and mostly sober for nearly four months—no coke, no weed and only two glasses of wine with dinner. Living more responsibly was the goal she pursued in lieu of having any others. "Sure, what the hell," she finally said, and Carla began rolling a joint on the glass coffee table. "It'll be fun," she said, "getting stoned while we're sitting here looking at the statehouse."

"Yeah, poor Buddy," Carla said. The city's mayor, Vincent "Buddy" Cianci, had recently been convicted in the Operation Plunderdome scandal and removed from office. Though many Rhode Islanders hated Cianci, an equal number loved him. He'd been mayor on and off since the seventies, and his leaving was bittersweet. The man who would most likely replace him in the November election was a Democrat and a homosexual. Allison wanted him to win.

Once Carla had finished rolling the joint, she held it up to the window and said, "Buddy, this one's for you." She handed the joint and a cigarette lighter to Allison. "Here, you take the first hit. It's your apartment."

Allison lit the joint and carefully brought it to her lips. The first, corrosive intake of smoke made her throat burn, and she coughed it back up.

"First time?" Carla laughed as the thick green smoke hovered over the sofa.

Allison tried to speak but couldn't. Swishing the smoke out of her eyes, she waited for the burning to die down, then croaked, "It just feels like it."

A second hit went down easier, so she passed the joint to Carla and picked up her wine. The Merlot tasted so good with the flavor of the smoke still in her mouth. "I love red wine and cigarettes," she mused.

After they'd finished the joint, they decided that it was a better idea to walk to dinner rather than drive back to Paragon on the East Side. Empire was nearby, but as it was more money than either Marlene or Carla had planned on spending, Allison offered to treat. Over their protests, she said, "Come on, you guys paid for dinner last week," which wasn't even true.

Empire stood on a busy corner in Downcity where patrons could watch well-dressed couples flocking into the Trinity Theater. The ladies arrived between seatings and were waited on by a sensational-looking Peruvian named Carlo. He and Carla shared a laugh over their similar-sounding names and made a point of saying to each other "Hi, Carlo," or "Hi, Carla," whenever he drifted past the table, until that became the joke of the evening.

With Carlo out of earshot, Carla whispered, "Ladies, that is the choicest piece of ass I've seen in a long time."

Marlene shakily reached for her third glass of wine. She'd had too much to drink at the apartment, and red wine usually went to her head. Without realizing what she was saying, she blurted, "*Bill's* got a nice ass."

Carla stared at her, then burst out laughing. "Oh, Marlene! The look on your face," she spluttered.

"What?" Marlene asked, leaning a little off-balance in her chair.

"Well, if you don't mind my saying," Carla said, "Stuart's got a nice ass, too."

It was Allison's turn to make a comment, but she didn't particularly feel like talking about Heath's ass. Her experience up in the mountains had changed her mind about a lot of things, men in particular. The biggest realization was that after five years of being sexually active, she'd never once had an orgasm. It wasn't a realization per se, more like a gradual awareness of what she'd always known to be true. The closest time was up on the mountain, a few days after Henry Savage had gone back to Washington, when she and Marlene were walking naked in the forest and took a nap together on an exposed shelf of rock, and once Allison was sure Marlene had fallen asleep, she lay on her side and touched herself until a golden shiver told her to stop. That, of course, was an extraordinary experience, something that could never be repeated.

After dinner, they decided to stop for a nightcap on Richmond Street. The Mira Bar was a gay club with a tiny dance floor, a DJ on a riser and multiple TV screens showing soft-core erotica—black-and-white videos of men kissing, caressing and giving each other hot-oil massages. Women liked coming to the Mira whenever they felt like dancing without being hit on by jerks. Allison, Carla and Marlene were in just that mood, so they showed their IDs at the door, paid for their drinks (the bartender knew Carla and charged her for only one) and took a seat on the balcony. Marlene had never been to the Mira before, and the sight of so many muscle-bound men in tank tops intimidated her.

As she and Carla chatted, Allison scanned the dance floor for anyone she might recognize. A few years ago, when she was still doing Ecstasy, she liked to stop off at the Mira before turning in for the night, but she was sure that most of those old friends had left Providence for New York or L.A.; it was that kind of crowd, always searching for something better to do. No one looked familiar until her gaze fell on a quiet spot near the front of the club. "Oh my God," she said and grabbed Carla's arm.

"What is it?" Carla asked.

"My father's here. I don't fucking believe it."

Gregg Reese was standing by the bar with another older gentlemen, whom Allison didn't recognize. They were waiting to pay for their drinks, which had just been served. Gregg had a bottle of beer, while his friend held a clear cocktail in a long, slender glass. The other man was tall enough to reach over the crowd and hand the bartender his money.

Allison stopped watching. "Fuck. What do I do?"

"Why don't you say hi?" Carla suggested. "It's really no big deal, honey. Your father's a grown man."

"I know, but it's like . . . *Eww.*" Allison would've left it at that, except for curiosity about her father's boyfriend. She'd heard rumors about his seeing someone but found it hard to believe; he'd always struck her as more celibate than actively gay. From one hundred feet away, the other man looked about Gregg's age, which was a good sign. At least he wasn't being taken advantage of by some young colt. "All right, what the hell," she sighed and got up from the table. Heading downstairs, she tried keeping her father in sight, even as the swirling, writhing bodies of the dancers crowded her on all sides. Soon she found herself tapping him on the shoulder. "Daddy?"

Gregg turned around. It took him a moment to recognize her in the darkness, then he smiled. "Honey! What are you doing here?"

Allison instantly regretted coming over. "Just hanging out with some friends. Marlene Breen's here, and Carla Marshall. I put dinner on the AmEx. I hope that's okay."

"Oh, sure, sure," Gregg remarked absently, then hooked his arm around the man standing next to him. "Allison, let me introduce you to a friend of mine, Donald Kress. Don, this is my daughter, Allison."

She nodded and said hello. Kress was an appealingly homely man with a white, neatly trimmed beard, cherry dimples and supple lips that looked stained with red wine. He and Gregg were wearing matching Polo shirts, the only difference being that Gregg also had on a blue blazer. Kress's suntanned arms were covered with liver spots.

"Delighted, my dear. I knew we'd meet, I just didn't know when." He spoke with a lilting southern accent that sounded almost maternal. Allison found him gentle, cheery and unpretentious.

"Did you two go out to dinner?" she asked.

"That would've been a good idea," Kress said. "I'm afraid that cookin' isn't my forte." To be funny, he pronounced "forte" wrong, with a silent *e*. "I thought we'd try a little Cajun tonight, but it wound up tasting like Chinese takeout."

He and Allison laughed, while Gregg smiled at him. "I thought it tasted fine," he said. "Sometimes it's nice just to eat at home."

"Yeah, if you're married to Craig Claiborne," Kress joked. "Allison, I understand you just flew the coop?"

Allison rolled her eyes. "Yeah. The place is still a mess, but I got lucky on the rent."

She described the apartment to Kress, who listened raptly, interjecting comments like, "Oh! I love exposed brick!" and "I would *kill* for pink marble in my kitchen." When she was finished, he said, "Well, it sounds absolutely delightful. We're gonna have to come over with a housewarmin' present one of these days."

"That sounds like your department," Gregg told him and

turned to Allison. "Don's an antiques dealer. He's got a shop on Wickenden."

"Really? What's it called?" she asked. By this point, she'd forgotten all about Marlene and Carla.

Kress said, "I call it 'Oh, This Old Thing?' It's kind of a silly name, but I think it suits what I'm doin'."

"Hey, I know that place! You're in the same block as Z-Bar." Giving Kress a closer look, she said, "I thought you looked familiar. I bought a wedding present from you once."

"That's Rhode Island for you. This state freaks me out sometimes. I tell myself, I never should've moved up from Georgia. But then"—clinging to Gregg's arm—"I never would've met this wonderful person."

The two men kissed, and Allison allowed herself to feel happy for both of them.

Breaking away from Gregg, Kress asked her, "Do you think it's safe to use the bathroom here? You know what they say— don't bend over!"

"I'm sure it's fine," Gregg said. "I've used it myself."

Kress handed his gin and tonic to Gregg, then walked flat-footedly through the crowd on the dance floor. "He's a nice man," Allison said.

Gregg glanced nervously toward the front door, then back at her. She could tell that her presence was upsetting him, and she wondered if she should just say "Nice seeing you" and go back to her friends.

Before she could decide, he said, "I'm glad to hear that the new place is working out. I miss you at home, though."

"I miss you, too, Daddy." Allison realized she really did miss him and didn't know why she hadn't seen him more often. In a matter of weeks, they'd gone from being father and daughter to being two adults leading separate lives. "Have you heard anything from Mr. Pike?" she asked.

He nodded. Since the summer, his contact with Pike had been sporadic, but at least they were talking to each other again. "He's getting married," Gregg said.

Allison stared. "To whom?"

"Sarah Cranberry. They're planning a quickie ceremony up in New Hampshire next month."

Having processed this information, all she could do was laugh. "Go figure."

"Yeah, go figure." He smiled to see her in a good mood. "Any word from Heath?"

References to Heath always made Allison feel like people were worrying about her, and she didn't want them to. "Yeah, he calls me every now and then. It sounds like he's having a great time in L.A."

"So, no hard feelings?"

"Nope. No hard feelings." Softly, she added, "Everyone's happy."

"That's good."

They ran out of things to say and waited quietly for Kress to return from the bathroom. Already, they felt more comfortable with Don as part of the group than without him. She could imagine all three of them spending time together—no pressure, no hang-ups, none of the uneasiness that had hampered her relationship with her dad in the past. After a year out of college, she'd learned not to expect too much from either herself or her parents but to embrace everything, especially the mysterious, the eccentric, the whimsical. Life was neither as serious nor as intimidating as she'd once thought. Life was about trying to smile as much as possible.

Gregg said, "Oh, before I forget, would you like to have Thanksgiving with Don and me?"

She answered immediately, "Yes, I'd love to."

He looked startled, as if he'd expected her to make up an

excuse and decline. "I thought you might want to be with your mother this year."

"Of course not. I want to be with you."

Rather than spoil the moment, he took a sip of Don's gin and tonic. "Oops, that's not my drink," he said.

His nervousness touched her. "Look, I should probably get back to Carla and Marlene."

"Yeah, I guess so." Gregg's hands were full, so he just leaned forward and gave her a kiss. "Good seeing you, honey."

Before she left him, she said, "By the way, tell Don I approve."

"I will," he said.

The next morning, she invited him to lunch, and they met at Steeple Street, a fairly run-of-the-mill sandwich place on the East Side. By coincidence, their waiter was the same Carlo from the night before. Recognizing her, he exclaimed, "Ai! You're not supposed to see me here!"

Allison laughed and said to her father, "That's Rhode Island for you."

4

Record of live web chat with film director Heath Baxter,
10/12/02, 16:04.33 PST.

WebModerator (**GS266**): Welcome to our forum with Heath
   Baxter, director of The Independence Project, who's in
   L.A. right now, working on a new feature for Miramax.
   Heath, thanx for being here.
HeathBaxter (**surfergrrl03**): Thanks for having me.
GS266: We've got 47 UIN logged in, so if you have a question
   for Heath, give us your nick, a /s /l, so Heath knows who
   he's talking to. K?
surfergrrl03: Sounds cool.
GS266: K
jillslut17: Heath! Sup Jill, 16 /f /Dallas Ft Worth area, wanted
   to know about the new project, r u almost done with it,
   heard u were working with Chloe Sevigny / Marilyn
   Manson / Nic Cage what's the deal and where can I get
   DVD copies of TIP 4-17??
surfergrrl03: Hi Jill. Don't know about DVDs, if there's

anything out there, I haven't seen it so take heed. Ummm, hard to type this fast. Nic Cage, no, M. Manson, unlikely, Chloe, no comment but stay tuned.

GS266: What about the new project if u could tell us just in general

surfergrrl03: Still working on the script. I like to know what I'm doing before I start working with actors, technical crew, etc. Obviously, TIP was different because we had like no budget, no permission to shoot etc so we had to make do. Studio backing really helps, and Miramax has been totally cool so that's cool.

GS266: And if u could give us an idea—story, characters, who's on the soundtrack thx

surfergrrl03: It's kind of hard to say cuz of the evolutionary nature of film, like I can't visualize the end result when I'm still meeting with cast members and that kind of preliminary sh*t. Like TIP was crazy that way.

GS266: Totally, but if u had to summarize it in one word or ten words, or like five words

surfergrrl03: Five words, I would say spiritual, religious, transcendental, pagan and f*cked up.

GS266: Good let's get another question

Progfan2000: Bill, 24 /m /Oakland, Heath I'm an independent filmmaker and I was wondering how u shot fragment 27b looks like the screen is tinted for night effect but there's lens flare in the upper right corner at 5:03.17, so I'm like what. Did u do that in post?

surfergrrl03: Bill, everything was in post cuz of time restrictions. I don't remember using any gradient tints during the shoot, so maybe what you're seeing isn't lens flare but a problem with your download.

GS266: I know what Bill's talking about. I thought it was lens flare too, and I was like whoa

surfergrrl03: Totally. I don't know, but I'm moving my site to a different server, so that should help to clear it up.

Progfan2000: Thx. BTW, have u heard of a prog-rock group from the 70s called Mirthrandir? Their awesome! Check out Grobschnitt, Gentle Giant, Wallenstein, Van Der Graaf Generator, Banco del Mutuo Soccorso, Area, P.F.M., Magma and Goblin—did the soundtracks to those Argento flicks.

surfergrrl03: Cool, I'll write 'em down.

GS266: Good new question

hafunny77: Heath wondering what you think about sudden fame sudden success for TIP and what advice for other artists.

GS266: hafunny77, let's have your name, a /s /l.

hafunny77: 34 / m / Orlando, Kevin

surfergrrl03: Thanks Kevin. I guess I feel cool about everything. I miss a lot of my old friends from back east. Just been so busy. My advice is to stay focused on what you want to do and not worry so much about the business side of things, like with TIP I made with no studio support no professional actors just some friends working on weekends, and that's true of writers, filmmakers, visual artists, whatever, sometimes its easier to focus and stay true to yourself when there's no expectations or pressure from the outside.

GS266: Good advice. Let's hear from someone else

Oluckyman01: BAXTER YOU SUCK FUCKING ASSHOLE NO TALENT HOW PEOPLE LIKE YOU MAKE IT BLOWS MY MIND TOTAL HYPE I SHUDDER TO THINK WHAT YOUR SHIT'S GOING TO LOOK LIKE PROBABLY SOME WHINY GEN-X BULLSHIT LIKE LINKLATER OR WHATEVER YEAH I CAN USE A SUPER 8 TOO I CAN TAKE HOME MOVIES TOO DOESN'T MEAN THAT I HAVE ANYTHING

MEANINGFUL OR RELEVANT TO SAY ALL THIS IS
JUST CORPORATE BULLSHIT PEOPLE NEED TO JUST
CHILL AND REALIZE THEY BEEN HAD
GS266: Oluckyman01 is banned. Let's move on
pretty_princess: Hi Heath, my name's Kelly 20 /f / I live near
Phoenix but hopefully moving to L.A. this spring. I was
wondering if u had a g/f and if not if u wanted to hang out
sometime. My favorite TIP downloads are f-4a and f-19a b/c
you're in it. Why don't u do more acting? xoxoxoxoxox ☺
surfergrrl03: Thanks Kelly. First let me answer the other
question from the person who didn't give his or her name.
I'm sorry if you don't like my work, and I can understand if
you think that everything is corporate or orchestrated or
overhyped, because in a sense that's true. But the fact is that I
struggled hard to get where I am, and I'm not going to give it
up just because some people think things are bullsh*t.
GS266: Cool point taken
surfergrrl03: And as far as my own work goes, I'm not
hurting anyone, nor am I stealing chances from other
artists who want to be in the same position. I'm just trying
to make something lasting and beautiful.
GS266: word and then Kelly had a question
surfergrrl03: Right I'm sorry. Hi Kelly. Yeah I'd love to hang
out sometime—whisper to me later. No girlfriend at the
moment. I was seeing someone before I moved to Cali, but
couldn't make it work out.
GS266: that sucks
surfergrrl03: you know whatever. But right now, I'm so focused
on what I'm doing, and getting my script together, that
maybe I just need to do that and nothing else for awhile.
GS266: Any more questions for Heath?
surfergrrl03: That a**hole must've scared people away. Is
Kelly still out there?

aceventura782: Hi Heath I read on tipchat that there's an alternate version of f-44a/b that has better resolution and a different ending, six seconds longer or something. Please comment on that, and also comment on whether you're going to release another batch of frags before the feature comes out, and also if f-81b still exists in the vault, and if so when do we get to see it?

GS266: Ace, you sound pretty hardcore How bout your name a /s /l? thx

aceventura782: Rick 15 /m /Newton Mass

surfergrrl03: Thanks Rick. First things first, don't expect to see the full-length until winter '04 at the earliest, maybe even spring or later. As far as alternate versions go, I don't know about the specific one that you mentioned, but as I've said before, the vault's already been cleaned out, so unless someone's got a fifth generation dub, which I highly doubt, that stuff's gone for good. Sorry! ☹

GS266: Cool maybe u could talk about how you're coping with L.A. and like how different it is from the New York scene and sh*t.

surfergrrl03: Well, I'm not from New York, but I know what you mean, the whole east coast west coast thing. My friend Brian and I talk about once a week, and it really helps to keep me grounded.

GS266: Brian the beach boys dood

surfergrrl03: That's right. Sometimes I feel like he's my only real friend out here, not that I haven't met a bunch of cool people, because I have, like Michael Moore and John Singleton. But I think that Brian understands me in a way that's different, you know, like he's been talking to me since I was a kid.

GS266: Totally I feel the same way about Todd Rundgren

pretty_princess: Hi Heath it's Kelly again, sorry, I was afk I saw what u wrote about me—that's so sweet! Like u were thinking about me and stuff.

GS266 Kelly do you have a ?

pretty_princess: Not really just that I'm probably going to be in L.A. for Thanksgiving, so we should get together—do u like Ethiopian food? I know the joke is that there's no Ethiopian food cuz Ethiopians don't have any food, but it's actually really good!

surfergrrl03: K Hold up and we'll go private.

GS266: If there's no other questions, Heath maybe u could wrap it up with a few last words, like something inspirational or whatever. But make it quick, k? thx

surfergrrl03: I guess I would say that you shouldn't worry so much if you don't know what you're doing, cuz that's actually a good thing. Don't make plans—I mean it's okay to make them, but don't adhere to them too closely, you know? And read a lot and listen to interesting music and watch a lot of interesting movies. That's it.

pretty_princess: Hi Heath it's Kelly again. I think that's so sad what u wrote about not having any friends in L.A. U shouldn't say bad things about yourself, k? I don't have any friends here in Phoenix either.

surfergrrl03: Sorry to hear that.

GS266: Yeah we all are Heath thanks for coming

surfergrrl03: Thank you. It's been fun.

GS266: Spring '03 for the new material? That's awesome

surfergrrl03: Nope, like I said, it's going to be early '04, maybe even the summer, but definitely sometime soon.

GS266: Looking forward to it

surfergrrl03: yep it's gonna be beautiful

END OF SESSION

5

One night in late October, Marlene came home from her shift at Zales and found Stuart still working in his office. The lights were off in every other room of the house, and the only sounds were the hum of Stuart's computer and some nondescript jazz on the radio.

His back was to her when she came into the room. "My head is throbbing," he said. "Do you mind if we order a pizza tonight? I'm too tired to cook."

She stepped out of her shoes and left them by the door. "No, that's fine. Wanna see my new bracelet?" she asked. With the commission that she'd earned that day, she'd treated herself to a sixty-dollar bracelet, which she thought looked sexy around her ankle.

He turned away from the computer and glanced at her hands. "Where is it?" he asked.

She pointed down at her right foot. "There. It's an ankle bracelet."

He admired it as one might admire a child's drawing. "Nice, but you've got it on the wrong foot."

"I do?"

"You're supposed to wear it around your left ankle."

"Really? Why?"

"Because you're married."

"I don't think so, Stuart. I don't think it works like that."

He shrugged. "Okay. Fair enough."

She didn't want him to be unhappy, so she bent down and took off the bracelet. "No, I'm sure you're right. Here, I'll just fix it," she said, transferring it to her left foot. She stood back up. "There—better?"

"It's fine either way, Marlene. You didn't have to change it for my sake."

She smiled uncertainly and put her arms around him. The tension in his neck and shoulders failed to melt under her caress.

"Have a good day?" he asked.

"Pretty good. I sold an engagement ring. This poor kid was going to give it to his high-school girlfriend."

"Why does that make him a poor kid?" he asked.

Boy, she thought, *he's not letting me get away with anything.* "No reason, just . . . he was sweet. How about you?"

"What?"

"Did you have a good day?"

He slouched and put his head in his hands. The computer screen in front of him was filled with words, and she wondered how long he'd been staring at the same sentence.

He sat up suddenly and pointed an angry finger at the screen. "Listen to this and tell me which version you like better." Reading from the screen, he said, " 'After Joseph's death in 1733, Nancy became even more promiscuous and eventually took one of her own offspring to bed.' *Or:* 'Nancy became even more promiscuous after Joseph's death in 1733, and eventually took one of her own offspring to bed.' "

Marlene closed her eyes tightly. "I can't tell the difference, hon."

"Fuck. Goddamn it. This is driving me crazy."

She sighed, disappointed to find him in such an edgy mood. Her plan for the evening had involved a glass of wine, a stack of catalogs and maybe a nice foot massage. No spot quizzes. All in all, she preferred her husband when he wasn't working.

"Anyway, I'm going to have some wine," she said. "Do you want anything?"

She'd turned away when he said, "I'm sorry, hon. I'm still in work mode right now, that's all. I'll be done in five minutes."

"That's okay. Take your time." Picking up her shoes, she went into the bedroom and stripped off her clothes. Once she'd undressed, she opened the closet and put on a pair of jeans and a T-shirt. Being naked was now a temporary, transitional state, like passing through a room without lingering there.

Downstairs in the kitchen, she poured herself a glass of wine and sat down to read the paper. Stuart joined her fifteen minutes later. His hair looked a mess, like he'd been pulling at it all day.

"What do you want to do tonight?" she asked. Thus far, pretty much all she'd seen of him was the back of his head.

He stood at the refrigerator, scanning the shelves for a beer. "I don't know. What do you want to do?" Reaching for his beer, he unscrewed the bottle cap and slumped over to the table, where he dropped into the chair across from her.

"Maybe we could take a bath together after dinner," she suggested.

"A bath."

"There's some champagne in the basement, I think."

He finally rewarded her with a smile. "What's the celebration for?" he asked.

She took his free hand, the one that wasn't holding the beer. "Just because I love you," she said.

He laughed, though his heart wasn't into it. They'd had days like this before—days when neither one of them felt like talking—but there was always the awareness that they *ought* to be talking, ought to be trying harder. Stuart didn't seem to have that awareness anymore.

They ordered a pizza, ate in front of the TV, then made waves toward going upstairs. Marlene offered to draw their bathwater, but Stuart abruptly decided not to join her. "I don't think I'd be much fun tonight," he apologized.

"That's okay, honey. It was just an idea." She stood and kissed him gently on the cheek. "I think I'm going to have a quick soak anyway. I still feel sticky from work."

Once upstairs, she decided to take a shower instead of a bath. With her hair in a wet tangle and the water streaming down her face, she looked as miserable as she felt.

Later, in bed, she asked him if he still found her attractive. "Of course I do," he said.

"Because *I* do," she replied hotly.

He modestly lowered his eyes. "Thanks."

"No, I mean me. *Me.* I think *I'm* attractive. I've never felt attractive before, but I do now. I've lost six pounds this month, Stuart. That's a real accomplishment. I'm actually *proud* of myself, you know?"

He felt like she was goading him into having sex. "You've always been attractive to me. I've told you that." To prove his point, he willed himself to get an erection but couldn't sustain it for more than a few minutes. When he pulled out of her, the condom that they'd been using stayed inside, like a crumpled-up, defeated version of himself.

The next morning, he woke up early to get a jump on the

pages he wanted to finish that day. Marlene generally slept until nine, so he was careful not to wake her. Going into the kitchen, he started the coffee and sat down to browse through the over-eighteen listings in the *Providence Phoenix*. One ad called for a personal foot slave, while another, posted by an over-weight black woman, sought an effeminate white man to wear her clothes and masturbate on demand. Reading the listings aroused him, and he wondered why he was continually drawn to the dark side of sexuality. In his mind, sexuality *was* dark, or maybe only his personal experiences of it were. He'd never had the kind of sexual experience that made him feel lighter inside.

He worked from eight to eleven, taking breaks only to go downstairs for more coffee. The memoir that he'd been working on for Gregg Reese was a patchwork of rumors, history and out-and-out fabrications. Some of the material had come from notes Gregg had provided, while some he'd made up on his own. Some even derived from sources who weren't directly related to the Reeses, such as Sarah Cranberry, who'd divulged much of her family's history to Stuart during those cold nights in New Hampshire. It was fun to distort the truth, Stuart thought, rather than having to invent a story from scratch. Gregg encouraged these flights of fancy, no matter how strange or incongruous. It didn't matter to him, for example, that the Reeses were originally from South County while the Cranberrys were from the East Bay. Everything belonged in the book.

At noon, when Marlene left to pick up something for lunch, Stuart went into the bathroom and jerked off. His body was filled with nervous energy from writing all morning, and he needed some quick relief. Asking Marlene for sex would've taken too much time out of his day.

She could read the guilt on his face when she returned. "Did you jerk off while I was gone?" she asked.

He reacted indignantly. "What are you talking about?"

"Nothing, it's just that your face is all red, and your hair's messed up. You look like you've been jerking off." She set two deli sandwiches down on the kitchen table. "I don't mind, Stuart. You're free to do whatever you want."

He laughed to hide his embarrassment. "Well, I *didn't,* okay? As a matter of fact, I've been working on this fucking Reese book all morning."

"I was just asking. Don't get mad, eat your sandwich."

Stuart wasn't hungry. "Why did you say that just now?"

"No reason. I was just making an observation."

She pushed one of the sandwiches toward him, but he pushed it back. "Some observation. That's like saying, 'Hey, did you just take a shit?' "

Marlene calmly unwrapped her sandwich. "We're married, Stuart. We're allowed to be open with each other."

Rather than argue with her, he reached for his lunch. A few bites into his sandwich, he asked, "So what are you up to this afternoon?"

"I don't have any plans. Don't worry, I'll stay out of your hair."

This response didn't invite further conversation, so he said nothing and wolfed down the rest of his food.

After lunch, he went back up to his office and polished off half a dozen pages of the Reese book. When he came downstairs, he found a note from Marlene saying she was walking to Acme Video to rent some movies. Acme was a small, independent store that specialized in rare, imported and art-house films of the sort that people like Heath Baxter liked to watch.

When she got back, she said, "I'm having dinner with the girls tonight, so I picked up a few extra videos in case you got bored. What's the name of the actor that you like so much?"

He shook his head. Marlene was always asking him questions that were so vague he often couldn't guess what she was talking about. "I like a lot of actors. I like Malcolm McDowell," he said.

"No, that Polish guy—the one with the bug eyes."

"Oh, Klaus Kinski."

She brightened. "That's it. The man at Acme helped me pick a couple out. I couldn't remember what the actor's name was. I kept saying, 'Bug eyes, bug eyes.' "

"Yeah, well, those guys at Acme know everything." Stuart walked over to the table, where she'd set the videotapes. He'd already seen both of the films, *Fitzcarraldo* and *Aguirre, the Wrath of God*. He wondered what movies he would've chosen for her but then realized he had no idea. *I don't know what she likes*, he thought. *I don't know anything about her.*

Setting the cassettes down, he said, "I didn't know you were going out tonight."

"It's my regular night, Stuart. Do you want me not to go?"

"Oh, no, have fun. I'll just miss you, that's all."

"Are you sure? Because I can cancel."

He put his hands on her shoulders. "Marlene, relax. I'm not going to run away. I'll still be here when you get home."

They had some time to kill, so they had a glass of wine in the living room while waiting for Carla to pick her up. A compact disc played softly in the background, part of a classical music sampler Marlene had bought at the mall.

"I was just thinking," she said, "why don't we move out of town? There's no reason for us to stay here anymore. You can write wherever you want, and I can always do . . . something."

"Where would we go?" he asked.

"I don't know. Maybe Connecticut?"

"If we're going to move to Connecticut, we might as well

stay in Rhode Island," he said. This logic made no sense to him, but he didn't care. "What brought this on? Aren't you happy here?"

"*You're* not, Stuart. You're not happy. You're not happy with me, and you're not happy with yourself. I've made you unhappy."

She became teary eyed, and he put his arms around her. "Honey, I thought we were over this. What can I say? I'm happy enough. This is as happy as I'm going to be."

She knew she was annoying him, so she made herself stop crying. "You're right. Anyway, Carla will be here soon. I should do my makeup."

He took her arm and pulled her back down on the sofa. "Wait a minute. Don't just run off like that. I don't get it, Marlene. You seem perfectly fine all day, and then you're a wreck."

"I'm trying, Stuart."

"What do you mean, you're trying?"

"I'm trying, that's all." His grip loosened on her, and she stood up. Dabbing at her eyes, she said, "Don't worry about me. I'm just being a silly woman."

She went off to finish getting ready, and Stuart turned up the volume on the music just as the final, decisive chord of a symphony erupted. He wasn't sophisticated enough to know who the composer was, nor did he particularly care.

Carla came round at six, and Marlene left with many promises not to stay out past eleven. Stuart spent the first hour trying to watch *Fitzcarraldo* but couldn't concentrate. His conversation with Marlene had put him in an unsettled frame of mind. Going to the stereo, he read the composer's name from the back of the CD case: *Robert Schumann.* The name of the CD was *15 Romantic Favorites,* and the picture on the cover showed a couple nuzzling in front of a seaside sunset and toasting each other with flutes of champagne. Their silhouetted profiles were perfect complements to each other. This was what Marlene thought about, he realized, when she thought about love.

Later that night, he greeted her naked at the door, led her upstairs to their bedroom and—ignoring the fact that she'd had a bit too much wine with dinner—undressed her, laid her down in the sheets and made love to her.

6

Pike and Sarah were married in North Conway on the first Saturday in November. Among the guests were Stuart and Marlene Breen, Allison Reese and Heath Baxter, who'd flown in from California. Allison's mother, Renee, was delighted to hear about the wedding and came over from London. Only Gregg couldn't make it, but he sent his regrets along with a case of expensive French wine.

A hastily arranged ceremony took place in the meadow behind the ski lodge, where a stage was set up for a band to perform after the exchange of vows. The day was sunny and brisk; in another week, the first light snows of the season would be falling on the summits.

Pike got dressed in one of the guest cabins, while Sarah and her attendants made themselves ready in the master bedroom. When Heath arrived in his rental car, a caterer informed him that Pike wanted to see him before the service. Heath followed his directions to the cabin where the groom was combing his hair and nursing a watered-down Scotch.

Pike shook Heath's hand and pulled him in for a bear hug. "How's California treating you?"

Heath winced, still feeling self-conscious about his L.A. tan. "Oh, it's okay. It's been really hectic out there."

"I thought Californians were supposed to be laid back."

"That's what I thought, too."

Pike smiled at his protégé. "You don't have any regrets, do you?"

"No." Heath looked away. On the floor was a suitcase Pike had already packed for his honeymoon. Heath yawned. "I'm sorry, being on a plane always makes me sleepy," he said.

"Not me. I love flying. Do you know what I love the most about it? Getting drunk. There's nothing like a stiff Bloody Mary at thirty-eight thousand feet." Pike finished combing his hair, then dropped the comb in his suitcase. "Sarah and I are going to Bermuda for our honeymoon. Have you ever been?"

Heath shook his head.

"You should. You need to get out more, Heath. Do some traveling."

"Where would I go?"

"Anywhere! Throw a dart at the map, I'll pay for the tickets." Turning to a mirror on the wall, Pike began to knot his tie. "Of course you probably don't need my money anymore, Mr. Big-shot Hollywood Director." He laughed. "I'm just kidding. We're all proud of you back home." Catching Heath's eye in the mirror, he said, "Allison's here, you know."

"I know."

"Are you going to have a problem with that?"

Heath shrugged. "No."

"Good. I want everyone to be happy. Life's too fuckin' short." The knot fell apart in his fingers, and he started over. "You know, I always wished that you two had stayed together."

It seemed an unlikely thing for Pike to say. "Why's that?" Heath asked.

"Oh, no reason. I guess I'm just in a romantic mood today."

Pike's Folly

After Pike had finished getting dressed, he and Heath joined the other guests behind the ski lodge. The decorations that Sarah had picked out were lavish, with a thousand blue and white garlands hanging like vines from a yellow tent that extended the length of the meadow. Five rows of folding chairs faced the stage, whose curtains were drawn to hide the band's equipment.

Pike spotted Marlene and Stuart in the crowd of guests and walked over to greet them. Stuart looked much the same, but Marlene was nearly unrecognizable. She'd lost some weight—not too much, just enough to accentuate her natural shape, which was appealingly plump. Her black hair, worn short in the spring, now fell to her shoulders, giving her a more youthful, less severe appearance. In addition, someone had taught her about makeup. Gone were the days of heavy rouge and silver-blue eye shadow. For the first time, Pike could see her face.

"Marlene, you look sensational," he said, kissing her hand. "You make me want to move back to Rhode Island."

She blushed. She hadn't seen Pike since her trip to the mountains and still thought of him as a beautiful wizard of a man. "Thank you," she said.

"So you're staying in New Hampshire, then?" Stuart asked. His arm was around Marlene, and he seemed proud to show her off.

"We're not sure," Pike said. "We might hold on to the brownstone, in case we ever feel like driving down for the weekend. I like the pace up here. Nice and slow."

Stuart couldn't take this seriously. "Well, if you ever get bored, you can always go back to Mount Independence."

"Not anymore—I sold it." Marlene and Stuart stared as Pike explained, "Back to the government. Really, guys, I didn't need it anymore. I'd already had my fun with it."

Given all the hard work Nathaniel had put into the project, it seemed rash to just turn around and sell it. Ah, well, Stuart thought. On his wedding day, the man should be allowed to do whatever he wants.

Across the banquet area, Heath was talking to Allison, who'd driven up with the Breens. Though she and Heath had spoken on the phone recently, they hadn't actually seen each other in two months. He had expected to feel awkward around her and did. His only consolation was that he'd be back in L.A. in another forty-eight hours.

"Weddings always make me sad," she said. Her hair was done up in golden curls that left the back of her pale neck exposed. "I guess I don't like ceremonies. If I ever get married, I don't want a ceremony. We'll just fill out the paperwork and that's it."

Heath didn't want to think about her getting married. It was fine for them not to date anymore, but he hadn't yet reached the point where he could chat casually about it.

"We don't have to talk, you know," she said. "I think the service is about to start anyway."

On stage, in front of the curtain, a microphone was being set up for the justice of the peace, who'd just arrived and was looking for a place to leave his jacket.

Heath drew closer to Allison. "I think you'd really like L.A. I mean, not to *live* there but . . . well, you know what I mean."

"It sounds nice," she said dully. From her purse, she pulled out a pair of tortoiseshell sunglasses and put them on. "Right now, I'm happy being in Rhode Island. Did I tell you I met my father's boyfriend? We're having Thanksgiving dinner together." Twisting the knife a little, she asked, "Do you remember Thanksgiving last year?"

"Yeah."

What he remembered was spending the night at her father's

house, staying up late, drinking too much and, in the end, being too exhausted to have sex in her room, something they'd never done before (and now never would).

Allison laughed. "I just remember getting so high on that hash I brought down from Amherst."

"Yeah, that was pretty crazy."

"I was such a stoner back then."

"You were great," he said impulsively. "I liked everything about you."

Just in time, Pike joined them with a special guest. Heath felt silly meeting Renee Reese now, after breaking up with her daughter. She was a handsome blonde in her late forties— taller than Allison and with a habit of showing off her lean, equine profile. Her hair was pulled back in a tight bun, and her immaculate dress from Armani smelled hideously of cigarettes. She and Pike were holding hands.

"Pleased to meet you," she said in a clipped voice. "Shall we all sit together?"

"You three sit," Pike said. "I have work to do."

Renee pulled him down for a quick kiss. "Good luck, champ. Don't lose touch, okay?"

"I won't," he promised, and wrinkled his nose at her. "I always liked it when you called me that. Sarah calls me 'chief,' and you call me 'champ.' I've known some pretty neat women in my time."

Renee glanced sidelong at Allison, then back at Pike. "It's not us, it's you. There's nothing sexier than a man who knows what he wants."

This pleased him immensely. "Well, you knew me a long time ago," he said, and they both chuckled.

Before going, Pike asked Allison to wish him well. Slightly dazed, she said, "Congratulations. We'll be around for the reception."

"Good. That's the fun part, anyway. We always have fun together, don't we?"

The question puzzled her. "Sure we do," she said.

Beaming, he took her hand. "That's what I like to hear. I like to see you having a good time. Nothing wrong with that."

Renee added, "Now *there's* some good fatherly advice," then nipped off to find the bar.

An announcement from the stage called the guests to their seats, and the justice of the peace, an old acquaintance of Sarah's from North Conway, began the ceremony. They'd decided not to have a full wedding party, only a pair of flower girls for the bride. Elaborate wedding processionals had always struck Pike as dull and pretentious, and he preferred the focus to be on himself—and his wife, of course.

In place of the traditional wedding march, a loudspeaker played the classic seventies pop song "Make It with You" as Sarah stepped briskly down the aisle, preceded by her two attendants. She wore a white pantsuit that complimented her figure better than a conventional wedding dress. Allison recognized the flower girls as part-time workers from the ski lodge.

Sarah reached the front of the stage early, and she and Pike waited for the song to finish. As they stood together, he winked at her and whispered something that made her laugh. Those in the first two rows also laughed, even though they couldn't hear what he'd said. Then the music stopped, and the justice of the peace unfolded his speech.

Sitting next to Heath, Allison said, "Sarah looks big enough to kick Pike's ass," and they snickered together, drawing glances from the people around them.

When it got time for the couple to exchange their vows, Pike went first. His speech was predictably grandiose and dealt mostly with himself. Still, it sounded charming coming from him, and few people noticed that he'd referred to Sarah only once, and in the very last sentence. Her vows were more straightforward—I promise to love, honor, obey, etc. Both she and Pike fought hard not to crack up during the ordeal.

After the vows, Pike produced a ring from his jacket pocket and slipped it on her finger. The ring was encrusted with two-karat diamonds that outshone the chunky engagement ring he'd given her eight weeks ago. Together the two rings looked gaudy but somehow right for her hand.

The justice of the peace pronounced them husband and wife, and they gave each other a polite, chaste kiss. Once the applause had died down, Pike announced to his guests, "And now, Sarah and I would like you to stay for a special treat. This is dedicated to our good friend, Heath Baxter, who came all the way from California to be with us. Heath?" He searched for him in the crowd. "Come back home, buddy, okay? New England misses you."

Heath did his best not to look at Allison, whose presence he could feel close to him. At this point, all attention turned to the stage, where the curtain had opened to reveal an eight-piece band standing with their instruments. At the piano sat a large, pale man whose brown hair was neatly slicked to one side and whose clumsy hands were poised tentatively above the keyboard.

Heath took a closer look. "Shit! That's Brian!" he shouted.

Colored stage lights blossomed overhead, transforming the occasion from a wedding to a concert. The band's first number was "Love and Mercy" from Brian Wilson's 1988 solo album. Brian normally liked to end his shows with the tune, but this was a special gig, and he'd wanted to change things up a bit. Most of the audience didn't know the song and in fact didn't recognize the man on stage. It wasn't until later, after he'd sung a couple of Beach Boys warhorses, that they put two and two together.

The lyrics to "Love and Mercy," like those of so many Brian Wilson songs, were dopey and earnest, and Brian sang them slightly behind the beat, as if he couldn't quite remember them. With his Ray-Ban sunglasses and Hawaiian shirt, he looked like a performer in a karaoke contest and at times sounded like it too. He no longer used his upper register—the famous falsetto that had harmonized for years with his brothers Carl and Dennis, his cousin Mike, his friends Al and Bruce. Instead, his voice sounded gravelly, broken, human, frail. If his voice had once been an honest reflection of who he was in the sixties, this was an honest reflection of who he was now.

At the last chorus, Brian asked the audience to sing along, and while most people were still unfamiliar with the song, the chorus was simple enough for them to catch on. As Pike slow-danced on stage with his wife, the guests of his wedding joined the band in singing:

Love and Mercy, that's what you need tonight
So, love and mercy to you and your friends tonight

When the song ended, Brian launched the musicians into a tight rendition of "Be True to Your School," "Do It Again," "Surfin' U.S.A.," "Little Deuce Coupe," "409," "Fun, Fun, Fun," "I Get Around," "All Summer Long," "Surfer Girl," "Wouldn't It Be Nice," "California Girls," "Barbara Ann," "Good Vibrations," and, last, "God Only Knows." Closing out the show, he wished Pike and Sarah a happy life together, then followed his handler around the side of the piano and off the stage. And everyone went home with a smile.

Three days later, on election night in Rhode Island, the Allison Fund won a narrow victory, passing with 51 percent of the vote. In a crowded room on the first floor of the Biltmore Hotel in downtown Providence, an elated Gregg Reese gave a televised press conference, where he said, "There are so many people I have to mention. I'd particularly like to thank my wonderful daughter, Allison, who's stuck with me through a couple of hard years—thanks, hon. Also Celia Shriver, for her untiring commitment to the Reese Foundation. And my mother, Keeny Esther Reese, who is no longer with us, but whom we remember for her vision, her love of life and her leadership of the Reese Foundation for nearly four decades. Senators Chafee and Reed, and Representatives Kennedy and Langevin. And my good friend Donald Kress, and the many volunteers who helped make this possible—too many to name, but you know who you are. My deepest thanks. You have no idea what this means to me."

By 1760, development around the Great Swamp had increased to the point where few people could afford more than half a dozen acres for their crops and livestock. On the site where a Benny's Home and Auto Store now stands in South County—Summer Special, Goodyear Tires, Free Alignment—the shanties and cabins and homesteads were already crowding one another, as the duplex condos and public housing projects would later crowd the streets of Peace Dale, Kingston and Wakefield. A great change, something epochal and large scale, was imminent. In another fifteen years, Americans would unite to fight their British overlords and declare their belief in their own sovereignty and the equality of all men. The age of European imperialism was coming to an end.

By the time Sander Reese was old enough to take charge of the family business, it had become something of an anomaly in southern New England. His mother had left him with a considerable fortune and the means to sustain it, but Sander had no intention of following in her footsteps. Recognizing the changes taking place in the colonies, he sought to make his own contribution. How could a people who believed in brotherhood and equality condone the actions of the Reese family? In the name of democracy, a lasting change was in order. From now on, the Reeses would devote themselves to public charity rather than their own hideous, selfish pursuits. This was meet and right. This was American.

In the meantime, the problem of what to do with the slaves still on the property remained. Setting them free would've been unfair, as most of them lacked the skills to survive on their own. The quickest solution was to put an end to the poor girls' lives and make a fresh start from there.

And so on a stormy day in 1760, the thirty-seven Native American girls whom the Reeses had abducted, exploited and robbed of their innocence were rounded up and summarily executed. Following this carnage, a hole was dug in the middle of the stone pen, and the bodies were dumped into it. Sander didn't participate in the killing himself but watched from a vantage of a hundred feet away. His only counsel was an old soldier named Burt, who was sympathetic to the cause against England. Sander later described the scene in his unpublished autobiography:

"You did the right thing, sir," Burt said to me. "It's a bad day, sure, but necessary. Only good times from now on, yea?"

I nodded but couldn't share Burt's enthusiasm. Damn this confounded chill, I thought, and tightened my greatcoat around my shoulders.

When a young cadet came by to report on the progress, I told him, "You make sure that hole is well filled, do you hear?"

The boy clicked his heels and scampered to do my bidding. Once he was safely away, I said to Burt, "As soon as we're through here, I want a carriage waiting for me at the main house. I don't wish to spend another night in this place."

"Where are we going, then, sir?"

I stared at the soldier, thinking him mad. "Where else, man? To Providence!"

Endnote

On September 28, 2004, Nonesuch Records released *Brian Wilson Presents Smile*, a newly recorded version of the Beach Boys' "teenage symphony to God."

Acknowledgments

Thanks to my family, both new members and old, and Gary Fisketjon, my amazing editor. Thanks as well to Richard Abate, Susan Aylward, Regis Behe, Nayon Cho, Claudia Cross, Wieland Freund, Joshua Furst, Evan Gaffney, Gina Gionfriddo, Gordon Haber, Victoria Häggblom, Gabriel Haman, Edward Kastenmeier, Kate Lee, Matt Lee, John Malicsi, Adam Mansbach, Joseph McElroy, Peter Mendelsund, Dean and Marianne Metropoulos, Joe Michaels, Sheila O'Shea, Chuck Palahniuk, David Plante, Peter and Susan Straub, Alex Suczek, Virginia Tan, Liz Van Hoose and Curtis White.

A NOTE ON THE TYPE

This book was set in Minion, a typeface produced by the Adobe Corporation specifically for the Macintosh personal computer, and released in 1990. Designed by Robert Slimbach, Minion combines the classic characteristics of old style faces with the full compliment of weights required for modern typesetting.

Composed by Creative Graphics,
Allentown, Pennsylvania
Printed and bound by R. R. Donnelley & Sons,
Harrisonburg, Virginia
Designed by Virginia Tan